Mason's RESOLUTION

A DEMENTED SONS MC NOVEL

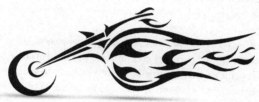

KRISTINE ALLEN

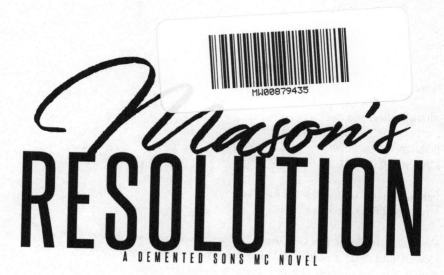

ISBN-13:978-1975746933
ISBN-10:1975746937

Published in the United States of America.
First published in September, 2017.

Cover Design: Clarise Tan, CT Cover Creations ctcovercreations.com
Cover Model Photo: Courtesy of Aleksey Satyrenko
Editing: Virginia Cantrell, Hot Tree Editing hottreeediting.com
Formatting: Champagne Book Design champagnebookdesign.com

Mason's Resolution is a full-length, standalone novel. It is the second book in the Demented Sons MC Series. This book will contain some spoilers if read before *Colton's Salvation*.
Colton's Salvation is the first book in the Demented Sons MC Series and is also a full-length standalone novel available now.

Dedication

To my main man… my real life husband who rolls his eyes and laughs at me as I look through hundreds of pictures of half-naked men trying to find the perfect cover model. You know you're my number one. I love you, Marty!

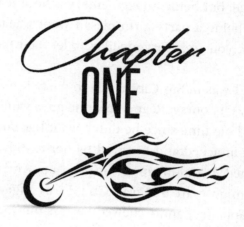

Chapter ONE

Becca

I STOOD AT THE DOOR OF MY BEST FRIEND'S HOME AND TRIED TO work up the courage to knock.

Shit, how was I going to explain why I was there with all my meager belongings packed in my car? A frustrated breath expelled from between my lips.

I just didn't know where else to go. I really didn't know if it was the best place to stay, considering I knew *he,* who ridiculously preoccupied my thoughts, was there in the same town, but Steph was my best—if not my *only*—friend. Telling myself I would just have to ignore him if I saw him seemed easier said than done.

Shit.

Sighing, I reached up and knocked on the door.

Seven Months Earlier

I had always wanted to go to Vegas. So, when Stephanie called me and told me she was getting married and she wanted me to be her maid of honor, heck yeah baby, I was there. Sure, I had been a wild child in college, but being an elementary school teacher kind of put a damper on being a party girl unless I went waaaay out of town. I don't care who you are, everyone likes to let their hair down every so often.

So, there I was in Sin City, ready to party it up for Steph's bachelorette party. Of course, Reaper and the guys would be in the background the whole time since he didn't want her out of his sight after she had been attacked and tortured by her ex-boyfriend. Yeah, that really happened. I couldn't make this shit up. And who could blame him? What a nightmare that was. God, I was angry she hadn't called me after it happened, and I chewed her ass out for it. She'd said she was embarrassed by the situation and didn't want to burden me with it, but dammit, we were supposed to be best friends. It was our job as best friends to be there for each other.

Anyway, I was dressed to kill for the party that night, because if I could, I was getting fucking shit-faced and laid. My relationship with Trevor was a dismal failure and had been the most miserable, boring, shitty year and a half of my life. I'd tried to live a "respectable life"—yes, air quotes and all—and keep the image of a proper school teacher, but it wasn't *me*. Now let me clarify. I'm not saying I wanted to run around and be a slut or a drunk, but I wanted to be able to go out and have a good time occasionally.

Not Trevor. Trevor was stable, responsible, reliable, had a great job on the Air Force Base in Omaha, blah, blah, blah, blah, blah… and he was boring. God, he was soooooo boring. His idea of a night out was to go to the movies and home again. Eating out would be a waste of money when we had a pantry full of food at home. Popcorn with your movie? Forget that shit. That was "over-priced and wasteful." So? Movies and popcorn went together like peanut butter and chocolate. It should be illegal to have one without the other. Sorry, I digress. He sucked in bed. Like really "sucked monkey balls" bad. He insisted on the lights being out and only ever being in the missionary position. Really? Ugh. And an orgasm? What the fuck was that? I hadn't achieved one without the help of my hand or BOB since the day Trevor and I moved in together. He hated me getting dressed up, doing my hair, wearing makeup—all things he considered "pretentious." What he wanted was some librarian-type, or better yet, an Amish woman. Yeah, that was what he should have found, an Amish chick. So breaking things off with him before I came to Vegas was the plan. The reality was he begged me to work on things when I got back. He wanted me to "go have a good time with the girls," and then we would discuss things when I returned. He said… wait for it… he could "try to change." Sheeeit. Okay. Sure.

Yeah, discuss things? No. I was so done, but I didn't want to keep arguing with him, so I decided to let it lie until I got back.

So, there I was in my tight, short, red dress with my boobs flashing ample cleavage, and matte black, six-inch heels. My dark auburn hair was tamed with a shit-ton of hair product, but the curls were still on the riotous side and fit my mood. I topped the look with some "fuck me" deep-red lipstick and looked at my reflection in the hotel mirror with satisfaction. I'd gotten a light fake-bake tan and was fit from hours spent at the gym in an effort to be away from Trevor.

Man, I was so stupid for thinking I could make my parents happy and conform to society's expectations of the good little school teacher by hooking up with a dud. My parents never thought I would curb my wild ways and settle down, so I tried my damnedest to show them they were wrong.

Unfortunately, maybe they had been right after all. I was a free spirit. I loved life and believed it should be lived to the fullest, every second of every day. It was amazing, but short, and we should enjoy it while it was ours.

We all met up in the lobby. It was me, Steph, Kristina, her nurse from the hospital who she had ended up keeping in touch with and becoming great friends with—yeah, I was a little jealous—Pam, her married friend from Des Moines who also used to babysit Remi for her, and her high school friend, Letty. We giggled and shouted as we headed out to the first stop—a male revue at the Hard Rock Hotel and Casino.

Steph had laughed and said she didn't need a male revue because she had her own personal male revue at home, to which I gagged in mock disgust and, truth be told, more than just a little bit of jealousy, because let's be honest, Reaper was freaking hot and she was a damn lucky girl. My foot went down on this one though, and the rest of the girls backed me up. This was her bachelorette party, and much to Reaper's displeasure, we were going to drool over some sexy-ass abs and butts. *Whooooo-Hooooooo!* Hey, not all of us were getting married, and even for the ones who were, they were married, not dead, sheesh.

We were preparing to load up in the limo, which would be followed by Steph's SUV with the guys in it. That was when I saw him. Fucking hello hotness. Naturally, I had to know. So, I asked, in an oh-so-nonchalant way, who all the guys were. Steph told me his name was Mason, but they called him Hollywood. He was tall, had a freaking kick-ass toned body, dark blond just-been-fucked messy hair, and light hazel eyes. Yum. Oh, and did I mention he was hot? Oh yeah, totally hot. I'm talking lick-every-muscle-on-that-gorgeous-body-head-to-toe hot. Of course, he was chatting up Kristina, which only fueled that little shit-stirring green-eyed monster and made me a little *more* jealous of her, which really sucked because she was a sweetheart. I felt like such a bitch. A really jealous bitch.

He laughed at something she said, and when I shouted, "Let's go, girls!" he looked at me for the first time. When our eyes met, my girly parts tingled and my breath caught for a second.

Wow. Did I really just feel that shit?

His eyebrow rose and his eyes slid leisurely up and down my body. *Like what you see, sexy?* I winked and headed out to the limo, adding a little extra sway to my ass. I had no intention of hooking up with one of Reaper's friends, but Hollywood was panty-melting hot, and if he was going to look, then, hey.... So I strutted as I approached the limo, sat on the seat just inside the door, and slid my legs in slowly, one at a time. I knew he was watching, and it gave me a sense of empowerment I hadn't felt in a long while.

Tonight was going to be fun. I planned to find some sexy hunk of anonymous man to scratch my itch, so to speak, and call it a good night. As they say, what happens in Vegas, stays in Vegas. With each sip of my champagne, I felt myself breaking out of the stifling shell I had built around myself over the last few years.

Yes, it was going to be a good night. I could feel it in my bones.

Hollywood

I was so fucking happy for my buddy, Reaper, and his girl, Steph. After all the hell he'd been through, he deserved someone like her. It was crazy that she was the same girl he'd carried around a picture of on that old useless cell phone through our last deployment together. Who would have thought they would find each other again? Some crazy shit. They were fucking insane about each other and had the cutest little girl. Damn, they were gonna be in trouble with that little one someday. I laughed to myself at the thought. Better them than me.

Vegas was a well-deserved and much needed vacation for all the brothers and me. Things had gone well with the drop-off a few months ago, despite shit going down with Reaper's old lady and him having to miss it all. Thankfully, we hadn't needed him, but I'd taken over just in case. I was a pretty good fucking shot too, even if I had been his spotter and he was the sniper back in our military days.

We'd been a tight pair when we were together in the Army. Shit, as a sniper team, you had to be. Then, we lost touch for a while after we both got out. Before I left for home, I'd begged him to come back to Iowa with me, but he said he needed to get his head straight first. I figured he would contact me when he was ready, but I never heard from him and his number had been disconnected. So, I followed my plan by beginning the prospect phase with the Demented Sons MC, and a while later, I found him again, thanks to Hacker's mad skills on the computer. When I went down to Texas to pick up a bike for a customer, I stopped by his place. Fuck, I was glad I got him to come back with me, because honestly, I don't think that poor bastard would be alive today if I hadn't. He was a fucking mess. We both had been, but luckily, I had my family and the MC, whereas he'd had no one. I loved him like a blood brother, probably even deeper than my love for the rest of the brothers in the MC. Reaper and I'd been through a lot of shit together, like life-and-death shit overseas. That tended to bring people pretty fucking close.

It was good to see Kristina again. She was witty and funny, and she always made me laugh. She was also fucking smoking, and at one time, I would have loved to have gotten a piece of her gorgeous little ass. Lord knew I chased it for an entire week while Steph was in the hospital and she was Steph's nurse. Of course, she just laughed and brushed me off every fucking time. It really was a blow to my ego, I'm telling you. When she finally told me she was dating someone though, I backed off, keeping it to harmless flirting. Maybe most guys would have gone after her anyway, but not me. My sister's husband fucked around on her, and I watched her fall apart and sink into a deep depression before finally dragging herself back out of it. It took her forever to move on after divorcing his stupid ass. I vowed to her that I would never fuck around with a married woman or wreck a relationship—not just because of the hurt it caused, but because it went against the grain. My own personal experience with getting shafted was one I would never put on anyone. Fuck that shit. Which was another reason I shied away from relationships. Too much bullshit.

When I heard Becca, the maid of honor, round the girls up to leave, I looked over, and *holy shit*. What a fucking beauty. She looked straight at me, and my heart jumped and sent a current straight to my dick. I grinned at her and gave her "the look" that had never failed me in the past.

She was a straight fucking knockout. I always had a thing for redheads, and she had a deep, rich auburn head of curls that begged to have a man's hands buried in it. Twisted in it. The thought of those plump, red lips wrapped around my dick made my grin even bigger. As my gaze wandered down over the red dress she'd poured her sexy ass into, I wondered if her tits would pop out if she took too deep of a breath, 'cause I would sure as shit like to be around to see that. She had nice curvy hips that were perfect for grabbing onto when… yeah, sorry, my mind went there. All the time. It was just one of those things I'd never been able to help. Beautiful women were my addiction, and I made sure they were well satisfied when they were with me. She also had toned, tanned legs that I knew would wrap around me perfectly—and could she please leave the heels on while she did it? *Damn.*

She winked at me, and I knew she saw me checking her fine ass out. I didn't give a fuck. As she shook that ass and climbed into the limo, the last thing I saw were her long legs sliding in. Jesus. She was stunning, and if it was my lucky night, she would be mine. I felt a "challenge accepted" smirk spread across my face. If I played my cards right, she would be screaming my name by the end of the night. After all, this was Vegas, right?

Chapter TWO

Becca

TRULY, I THOUGHT I'D DIED AND GONE TO HEAVEN. I'D NEVER HAD so many hot-as-hell men dancing in front of me, and never dreamed I would have, either. It felt so damn good to be able to let loose and have a good time without having to worry about how people would look at me. It was beginning to make me seriously question my choice of careers. I don't know what the hell I was thinking. I loved being an elementary school art teacher and working with all my kids, but I just didn't know if it was worth completely stifling my personality like I was letting it. Don't get me wrong. Like I said, I didn't want to be a whore, by any means. But shit, if I wanted to go out and have a few drinks, I didn't want to be looking over my shoulder for parents or fearing people would look down their noses at me.

I must have shoved about a hundred bucks down G-strings, allowing my fingers to wander slightly against their smooth, slick skin. Yum. I was sure half of them were probably gay, because that's how it went, but they were damn hot. And holy six-pack, can you say buff? It felt like I was in my very own *Magic Mike* movie. Steph laughed her ass off at me and the rest of the girls. The guys sat back with their arms crossed like some kind of Persian guard, keeping a close eye on us as they continuously glared at the dancers. *Ugh. Please.* And Hollywood gave me the evil eye every time one of the dancers rubbed up against me or gave me a lap dance. *What is his deal?*

As I finished off my fourth apple Crown and cranberry, feeling the sweet, cool liquid run down my throat, I knew I was getting beyond tipsy. I totally should have eaten something before we left. Screw it, I was feeling good and having a great time. Pam bought a round of buttery nipple shots and we all toasted by clinking the rims together. On the count of three we bottomed up. The girls cheered me on as I used my tongue to lick every drop from inside the glass. As the tip of my tongue ran around the top of the glass, I looked up and straight into Hollywood's eyes. I couldn't tell if he was scowling at me or in pain, but he sure didn't look like he was having a good time. So, of course, I teased him a little by wrapping my lips around the top of the shot glass. Oh yeah, that was totally a scowl. I watched his jaw clench and a muscle jump in his face as his nostrils flared slightly. I was tipsy enough to stick my tongue out at him in a completely childish gesture. *Take that, you judgmental party pooper.* He turned away, pushing through the crowd as he walked away.

Damn, he really disliked me. Asshole. What did I care what he thought of me, though? I didn't owe him diddly shit. He wasn't my dad or my big brother. Hell, the way he made my body respond just by looking in my direction, we better not be related or I had more issues than being stifled. A giggle slipped out at the thought. Shit, yeah, I was getting way more than tipsy.

After the dancers finished their final performance, we headed out to the next bar. The limo ride included another glass of chilled champagne. I loved the feel of the bubbles tickling my nose as I drank, and then the way they floated across my tongue and down my throat. It brought an unbidden vision of me sharing some of the champagne from my mouth to Hollywood's before I took him in my mouth, letting the bubbles tease his cock. Jesus, I was so very naughty.

And so very drunk. I laughed, again.

We arrived at the bar and were ushered to the front of the line because of our reservation for the bachelorette party. Thank God, because the line was crazy long. The bar was absolutely hopping by the time we made it inside, with music blasting in surround sound and colored lights flashing and spinning. My favorite song was playing, and I squealed as I grabbed Letty's and Kristina's arms and proceeded to drag them out on the crowded dance floor. The bass pumped so loud I could feel it reverberate from my feet to my chest and take hold of my heartbeat.

As we danced to the next song, hands slid around my waist and rested on my hips as a male body pressed up against my back, bumping and grinding to the beat of the music. I glanced over my shoulder into the smiling face of a nice-looking guy who was a little shorter than I usually went for, but he was cut, had muscular arms, a great smile, and rich chocolate-brown eyes. *Mmmm, he might do for the night.* I flashed a smile, looked up at him, and pressed closer against him. Letty gave me a thumbs-up, and we continued to dance as a couple of guys joined them, too.

We must have danced through four songs or more, and I was sweating like crazy from shaking my ass. As I gathered my damp curls, holding them up off my neck to try to cool myself, I felt his lips touch my shoulder, followed by his teeth and then a soothing stroke of his tongue. God, I loved it when a guy kissed my neck and shoulders. My eyelids fluttered closed as my head fell back and my mouth fell open in a sigh.

Oh yessssss.

He spun me around and slid his arms around me to rest his hands at the top of my ass as a slow song started up. Pressed up against his body, I could feel his erection, and I knew he could be mine for the night if I really wanted him. We swayed to the music, and he kissed my ear, then my neck. He pulled back to look me in the eye. His smile was radiant as he leaned into my ear to be heard above the noise and told me he wanted to take me home. Bingo.

I gave a sly smile and coyly said, "Maybe." It didn't pay to appear too slutty. Right? Then he kissed me… and I had to say… that part was a little disappointing. Sorry to disappoint, but there were definitely no fireworks. He wasn't a very good kisser, but I wasn't planning on marrying the guy; I just wanted to get laid. Hell, it could be worse.

He followed me back to the table and offered to buy me a drink. Since I was starting to lose my buzz after all the dancing and sweating, I graciously accepted. Everyone introduced themselves, and Steph gave me a questioning look before she leaned over to tell me to be careful and asked me if I was sure it was a good idea to hook up with some stranger I didn't know. My droll look and raised eyebrow told her she was pretty much the pot calling the kettle black after taking her fiancé home for a one-night stand back in college. Look where she was today. How could she fault me?

She laughed and held a hand up to me as she said, "Okay, okay, *okay!* 'Nuff said." We both laughed and hugged, and then I kissed her cheek. Dang, I loved her. She really was my very best friend. Nah, screw that. She was my sista from another mista.

It wasn't long before I desperately had to pee. Excusing myself, I headed through the pulsing crowd to the bathrooms, guided by the neon *Restrooms* sign in the back corner. Thankfully, there wasn't much of a line, and I was able to get in quickly. After doing my business, I washed my hands, fluffed my hair, boosted the girls, and checked my makeup. A quick blot with a paper towel pulled the shine off my face. Yep, good to go.

A hand snaked around my upper arm as I exited the restroom and pulled me off to the back of the corridor.

"Hey! What the…?" I didn't get another word out before I was pressed up against the wall with his hands holding me immobile by the tops of my arms. Flashing hazel eyes met mine just as I realized it was Hollywood. His mouth pulled in a tight line. I watched him close his eyes momentarily, as if he was fighting to keep his cool. He then took a deep breath before looking at me and blowing out the air he had held in his lungs.

"Jesus fuck, Becca! What the hell do you think you're doing? You're all over that guy, and you don't even know him. You were acting like you were planning to fuck him right there on the dance floor," he spit out. "Please tell me you aren't trying to pick him up. You've *got* to be smarter than that, Becca…. Besides, he looks like a fucking tool." His frustration was evident in his every breath and movement. What the ever-loving hell was up with him? Why did it matter to him if I screwed every guy in the bar? And why did my body start doing these crazy things just because I was close to him? Breathing the same air. Catching fire where our skin touched.

Whoa. What's up with this shit?

"What's it to you? You aren't my keeper, you know. I don't even really know *you*, for that matter. I'm a big girl, and I can make my own decisions. Shit!" He really was too much, and damn, he needed to back the fuck up. Being up close and personal to him had my nipples tightening and poking through the thin fabric of my dress. They felt abraded by the fabric and the friction of brushing against his chest. I wasn't completely sure, but I thought I felt his hard cock press against my hip. I pushed closer to him. Oh my Lord, yes, it was, and may I say, he felt very well blessed. Oh, who was I kidding? More like *huge*. Then my heartbeat picked up speed and fluttered in my chest like a thousand tiny butterflies.

"*Fuck,*" was all he said before he lowered his head and ran his tongue along my lower lip. Threading his fingers through my hair, he tipped my head and claimed my mouth with his in a savage and blatantly hungry kiss.

Now this man… this man could kiss, was my last coherent thought as I grabbed his ass tight and pulled him closer to me.

Hollywood

The last fucking thing I planned to do was kiss her. I was pissed at her, dammit! But she had been driving me insane all night. Watching her grope and rub against those half-naked strippers set my teeth on edge from the start. It got worse when I watched her lick every last drop of her shot with that little pink tongue. When she placed the glass in her mouth like it was a cock, it was seriously all I could take. I almost fucking shot my load in my pants. I had to fucking walk away before I made a complete ass out of myself.

Why was she pissing me off so much?

Just when I thought I had cooled off, that fucking asshole was grinding against her and running his hands over her body on the dance floor. Yeah, by then I was damn near seeing red. Hell if I could explain where all the possessive feelings were coming from. I was pretty sure some of it had to do with the fact that her best friend almost died at the hands of a guy she *thought* she knew. So, part of this had to be about her safety and the fact that she was treating that safety with absolute disregard. Right? I mean, I barely even knew this girl. Sure, I had hoped to get lucky with her tonight, but I didn't want to be her boyfriend. Fuck no. Plus, I felt an obligation to keep her safe for Reaper and Steph. Besides, I didn't get attached, nor did

I do relationships. That just wasn't me. Hell, I wasn't stupid. I was blessed with good looks, so finding hot women who were willing was no issue. I fucked them until the novelty wore off and moved on. Things were a lot less complicated that way.

When she walked off from the group, I couldn't help but follow and wait for her to emerge from the bathroom. She sputtered when I grabbed her and pulled her down the hall farther. I totally lost my shit and chewed her ass out. The sight of her plump, red lips parted in astonishment broke me, and I had to taste them. That's how I found myself with her hot, panting body pressed up against the wall of a night club and my mouth devouring her like I was starving and she was my first taste of food in a month.

She tasted like cranberries, and she smelled fucking amazing. She had on a rich, musky perfume that teased my senses. It wound up around me, through my nose and around my body like a serpent. The moan that slid across her tongue and into my mouth as I dropped my hands from her hair and grabbed her ass left me undone. I slid my hands down to her thighs and lifted her up to straddle me as I braced her against the wall. Her skimpy red dress slid up her thighs as she wrapped her legs around me and fisted her fingers in my hair, deepening the kiss.

Groaning, I broke away for air and rested my forehead against hers. We both panted breathlessly. Her pulse pounded in her neck, and I couldn't resist running my tongue along it. It was as if I could taste her excitement. Her skin was salty from the fine sheen of sweat, but still sweet, and I wanted more. My teeth nipped her skin as I nuzzled along her neck and shoulder.

"Becca, I know this probably sounds crazy, but I can't let you go anywhere with that guy. It's killing me to watch you with him. I want it to be me. I need it to be me. You have to know you affected me from the first second I saw you. If you aren't on board with that, you need to let me know now, and I'll walk away." I inhaled a ragged breath. "Because I'm not going to sit by and watch you do this with someone else. So, if you want him, say so and go. Otherwise, we're going out to the limo and heading back to the hotel. You hear me?" In my mind, I begged her not to say no, but she needed to have a choice. I didn't force myself on anyone. Ever.

"Yes. Jesus, yes, Hollywood, please." Her whispered plea had my cock surging toward the heat at the juncture of her thighs, exactly where it wanted to be buried. My body pressed harder against her to relieve some of the tension, but fuck if it didn't make things worse. With a groan, I slid her toned legs down to the floor and straightened her dress. Taking her hand firmly in mine, I pushed my way through the crowd to the front door. The night air was cool on our heated skin, bringing goose bumps to hers, as I tucked her in the limo and told her to wait there.

My legs carried me back into the bar on autopilot, and I found Reaper with his arms around his bride-to-be's waist as he kissed her shoulder. Shit, I knew he couldn't stay away from her all night. I laughed at him, and he gave me a dirty look that said, "Fuck off." Steph blasted me with a huge smile. Her smile faltered when I said Becca wasn't feeling too hot and asked me to take her back to the hotel. When she wanted to wrap everything up early, I told her no and tipped my head toward all the girls out dancing and having fun on the dance floor.

"Becca said she didn't want to cut everyone's night short, so I'm gonna make sure she gets to the hotel okay, and I'll send the limo back for you all as soon as we get there."

Reaper raised an eyebrow and gave me a knowing smirk, which earned him the same "fuck you" look in return. After everything we'd been through together over the years, we knew each other as well as we knew ourselves and could easily communicate without words. Still, he leaned over toward my ear so I could hear him over the noise.

"You've been looking like you want to break every fucker that got close to her tonight. I'm not stupid, you know. Don't fuck with her and break her heart, bro. That's Steph's best friend, and you know she'll kick your ass."

"Shit, man, don't get your panties in a wad. I'm just making sure she gets back safe, that's all." With a grin, I left before he could say more.

Chapter THREE

Becca

HOLLYWOOD CLIMBED IN THE LIMO AND, AFTER TELLING THE driver to take us back to the hotel, closed the privacy screen. For a minute, he just sat across from me with a brooding look on his face. When he spoke, his voice was strained and hoarse.

"Come here. Now."

I raised my brow at his commanding tone, but if I was honest, it fucking turned me on. Yep. Panties officially, and totally, soaked. Lordy, he really was the full package—good looking, alpha male, ripped as hell, tall, a phenomenal kisser, and he felt very well blessed in his… umm, yeah… *that*. I decided I would follow his commands, but on my terms. Dropping to my hands and knees, I crawled over to him in a sultry manner and rested my hands on either side of him. *Okay*… so I *tried* to be sultry… Anyway, moving on….

The leather of the seat was cool to the touch. When I slid my hands up his outer thighs to the waistband of his distressed-looking jeans, his hands flew to stop mine. I looked up to his face in question.

"What? You don't want me to set you free? Isn't this why you wanted me over here?" I pulled my bottom lip between my teeth. He was breathing harder and had an intense look on his face. He sat slouched back in the seat with his hands still holding firm to mine.

"Becca, Jesus, I'm not trying to fuck you in the limo. Not for the first time. I just wanted to hold you. I just needed to taste you and touch you," he rasped. His hands clenched mine briefly, and his eyes flashed to mine, appearing more gold than before.

When I leaned forward and brushed my lips against his, the faint taste of beer lingered on his lips. We kissed deeply before I broke off and ran the tip of my tongue along his jaw until I reached his ear. Nipping it softly, and intentionally misconstruing his statement, I whispered, "Well, what if I want to taste you too?"

"Aww, fuck me," he whispered to himself, his resignation clear in his expression and tone.

After extricating my hands from his, I proceeded to unbutton his jeans and was pleased to see he went commando. My lips curled in delight. *Hell, yeah.* It was too tempting not to run a fingernail lightly down to the base of his member. His sharp intake of breath as his lids lowered halfway told me he wanted this, even if he wouldn't admit it.

The knowledge made me bold, and I grasped his ever-hardening cock in my hand, stroking firmly and softly in an alternating pattern. And holy shit, I was correct in my assumptions—he was probably the biggest I had ever seen. My fingers and thumb didn't even touch when wrapped around him. He was like silk-encased steel, and he was hot and pulsing in my hand.

There were obviously no complaints over my actions, as his

silence continued, broken only by his harsh breaths. His precum glistened at the tip of his silky-smooth head, so I leaned forward to catch the shiny drop with my tongue. Jesus, his taste was like an aphrodisiac, and I quickly took him as deep as I could, allowing my tongue to swirl around him as I sucked and stroked him. God, I loved the feel of him in my mouth, but I was willing to bet it wouldn't be half as good as having him between my legs.

"Jesus fucking H. Christ. Shit, Becca. Stop. Fuck, you're going to make me come if you keep doing that. You need to stop." He was groaning with his head flung back on the back of the seat. Despite his words, his fingers reached down to entwine in my hair and gently encouraged my rhythm.

He didn't hurt me or force his massive cock down my throat like some guys tried to do. Even in his moment of abandon, he was considerate, and I appreciated that.

Some women hated giving a guy a blowjob. Hell, I loved having that kind of power over them, and it was an especially intoxicating feeling considering how in control he had seemed all night. One of my hands remained wrapped around his firm cock, while the other slid to gently massage his balls.

Oooooo, he manscaped. Nice.

There was no way I was stopping until I tasted him. When he began to massage my scalp with his fingers, I moaned. The vibrations must have been enough to set him off because I felt his balls tighten up and pull closer to his body. Then he tensed and murmured encouragement and disjointed words as his cock seemed to swell even bigger.

"Oh God, Becca, yes. Suck me harder. Fuck. Jesus. You're doing so fucking good. Shit. Gonna come. Stop. I can't… No. Don't stop. Shit. Shit. Shit." He bellowed right as I felt his cock swell and pulse with his hot release washing over my tongue and hitting the back of my throat. I continued to lick and suck as if I was trying to collect every last drop, which I was.

First, let me tell you, I had never—and I mean *ever*—swallowed when giving a guy head, but for him? For him, I felt insatiable when it came to the taste of him. He started to jerk and spasm as I continued to lick and suckle his cock. He roughly pulled me up to straddle his lap, my dress scrunching up to the tops of my thighs. Just to fuck with him, I slowly licked my lips while staring him dead in the eyes.

"Fuck, that's enough. Too much, baby. Dammit, I can't handle too much of you doing that… It's so fucking sensitive after. Thank you, that was…. Shit, that was fucking amazing." He kissed me, and I knew he tasted himself—damn, that was hot as hell.

His hands roamed up and down my back, squeezing my ass and pulling my core tight to his cock. My wet panties rubbed along the length of his semi-erection, and I felt my pussy tighten in anticipation.

God, I wanted him. Now. Desperately. Reaching down between us, I grasped him in one hand, stroking him until he was fully erect again. He gripped my hips firmly in his calloused hands. Then I slid my soaked panties to the side, intent on sliding him into my slick folds.

He broke away from the kiss to exclaim, "Fuck, reach around me and grab the condom from my back pocket." His sexual frustration with the delay was evident in the drawn look on his face.

Dammit, what was I thinking? I had never fucked a guy without a condom either. Too many diseases out there. What the hell was it about this guy that had my safety practices and my very sanity flying out the window? It was as if I couldn't think straight with him this close to me. My head dropped and my face buried in his neck.

"Shit, please don't think badly of me. I *never* have unprotected sex. I'm on the pill, but still, I don't. I swear. You make my brain turn to mush." I'd been on the pill forever, but I still used condoms with Trevor. It was like subconsciously I wanted to keep a barrier between us.

Now Hollywood probably thought I did that with everyone and I was a slut full of all kinds of crazy funk. Damn.

"I haven't been with anyone since I was tested a couple of weeks ago. I'm clean, but do you trust me? I always wrapped my shit. I have a condom on me, but I really didn't plan on us doing this here, babe." He rested his head on my shoulder with ragged breaths escaping his mouth and tickling the top of my breast.

"I trust you." How I knew I could trust him after just meeting him was a complete mystery to me. I reached down between us and guided his cock to rub on my soaking wet folds until it slipped in the opening.

Shit, he was big.

There was a faint burning as I felt myself stretch to accommodate him. It was borderline painful but amazing at the same time. Trevor and I hadn't actually had sex in months before I told him I was done, and he had absolutely nothing on Hollywood when it came to size. His excuse was always he was tired, or he just came to bed long after I did and I was already sleeping. Part of me wondered if he wasn't getting it somewhere else. I was a sexual being, and I would never have complained if he had woken me to have sex, but nope. Not him. So anyway, I knew I was tight, and I prayed Hollywood would fit as he held me up above him and slowly stroked in and out with just the tip until he eased in further with each stroke.

"Please. I need to feel you inside me. God, please." No, I wasn't above begging by this point. My nerves felt frayed and overworked. A frantic need to have him fully encased in my sheath overwhelmed me. My body was expectantly quivering. At my breathy request, he looked me straight in the eye with determination, grasped my hips so tightly I felt his fingers digging into my flesh, and drove deep.

Holy Shit.

Hollywood

Fuck. Me.

Shit, she was fucking tight. Damn if I didn't have to hold her still for a moment because I was afraid I would lose it right then and there. Even though we were fucking in a damn limo, I needed this to be good for her. No man wanted to be known as a one stroke wonder, either.

Okay, I'm not gonna lie, fucking in a limo was amazing. Thrilling. Hot as fuck. But I hadn't had anyone this tight in a while, and I also hadn't experienced the incredible sensation of nothing between my dick and a warm pussy either. Never in my life had I gone without a wrapper. *Ever*. No love without a glove. Don't make a mistake, cover your snake. Armor the tank before you enter the flank. You get the idea. It was like my brain short-circuited with her and all my rules burned out, followed by a wisp of smoke. She was going to be the death of me, one way or the other. Call it a premonition.

She bit my shoulder, leaving my T-shirt damp where her mouth was. Fucking A, I couldn't take much more of this shit. I needed to fuck the shit out of her. Slamming up into her, I felt my dick bottom out in her tight pussy. Her dress was covering her ass, and I wanted to feel the firm, smooth globes in my hands, so I gathered it up around her waist. She had on some kind of skimpy-ass, barely there panties that had the bottoms of her cheeks hanging out.

My hands alternately squeezed and smoothed circles on both ass cheeks as I pumped into her with a steady pace. Without warning, I smacked her ass. Her pussy instantly clamped tight around me, and she moaned. My hand resumed circling on her ass to soothe the sting.

Fuck, she looked so incredibly sexy riding my cock. Her cheeks were flushed, and her jade green eyes were glazed over with pleasure. Those plump, red lips were still swollen from sucking on my cock, and that was a *major* fucking turn on. Beautiful tits swelled above the top of her dress neckline, and I couldn't stop myself from licking across the tops and down into her cleavage. The thought of my cock sliding between her luscious breasts battled with the thought of her nipples rolling under my tongue and had me pumping faster. I reached up and pulled her dress down to allow them to rest on the top of the dress, putting them on display. One side of her dress slipped down over her shoulder.

"Come for me, Becca. Fucking hell, come all over my cock." I continued the onslaught to her pussy walls, feeling her body begin to tense before she tightened around my cock.

"You're close; I can feel it. Fuck me hard and come. Do it, baby, now," I demanded. The need to feel her hot core throbbing around me was all-consuming. She bit her full lower lip and moaned. "Yeah, that's it. Fucking let loose, baby girl. Hurry or I'm getting there without you." Her magnificent tits shook and bounced with each thrust, and I bit down on them one at a time, then licked and sucked them reverently.

She shouted as her walls clenched around my cock in tight, rapid spasms. I felt a flood of wetness as I continued to fuck her for all I was worth. Jesus, I needed to fill her with a desperation that felt primal. Her tits bounced franticly by this time, as I fucking slammed deep into her until I felt myself on the verge of exploding.

Tension started low in my back and snaked up my spine. Her ass slapped against my thighs, and I grabbed it, digging my fingers into her ass cheeks to pull it tight to me as I unloaded in her with a roar. I felt like a fucking caveman. It was like my cum spraying inside her marked her as *mine*.

Fuck. I buried my face in her hair, inhaling the scent that was just her, and held her tight to me as my cock pulsed every last drop into her.

What the fuck *was* that?

We were both fucking panting like rabid dogs. Jesus, you have no idea. The back of the limo smelled like straight sex. Hopefully it cleared out by the time everyone else climbed in later tonight, or we were busted for sure. Not that I cared, but she might.

When we felt the limo slowing to a stop, she quickly jumped from my lap, straightening her dress and nearly sending me into shock simply from the loss of contact and her incredible warmth.

Shit, what had this woman done to me? I reluctantly tucked my cock back in my pants just as the driver opened the door. She was flushed, her hair was a mess, and there was no denying she had been well satisfied. Our eyes met, and we both started laughing.

I tipped the driver as Becca grabbed my hand. Together, we entered the hotel and rode the elevator up to the floor where we all had rooms. As the elevator made its slow ascent, my hand slipped up the back of her dress and along her thigh to slip a finger in her wet panties. On my way up, I felt our mixed cum running down the inside of one thigh, and I rubbed it into her skin. Looking deep into her eyes, I knew she was aware of what the fuck I was doing.

"Your room or mine?" she asked me in a husky whisper.

"It doesn't matter to me, but I'm crashing in a double room with Hacker," I confessed. She ran the tip of her tongue along her bottom lip in a sexy-as-hell way and led me to her room. Fucking hell, I was glad she had gotten a room to herself, but I would have totally locked Hacker out of the room if need be.

We barely made it through the door before we were ripping each other's clothes off. I needed her naked body exposed to me, her silky skin sliding against mine. It didn't matter that I had just come twice in the limo. Mystical voodoo was all I could attribute it to, because God knew the last time I was this fucking horny.

Grabbing her by the tops of her legs, I lifted her around my waist and carried her to the bed. When I tossed her naked ass on the center of the mattress, her chest shook as her body bounced on landing. God, she had perfect fucking tits. I could lick and squeeze them all damn day and be a happy man. An extremely happy man. Her glorious, deep red hair spread wildly across the stark white of the sheet and pillows. That bottom lip held between her teeth as she looked at me with a total "come fuck me" expression broke any resolve I was holding onto.

My eyes scanned slowly over her body, taking in those perfect mounds topped with tightened, dusky, pert nipples; her flat, toned belly; the full curve of her hips; and those long, sexy fucking legs.

Fuck Me. The carpet matched the drapes.

I climbed on the bed, spreading those perfect legs, licking and biting up the insides of her thighs. Her skin was silky smooth against my cheek and lips. The dark red hair at the apex of her legs was trimmed close and in a thin strip that seemed to point straight to that wet piece of heaven. The scent of her arousal invaded my senses, and I rested my head on her belly as I breathed her in deeply. She smelled like us.

Her delicate hands grabbed my hair, pulling me up her body. My weight resting on one forearm, I ran my fingers through her deep red hair before fisting it to tip her head back where I could have better access to her neck. I rained kisses down her throat, biting her shoulder, and back up to suck her skin into my mouth. She tasted sweet like sugar cookies and ripe berries. When she spread her legs open farther for me to be able to nestle closer to her, my cock probed against her warm center of its own volition.

"Yesssss. Mmmmm, Hollywood…" Her voice was a plea, and my cock slipped in to be surrounded by her slick warmth. She was killing me. Second by second, minute by minute, she was drawing me into her, to a place where I would eventually lose myself completely.

"Harder. Faster." Her hands roamed over me, and her nails scored my back. My pace increased at her demand.

"Mason. My name is Mason. Say it."

"Mason," she breathed out.

My chin pulled close to my chest, my heart beating in a rapid-fire rhythm, I lost myself in her.

The room was filled with the sound of our breath, slight moans, and the slapping of skin on skin. There was no way I would have thought it was possible, but she tightened even further around my length, and I couldn't hold back any longer. My cock burst with hot cum, emptying into her to overflowing. As I continued to pulse inside her, I reached between us to circle her clit with a firm touch. She arched off the bed, gripped her legs around me, clutched my shoulders in her hands, and screamed my name. God, I had never heard a sweeter sound in my whole fucking life.

"Fuuuuuck." My mind was scrambled.

We lay there for a moment before I rolled off her and sat on the edge of the bed. My head hung down and my arms rested on my thighs. *Jesus.* My lungs struggled to draw in a deep breath, and I threw my head back in supplication. *God, help me.*

She crawled off the bed and grabbed my hand. "Come on, sexy. Let's clean up a bit." Mindlessly, I followed her to the shower. As we stood with the hot water running down our bodies, my fingers reached up to trail lightly over the rivulets streaming down her chest. Circling a nipple with my index finger, had it puckering under my gentle touch. Her head still tipped back in the water, I looked up to watch her eyes close and her luscious lips part. She was beautiful. In a simpler world, I could've been tempted to keep her.

Her chest heaved with each breath she took. Needing to taste her, I leaned down to bury my nose behind her ear and allowing my tongue to trail down her neck. Nipping and kissing my way down, I knelt in front of her and slid my hands from the back of her thighs up over her perfect ass. Her silky skin was flawless and addictive. Squeezing her tight in my hands, I placed a gentle kiss on the deep red curls at the top of her pussy. She was a goddess. Venus rising from the sea. If she was mine, I would worship her body daily – show her how precious she was to me. If only I were a different man…

In resignation, I stood. Accepting this was just for tonight was difficult for me, and that in itself was abnormal. Just the thought of telling her goodbye left a bitter taste on my tongue. Completely out of character, I had to remind myself I didn't want a forever with *any* woman. Shoving all thought to the back of my mind, I poured body wash into my hand and began sliding it sensuously over her curves.

We took turns lathering each other and rinsing off, before I turned off the water. The thick white towels hung on the rack, and I grabbed one to gently dry her body head to toe. After wrapping it around her, I reached for my own and briskly dried off.

With the towel carelessly discarded on the floor, she flopped naked on the bed and looked me in the eye with a wicked smile. "Holy shit, Mason. That was fucking amazing. You're absolutely incredible." I crawled onto the bed and ran my tongue around first one nipple then the other before looking up into her sparkling eyes.

"Who are you telling? Damn, I can't get enough of you." My tongue flicked her nipple before I bit it lightly. A groan slipped from my lips as her fingers threaded through my hair, holding me close to her chest. I nipped the bottom side of her breast and worked my way down to her downy curls between her legs.

Having my face buried in her was heaven, and I ate her pussy like a famished man placed before a feast. She reached down to grab my hair, pulling me closer. Could a man be smothered in pussy? 'Cause goddamn, what a way to go.

I nipped her clit before I licked her from there to her ass. She thrashed and groaned as I slid two fingers into her tight, wet passage, curling them to stroke her G-spot. A few well-placed strokes on that sensitive area, and she shattered quickly, with her walls throbbing and squeezing my fingers as she screamed my name. What a beautiful sight and sound. I continued to use my tongue to lave her until I felt I had licked up every drop of her creamy release.

She tasted so damn sweet, and I slid up her body to kiss her. She was going to taste herself on me and know how amazing her release was. Her tongue stroked mine without hesitation as she wrapped her legs around my hips to pull my straining cock toward her soaking wet pussy. Never let it be said I couldn't take a hint.

Without hesitation, I plunged in balls deep and groaned into her mouth when I felt her warm sheath grip me. Though I planned to take my time, it was as if I lost my fucking mind when I was near her, inside her. Breaking from her lips, I reached down and threw her legs over my shoulders, angling me better to fuck her furious and deep. Shit, I knew I wasn't going to be able to hold off.

Dammit, I normally have better control than this.

We came together in a massive explosion that left us breathless. Our mixed cum was pushed out of her warm pussy with each slow stroke I made in my effort to extend the pleasure as long as I could. She felt so freakin' good I didn't want to leave her body. Being in her was like nothing I'd ever experienced—it was like nirvana.

Finally, I collapsed on the bed next to her and gathered her close to my side. She had utterly exhausted me, and I could barely keep my eyes open. We were both covered in a thin sheen of sweat, but it didn't stop me from pulling her top leg over mine.

Her hand drew circular patterns on my chest as I absently ran my hand up and down her back from her shoulder to her curved ass. If I thought fucking her would get her out from under my skin, I was terribly wrong. After having just this small sampling of her, I was afraid I would *never* get enough of this wild child.

Chapter FOUR

Becca

Hollywood's breath slowed then evened out, and I knew he was sleeping. Shit, that was probably the best sex I'd ever experienced. Ever. I could live with sex like that every day for the rest of my life and die a very happy and replete woman. Something told me it wasn't just because he had a body to die for and the biggest cock I'd ever seen. There was a weird and powerful… I don't know… *connection* between us. Just the smell of his skin under my cheek made me want him again, which was crazy because we had already gone three rounds. I didn't even know a guy was capable of doing it twice, let alone three times—not including the blowjob in the limo. Damn. Talk about stamina. He was like some kind of sex machine.

In all honesty, I could see myself falling asleep in his arms every night. There was just such a "rightness" in the way I fit into his arms and against his body. We had just met, and the logical part of me knew this was insane. It would be interesting to see where things could lead, but unfortunately, we lived three hours apart, and I was definitely not into long-distance relationships. They never worked. Tried that after college. Never again.

The reasons I couldn't get attached to this man were an absolutely endless list. For one, I still needed to get Trevor to accept that we were over. I didn't know why I wasn't firmer before I left and forced him to comprehend I was D-O-N-E, done. Looking back, I should've never agreed to discuss things when I got back, but I wasn't in the mood to argue the day I left. I'd just wanted to leave, so I took the coward's way out and agreed to talk more when I returned.

Stupid.

I traced over the colorful tattoos that decorated his arms and the left side of his torso. My fingers skimmed his skin in a feather light touch so I wouldn't wake him. They were bright and colorful and seemed to reflect a positive energy. Initially, he had appeared to be a normally happy person. So why had he been so broody and bitchy while we were out tonight? It was a strange contradiction to his ink and the persona he gave off. The only reason I could think of was that I had pissed him off in something I said or did, but the alcohol I consumed pretty much hazed and erased most of the night prior to the limo ride from my mind.

As my fingers continued to absently trace the ink on his left arm, I felt uneven ridges. Lifting my head to look where I was tracing, I noticed he had some scars that his tattoos camouflaged. My lips kissed the scars gently as my mind tried to make sense of them and how he could have gotten them. My tongue slipped out and ran over his nipple that rested in front of my face. The stimulation had him fidgeting in his sleep, pulling me closer. A small smile spread across my face at the power I had over his body, even in sleep.

As I rested my head on his firm chest and stroked his sculpted abs, I breathed in his scent, which was a combination of a light cologne, sweat, sex, and something that was just… Mason. It was an intoxicating scent, and it lulled me into a deep sleep filled with passionate embraces with this god-like man.

I woke to kisses along my shoulder and large, calloused hands holding my breasts and stroking along the side of my body. Shivers broke out across my skin as I nestled my ass back into his hard cock. The heat emanating from the satin skin encasing his beautiful appendage seemed to ignite a fire between my legs, and I arched my back, trying to create a better angle in hopes he would enter me.

Jesus, what a way to wake up.

The kisses became love bites and licks, causing me to moan at the sheer ecstasy of the sensations he ignited. His hands stroked along my skin, leaving chills in their wake. That silky-smooth skin slid back and forth across my ass and slipped briefly between my thighs. It was like being on sensory overload. Finally, his cock settled in my folds, which his fingers had deftly lubricated and separated. He tortured me with a slow and teasing pace until I couldn't stand it anymore. I pulled away to climb on him, straddling his hips.

With a grin, I slid my wetness up and down the length of his engorged cock. I leaned over, crushing my breasts against his chest. My lips were magnetically drawn to his, and I had to kiss him. Then after biting and licking his neck briefly, I sat up smiling.

"So, you call Colton 'Reaper,' and they call you Hollywood. That's your nickname?" I continued to tease his cock while I nibbled and sucked on his fingers that had reached up to touch my face. Growling, he flipped me to my back. I laughed and wrapped my hand around his cock, guiding it back to the center of my wet heat.

"It's called a road name, and, yes, it's Hollywood," he said, sounding barely contained as he thrust in me with a guttural moan followed by a mischievous grin.

"Mmm, Hollywood. Why? Because you're a porn star in bed?" I giggled as he continued to stroke in and out of me in that slow, teasing stride. At my last question, he raised an eyebrow and slammed deep into me.

Ohhh, yessssss.

The man was freaking incredible in bed. Where had he been all my life?

His cock jumped in me as he laughed. "No, it's because they say I'm a pretty boy and I'm more suited to Hollywood than a motorcycle club." He never missed a beat as he smiled, kissed me gently, and nibbled on my jaw and neck. He then whispered in my ear, "I know this is going to sound insane, but… come back to Grantsville with me. I'm not ready to let you go. We have something… I don't know… I don't make a habit of asking this, so bear with me… Come back and see where whatever this is between us goes." My heart hammered in my chest, and I pushed him up and looked at him in question and surprise. His face flushed, and he gave me a puppy dog look in an attempt to make light of the situation.

Mmmm, the badass boy has a soft side…

"Hollywood, it's not that easy. I have a job. Family."

When my phone went off, I groaned at the poor timing. Dammit! I stretched over to the nightstand to grab my phone and answered it without looking at the caller ID. I knew it was Steph calling to make sure I was up. We were supposed to go get our hair done before lunch, and the wedding was this afternoon.

"Yesssssssss?" I drew out the greeting as I smiled at Hollywood.

"Tell them you're fucking busy and you'll call back in an hour or two." Hollywood continued his slow, steady assault on my body as he grinned at my attempt to remain "normal" on the phone. My eyes rolled back in my head at how good he felt. When he leaned down and nipped my nipple, I couldn't help but shake my head and smile at him, though. I smothered a groan as he thrust deep and hard before picking up the slow and steady rhythm again.

"Who the hell is that and what is he doing in your room at seven thirty in the morning?" Stunned, I sat up, dumping an unprepared and dumbfounded Hollywood off me when I realized who was on the phone. Trevor. Shit.

What.

The.

Hell.

Dammit! I looked at Hollywood and the shock on my face along with my dislodging him had him frowning in consternation. "The fuck? Is everything okay? Who is it?" Hollywood questioned.

Oh shit, shit, shit. Damn, Trevor had piss-poor timing. And why was the asshole calling me anyway? I waved at Hollywood to be quiet. I would have to explain to him after I hung up, but first I needed to get rid of Trevor. Damn, I should've stuck to my guns with him. I really wasn't ready to deal with him this morning.

"It's one of the groomsmen. He came to get me to take us all to breakfast. So, I need to get going." Dammit. I didn't want to get into all this with him in front of Hollywood. Of course, this caused Hollywood's frown to deepen as he sat up in the bed, resting his arms on his raised knees. He was so comfortable in his nudity. It was sexy as hell. The sight of his erection, still wet from me, had my core clenching in lust, and I cursed Trevor for being an ass and having terrible timing.

Trevor didn't sound overly convinced, but he told me he was just checking on me to make sure I was okay and to see if we had a good time last night. *Oh, Trevor you have no idea.* I felt my cheeks flush at the thought of last night's entertainment—and I didn't mean the strippers.

"Look, Trevor, everything is fine. I need to go. I'll talk to you when I get home, like I promised. Okay?" I just wanted him to hang up the damn phone so I could get back to my morning wake-up call. Unfortunately, the object of my desire had gotten up and appeared to be in the process of gathering his things. Ending the call, I looked at Hollywood in question as he dressed in his clothes from last night.

"What are you doing? I was hoping we could finish what we started. Do you have to go?" I gave him a teasingly sultry look.

"Evidently, there are a few things you forgot to mention. If you had, I would have told you I don't fuck around with married or committed women. The fact that you could fuck me like you did, when you have a relationship back 'home'? Jesus H. Christ. People like you disgust me. You have no morals or concept of commitment. You are exactly the reason I will never settle down with one woman. You're all the same. To think I thought you were something special and there was a chance… You know what? Never mind." I watched, speechless, as he pulled on his shirt and ran his hand through his dark blond hair, causing it to stick up on end in a sexy-as-hell way. He looked at me with such contempt, it had me reaching down to grab the sheet in an effort to cover and shield myself from the hatred pouring from his eyes.

My mouth wouldn't close, let alone form coherent words. My heart felt as if someone had ripped it out, still beating, and thrown it to the ground to stomp on it. There was such an ache in my chest I could hardly breathe. He had totally misunderstood the phone call because he didn't know the situation. Even though he read everything all wrong, I couldn't seem to comprehend exactly what had set him off to such an extent.

"I hope you have a nice fucking life, Becca." My name came out sounding like a curse or a bad taste he was trying to expel from his mouth, and without another look in my direction, he stormed out the door, slamming it closed. I felt like this had to be a bad dream. I physically hurt, and my eyes burned with the tears threatening to fall. *What the hell had just happened?*

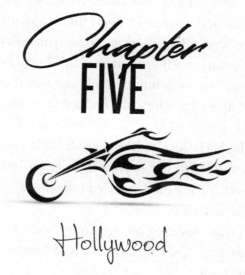

Chapter FIVE

Hollywood

EVEN THOUGH I HADN'T KNOWN AT THE TIME, I COULD NOT fucking believe I had been "the other guy." Never had I cheated on a woman, nor had I been one to pull someone from a relationship.

Relationship. The word itself damn near gave me hives. Because I just didn't do relationships ever since I found out my high school sweetheart had cheated on me with my best friend as soon as I left for basic training. When Lorie had been caught with Johnny, his sister had been the one to tell me after I called his house to talk to him because he hadn't answered his cell. She meant well, but to hear about that over the phone when you knew there was nothing you could do about it? That had devastated me. My trust in women had gone straight to shit.

After I came home, it burned a little every time I saw them. It was hard for them to deny they had been together since he knocked her up almost right away. They were surprisingly still together, and now, years later, I couldn't give a shit less. I wish them well.

What I had done was made sure every girl I had been with since then knew up front what the deal was. The thing was, I had made a promise to my sister, too. Never fuck with someone who was committed. After her husband had cheated on her with a woman who *knew* he was married, I swore to her. I fucking *swore*! Dammit!

To make it worse, I still wanted to bury my dick in Becca. It was like she had woven a spell around me, and I was addicted to her after a single night. Fucking bitch! While she was there sucking on my dick and fucking me senseless, she had a damn husband or boyfriend back home.

The real kicker? Despite how sick it made me, I still craved her body. I could still smell her on my skin. It was intoxicating. God, I needed a shower. Sitting on the closed toilet lid, I held my head in my hands. I felt like such a piece of shit.

Hacker started banging on the door. "Hurry up, man. I have to piss!" Standing, I opened the door and told him to go. I would shower after he was done.

"Damn. What the fuck happened to you? You don't look like a guy who enjoyed himself last night. I figured, when you didn't come back to the room last night, that you were off somewhere making some hot piece scream your name. Instead, you look like someone just kicked your fucking puppy. Shit, bro. You okay?" I shook my head and waved him toward the bathroom. Hacker looked at me in confusion before closing the bathroom door.

I flopped on my bed and stared up at the ceiling. No matter how hard I tried, I couldn't clear my mind of the images of her body and the way she moaned as I slid deep inside her heat.

Fuck! Stop it!

I turned over, punching the pillow several times in frustration.

Shit, the wedding was today, and I would have to walk down the fucking aisle with her and stand across from her as Reaper and Steph said their vows—vows that obviously wouldn't mean shit to someone like Becca.

Hacker came out of the bathroom, and I grabbed my clean clothes and headed in. Turning on the water as hot as it would go, I stood there staring at my reflection in the mirror as steam filled the bathroom, finally obliterating my image.

The shower curtain rings screeched as I slid the curtain open and then closed after climbing in and standing under the hot spray. Both palms splayed on the wall as I hung my head, allowing the water to wash over me. It streamed down my face, forming a thick torrent that gathered my tears and washed them away to the shower floor and swirled down the drain. What the ever-loving fuck? Jesus, I felt like a pussy. Here I was a grown man sitting here crying over a woman I had just met and screwed. But, shit, I actually felt like we clicked, like maybe there could possibly be more with her—not that I would go so far as to say the "R" word, but hell, maybe… Like I said, that hadn't happened to me since Lorie and Johnny burned me. Except instead of being something special, I find out she duped me into being the one thing I never wanted to be.

How did she get to me so fast? Before last night, I barely knew she existed. Damn, I could still see her face flushed in embarrassment when she knew she had been caught with the phone call this morning. What I couldn't believe was she thought we would pick up where we left off after she ended her call with *him*. Damn, she was a piece of work. A sexy, beautiful, wild, quirky piece of work. I couldn't believe I had asked her to come home with me. I couldn't believe I thought we might actually have something. What the hell had I been thinking? *Fuck!* That just wasn't like me—I knew better. She just reiterated my stance on relationships and women in general.

After finishing with my shower, I dried quickly and dressed in a black tee and a pair of broken-in jeans that had seen better days, but who the hell cared? I needed to get out of here for a while. Feeling the wind on my face and the rumble of my bike flying down the highway were what the doctor ordered to clear my head. I still had plenty of time to make it back to get ready for the wedding, and I wasn't going to worry about being early. Besides, if I was a little late, I wouldn't have to be around *her* any longer than I had to. Man, I didn't understand how someone as sweet as Steph could be friends with someone like her. Steph was one of the rare ones. Shit, Steph probably didn't even really know her "friend" anymore.

Stepping out of the bathroom, I padded barefoot to sit on the bed then stretch on my socks and put my boots on. Hacker was lying in his bed propped against the headboard with his arms behind his head. I felt his eyes on me as I tightened the laces of my last boot.

"You want company?"

"Hey, it's a free road. You can do as you like. You're welcome to join me, or you can stay here." Hacker was a smart guy, and I knew he could tell I was pissed, but I didn't want to talk right then. What I needed was to get out and away from the walls that felt like they were closing in on me.

There was absolutely nothing like riding my bike to calm my emotions and soothe my mood. It was as if the wind rushing past grabbed all of the negativity and self-depreciating feelings clinging to me and ripped them off until the last grasping tentacle of despair and anger left me. My bike had been one of my saving graces after I was discharged from the Army. The shit Reaper and I had been through during our many deployments together were things that no one should have to experience. Just because we were good at our jobs and able to compartmentalize it while we were active didn't mean it didn't weigh heavy on us. There were so many times I was afraid we weren't coming home, I couldn't begin to count them. I tried not to let all that stuff eat me alive, but it was hard.

PTSD was a bitch, and there were times I did better than others. Thankfully, I never found myself scraping bottom to the extent Reaper did, and shit, it tore my fucking heart out when I found him in that shithole in San Antonio after he was discharged. People talk about how the VA is there for soldiers after they get out, but mostly it's total bullshit. It's so damn easy to slip through the cracks. Reaper was living proof of that—almost *not* living proof. I can't even let myself go down the what-if-I-hadn't-found-him-when-I-did path. It tears me up inside some days.

Honestly, I was lucky. After the IED explosion in Afghanistan that claimed the lives of our interpreter and a young specialist, it took months of recovery for us. Physically that is… Mentally, I think we're still recovering. Sometimes that day runs through my head on repeat.

The Humvee we traveled in rocked and jolted along the crappy dirt trail they called a road in this godforsaken hellhole named Afghanistan. We were in a small convoy headed to a rendezvous point where we would meet up with a trusted informant and then break off and get into position to take out a key member of the fucking piece of shit Taliban. Reaper, he was SSG Alcott to me then, and I always said it was a hopeless cause, because it just seemed you kill one and another sprouted up to take his place, but it was our mission, and we were damn good soldiers. There hadn't been anyone on the road as we traveled, and it gave an eerie, unnatural feel to the land. We were all on edge and alert, watching for anything that seemed out of place or suspicious.

We were about fifteen clicks out from the rendezvous point when we hit a large rock, causing us to swerve and nearly go off the road. It scared the shit out of me. Suddenly, there was a loud explosion, and none of us heard anything for a few minutes, but we flew through the air, tumbling over and over. Debris in the Humvee flew around inside like missiles, hitting us repeatedly before working its way out a window as we tumbled. We thought a camelback or canteen had busted open, mixing with all the dirt and dust because it splattered all over us inside the Humvee.

My hearing slowly returned, along with a constant ringing sound, as we came to a stop at an angle against a bunch of boulders and rocks. The driver's side of the vehicle was caved in and mangled. I heard screaming coming from up front, and I realized it was Reaper. My legs were numb, and when I looked down, they rested at unnatural angles, and my ACU bottoms were charred and bloody. The smell around us was revolting. Burning flesh was a smell you never hoped to experience, and if you did, it was not one you were likely to forget.

The driver was covered in blood, and he looked at Reaper. He mumbled something, but I still couldn't hear well, and then I saw him cough and gurgle before blood ran out of his nose and mouth, dripping down on Reaper. Through my muffled ears, I heard Reaper yelling, "No, no, no, no, no, no, no!" I tried to get out of the Humvee, but my legs were jacked up. When I looked next to me, the interpreter was staring sightless at the roof of the Humvee with one remaining eye. The left side of his head and where his arm and shoulder should be was just… gone. Gaping, mangled flesh edged the area. My hands ripped at the straps holding me in, and I started screaming before Reaper yelled for me to hold on and asking if I was okay. My eyes looked back to my legs, trying to see if I had hallucinated and maybe they were gone, too. Why wouldn't they work? It felt like I was suffocating. Part of my brain knew I was hyperventilating; the other part felt I was coming apart at my seams.

Voices shouted and gunshots exploded around us as bullets pinged off the rocks. I had no idea who was shooting or what the condition of the rest of the convoy was. I was trapped, and my crazed eyes looked around me as my head twisted in a wild scan to see where things were happening. The gunshots tapered off before they finally stopped. We heard yelling and boots running in various directions. No matter how hard I tried to see outside the Humvee, it was hopeless. We were lying on my side of the vehicle, and all I could see was the rock out of my door. "SSG Alcott! SGT Lange! SPC Thompkins! Is anyone still in there?" That was when the adrenaline started to fade and the pain started to set in. I remembered excruciating pain, moaning, and then blackness. That was the beginning of the next few months of hell...

We had med-evac'ed into Germany first. After that, they shipped us to BAMC, Brook Army Medical Center, down in San Antonio, Texas. I sat by Reaper and talked to him every fucking day. They had him in a medically induced coma for what felt like forever because of his severe TBI and the injuries he suffered. Sometimes I thought he heard me; other times I just prayed he did. He was wrapped up and wired up to so many machines it scared the shit out of me. There were countless times I would sit by his bedside in a wheelchair and doze. After he finally came around, he gave me shit about both my lower legs being casted and how would I chase girls with them. Those were the few moments that he seemed like the old Colton I knew. Most of the time, he just lay there staring out the window.

The doctors and nurses tried to explain his injuries to him, but he didn't want to listen or talk to them. When he finally asked me, I explained to him he suffered fractures to his left arm, the side of his skull, three of his left ribs, his left leg had a rod at the thigh, and the lower leg had pins, plates, and screws. It killed me to have to tell him what we had thought was mud from the dirt and a busted canteen was all of our blood being tossed around inside the Humvee. A fucking human milkshake. If we hadn't hit that giant-ass rock in the road, we would have all been killed instantly, but they said it set us off-track just enough.

We lost a few good friends that day in the firefight that ensued after the explosion, not including our driver and interpreter in the Humvee with us. It fucking sucked, and it tore me apart inside at nights while I lay alone thinking. You do a lot of thinking laid up in the hospital with nothing better to occupy your time.

Reaper and I spent Christmas and New Years in the hospital. Yeah, I had suffered mild burns and breaks to both of my lower legs, but they healed long before Reaper did, so I used to walk in Reaper's room—first with my walker, then the cane—and made it my mission to get him to mentally come back to me. I gave him shit and talked his ear off in an attempt to get any kind of response out of him. Even after I was released to the Warrior Transition Unit, or WTU, I went to the hospital daily, whether I had a therapy appointment or not. We were brothers, maybe not by blood, but in every sense that mattered.

In a last-ditch effort, I went to see Reaper one more time before I left to go home. I had already spent a week of my terminal leave with him trying to convince him to come up to Iowa after they discharged him from the Army. Every time I'd asked him, he always said he would think about it. He never called me, and I was worried as hell about him. When you lived through all the shit we had, you ended up with a bond most people would never understand. Brotherhood.

My family was supportive, and I was lucky I had them to help keep me grounded after I went home. My dad had been a biker my whole life, so it was second nature for me to ride a bike before I even drove a fucking car. Scared the crap out of my mom, but she never once told me no. By the time I joined the Army, I probably had more experience on a bike than a lot of the guys I was stationed with put together. So, it was no surprise to anyone when I put a lot of miles on my bike after I got home… just riding with no destination in mind.

When I was finally accepted as a prospect for the Demented Sons MC, I felt I had gained some of the camaraderie back that I felt lacking after the Army. We were more than that, though… we were a family. But without Reaper, something was still missing. After numerous voice mails with no reply, the last time I called, his cell had been disconnected. I literally felt as if I had been torn in two when I couldn't get in touch with him. Hacker had mercy on me and tracked him down, because having served, he understood the bond you have with those you deploy with. With me being a prospect, he shouldn't have, but we kept it between us, though I had no idea how I was going to get to him. As a prospect, I really didn't have the luxury of running off whenever I wanted. It sucked big time.

Nightmares plagued me, but I dealt with it as best I could. Going into grocery stores, malls, department stores, and places like that was awful. I fucking hated it. The crowds had my skin crawling and my senses on overdrive. When I first got home, I drank a lot too, but after riding my bike home drunk one too many nights, my dad had my ass and told me he worried every damn day about me coming home from combat in a fucking box and he would be damned if he was going to let me climb in one of my own volition after I was lucky enough to have made it home from that hellhole alive. I remembered thinking I was glad *he* thought I was lucky, because I swore it felt like I'd never be whole again… like a part of me was left back in that shithole, never to be recovered.

I decided to get help with counseling for a while. God, I hated the fucking meds they put me on at the VA. They made me feel like I was swimming in syrup half the time, and I couldn't bust a nut for shit. I felt like a freak whenever I had sex with a girl. It sucked. The pain pills made me high, and they became a little too easy to take. That scared me too. So, I quit taking the shit, and with Hacker, Gunny, and my dad's help, I quit drinking so heavy. Sure, I may use a little weed every so often when shit gets especially bad or I can't sleep, but not enough to really get high, just to take the edge off.

The most important thing I did, though, was making it my mission to enjoy life and appreciate the gift I had been given by coming home in one piece, as my dad put it. Maybe a broken, slightly scarred piece, but one piece just the same. So many didn't.

For the most part, it worked. I kept my ink bright to remind me of the happiness I had all around me. I loved my brothers in the MC, and the day I got patched was one of the best and worst days of my life. The gauntlet I had to run with everyone getting a hit in left me bruised and battered, but it was a rite of passage, and I accepted it with honor. But shit, it fucking hurt. Damn.

All in all, I had a great life. Women loved me, and I loved women. My little family was there for me, and I had my brothers in the club. It was easy to tell myself I didn't need any more than that.

When the prez, Snow, told me I was going along with Gunny to a small town outside of San Antonio, Texas, I knew there must have been divine intervention involved in that shit. Call me crazy if you want, but some shit in life makes you believe in fate.

We were heading down to pick up a bike we had been hired to customize for some rich fucker. Gunny was my sponsor in the club, and as a Marine, he had deployed to Iraq a few times before getting out. During our time together, I talked a lot about Colton; he wasn't Reaper until he came home with me and joined the club. We made a detour to the shitty neighborhood he had holed up in and pretty much dragged him with us. There was no way in hell either of us was leaving a brother in arms behind like that. We never admitted it out loud, but even hardened as we were, it scared the shit out of us.

Now here we all were in Vegas with Reaper, where he was preparing to marry the love of his life and mother of his child—soon to be children. Returning to the hotel, I pulled back into the parking lot with Hacker rolling up next to me as I backed into a parking spot. Killing the motor, I sat for a minute in silence, listening to the occasional ticking of my motor. Hacker threw a questioning look my way, but I appreciated his silence. The ride distracted me and calmed me, as I hoped. *Thank God. Now if only I could get a certain redhead out of my mind and move on.*

Chapter SIX

Becca

WHAT A SELF-RIGHTEOUS BASTARD. THE MORE I STEWED ON THE events of this morning, the angrier I became. It wasn't like Hollywood had worried about whether I was with someone when he pinned me up against the wall in the club… or when he was screwing my brains out in the limo. How dare he be so accusatory and condescending to me when he didn't even know the entire story?

Like I said, Trevor's call had definitely been unwanted and occurred with horrible timing. If I had thought to look at the caller ID, I wouldn't have answered and I would've dealt with Trevor later. For the thousandth time, I questioned myself regarding my stupid decision to agree to talk about our relationship when we got back. Damn me for being non-confrontational and not wanting to deal with a big blow up right before I left. Now it'd come back to bite me in the ass. Shit.

Hollywood was so different from Trevor and every other guy I had dated, if the truth be told. He was funny, sweet, hot, gorgeous, sexy, and hot. Oh, did I mention hot? Geez, there had to be a better way to describe him, but hot just described him… singe-your-heart hot. Set-your-nerves-on-fire hot.

His eyes were an amazing blend of a tawny gold and a dark green, making them possibly the most beautiful hazel I had ever seen. His dark blond hair always stood up in a short, wild mess like he had just rolled out of bed and run his hands through it, calling it good. He seemed like he was a tease and a happy guy at first. I caught a glimpse of that side of him again this morning before the phone call. But physical attributes aside, he was the perfect blend of sensitive lover while being a total alpha when he wanted something. He also seemed secure in himself, happy in his skin.

His hot and cold threw me for a loop, though. He started out flirty, got pissy, turned hot and sex-driven, then sensual, loving, and funny, and then pissy again. If I was honest, and if we were closer, I could have seen us finding a way to see what developed, but I sincerely didn't expect much more than a little fun last night. The more I considered it, I wondered if he only mentioned me going home with him because he knew I wouldn't. And why had he been angry last night before we left the club? Surely he wasn't jealous? That was impossible. He didn't even know me. Maybe he'd decided to rock my world after the bachelorette party and got pissed when he thought I was hooking up with the other guy instead of him. Maybe? Funny, I couldn't even recall that guy's face now.

Oh, well. To hell with Hollywood. I probably wouldn't ever see him again after the wedding anyway. It didn't do me any good to sit here and brood over him and his up and down attitude. We had a great night full of great sex—exactly what I had set out to do. No harm, no foul. So why did my chest still ache when I pictured the look of disgust on his face before he walked out my door?

The laughter and tittering of the girls as we all sat and had our hair and makeup done at the salon was grating on my nerves. I felt wound up and on edge. The constant conversation around me was nothing but a wordless drone that drilled through my head. Shit, I needed some Tylenol for my pounding headache. The smell of hair chemicals in the salon wasn't helping either, and my nostrils felt like they burned from it.

My hair and makeup were done, and the stylist turned me toward the mirror for my approval. I didn't even recognize myself in the reflection that stared back at me. Over the last few years, I had rarely applied makeup, with the exception of last night, and my hair ended up in a ponytail or braid more often than not. I always felt like I had the "good girl" elementary school teacher image to uphold. Not to mention, Trevor felt too much makeup was a sign of vanity, and he didn't really approve.

The stylist had outdone herself. My deep auburn locks were swept up in a sleek twist that ended in a tumble of curls. She had captured the usual wild tangle into smooth ringlets that cascaded down and teased the top of my left shoulder. My makeup was soft, but my eyes were dramatic and appeared to be a deep jade color framed by a thick fringe of lashes. I never felt like I was ugly, but she made me look… well, just, wow.

When the first thought in my head was to wonder if Hollywood would think I looked good, I gave myself a mental kick. Ugh! What the heck was wrong with me? Who cared what he thought? Well, actually I hoped he ate his heart out. Ha! Jerk. I was looking forward to sliding the silky, form-fitting, black bridesmaid dress on and strutting my stuff. A smug smile spread across my face. I would show his ass.

I was starting to look forward to antagonizing him and pouring it on thick. You see, I knew how to work myself and my body. Just because I had tried to maintain a low-key appearance and life for the last few years didn't mean the real me wasn't buried deep inside. Now, I felt like a butterfly breaking out of its chrysalis of self-imposed restraint to be the person I should have been all along. I took a deep, cleansing breath. Damn, it felt liberating.

Steph and Reaper had chosen a little chapel called the Graceland Wedding Chapel with the officiator of the wedding dressed like Elvis. They decided not to have Elvis walk her down the aisle though, as that was an honor reserved for her father. It was sweet and an experience they would never forget. The bright smile on my face had been in place since we arrived, and I couldn't have held it back if I tried. Just seeing how happy Steph was made me feel warm and fuzzy inside. Her husband-to-be was hot as hell, lucky bitch, and she would have her beautiful baby girl, Remi, as her flower girl. They would all be a real family, finally.

I remembered being with her the day she found out she was pregnant. She'd been terrified with no idea where Colton, aka Reaper, was back then. She was strong, and I was so proud of her for having Remi, working hard to be what and where she wanted in life, and for being a survivor. After everything she had been through, she totally deserved every bit of this happiness.

We all stood around, looking in the mirrors set up for us to get ready with to double check our hair, makeup, and dresses. All of our dresses were different styles, but each of them were black and classy. I wore the same black heels from last night. They had a black platform with five-inch heels, and I loved how they tighten up my calves, making them look even more sculpted and firm. For the second time this trip, I thanked my escape time to the gym for having a tight butt, and thanked the booby fairy for her blessings. *Yeah, Hollywood, eat your damn heart out.*

My heart gave a little gallop just from his name running through my mind. For the first time since arriving, my smile slipped.

Disgusting. Jesus. I needed to get a grip. Yes, he was gorgeous and a good lay, but that was all he was. I couldn't even stand him anymore. There was no reason he should be taking up so much real estate in my head. So, tossing him out of my head like a piece of trash, I pasted my smile back on my face and finished settling Steph's veil around her shoulders. She was a beautiful bride. Stunning, really.

"God, Steph, you look beautiful. I'm so damn happy for you. Who would have thought we would be here today? Destiny has a crazy way of twisting and turning until your life gets to where it's supposed to be, huh, chica?" Tears welled in her eyes as she hugged me.

"I love you, Becca. Thank you for being there for me through the pregnancy and all. I wouldn't change any of it if it meant I wouldn't be where I am now."

The wedding music began to play, and we all kissed her on the cheek as we exited the room, leaving her to her father. He was such a handsome man, and he looked like he was going to burst with pride or collapse from the stress of giving away his baby girl. A chuckle escaped me, imagining my own dad someday. Hopefully. I sighed. Someday, I hoped this would be me getting ready for my own wedding.

Being the maid of honor meant I had to walk down the aisle with *him* since he was the best man. *God, give me strength.* I tried not to make eye contact as I reached to hook my arm through his as we prepared to start down the aisle toward the little Elvis impersonator. The other members of the wedding party, who had walked before us, awaited on either side of the archway ahead. When my hand touched the crook of his arm, I felt a jolt of energy and the heat of his arm through his crisp, white, long-sleeve shirt. There went my heart again.

Breathe, Becca. Deep breaths. It was just primitive sexual tension, that's all. That's what I kept telling myself. God, he smelled so damn good. *Okay, maybe not so deep of breaths.* My appreciation of his firm muscles under that white shirt was strictly a result of appreciating a beautiful male form, not because they were *his* muscles. Definitely nothing to do with him. Nope.

As we separated at the archway, I snubbed my nose to him and turned the other way to take my place. We glared at each other from our respective sides as we waited for the bride to walk up the aisle. I noted Colton's—ugh, Reaper... I needed to remember to refer to him as Reaper—curious expression as he looked between the two of us, and I pasted my fake smile back on. He raised an eyebrow at me and gave me a questioning glance. I smiled bigger and was so relieved when the wedding march began to play, pulling his attention to his bride as she slowly advanced down the aisle toward him.

Reaper and Steph were exchanging vows and rings. So, what did I do? I resumed glaring at Hollywood. *I hope he chokes on wedding cake later.* Why did he make these evil thoughts swim in my head? My teeth ground in frustration. Thankfully, it was a brief ceremony, and before we knew it, we were headed back to the banquet room at the hotel for the reception.

The toasts, congratulations, and dinner were a blur of laughter and smiles. Despite my own inner turmoil, I was truly happy for them. When it was time for the bride to throw her bouquet, I joined the single ladies but hung back behind everyone else. Truth be told, I would have been just as happy to stay seated for the whole bouquet thing. When it smacked me in the face, I reached up, pulling it to my chest by sheer reflex. My mouth gaping open as all the girls teased, patted, hugged, and kissed me, I stood staring at the bouquet like it was a viper. When I raised my gaze from the deep red roses, my line of sight collided with Hollywood's. He stood there with his arms crossed over his chest, and if looks could kill, I would have dropped dead on the spot.

What the hell? Asshole.

I made the excuse of having to use the restroom to freshen up and pee, and rushed toward the door with my nose buried in the fragrant roses as I walked. The petals felt like the finest velvet, and I couldn't resist rubbing my nose on them again. Roses were my favorite flower, and these were beautiful, but I didn't deserve to catch the bouquet. I didn't even have anyone. At this rate, I never would. A heavy cloak of melancholy settled around my shoulders.

When I returned to the reception, it was just in time to watch the bride's dance with her father end and the one with her new husband begin. It was a magnificent sight. Steph was a radiant bride, and Reaper beamed with love and pride. It didn't hurt that he was absolutely striking in his white shirt and bow tie, despite being dressed in his biker vest thingy now.

When the bride and groom's dance ended to deafening applause and whistles, they called the bridal party to the dance floor for their dance and my feet froze to the floor.

Shit. No. No, I wasn't dancing with him. No way. Oh Lord.

There he stood, in the middle of the dance floor, dressed the same as Reaper now, and his eyes met mine once again. He waited with a haughty expression, which I did my best to replicate. Huffing, I grabbed myself by my big girl panties, gently set the bridal bouquet at my seat, and walked toward him.

I stepped into his arms as the music began to play, and my heart leaped at his touch and raced at being so close to him. He pulled me closer and my nipples hardened as they encountered the leather of his vest with only the thin black fabric of my dress separating them. My eyes closed, and I took a deep breath, attempting to collect myself, but that was a big mistake. Because when I did, I breathed in his cologne, and I felt my face and chest flush with the pleasure of just inhaling his scent. Spicy, exotic, and leather… Why did he have to smell so damn good? Hell, if my hooha didn't clench just from that and his touch.

"So, congratulations on the bouquet. I guess that means you and *Trevor* will probably be next." His voice was strained and snide. My eyes flashed open in hurt and annoyance to see him looking down at me with a blank expression.

Why was he being so hateful? God, he was such an ass.

"Doubtful." My voice snapped out. I just couldn't get any other words out at that point. I knew I would sound breathless and shaky if I did. My body was screaming for him just by being this close to his. It was as if my very soul sensed his was close and put every cell in my body on high alert. Traitorous damn body. I looked away so I didn't drown in the green that had taken over his beautiful hazel eyes. It wasn't fair that he was so freaking cute but such a damn jerk.

As he spun me at the corner of the dance floor, his hand gripped my hip tighter to keep us together through the turn. He was an amazing dancer, I hated to admit. When his hand slid down across the curve of my ass, I jumped and my shaken gaze collided with his. His nostrils flared, and the muscle in his jaw jumped as he pulled me even closer so that we were nearly touching head to toe. His erection was enough to be felt through his black denim, and I was completely stunned. My ego started to feel a boost knowing, even with the contempt he felt for me, he still desired me. Without meaning to, my lips curved into a satisfied smirk.

I swear he growled. Yes, *growled.* Guess he didn't like being turned on by me.

Too damn bad, asswipe.

When we turned at the next corner, he spun us off the dance floor and proceeded to drag me along by my hand down the hall that led to the bathrooms. I protested to no avail. He kept pulling me along, past the bathrooms and entered a door at the end of the hall.

"Ummm, it's a storage closet? Is there something you needed, Hollywood? Perhaps you wanted to mop the dance floor? Need more toilet paper?" Yeah, the sarcasm was rolling off my tongue. I was such a bitch. Oh well, if he didn't like it, he shouldn't have been such an ass to me. The door closed with a sharp click.

"Yes," he said as he grabbed me by the waist, setting me on top of a table along the wall. "Dammit all to hell. I fucking hate myself for it, but I need you." His lips crashed to mine with a ferocity that took my breath away. Our tongues battled and tangled as he slid my dress up my thighs to spread my legs and step in between my knees. His hands grabbed my ass and roughly slid me closer until my hot core was flush with his encased erection. With a satisfied moan slipping from my lips into his mouth, my hands threaded through his hair. *Fuck it.* Despite my mind's resolve to snub him, my heart and body craved him. The kiss was like none other I had ever experienced. Wild, passionate, and consuming.

His warm, calloused fingers slid up my inner thigh to cup my throbbing core. My panties were soaked, so there was no denying my arousal. His small groan told me he noticed. When a single finger slid them to the side and dipped in and out of the moisture pooling there, my hands clutched tight to the back of his neck and shoulder. In desperation, my hips tilted, trying to pull his probing fingers deeper inside me.

Without warning, he pulled away from me. His eyes were wide, and his hands fisted before he banged them on his head.

"Shit! I can't fucking do this! What are you *doing* to me?" He turned to slam out the door. My arms, which had remained outstretched and suspended in my shock, fell helplessly to my side. For the second time that day, he left me sitting with my mouth hanging open and panting in sexual frustration like I had run a marathon.

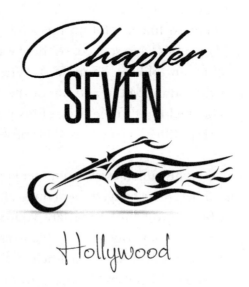

Chapter SEVEN

Hollywood

SLAMMING INTO MY ROOM, I PULLED OUT THE SMALL DUFFLE I had brought and stuffed my few belongings into it. I dug out my cell phone and sent off a text to Reaper, apologizing for ditching out early from the reception. Then I called Snow and told him I had to take care of a few things and I would meet everyone at the hotel in Gallup, NM.

We had taken the longer ride down across I40 instead of the more direct route through Denver due to the temperatures and weather in early October. We had brought trailers with the SUV and truck, so if we got tired or the weather got bad, we could take turns riding, driving, and hauling. Two days and nearly 1800 miles is a long time on a bike, even if you love the hell out of it.

Snow asked if I wanted someone to ride with me, and I told him no, I was good, and to let everyone enjoy the reception. I would stow my cut to avoid any issues on the road since I would be riding solo. You just don't go flashing your colors around in another MC's territory. Snow told me to be careful, which I always was. After tapping out a quick text to Joker and Hacker, I stuffed my phone into my inner pocket of my jacket.

With careless regard for my shit, I shoved the bag and my cut in the saddle bags and climbed on. I had always ridden a soft tail, but decided to spoil myself after returning home from the Army, and bought a black Street Glide. I fucking loved this bike.

Damn, I was so pissed at myself and her, I was shaking. Searching my pockets, I found the stub of a joint, stuck it between my lips and lit the end. A couple of puffs and I felt my tension ease. A couple more and it was pretty much used up. Far from high, but feeling calmer, I tossed it to the ground and exhaled the last breath I had held.

Jerking on my helmet, I settled in and zipped my jacket up all the way. Clutch, brake, and then I was putting her in neutral before flipping the engine switch and hitting the start button. She purred to life with a deep rumble, and I gunned the throttle to blow out the dust. Shit, I loved the Rinehart true duel pipes I had added. Best sound, ever… next to the little sighs and moans Becca made as our bodies collided…

What the hell? Fuck me.

Let's go, baby. We need some asphalt under our wheels.

There would be about six hours to think on the way to Gallup. As I eased on the throttle, I left the situation tearing at my heart and dick behind me. Too bad it didn't flush this fucked-up situation from my mind as well.

It was late and the roads had been nearly deserted most of the night.

At about two in the morning, I pulled off the interstate and up to the hotel we stopped at on the way down. Of course, I had made good time, and let's just say I was lucky I hadn't encountered any damn cops. Habit had me backing my bike into a spot in front of the hotel. My head was screaming, and I had hoped to have a drink at the bar before I hit the sack, but I didn't make it before closing time. Oh well, I walked over to the 24-hour convenience store across from the hotel and picked up a fifth of Jack. Yeah, I may not drink much anymore, but tonight was definitely a Jack night.

After checking in, I dropped my bags in my room and walked to the chair in front of the open curtains without turning on the lights. Restless, I sat staring out the window at the night lights, tipped the bottle up, and tried to forget her.

Damn, she'd lured me like a siren and woven her very essence through my veins. Her face flashed like a strobe light in my mind with all her beautiful expressions a kaleidoscope in my head. Visions of her laughing with her eyes twinkling, angry with eyes dark and gleaming, and painfully clear was the expression on her beautiful face as she was lost in passion, on the brink of imploding. That was when her lips were full and red, her mouth parted with her gasping breaths, and her lashes casting shadows over her glazed jade eyes.

She was under my skin, and I couldn't stand it. Never had I been so hung up on a woman. And of course, I had to become obsessed with an unfaithful bitch. The problem was, she had her claws in me after one night, and I was on the verge of throwing away all my morals and promises for her sweet, addictive pussy. That was why I had to leave. The only cure I could think of was to find someone else to bury my cock in until the memories of her were nothing but hazy photographs in my mind. If I could lock her away with the memories of all the shit from my deployments, including the accident in Afghanistan, I knew I would be okay. Yeah, just lock it all away—easier said than done.

It didn't take me long to polish off the bottle in the mood I was in. Good thing I hadn't bought a bigger bottle, because I could have kept going. When I stood up, the alcohol hit me like lightning, and I swayed on my feet.

Whoa. This was why I quit drinking so much of that shit.

Boots kicked off, I flipped back the bedspread and crashed face down on the bed. My heavy eyes drifted closed, and I fell asleep with green eyes, red lips, and deep auburn hair racing through my mind. I could have sworn I even smelled her perfume.

Shit, I was so fucked.

Chapter EIGHT

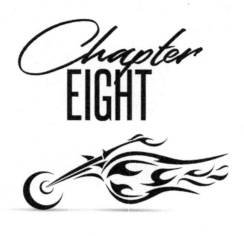

Becca

TREVOR FOLLOWED ME THROUGH THE DOOR AND TOSSED HIS KEYS to the table. Shit, I wish he would have let me take a cab home from the airport. What the hell was I thinking telling him when I was flying in? The silent ride home was tortuous. It made me just want to crawl in bed and pretend the trip to Vegas never happened.

Couldn't I just go upstairs and pack my bags? The furniture that was mine didn't even seem to matter. He could keep it, or I could get it another time. Of course, he wanted to talk *right fricking now*. Damn him. What had I ever seen in him, other than he was good looking, had a good job, and seemed so respectable? Which sure as hell didn't really seem so important now.

"You shouldn't wear so much makeup, Becca. It makes you look cheap. What would your students and their parents say if they saw you looking like that? Appearances are important, baby. I've told you this before. No one wants their child being taught by a loose and easy woman. Right?" My teeth gritted in frustration as I looked in the mirror over the hall table to make sure I hadn't gone heavy with my face this morning. After all, I did have to cover the dark circles I woke with after a fitful night.

Wait. What did my makeup have to do with being easy or not? And why in the holy hell did I look right away, intent on fixing whatever he said was wrong? Sheesh, he really was an idiot, or maybe I was the idiot. How did I let myself fall into his controlling manner? It was like I never even saw it, or more likely, I inadvertently allowed it because I was trying so hard for "respectability." I was *really* beginning to hate that word… Respectability. What I had lost sight of was the simple fact that I couldn't expect other people to respect me if I didn't respect myself.

"You know what, Trevor? Newsflash: I'm not really wearing that much makeup, and I was *still* told I looked good today." His eyes widened in shock at my uncharacteristic response. He had some issues if he thought I had a lot of makeup on, especially now that most of it had worn off since I put it on this morning. God, he was starting to piss me off. He had me feeling like a completely different person than I was before him, and not in a good way. Then, I was carefree, bubbly, and happy. The last time I felt happy with him was… hell, I hardly ever felt happy anymore. In Vegas was the happiest I had been in forever.

Trevor always seemed so boring but… *safe*. There was never a concern that he would pull me back into my former wild behavior. What I hadn't realized was that he had molded and manipulated me into what he wanted me to be, and I completely and totally drank the Kool-Aid where he was concerned. I'd lost sight of myself and the fact that I could mature and still have fun. It didn't mean I would go insanely crazy just because I had a few drinks or went dancing. God,

I needed to get away from him already. Just being back here, I could feel the tension creeping in, constricting my skin and the very air I was breathing.

"Hey, you know what? I think I'll go wash my face, swing by my mom's real quick, and then head to the gym. I really slacked on working out while I was gone, and I ate way too many carbs." A false smile plastered on my face, I rushed upstairs to the bathroom. When I got there, I scrubbed the makeup off, pulled my hair up in a tight, high ponytail, and threw on a work out T-shirt and some yoga pants. Grabbing my car keys from my dresser and a light jacket from my closet, I quickly descended the stairs, each step a staccato echo of my heartbeat.

There was no sign of Trevor when I grabbed my purse from the table. He must have been in his office. Good, because I didn't really want to talk to him anymore. I needed to get some fresh air and see my mom. Maybe she would have some of her homemade coconut cake waiting for me. Of course, that would mean extra miles on the treadmill, but it would so be worth it. The thought brought a genuine smile to my face.

I took the long way around, taking Shore Drive around the lake to East Manawa Drive and then to Navajo Street. Driving on the curving road bordering Lake Manawa never failed to calm me and bring back memories of my childhood growing up on "Lake Manaswamp." It had been dubbed that for as long as anyone could remember. My friends and I used to party on the beach, and, of course, we made out and drank in the park and in the random parking lots that surrounded the lake.

While there were a lot of really nice houses around the lake, my parents' house was a little rambler that was now squeezed in between two big fancy houses. We weren't directly on the lake, but close enough. It was much older than many of the houses around us, having been built years and years before they were, but it was home.

I parked in the driveway, in front of the chipped "Semi Parking

Only" sign I had bought my dad for Christmas my sophomore year of high school. Just the memory of his face as he nailed it up on the side of the house where the driveway was had me grinning. He had been so proud and tickled. Since the spot was open, he obviously was out on a run. Dang, that had me more than a little bummed, because I loved seeing my dad and hearing his booming laugh.

The rust-colored red paint on the house was peeling in spots, and I made a mental note to offer to help repaint it next summer. Dad didn't always get around to repairs on the house because he was gone so much. Mom tried, but she wasn't super handy, having come from a family where she was the only girl who really never had to do anything for herself. She was spoiled growing up. One thing my mom could do, however, was grow beautiful flowers and bake. She was also incredibly creative and had, at one time, aspirations of doing graphic design.

Honestly, I couldn't believe I didn't end up around 500 pounds with all the delicious baked goods that poured out of her oven over the years. It never ceased to amaze me how she and my dad had hooked up, because they were so totally opposite. My mom was like me, artistic, maybe a little of a flower child. Dad was gruff, a work-with-his-hands type of guy. He drove a truck, fixed shit when he was home, and tinkered in his shop on God knows what when he had free time. They loved each other though, there was no doubt about it. The love in their eyes when they looked at each other warmed my heart. That was what I wanted someday. I just didn't know if I would ever be that lucky. Maybe luck had nothing to do with it. Maybe my own fear of losing control over my newer "good girl reputation" was actually what was holding me back.

As if I had conjured it with my thoughts, I walked in the house and the aroma of my mother's baking engulfed me. *Ahhh, home.* How was it that a simple smell could have nostalgia flood back over you and leave you feeling like a kid again… safe… with no worries, just the stress of school work or how you would respond to an invite to the SnoBall dance? It was as if stepping through the doorway was like stepping into a time warp.

"Becca, honey? Is that you?" My mom peeked around the doorway from the kitchen to the living room. Her smile was wide and bright as she blew a stray strand of blonde hair from her face. Despite not seeing eye to eye with my mom, I loved her. She was still beautiful to me, and I hurried over to hug her and kiss her cheek as she continued to stir what looked like frosting in a mixing bowl. Her green eyes lit with laughter when I told her how beautiful she was.

"Girl, you're so crazy. You know I'm old and out of shape and the wrinkles are taking over! What do you want?" She winked at me and tipped her head over to the counter where I noted a cake resting on a cooling rack. This had me clapping my hands and jumping up and down just like the child I felt take over as I entered the house. My mom continued to laugh at me as she told me to sit down and tell her all about Las Vegas.

"It was fun. Steph was gorgeous, as always. The wedding was sweet, and the food at the reception was good. Steph's husband is so incredibly hot, and you can just tell he loves her so much. It reminded me of you and dad." I knew I had a wistful look on my face. Jealousy was creeping in again, and I fought down the green-eyed monster that was clawing up my throat. It didn't seem fair because I had always wanted what my parents had, and now my best friend seemed to have it too. Not that I begrudged Steph and Colton one iota.

"I'm just still so shocked! A *biker!* I would never have thought that sweet studious little girl would hook up with someone like that." Mom tsked in slight disapproval.

"Oh, Mom, he's nice. And he used to be a soldier in the Army. He's a war hero with a purple heart and everything." How I wished my mom wasn't so hung up on occupations, income, and appearances. For crying out loud, my dad did a short stint in the Army before he got out and became a truck driver. He wasn't a Wall Street tycoon, and that had done them just fine.

"Oh really? Hmm, I didn't know that. But a biker mechanic… surely he could have found a better job than that after the Army. Now Trevor, he got a good job after he got out of the Air Force. Surely, that boy of Steph's could have found something like Trevor did."

Ugh! Mom, please!

"Mom, Trevor was an admin assistant in the Air Force for three years. He never deployed and rarely left his office." In frustration, I rolled my eyes. Trevor rarely talked about his service time, and I didn't really ask because there wasn't much to talk about. He spoke more about his job now, as a government employee, than his service time.

"But it's what he does now that's important. He has a good job with good benefits and a nice retirement. He is such a great catch for you, Becca." Great, now I needed to tell her I was ditching him. Her hero, Trevor. For the life of me, I never understood why my parents felt like he hung the moon. Every time we were over to the house, he charmed the pants off them though, so I suppose it made sense. Well, this wasn't going to go over well.

"Yeah, about that…" I sat at the table, tracing the woodgrain with my fingernail. "I told him I want to break things off." My eyes stayed trained to the tabletop, flicking at a couple of stray grains of salt. Meeting my mom's gaze briefly after this news seemed tantamount to telling her I had murdered someone or something. So, I looked back down swiftly.

"What?" The mixing bowl dropped to the table with a loud *thunk* as she dropped into the chair next to me and reached over to my chin to bring my eyes to hers. "What on Earth happened?" My mother looked like I told her I just robbed a bank. Great.

"Mom, we just don't click. We are so different, and he is so… just boring, Mom. I don't love him, and I don't see myself *ever* loving him. When we met at the Storm Chasers game, I thought he was cute and polite. I should have realized when there was no real spark that he wasn't the one. It has just gotten worse over time. Now he just makes me feel stifled and smothered." The desperation in my voice and eyes pleaded with her to understand.

"Baby, don't be hasty. Talk to him. He's a really good man, and I feel like he really grounds you. He loves you, and I'm sure he just wants what's best for you, honey." My mom tried to make me see what she did, but that was a vision I couldn't conjure.

"Can you please let me make my own decisions? Trevor doesn't ground me. He tethers me to the ground. There's a difference, Mom. God, I wish I had never even started dating him." Knowing I wouldn't get anywhere with her, I got up to leave.

"Becca! Don't you dare screw this up! That man accepted you despite your wild-girl past, and he helped you grow up and become a mature adult! Life isn't about running around partying and painting happy little trees and sunshine everywhere." She had me wanting to growl in frustration at her obstinacy.

"Love you, Momma, but I need to head home to get some supper started." Kissing her on the cheek, I once again took the coward's way out with her and left.

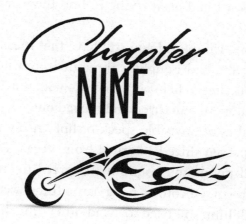

Chapter NINE

Becca

LORDY, I LOVED THE KIDS IN MY CLASS, BUT IT WAS MONDAY, AND the twenty-four fourth graders in my last class had been in rare form. My coffee was gone before I knew it, and I looked at the clock to see if I had time for another cup. A resigned breath escaped my mouth, and I slouched further in my chair in the teachers' lounge. Hopefully, the next bunch ran off some of their energy in the P.E. class before mine. Ugh!

"Break's almost over, girl." Josie had to go poking me with her proverbial stick. She and I had several education classes together in college at Iowa State, and I loved working with her. We had gotten pretty close, but nowhere as close as Steph and I were. She was from a small town not far from here, but with no jobs available in her area, good old Council Bluffs was the closest area with positions. So, there we were, both dreading going back to class. Mondays were the worst because the kids had been out of their routine for two whole days, and it was like starting at square one with them every Monday.

Giving her the stink eye and sticking my tongue out at her, I got up to rinse out my mug and place it on the drying mat by the sink. Leaning against the counter, I folded my arms and prepared to ask her the question I had been trying to find the words for during our entire break.

"Hey, Josie. Umm, did you still have that room you were trying to rent out?" She had bought a three-bedroom house and usually had two roommates to help with the payment, but Tanya, her second roommate, had gotten married and moved out.

I brushed at an invisible speck of lint on my blouse. Over two months had passed since I returned from Vegas. Two months since, at Trevor and my mom's hounding, I agreed to "try to make thing work" with Trevor. Of course, not a damn thing was different, and yet I was still with him, so I tried to avoid him as much as possible. Who was this pushover bitch and what had she done with the Becca I used to be?

"Actually, yes, I do. Why? Who do you know that's looking? Do I know them? It's not some weirdo, is it? I require references, you know." She crossed her arms over her chest, tipped her chin down, and gave me the raised eyebrow look. Josie was a darling, but she was very reserved, and I imagined she had been a bit of a nerd in high school. In college, she was quiet and kept to herself unless we had a study group together. She could be super pretty if she would think of getting contacts and doing a little something with herself. It was oh so wrong, but I couldn't help thinking she was who Trevor should have hooked up with. She was just sweet and kind of, well, *plain*. Mousy brownish-blonde hair, parted in the middle, straight as a board and long, and no makeup *ever* topped off her dang-near Laura Ingalls look.

"Well, funny you should ask… it's me. Most of my references would be the same ones you would use. The only rental reference I have is from when Steph and I were in college." Suppressing a laugh at her owl-like expression, I gave her a pleading look.

"Uh, yeah, okay. But if you don't mind my asking, is there something going on? I thought you and Trevor lived together and were like practically married. He's such a sweet man. Don't tell me he broke up with you? Or… no way. Don't tell me *you* broke up with *him*?" She was so nice, but evidently easily shocked and amazed.

Why did everyone have to seem so surprised I would want to end things with Trevor? First my mom, now Josie. Couldn't anyone see what he was like? Maybe it *was* just me. No, because Steph couldn't stand him. He didn't like kids, and he had been condescending to her anytime she and Remi came to visit me until she quit coming. Because he didn't want children, I wasn't supposed to want them. It was frustrating. Looking at the clock again, I saw I only had about five minutes to get back to class.

"I don't really have time to get into it now, but if you're okay with me moving in, I'd love to be able to do it ASAP." I clasped my hands in supplication at her and put on my best pout. She started laughing at my antics and told me I could swing by tonight to sign the rental agreement and move in any time after that. Hugging her tightly with a jubilant and profuse "thank you" pouring from my mouth, I told her I would be by tonight and, hopefully, moving in this weekend.

Maybe it was a small thing, but making definitive plans to move out and move on with my life lifted a huge weight off my shoulders. It was as if the skies were a little brighter and my heart was a little lighter.

You would think four days would be more than enough time to discuss with Trevor my plans to move out. Yet, here it was Thursday and

I still hadn't had a chance. Either he wasn't home, I wasn't home, or he was "too busy with work" to talk to me. He spent nearly every waking moment in his home office. Well, that was fine. I didn't need much time to tell him, and I was going to corner him that night. Period.

Dinner was made and waiting for him and the table was set. That seemed like as good a place as any to keep him in one place so I could talk to him. The second hand on the clock seemed to tick by in slow motion. My eyes would not quit looking at my watch, the clock on the stove and the clock in the living room. Sheesh. Five minutes after six. *Shouldn't he be here by now?*

The sound of the garage door opening had me rushing to the kitchen to dish up our plates. Trevor came through the kitchen door and set his briefcase by the doorway to the living room. He then came and bussed my cheek and told me dinner smelled excellent. Just the touch of his lips on my skin had my cringing inside, but I told him to have a seat and I would bring his plate over.

We ate in relative silence for a few minutes before I set my utensils down and rested my hands in my lap. A deep breath to gain my composure and calm my nerves was in order. This shouldn't be that difficult. However, even though Trevor had been boring and a little controlling, he had been good to me, letting me move in with him and not charging me a penny for rent or utilities. He covered everything, telling me it was his job as the man in the relationship. The part of that I never liked was him hinting that I wouldn't be working after we got married. Considering I had never agreed to marry him, because he had never actually *asked*, I always left that discussion alone.

"Trevor, I really need to talk to you. We still haven't discussed our relationship status since I came home. I have really thought about things and—" As usual, he interrupted me.

"Becca, dear, there is really nothing to discuss. I know you were feeling stifled, and that is why I let you go to Vegas before we discussed our relationship. I knew you would feel better after getting away for the weekend and having a little 'girl time' with Steph and the girls. Don't worry, things are still good between us," he finished. *Let me go to Vegas?* Was he serious?

"Trevor! That's not true. Things are absolutely no different with us. Yes, I was feeling stifled. It seems like I have been the one who has changed everything about myself. Initially, I felt like you would be good for me because you were steady and respectable, which I felt I needed to keep me grounded and reputable. We got along well, and then you asked me to move in and things have flowed along, and I got caught up in the current. I feel like I've gone so far to the other end of the personality spectrum and it's not fair to me." I tried to read his expression, but he just sat there staring at his food. My intent was never to hurt him, and I prayed he was okay.

"So that's it? You're just done? Over a year and a half put into this relationship and you're *done* just like that? I don't think you're thinking clearly, Becca. I think you're emotional and acting irrational. Maybe Vegas was a bad idea after all. We *are* good together, and I will *not* lose you. I really think you should take some time to think about your feelings. There's no need to rush into a decision." He slid his chair back and left the table. In astonishment, I watched him pick up his briefcase and walk into his office, closing the door after he entered.

"Why do you keep putting words in my mouth? Who put you in charge of my feelings?" I yelled after him.

My head fell to my hands. What a disaster. Why couldn't he understand and accept I was done? Was he dense? And why was it me who needed to think about my feelings and decide to stay? A true relationship should have give-and-take with equal input. That was part of the problem with our situation. The other part of the problem was the total lack of chemistry. No magic.

Call me crazy, but if and when I settled down, I wanted it all. This relationship, if you could call it that, was a farce. I wanted love. I wanted insane lust, amazing sex, friendship, and the give and take of a true partnership. Anything less was settling, and I didn't think I should have to settle any longer.

Chapter TEN

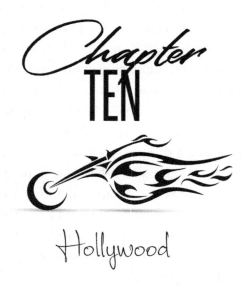

Hollywood

ROSALEE WAS STRADDLING MY LAP, FLIPPING HER FLAME-RED HAIR over her shoulder, as we sat in the big shop out at Reaper and Steph's house. It was the weekend barbeque, and the brothers and their families, or dates, were here to hang out, relax, drink some beer, and basically have a good time.

It was mid-December and too cold and snow-covered to have it outside. Rosalee's constant nagging about getting a property patch was getting on my damn nerves. I didn't want a damn old lady, and if I did, it sure as hell wouldn't be her. Sure, she had been a great distraction and had kept my bed pretty warm for the last few weeks, but that was all she was to me. She hadn't ever been introduced as my girlfriend, and I shouldn't have kept her around so long. I didn't even invite her! It sounded like it was time to cut her loose. Past time. And, God help me, if she popped her damn gum in my ear one more time, I would straight-up dump her off my lap.

"Hollywood," she whined in that shrill screech, "all the other girls keep asking me when I'm getting my patch. I'm getting tired of making excuses to them. It's embarrassing." She pouted, sticking out her red bottom lip. Jesus, that color of red looked hideous with her hair—unlike someone else who wore just the perfect shade to set off her auburn hair.

Fuck! Why did she have to creep in my head? Again!

"Look, Rosalee, I'm not going to tell you again. I've been straight with you. I'm not looking for an old lady in you or anyone else. I told you in the beginning this would be for as long as it lasted and that's it. Fucking drop it." She just couldn't get it through her thick-ass skull. It was bullshit about the other old ladies asking her about her patch, because I knew they didn't care for her. Actually, that was being nice. They hated her.

She continued to pout and rub her fake tits against my chest as she ruffled my hair and then licked my ear. Jesus, I really hated fake tits too. Fuck, she didn't even get a rise out of my cock anymore. Definitely time to shitcan her.

Pushing her off my lap, I stood and walked away from her without saying a word. Yeah, I was being a dick, and I didn't really give a shit.

Reaper and Steph were cuddled up in a lawn chair, and I watched his hand reach over and rub gently on her swollen belly. They still had about two months to go, but he coddled her like she was breakable. We all teased him, and Steph fought him tooth and nail when she wanted to do something he didn't think was "safe" for her, like continuing to run the Oasis. Funny thing was, I felt a little jealous of them, wondering if that would ever be me. My old man was forever ragging on me about a grandbaby to spoil and teach to ride a bike. My answer was always: "So you want me to knock a girl up so you can have a grandbaby?" That earned me a scowl and a grumbled "Hell no!" every time. I chuckled at the thought of my scruffy, bearded biker dad as a grandpa to a handful of a little girl like Reaper's girl, Remi. That would serve him right.

Without thought, I plunged my hand down into the beer tub and pulled one out. The icy water ran off the bottle and my hand, trailing along the concrete of the shop floor. *Shit, that was cold.* My hand tingled from just the short submersion. The cap got tossed in a trash can as I passed, and I tipped the ice-cold bottle to my lips. It didn't matter what time of year it was, a cold beer always hit the spot. I just knew to watch how many I had because they invariably went down too damn good. Right now though, I didn't care.

Hacker stood talking to Dice, the club secretary, and Soap, one of the prospects. As I approached, they greeted me with shit-eating grins and a head nod toward Rosalee. Of course, Hacker and Dice had to give me shit about her. Motherfuckers. Hell, she was really becoming more trouble than she was worth.

"Fuck you, assholes. That bitch is getting on my damn nerves. I'm ready to cut her ass loose. A steady piece of ass isn't worth all her bitching, whining, and nagging about a property patch. She's a fucking biker whore, and no one in their right mind would make her an old lady. Shit." Metaphorically biting my tongue, I took another swallow of my cold beer. The condensation ran down the side and dripped on my chin, so I rubbed it off with the back of my other hand, hearing the scrape of whiskers.

They laughed and slapped me on the back.

"Just giving you shit, dude. How's your old man doing? We don't see him much in the winter. He hanging in there?" Hacker always remembered my old man and would sometimes go over to see him. Of course, he had known him since we were in high school and played football against each other. We became friends after football camp the summer after our freshman year. We had stayed friends ever since.

"He's got cabin fever something fierce," I said with a laugh. My old man had been older when he had my sister and me. Our mom was fifteen years younger than he was, but they were insane for each other and us kids. We were a close family, and I loved him like crazy. He had never joined an MC, but had always been friendly with the Demented Sons and would often hang out with them and ride with them. Not being able to ride his bike in the winter drove him insane. If it was a nice day with sunny skies and no ice on the road, that crazy bastard would have his bike out riding.

"All this snow lately probably has him grouchy as an old grizzly." Hacker and I grinned at the shared thought of my old man cussing the snow every time it fell. Don't get me wrong, I hated it too, and I was just as guilty of riding any time I could, but I was also thirty-seven years younger than him.

Snow, our prez, and Cash, our treasurer, walked over and greeted us with a raised beer. We all bullshitted for a while.

"You ready for the run over to check the Shamrock tomorrow night? I want you and Hacker to take a prospect and scope things out," Snow asked before tipping up his beer. The MC owned a pretty profitable strip club over in Spirit Lake. There had been some complaints that the manager was skimming, and we needed to go check things out. Cash had been an accountant before he up and sold his business and joined the MC during what we teased him as being his "midlife crisis." There were rumors he had done some creative accounting and had been on the verge of going under. We didn't give a shit; he worked magic and kept us out of trouble.

"Hell, yeah. We'll go see what's up. Hopefully, it's bullshit, but if not, we'll deal with it." The club had been working hard to go legit over the last several years. Too much heat from the ATF, RICO, and general law enforcement had changed the dynamics of many MC's. It wasn't cool anymore to do time on behalf of a club. Fuck that. Not saying that we would put up with people fucking us over, though. Hell no. Don't mistake our desire to be legit for complacency. We still demanded respect, and most people knew not to try to screw us over. I said most because there were still the occasional dumbasses out there.

“Shit, you’re just looking forward to a free titty show, don’t lie! Hollywood’s the boob man.” Dice guffawed, and his salt and pepper beard seemed to bounce as he laughed.

My eyebrows waggling, and I grinned. “Sheeeeeeit, of course I’m up for free titties.” What red-blooded American man wasn’t?

“Besides, Dice, you’re just jealous that their titties don’t even touch your chest when you get a lap dance because your belly gets in the way.” His face progressively got redder before he finally burst out laughing.

“Shit, son, don’t let this belly fool, ya. I could whip yo ass up one side of the street and down the other any day of the week. And momma sho enough don’t complain about it, if’n you know what I mean.” Dice was from Louisiana, and he had a hot temper but was good at keeping it in check most of the time. He always said he was a lover not a fighter… unless he got pissed, of course.

We all laughed at Dice’s pelvic thrust actions, teased him about throwing out a hip, and finished our beers in good humor. So maybe I needed to shitcan Rosalee tonight and look for a new flavor of the month tomorrow night. Yep, sounded like a plan.

Two weeks into Cherry, I was pretty sure I was ready to shitcan her too. She was on stage dancing to My Darkest Days’ “Porn Star Dancing,” and I sat drinking my single beer at a table in the corner. After she got off work, I was going to have to tell her I was done. It had gotten to the point that I had to imagine someone else every time I fucked her if I wanted to get off. That blew, especially considering whose face always came to mind. That just straight up pissed me off.

What the fuck I was thinking by hooking up with a damn stripper, I'd never know. That bullshit you hear about strippers being a great lay? Yeah, it's bullshit. She was probably the lousiest lay I ever experienced. Besides being shitfaced drunk—another reason I rarely drank—her fiery red hair and body drew me in, and well, I guess I wasn't thinking with the right head, if you know what I mean. Another dumb Hollywood move for the books.

My beer was lukewarm from nursing it for so long. Pushing it over across the table from me, I leaned back against the wall to peruse the room. There were a few of the brothers laughing and drinking at a table by the stage, some preppy jock looking guys, a few regulars, and a group of business assholes sitting up on sniffer's row drooling and panting as Cherry shook her ass in their faces. One might expect this to make me jealous, but I really couldn't give a shit less.

After her set, she went backstage to change before coming out to rub her tits on my arm. Not sure why she thought it would turn me on after she had just been flashing her tits to half the bar, but whatever. She had on a cutoff tee that barely reached the bottom of said tits and a pair of cutoff jean shorts that left a generous portion of the bottoms of both ass cheeks showing. Her makeup was caked on from being on stage, and her hair was obviously in need of a refresher dye job as I could see her brown roots growing out. Shit, that was such a turn off to me. Natural redheads were where it was at, specifically dark red… *Ugh! Stop!*

She kissed me, and all I tasted was stale cigarettes and cheap whiskey. Jesus, I really must have been drunk as shit to have hooked up with her. Of course, it had lasted two weeks, mostly because I'd been put in charge of hanging out at the strip club with DJ and Cash to keep an eye on things here, so she was convenient, what with me being here nearly every night. Redheads had always been my downfall, but since Vegas, it was like they were an obsession. No matter how many I hooked up with though, none were the one I really wanted. There was never any true satisfaction.

"Not now, Cherry. I'm working." My hands wrapped around her waist, and I pushed her away from me. She pouted and ran her glossy black nails along my jaw and down my neck. My hand grabbed her wrist, stopping her progress and her touch.

"What's the matter, baby, you don't want a private lap dance?" She ran her tongue along her top lip. Maybe she thought that was sexy, but it just looked cheap to me. She looked cheap. Her other hand reached down to mold to my cock through my jeans. That caused her eyebrows to rise, and she smirked as she felt my semi-erection. "Doesn't feel like someone isn't interested."

This bitch couldn't take a hint. Never again was I hooking up with one of our strippers. It seemed like, if they got in your pants, they felt like they were queen shit because they were fucking a patch. My hand grasped her so I was now holding both of her wrists, which I pushed together and up against her chest as I shoved her away from me. A low growl erupted from my throat.

"Cherry, it's a dick. It would get hard if the wind blew, for fuck's sake. Don't flatter yourself," I said wryly. "As a matter of fact, leave. Hit the fucking road and don't let the door hit you in the ass on the way out. Go find another dick to fuck with. I don't need you anymore." It was obvious that she was pissed, and I probably hurt her feelings, but I didn't really care. Call me an asshole if you want. It's whatever. Damn, I was glad when she flounced off in a huff. It sure didn't take her long to climb in the lap of one of the brothers, either. Butch looked over at me with an inquisitive expression. With a wave that said, "Have at it," he grinned and grabbed her ass as she sat grinding on him.

Maybe I needed to just become a monk.

At one time, that would have been me, completely fucking happy to have any chick grinding on me or in my bed. Lately, however, I felt restless and unsettled, like there was something more. Yeah, I know it sounded stupid, but I was a fucking miserable asshole, wearing a fake smiling mask. Maybe it's just the fact that I hadn't been able to ride as much due the damn weather, with snow one day and freezing rain the next. Maybe it had nothing to do with sex, and it *definitely* had nothing to do with a certain sexy redhead who had taken up residence in my head. Nope. Not at all.

Who the fuck was I kidding?

Chapter ELEVEN

Becca

YEAH, I WAS A COWARD, BUT I COULDN'T TAKE IT ANYMORE. So, while Trevor was at work on Saturday, I began packing anything I had that wouldn't be noticeable and stuffed it in my trunk. I planned to just move out. If he didn't want to accept that it was over, I just wouldn't give him a choice. Loading the trunk in the garage prevented the nosy-ass neighbors from seeing what I was doing and mentioning it to Trevor. When I couldn't fit any more in the trunk and back seat, I left and headed to Josie's to unload. Monday would be the day I finished moving everything. I had arranged for a substitute for the day so I could move while he was back at work.

Three loads later, I figured I had probably reached the limit of trips without raising eyebrows. That didn't stop me from loading the trunk one last time for the first trip on Monday. Then I decided I needed to get out of the house. For one, I wasn't in the mood to see Trevor when he got home. For two, my dad had called to say he was home for a couple of days and asked when his favorite daughter was coming to visit. Yeah, I was his only daughter. My dad… I shook my head as I laughed at his humor.

Scribbling quickly, I left a note on the table telling Trevor I had gone to my parents for dinner. Of course, they didn't know I would be joining them for dinner, I thought with a devilish grin. Perks of being an only daughter? My dad loved me, my mom loved me despite disagreeing with me all the time, and I could invite myself at any time to eat because they would never turn me away. Aaaaaaaand dessert was bound to be yummy, knowing my mother.

On the drive to my parents, a guy on a bike passed me, causing *that man* to creep into my thoughts. Why? You would think after three months, I wouldn't even waste a second's thought on him. He was an ass. *He had a sexy ass.* What? Where the hell were these thoughts coming from? Crazy crap popping into my head. Unacceptable. Why, oh why, did that man have to be at the wedding? Why was Colton even friends with someone like him? Why was I even *thinking* about him? Argh!

Speaking of Colton/Reaper—Dang, I had a hard time getting used to referring to him by that silly nickname—I needed to talk to my Stephie. Lordy, I missed her every day. So, I dialed her number and listened to the ringing of the phone over my car speakers.

"Hey you sexy ho, you! How are you? You coming to see me any time soon?" Steph gave me crap about coming up there every time we talked on the phone. It didn't bother me… no, that's a lie because I wished I could go up there every weekend. Hell, maybe even every day.

"Hey hooker! How's married life treating you? How's that niece of mine doing? And what about my little niece in the oven?" Her laughter was a balm to my soul. We had a long-standing habit of slamming each other, but in a totally affectionate way. I'd never forget the looks on people's faces when we would greet each other in public back in college. Not everyone understood our form of humor. Fuck 'em.

"Well, what if it's a nephew? Huh? We decided to wait to see, but I think it's a boy this time. And married life is amazing, though sometimes I want to bury my foot in his ass. God, girl, he treats me like I'm made of damn porcelain. I keep telling him I've already done this once and I'm sure I'll be just fine this time too. Of course, that never seems to change anything. I have so much going on with the renovations at the Oasis, and I can't be there unless I sneak over without Reaper finding out. He's driving me crazy!"

I laughed at her tirade. It was obvious that he loved her and wanted her safe. Steph also did tend to get a little hormonal and crazy while she was pregnant, so I felt a little bad for him too. Someday I would have that kind of relationship. Inwardly, I sighed.

"So, how is Colt… ugh, Reaper, other than being overprotective? Everything good with him and his issues? God, girl, I'm glad he has had you and the guys to get him through all that." Steph had told me a little about Colton and his PTSD from his combat experience in the Army. During his last deployment, which he wouldn't really talk about, he had been blown up and lost two people in the vehicle with him and other friends in the incident. Then he spent months in the hospital and in rehabilitation to recover from his injuries. I also had found out that "*he*" was in the vehicle at the time. Damn if the thought of *him* going through all that as well didn't make my heart ache for him. Why was it so hard to even *think* his name?

"He's good. I mean, he has his ups and downs, but he's okay. I'm not so sure about Hollywood, though. Reaper says he has been a cantankerous asshole, which I cannot believe for a minute. Around me and Remi, he acts like everything is normal and perfect, but it seems like he's trying too hard to be happy. I worry about him." Jesus Martha, why did she have to bring him up?

I'm not going to ask. I'm not going to ask. I'm not going to ask.

"Why? What's going on with him?" *Dammit*. I asked. *Shit!* Why did I ask about him? *Argh!*

"He's just with someone new all the time. It's like he's self-medicating with sex. I keep telling him he's going to get something that makes his penis fall off." *Why?* Why did she have to say that? I was torn between being pissed to hear he was fucking around all the time and having my chest cave in at the realization that he was obviously not giving me a second thought.

"Oh." For the first time in maybe forever, I was speechless. Silence reigned.

"Oh? What do you mean 'oh'? Holy crap, Becca has nothing to say but 'oh' in a conversation. I have never known you not to have more to say than that. If I didn't know any better, I would almost think you don't like hearing he is with someone else." She laughed, and when I still didn't have anything to say, she got quiet. "Wait. Wait a minute.... Oh my God, Becca! Did you *sleep* with him in Vegas? I thought he just gave you a ride back to the hotel! Oh my Lord, you did, didn't you?"

"What? Why would you ask that? I never said I slept with him! You're crazy!" *Please, Steph, I don't want to talk about him*. I wanted to know every detail about him—wait! What? No!

I. Did. Not!

Thankful I was at a stop light, I banged my head on the steering wheel. At the annoying honk of the car behind me, I looked up to see the light was green. My hand shot up of its own volition to give them the one finger salute.

"Holy shit! You did too! Becca, you ho-monger, why didn't you tell me? Fess up! I want details. Holy hell, how was he? He's hot, I can't deny that, and he looks just, well, yummm. I think it might be a prereq for the guys in the club to be sexy as fuck. Well, there are a few that would shoot that theory to hell.... But I digress. Come on. *Share!*" Steph could be as relentless as a pitbull when she thought I was holding out on her. This was one time when I really wished she would just drop it.

"God, I really don't want to talk about it, Steph. Let's just say it was a disaster that I would rather not relive. The sex itself was off the charts, but other than that, the incident was… well, I don't know, it just ended badly. He's an asshole." He *was* an asshole, but he was invading my thoughts and mind all the freaking time no matter how many times I chased him out of there.

"Wait… Hollywood? An asshole? Are we talking about the same guy? He is one of the funniest, sweetest guys I know, even with all his hidden issues. Wait. Shit, Becca. Do you have a thing for him?"

My tongue refused to move.

"You do! Wait, what about Trevor? Did you finally get smart and dump him, then? Now that guy, he's an asshole. I don't even know what you saw in him, girl." Jeez, Steph could rattle on. As I pulled up to my parents' and put my car in park, I cringed at her accusations and questions about Trevor.

"What? No! Of course not! He never even crosses my mind. I couldn't care less what he does or who he does it with. You're talking fricking crazy." Lies. All lies. He invaded my *dreams*, if I was going to be honest with myself, for God's sake! Okay, yeah, I'll admit it. I think about him every damn day. I think about him every damn night. I think about him when I, well, you know… "And yeah, I'm actually moving out. Things have been over with Trevor for a while. I should have left as soon as I got back from Vegas. Correction, I should have moved out before I even left for Vegas."

My hands clenched on the steering wheel, and I shook it like I wanted to rip it off.

"Mmm-hmm, okay. You forget I know you, you little skank. Okay, fine, I'll drop it for now, but you're going to tell all soon." Her smug tone irritated the shit out of me. Brat. She was lucky I loved her ass.

"Gotta go, hooker! I'm here at my mom and dad's for dinner!

Love you! Byeeeeeee!" She was laughing, and I hung up before she could say anymore. My forehead fell to the steering wheel. Shit. What the hell was wrong with me? How could I possibly still be hot and bothered over an asshole like him? Not only didn't he give me a chance to explain, but he wanted to be all fucking self-righteous. I didn't like him. I couldn't *stand* him. Right? Right. Dammit!

The big semi-truck in the driveway was a comforting sight, and I took a deep breath to calm my nerves. My dad was exactly what I needed right now. Gathering up my purse and climbing out of the car, I prepared to invite myself to dinner. Pasting a smile on my face, I walked through the door only to be hit with the smell of pasta and the sound of my parents' laughter coming from the kitchen. My smile became genuine as I barged into the kitchen.

"Ta-da! I'm heeeeere! What's for dinner?" My parents turned at the sound of my voice, and I watched my dad's eyes light up and my mom's smile grow. Love from my parents was never in shortage, and I was thankful because it was just what I needed at that moment in time.

My dad's arms wrapped around me in a bear hug fitting his stature. It was obvious, from looking at the two of us together, where I got my red hair from. The only difference being his was graying, which I loved to tease him about, and he sported a full beard, big belly, and tree-trunk arms. My dad was a really big guy, and resting my head on his shoulder was as comforting as it was when I was a little girl. Tears welled behind my closed eyelids. Suddenly, I felt so overwhelmed and lost.

"Hey, baby girl." My dad gently pushed me back to look in my face. "Everything okay, sunshine?" The worry etched on my dad's brow made me feel bad because I was a grown-ass woman and he didn't need to be burdened with my problems.

"It's several things. But don't worry, Dad, I'll be fine." My eyes blinked rapidly to keep the tears at bay. He didn't believe me, but he respected my need to keep it to myself for now.

We had dinner, and I told my parents about my decisions, which went over like a lead balloon. My parents were upset with me. It actually seemed like my dad really wanted to tell me he supported whatever decision I made, but he was being supportive of my mom and her feelings. She chewed me out for, and I quote, "letting go of the best thing that would come around for me in a long time." She was convinced he was just amazing and I would have a hard time finding someone who "adored" me so much and could provide for me so well. Yeah, gag! It was frustrating because I never saw this "adoring" side of Trevor unless there was someone to impress.

Why their response surprised me, I'm not sure. It seemed I was one disappointment after another to them. It was no secret my dad had been brokenhearted when he never had the son he was so hoping for. I'm not saying he didn't love me, because he did and does. That didn't mean he wasn't a little disappointed I wasn't a boy. My next disappointment to them was my choice in careers. They had aspirations of me taking my artistic flair in a different direction than I had, that's for sure. Being a graphic designer just didn't do it for me, though. My passion was sharing my gift with children and watching their faces light up when they created something beautiful of their own.

My mother had gone on and on about how little teachers made and how there would never be any advancement, nor recognition. Honestly, I felt like my mom was trying to live vicariously through me because, when she got pregnant with me, she married my dad and dropped her entire life to be a stay-at-home mom. It was great growing up, but that had been her choice. It wasn't my fault she didn't go to school or develop her own career.

It was obvious I wasn't going to get the support I wanted and needed from my parents. "Thanks for dinner and dessert, Mom, Dad. But I better get moving." My dad laid a beefy hand over mine as I made to leave the table. I plopped back in my seat from my slightly raised position.

"Sunshine, we just want what's best for you, and we want you to be happy. Trevor can provide a good life for you. We hate to see you making any rash decisions, is all, baby girl." My eyes closed as I tried to gather my thoughts and calm my temper. Deep breathing wasn't working tonight. Rising from the table, I cast a hurt look at them both. My head shook back and forth in disbelief that they would so blatantly disregard my feelings like this. It was my life, not theirs.

Noisily, I placed my dishes into the dishwasher before turning back to them both as they sat quietly at the table.

"If you like him so much, maybe you should move in with him then. I'll see you both later."

When I stormed out of their house, my mom told me I was being an immature child and a fool. That was just icing on the cake. The look of pain in my dad's eyes when he tried to hug me before I left and I just brushed him off, felt like I had stabbed myself in the heart. I rarely did anything to hurt my dad, but he had never really taken sides like this before. He'd never *had* to. It hurt that he wouldn't stand up for me, even a little. Without looking back at the house, I got in my car and peeled out of the driveway.

Pretending I didn't care how my parents felt was a farce, but it was the only way to keep myself from totally falling apart. Being with Trevor had left me feeling bogged down and restricted. It was like I was suffocating and no one could see it but me. My own parents didn't support my decision to move on. How insane was that?

The back seat held my gym bag with extra workout clothes, so I drove to the gym to work off some of my frustration, hurt, and anger. After about an hour of sweating to some Avenged Sevenfold, Five Finger Death Punch, and Metallica, I calmed down and felt like I had my emotions somewhat under control. The important thing to remember was I knew I was doing the right thing. That was what I told myself over and over.

Thankfully, when I got home, Trevor was in bed. The part of me that had invested over a year into this relationship couldn't believe he never called, waited up for me, or even texted me to make sure I was okay. Shit, what if I had gotten in a car accident? You know what? It didn't matter. Screw him. I was out of here on Monday anyway. There was no point getting upset over his disregard for me.

Monday morning dawned, and I reluctantly woke, going through the motions of getting ready for work, knowing I wouldn't be going anywhere but to Josie's after Trevor was long gone to work. He ate the breakfast I made, filled a travel mug with coffee, and rushed out the door telling me he wanted me to make salmon, vegetables, and rice for supper. *Yeah, screw you, buddy. Make it for yourself.*

After I was sure he was well on his way to work, I began to stuff the rest of my clothes in a couple of large army duffle bags that had been my dad's. My furniture didn't consist of much more than a dresser, the kitchen table, and a few lamps—pretty much things I could replace without feeling much of a loss financially or sentimentally. The duffle bags both fit in my trunk, and I stuffed the random blankets, picture frames, and knick-knacks I had inherited from my grandmothers in around the duffle bags. Satisfied I had everything I needed, I reset my cell phone to factory settings, since he bought it and paid the bill, and left it on the table with a note explaining to Trevor that I needed to leave. Further explaining I had tried, on several occasions, to talk to him and tell him this, but he wouldn't listen and I couldn't stay with him. In the note, I tried to be tactful, despite wanting to tell him what an asshole he was. A smile crept across my face when I signed the letter:

Goodbye,
Becca

After climbing in and buckling my seat belt, I started my car and pushed the button to open the garage door. My heart stopped as I saw Trevor's car coming up the road as I backed out of the driveway. When I realized it just looked like his car, a relieved laugh slipped out and I scolded myself for being paranoid. Shit. It wasn't like I was robbing the man! I hadn't done anything wrong. The prepaid phone I had grabbed at Walmart last night went off, and I noticed a text from Josie.

Josie: Hey, girl! Started a roast in the crockpot but think I forgot to turn it down to low before I left. B home around 5. So excited to have u moving in!! See u then!

Her text made me smile. I started to feel that weight lift off me, and it actually felt a little easier to breathe. If I had only known things wouldn't stay that way…

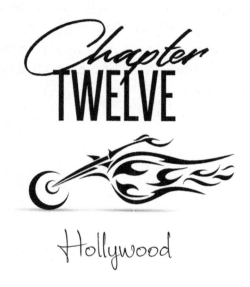

Chapter TWELVE

Hollywood

FOR THE FIRST TIME IN MONTHS, I DIDN'T HAVE A DATE, AND I USE that term loosely, for the weekly BBQ and get-together at Reaper and Steph's. It was actually nice to just sit and bullshit with the guys and not worry about someone hanging on me, demanding something, or pissing me off. Lounging like a serious lazy ass in a chair, I nursed my single cold beer for the night and laughed with everyone.

When I felt the hard belly push against my shoulder and soft hands cover my eyes and heard a whisper in my ear, I knew it was Steph before she even offered the requisite "Guess who?" Grinning, I said, "Unless someone else is suddenly growing a watermelon in their belly, it must be my beautiful Steph." Yeah, that earned me a playful punch to the damn arm and then a grouchy-ass look from Reaper that his woman was touching another man. So just to fuck with him, I pulled her around and into my lap. I gave her a kiss on the cheek and smiled at her.

"Hey, baby, how's that old man of yours treating you? You ready to leave his cantankerous ass and be my girl?" I winked at her and cast a sly grin toward Reaper. He growled, and I swore the shithead was grinding his teeth. Laughter burst from me before I could hold it back. Steph laughed and hugged me.

"Hollywood, honey, you couldn't handle me and my pregnancy hormones. Reaper can barely stand me, and he loves me and is married to me." Her grin spread even further as she kissed my head softly, ruffling my hair like the mom she was. We weren't that far apart in age, but she totally treated me like I was her little brother. Not complaining, I liked her spoiling me.

"Now, that is a true statement, baby. Damn, I feel like I've been in the dog house so much lately that when I meet new people, I don't know whether to shake their hand or sniff their ass." Reaper gave a cynical smile with his statement, and everyone busted a gut laughing. Reaper came over and kissed his wife before asking her if she needed a bottle of water. As he walked toward the cooler, he shouted over his shoulder, "And keep your hands to yourself with my wife, Hollywood, you fuck!" Laughter bubbled up from Steph, and I couldn't help joining in.

"Now, tell me about what happened in Vegas with Becca, lover boy." Steph caught me totally off guard with her softly spoken statement. Fuck! How did she know? I was gone before anyone knew I had been in her room that morning. Did she actually tell Steph? Wait. *When* did she tell Steph? My expression closed off as my jaw clenched.

"What the hell are you talking about, Steph? Who's been telling stories? I rode with her back to the hotel and left her in her room. That's it, end of story." My face remained neutral as I tried not to give her anything to go on. The last thing I wanted to do was talk about the one woman I obsessed over day and night. I was pretty sure it wasn't healthy.

"Oh, come on! Let's just call it a pregnant woman's hunch. Becca got all quiet—totally out of character for her, by the way—when I mentioned you. She tried to sound all nonchalant, but she forgets I know her too well. She finally caved, so there is no use lying to me." Steph appeared smug. Little shit.

My heart raced a little just from the sound of her name on Steph's lips. One thing I tried to avoid was even *thinking* her name. It was like, if I could just not speak or think her name, it would prevent my traitorous mind from conjuring her memory up every waking fucking moment. My dick was wanting to stir, which, by the way, was extremely awkward considering my best friend's wife was sitting in my lap. Too weird. Uncomfortably, I shifted in the chair to move Steph farther from my faithless dick that was ready and eager at the mere mention of that cheating, unfaithful bitch.

"Steph, it was nothing, really. Okay, yeah, we had a good time, and that was that. End of story. So, she doing okay? I mean, I'm just wondering because she's your friend and all. She told you about that night, huh? So, what did she say?" Okay, yeah, my worthless attempt at nonchalance was pretty sucky, I know. Hey, I tried. Shut up and get out of my head if you don't like it.

"Mmm, she said you are off the charts, big boy. So why didn't you ever say anything? She's a nice person. I would love to see the two of you together." The wheels were turning in her head, that was obvious. Oh hell no. No scheming woman was going to go matchmaking with me. Besides, didn't she care that her friend was in a relationship when she screwed me? Fuck that. No, I didn't need that crap in my life. Uh-uh! So, I carefully removed her from my lap as I felt my face burn up.

"Hmmm, look at that, my beer is empty. I guess I need to go get another one." Total lie, because I tried to keep my drinking to a minimum. A quick peck on the cheek, and I hauled ass away from her inquisitive mind and probing gaze. Shit, that conversation had gotten way too uncomfortable. Becca was going to become even more of a thorn in my side if Steph didn't drop this. *Fuck!* There I went and thought her name. Damn it all to hell.

Chapter THIRTEEN

Becca

TREVOR HAD COME BY THE SCHOOL FOR ME SEVERAL TIMES SINCE I moved out over three months ago. It had been easy to avoid any phone calls because he didn't have my number. When flowers started arriving at the school, I couldn't help but read the cards. Initially, I wasn't sure who they were from because it was so out of character for Trevor. It had me briefly thinking maybe he could change. Each card was a progressively more ardent request to come "home" to him. Some of the girls in the office thought it was so sweet and told me I should give him another chance. Not wanting to put my business out there, I just smiled and shook my head. Starting any kind of conversation would have just kept them going.

When he followed me home from school one day, I told him to

stop sending me flowers, that he was wasting his money and his time. Once again, I told him I didn't love him and I was moving on. He didn't take that well.

"Becca, you will regret not coming home. You belong with me, and you're being childish and foolish. Even your mom thinks we need to work things out." Oh my God! He was talking to my *mom* about us? That was going too far.

"Stop talking to my family! Stop sending shit to me at school! Quit stopping by the school! Trevor, we are through. Done. I moved out and it's over! You have no business talking to my family and friends. Jesus, what is *wrong* with you? You know what? Never mind. I don't care. Leave!" He was seriously pissing me off. Planting my fist in his arrogant nose was becoming more and more appealing.

He glared at me and slammed the door of his car after getting in. He revved the motor and peeled out in a screeching of tires, leaving behind the burning smell of rubber. Curtains moved at the house across the street. Great. Fricking nosey neighbors again. My shoes got kicked across my room as I entered and slammed my door. Then I felt guilty for slamming the door until I remembered the girls' cars were not parked outside, so no one else was home.

My hands held my head as I plopped on the edge of my bed. All I could think about was how Steph's ex had gone crazy and almost killed her. Deep inside, I knew Trevor wasn't capable of that though. He was too passive aggressive. He preferred manipulation and belittling. Prick. I said a small prayer that he would give up and move on soon. My arm rested over my eyes after I flopped back on the bed. Tears leaked out of my eyes at the spiraling feeling rushing through me. It began to feel like my life was never going to be stable again. Packing up my bags and hauling ass to Timbuktu sounded more and more appealing every day, I thought, as I felt myself doze off.

A knocking on my door woke me with a start. It was dark out already, and I certainly hadn't planned on sleeping that long—not that I was really even hungry or worried about sleeping through dinner, mind you. Josie poked her head around the corner of the door and looked abashed about waking me.

"Hey, Becca. I'm so sorry to wake you, but I think there is something you need to see." For fuck's sake. What now? How could my life get any worse at this point? Boy, was I about to find out.

Following her out to the dining room table with my slippers shuffling, she led me to her laptop, and I noted her social media account was open to the school's page. What I saw on the screen had nausea building in the pit of my stomach. What the ever-loving fuck?

Is this who you want teaching and influencing your children? The post read. Attached to the post were pictures of me in various poses at bars and parties. If someone didn't know better, they would think they were recent. Of course, I knew they were from the summer after I graduated, before I was ever hired at the school. It was my last summer of rebellion and living my party days, I remembered telling myself. There were pictures of me doing body shots, having random guys in the bar taking shots from my cleavage, me dancing with guys holding my boobs from behind. Oh sweet Jesus, there was even one of me competing in a wet T-shirt contest. Thank God for small favors that my nipples were fuzzed out where I knew they would be showing through my white tee.

Good God, these were all taken in Des Moines with my friends from college on the weekends I had stayed with them. That was the exact reason I hadn't want to party around home. Who the hell would do this? And why? And how did they get them on the school's page? My mouth was hanging open, and I knew I looked like a goldfish with it opening and shutting without words. My eyes felt like they might pop out of my head. Josie rubbed my shoulder and looked at me with sympathy.

"Becca, you need to talk to Nancy at the school ASAP to get those removed. I'm sure this will blow over. But I have to ask… uhh, when was this? I mean, we're elementary school teachers, and I guess I didn't think you, well, I guess… Ummmm, well." The more Josie said, the redder her face got. Poor girl. Did she grow up in a convent? She must be pretty embarrassed at seeing me like that, but I didn't really think the pictures were any worse than the things other people did in college. It wasn't like I was nude or having sex, thank God.

I had really tried to be a model teacher and to restrain my wild tendencies, so this was a bit of a blow to the gut, especially considering the pictures were several years old now. And how did someone get access to those pictures? They were all on my computer and a few were actual photographs that someone took a picture of, or uploaded. Something like this was simply an utterly hateful act.

"Jesus, no, Josie. These were all taken the summer after graduation. Before I ever got my formal offer of employment. I haven't changed much, so I guess it was easy to imply they were recent." My mind was running at 300 mph. It was hard to keep a coherent thought in my head.

"I just don't understand why someone would do this!" The nausea continued to build until I ran to the bathroom and vomited. I heaved until I had nothing left to vomit except my stomach lining itself. Tears poured down my face as I sat on the floor, leaning against the tub with my head resting on my knees.

Just when I thought I was gaining control of my life….

It looked like Josie's optimism was shot to shit, when a week and a half later, I was called into the superintendent's office. Mr. Strankowski was a kind, but stern-looking, fatherly type, and he did look truly sorry when he told me I was being put on temporary administrative leave due to the number of calls from concerned parents. The school had removed the post, but not before they were seen by every sanctimonious parent in the district, it seemed. As I left his office, my heart was heavy and I was near tears.

When I approached my house, I could see signs in the yard and papers flapping from the side of the house and front door from about three blocks away. What the heck was that all about? As I drew closer, my heart started pounding and my face felt like it was flaming. This was insane! What the hell? Were we in the middle ages or something? The amount of signs proclaiming me a slut, whore, and a "naughty teacher" was overwhelming. *Are you serious?* Someone had even spray painted "tramp" on the picture window. Oh my God, this wasn't even my house!

The nerve of whoever did this was over the top. They had done this in broad daylight, because it wasn't there when I left this morning. My mood alternated between anger, shock, hurt, fear, and embarrassment.

My car was slammed into park, and in a rage, I kicked over, ripped up, and pitched the signs in the trash can. Finding a paint scraper in the garage, I went to scraping the red paint from the front window as tears flooded down my cheeks. Tiny red flakes of paint rained down on my arms and landed on the ground like bloody snowflakes.

Josie was pulling into the driveway as I was still scraping the red letters from the window. Her face registered complete and absolute shock as she took in the overflowing trash can and the paint on the window.

"Josie, I'll get it all off, I promise," I sobbed. My entire body was shaking, and I was beginning to have difficulty scraping the last of the paint from the window. I just couldn't believe this was happening. She looked at me in disbelief then walked in the house with her hand over her mouth. I felt horrible. This was her home. Pain shot up my body as I dropped to my knees sobbing.

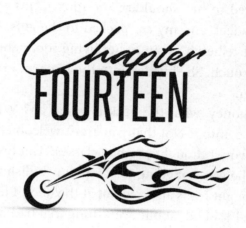

Chapter FOURTEEN

Becca

SO, THERE I STOOD ON STEPH'S PORCH, SEVEN MONTHS AFTER HER wedding, trying to get up the nerve to knock on her door.

This is where my life has ended up.

My career was in shambles, and I had turned in my notice. A poor reference was not on the top of my list of things I wanted, and I figured it would be better if I left while Mr. Strankowsi would still be willing to give me a good reference. Leaving of my own accord seemed a better option than waiting for my employment to be terminated. He had assured me it wasn't necessary to leave permanently, but self-preservation kicked in and I ran. *Coward*, my inner self whispered. That was me, it seemed, and I was disgusted with myself.

A deep breath filled my lungs, and my hand hovered over the

door. Knocking as I let the breath out, I waited for someone to answer the door. If I hadn't already cried every day since Josie asked me politely to vacate her home, and during the entire drive up here to Steph's, I would have started crying again. My eyes were swollen and red, and I knew damn well I looked like shit warmed over.

Footsteps approached the door, the knob rattled, and then Steph stood there with her month-old son wrapped in a fuzzy blue blanket and cradled to her shoulder. She took in my swollen, red eyes, the bag at my feet, and my car packed to the gills. Her concern was evident as she ushered me in to her living room and encouraged me to sit on the couch. She bustled into the kitchen, bringing me back a bottle of water.

"Becca, honey, what the heck is going on? Why didn't you tell me you were coming? Not that you aren't welcome, shit, but I'm surprised to see you. I thought you had classes." Her brow was furrowed, and I knew she was not going to accept any bullshit excuses. While I may have thought I was all cried out at the door, I felt tears slip down my cheeks as I told her about everything that had happened over the last seven months culminating in the vandalism at the house and the hate letters I had received, Josie asking me to leave, and ultimately, my resignation.

"I couldn't stay there anymore. My mom wanted me to stay with her, but after all the vandalism Josie's poor house suffered before she finally asked me to leave, I couldn't risk doing that to my mom. Besides, I was so tired of hearing about how wonderful Trevor was and how I should give him another chance. It was getting sickening and causing us to argue all the time. It's insane how much my mother thinks of Trevor. For the life of me, I cannot understand why she thinks he's so fucking perfect." It was like I couldn't even talk to her anymore. My own mother. It was breaking my heart.

"Don't worry, hon, we'll figure this out. You can stay here as long as you want. Or I can help you look for a place of your own. Rent and houses are pretty cheap here. Probably way cheaper than down in CB. It's up to you though, no rush. The selfish part of me is just thrilled to have you here. You know, I could actually use a hand down at the Oasis if you want something to do. I can pay you. I wouldn't expect you to work for free." The last she added, with a hand held up to quiet my arguments, when I tried to tell her she didn't need to pay me if I was staying in her home.

So that was how I found myself in the guest bedroom, curled up on my side in the comfy double bed of my best friend's house. Lying there staring into space, I let my mind wander. All the "what-ifs" in the world weren't going to change the state of my life. Nor would they stop me from wondering what things would have been like if Trevor had never called and I had taken Hollywood up on his offer to come back here with him after the wedding. Instead, my career and life were in shambles, leaving me feeling isolated and betrayed. My heart felt beaten and shredded. Hollywood hated me for whatever reason, and here I was in his town. God, my life was shit.

What am I going to do? My eyes grew heavy as my brain ran circles but never found answers.

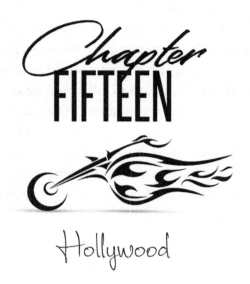

Chapter FIFTEEN

Hollywood

It was promising to be a beautiful day for the end of April, and I was enjoying the rumble and purr of my bike as the asphalt rolled by. The sun was just rising and the damp chill from overnight was still lingering, but I barely noticed as the wind whipped past. After spending the weekend with my family, I decided I would swing by Reaper and Steph's to ride to the shop with Reaper. I had to drive past their place anyway, and I loved seeing Remi and little Wyatt. My new nephew was a miniature of his daddy, no doubt, but much cuter in my opinion.

As I waited for the gate to open after punching in the entry code, I noticed an unfamiliar car in the driveway. Pottawattamie plates. *Who the hell was this?* Double checking the holster clipping my pistol into the back of my pants, I slowed and cautiously rolled up the driveway. I put my kickstand down and shut my bike off next to the strange car. Usually Reaper would come out if a bike pulled up, so when he didn't, I quietly walked up to the door, scoping through the windows for signs of anyone in the house. Just as I pulled my pistol out, the door opened and Reaper came out.

"Jesus, bro! Put that shit away! What the fuck is wrong with you?" He quickly scanned the yard, ensuring there was no threat he hadn't been aware of before shaking his head at me and waving me in. "You scared the shit out of me."

Okay, so he didn't seem concerned about the car and he looked right at it. Must be someone they knew.

"Whose car?" I asked as I followed Reaper into the kitchen toward the sound of voices and the smell of bacon cooking. Remi giggled, and I couldn't help but smile. My smile quickly faded, and I felt like someone had punched me in my guts when I stepped into the kitchen.

"Hey, handsome! You coming to join us for breakfast before you steal my husband?" Steph was all smiles and sunshine this morning. Remi jumped down from her chair and ran to me, wrapping her arms around my legs as she squealed, "Unco Mason! Unco Mason! I missed you!"

Steph gently scolded Remi to get back to the table to finish her breakfast and let *Uncle Mason* sit down for his. When I scooped her up and tugged on one of her dark, curly pigtails, she gave me a sticky kiss that smelled suspiciously like maple syrup. She went back to eating her food after I placed her in her seat.

My eyes stayed on Steph as I thanked her for my plate, and then I quickly developed intense focus on my food. Anything to not look at *her*.

Jesus, she was here.

Questions circled in my brain… *What's she doing here? Did she leave the asshole?* Hell, I didn't know if he was an asshole, or not, but in my mind, because she was with him and not me, he was just an asshole. No. No. No. It didn't fucking matter, and I didn't want to know. Okay, maybe I did, but I wasn't going to ask or engage her in conversation. Her voice, as she thanked Steph for her plate, felt like warm honey pouring over my body. It tempted me to taste her to see if her mouth would taste as sweet as the sound of the voice coming out of it.

What the fuck?

I shoveled my food into my mouth faster. The sooner I finished, the sooner Reaper and I could get on the road.

Of their own volition, my eyes darted in her direction repeatedly. In all seriousness, I really wasn't trying to look at her. Every time I glanced her direction, she seemed just as engrossed in her food as I was. During about the fifth glance in her direction, our eyes met when I looked up. Her cheeks bloomed in bright pink blotches and her mouth was slightly parted as her fork stopped halfway from her plate to her mouth. Despite the flush to her cheeks, she appeared pale, and I couldn't help but notice the dark circles under those captivating eyes, making her look strained and exhausted. Once we made eye contact, it was as if neither of us could look away. It was like being mesmerized.

Neither of us took much notice when Steph said she was taking Wyatt to change his diaper and feed him, nor Reaper taking Remi to the bathroom to wash her up and get her dressed. The silence at the table hung heavy. We just kept looking at each other, not saying a word, as if we were both waiting for the other to break into the quiet first.

Finally, I couldn't stand it anymore. I took another bite of my food, chewing it simply out of habit, because I sure as hell couldn't taste it anymore. After swallowing what felt like a wad of cotton, I placed my fork on my plate and looked up to her. She sat pushing the last of her food around on her plate.

"What brings you to town?"

"It's good to see you again."

"Sorry, you go ahead…"

"Oh sorry," we both spoke simultaneously each time, which brought out a nervous laugh from her. A fat curl fell from the clip she had holding the tumbling mass of red on top of her head. Without thought, I reached over to tuck it behind her ear.

Fuck!

The spark I felt when my fingers brushed against her cheek and ear unnerved me. For some reason, being this close to her made me feel like a bumbling teenager with his first girl. Shit, though. Stuff like this didn't happen to me. I grabbed myself by the balls, because I wasn't going to look like a bitch in front of her.

If her quickly indrawn breath was any indication, she wasn't unaffected by my touch either. Her eyes had met mine in a startled glance at our contact. She felt it too. Damn, I felt like I was going crazy, so I was glad it wasn't just me.

"Ummm, well, it's a long story that I would rather not get into right now. How have you been? You're looking, umm, good." Her cheeks remained flushed. The image I had been carrying around in my mind did absolutely no justice to how fucking gorgeous she was in the flesh, despite her weary appearance. Having her sit here in front of me was taking my breath away. When her compliment sunk in, I couldn't help but grin. She thought I looked good.

Shit, it didn't matter. I didn't really care. Right?

"Thanks. You don't look so bad yourself, Red."

She wrinkled her cute nose and smirked at me calling her Red, or maybe at my compliment—though calling her hair red was such an understatement. It was a rich auburn with fiery highlights and deep burgundy underneath. Shimmering in the sunlight that filtered through the kitchen window, it beckoned me. My hand ached to allow the silken strands to slip through my fingers again, but I stubbornly kept my hands on the table.

"You don't need to lie to make me feel better. I look like shit, and

I know it." She stood and gestured toward my plate as she prepared to take hers to the sink. When I handed her my plate, our fingers touched again. The plates momentarily shook in her hand before she took a deep breath and turned toward the sink to rinse the plates. There was that spark again, but this time my dick started to twitch as well.

Down, boy.

She turned and leaned against the counter with her hands resting on the edge on either side of her hips. The sun shining through the window behind her head illuminated her hair even further. Before I was aware of what I was doing, I stood and walked toward her until I straddled her legs and placed my hands on the counter at her sides, essentially corralling her. Leaning in until my lips grazed the shell of her ear, I inhaled her honeyed essence. God, she still smelled so sweet.

"I'm not blowing smoke up your ass, Becca. I thought you were beautiful the first night I saw you, and I think you're beautiful right now," I whispered in her ear. "I don't lie. You look like you have a lot on your mind, but that doesn't mean you aren't still fucking gorgeous or I don't still want you." Despite my resolutions to stay away from her, I tipped my head and leaned in to brush my lips across hers. What I intended to be a quick, chaste kiss, deepened into a possessive claiming when she parted her lips. A soft moan slipped from her, and those slender hands reached up to curl around the collar of my shirt.

Pulling away, pissed off at myself for giving in to my inner desires, I let out my inner asshole. "So, how's *Trevor*?" Her eyes widened and she tried to push me away.

"I don't want to talk about him with you," she ground out. "Let me go." She continued to push on my chest as her head dipped down and away.

She was killing me. She didn't need to be with him. Fuck.

My mind screamed that this woman was mine, and I wasn't going to let her go. Ever. How had I thought I could? Despite my promises to myself and my sister, there was something powerful between us, something that couldn't be ignored.

"Bec...," I whispered, and her eyes shining with tears met mine. Our lips crashed together again. The salt of her tears mingled in our kiss.

I wasn't sure how long we stood there devouring each other before someone clearing their throat broke through our haze. We broke apart quickly, and I watched her quickly dry her face, bite her bottom lip, and look at the ground. Her heaving chest and flushed cheeks gave away the effect the kiss had on her. My heart surged in my chest, it was beating so hard. After taking a deep breath, I leaned in to whisper in her ear before I turned to meet Reaper's questioning gaze. I grinned at him and walked out the door.

My bike was idling at a low rumble, and I was flipping through songs on my iPhone until Pop Evil's "Boss's Daughter" started to play. Reaper swung a leg over his bike as he looked at me and shook his head.

"What?" I asked him, as if I had no idea what he was thinking. He shook his head again as he smirked and started the motor. We pulled out of the gate and ran through all our gears in a mere heartbeat as we sped down the road toward the shop.

There was nothing like the freedom of racing the wind on a cool morning. The grin I couldn't keep suppressed stretched ear to ear as I raced down the road handlebar to handlebar with Reaper. We had a lot to talk about, Becca and I. Hell if I knew how, but Becca was going to be staying here and, come hell or high water, she was going to be mine.

Chapter SIXTEEN

Becca

MASON'S WHISPERED WORDS BEFORE LEAVING THIS MORNING RAN through my head as if on a perpetual loop. "This is *not* over. You are here and you are *mine*, Becca. Let it sink in good, baby girl." Absently scrubbing the dishes in the hot, sudsy water, my mind continued to wander.

Shit. I hadn't seen him in months, yet one touch of his hand against my cheek and ear as he tucked my hair behind my ear and my panties were wet. When he kissed me against the sink, I swore I was about three seconds away from climaxing just from tasting his mouth on mine. He hadn't even moved his hands from the counter on either side of me. The only contact had been our lips and my arms around his neck.

And in case you're wondering, *no*, I did *not* plan that and, *no,* I did *not* even realize my arms were moving until I felt the worn denim of his collar and the soft but prickly ends of his hair, which he still wore short in the back, under my fingertips.

The whole situation had me wondering what the hell was going on. Damn, I was a more than a little confused. When he left my room in Vegas, and then after the way he treated me at the wedding, I figured he truly hated me and never wanted to see me again. He had given me the cold shoulder when he first entered the kitchen this morning too. Then he suddenly reached out to tuck my hair back. His hand barely touched me, but I couldn't believe the current that shot through me at his touch.

He was still sexy as hell. The images of him I had tried to keep buried over the last seven months flooded back with a vengeance. The way his jeans rode low on his hips and snug on his ass, the feel of his abs and chest as I raked my nails and fingertips over them, the feel of his hot skin against mine. It was like yesterday.

Oh shit. Okay. Too far.

It was one thing to remember how good looking and hot he was, another to remember the intimate details of our one night together. But damn, what a night it had been.

Shit, I was in trouble.

What exactly did he mean when he said it wasn't over and I was his? Just the thought of his whispered words had my nipples hardening and tingling again. Lordy, I was really, really in trouble. Could he possibly still want me? Or was he just being an asshole, fucking with me?

"Sooooooooo… do you want to tell me why I just got a call from Hollywood asking me to invite him for dinner tonight?" Steph's smug question had me at a loss for words. The glass I had reached to set on the dish drying mat nearly slipped out of my hands. Lost in my head, I hadn't even heard her come back in.

"Honestly, I have no clue." A fluffy puff of suds was left in the sink after I pulled the plug to drain the water. The slight sounds of the tiny bubbles popping sounded like firecrackers going off in the silence of the room. My soul felt raw. It felt like any words I spoke were inadequate to answer the questions I could see spinning in her mind.

Turning slowly, leaning on the counter in the same spot Mason had kissed me had my heart rate jumpstarting as a deluge of feelings rushed through me. Holy hell, I was screwed. My arms crossed in an unconscious protective manner over my chest. There was a defiant spark in my eyes as I met Steph's eyes.

"Hey, hoochy momma, don't look at me like that. I highly doubt he is dying to come have dinner with me and Reaper, so that leaves little ol' you. Hmm, I wonder why that is? I think Hollywood wants to try for round two with you." Steph may be my best friend, but I seriously could smack that smirk off her face right now.

Grrrr.

"Bitch, please. He and I had one single night seven months ago. It's highly unlikely he's pining for me or wanting to rekindle anything." My attempt at dry humor and sarcasm was met with laughter from my supposed best friend.

Wench. I may have to rethink the whole best friend concept, I thought with a scowl. Evidently, my attempt at the evil eye wasn't scaring her, so I had to resort to drastic measures.

Yep. I stuck my tongue out at her.

We both erupted into gales of laughter after that. After the laughter died down, we each took a bottle of water from the fridge and carried it out to the porch. Steph set up the baby monitor to listen for the kiddos as they napped and we each stretched out on a padded patio chair. This was the first time I had been up to the house Reaper had bought for her, and it was easy to see why he had chosen it. It was serene and had plenty of room for Remi and Wyatt to run and play over the years. The air smelled clean and refreshing. You could hear the peaceful whisper of the spring air through the budding trees and the twitter of little birds. I loved it already.

"So, what are we making for dinner?"

"We? Do you cook with a mouse in your pocket?" I teased. My twisted sense of humor made me giggle. Steph gave me the you're-a-real-smartass look. We sat and made dinner plans until we heard Wyatt fuss over the baby monitor. She started to get up to get him, but I told her to sit and rest, I would go.

Wyatt was in his crib kicking his legs when I got to the room. Cooing over him, I scooped him up and snuggled him close as I walked to the changing table to clean him up. After he had a fresh diaper on, he smelled so sweet. My heart ached as I held him, wondering if I would ever experience the joy of being a mother. His dark, downy hair was so silky under my cheek. When he started rooting around on my chin, I laughed and knew it was time to go to Mommy.

The ache began again as I watched Steph settle her infant son to her breast. My thoughts wandered as I watched the incredibly sweet moment with a slight smile on my face. The vision came unprompted to my mind of me in the same position with a golden-haired baby held to my own breast as I watched him suckle. In my daydream, I looked up to my baby's father as he leaned over the back of the bench I sat on, to tenderly kiss our son's head and then my cheek. The amount of love that surrounded our little family was unbelievable, and I couldn't help but smile in overwhelming bliss. As my gaze moved up into my dream world husband's eyes, I was startled to meet familiar, beautiful, dark-lashed, light hazel eyes reflecting the love that bloomed unrestrained in my heart.

Oh Shit. What the hell was that? I'm losing my ever-loving mind!

Shaking my head, I jumped up from my chair. When Steph asked me if I was okay, I gave a false smile. "Of course, I'm fine. Why wouldn't I be? I'm just going in to start supper."

Jesus. For some insane reason, my mind had conjured Hollywood up as my future husband and father of my child.

Good God, I needed to get a grip.

Hollywood

Yeah, it was ballsy of me to invite myself to dinner at Reaper and Steph's, but she loved me and I knew she wouldn't mind. After the brief discussions we'd had, I also knew she wouldn't mind playing matchmaker between me and Becca. And with the chemistry that had exploded this morning, I needed to see Becca again ASAP. Something deep in my soul called to her, knowing she belonged with me.

Mine continuously circled in my head. The visceral desire to claim her body and soul was overwhelming.

She hadn't looked happy, and I was determined to find out why. She may not be with that Trevor guy, but I wasn't sure what the details were with all that. The sooner we talked, the better. She was mine, and there was no way she was leaving here until she admitted it. It was obvious she felt the connection; it just remained to be seen if she felt it as deeply as I did. The startled look in her eyes when our skin touched made me hope so. Now, I just needed to be able to get her alone tonight to talk to her.

"Stop. My plans really are to just talk to her. That's it. Okay, fine. Yeah, if she let me kiss her again and wrap her firm body up in my arms, then hell yeah, I'm going to do it. Quit making it sound like I have nefarious plans to seduce her," I mumbled.

I needed to quit talking to myself. *Jesus.*

The rest of the afternoon seemed to crawl by in slow motion. It was my job at the shop to do the custom paint jobs on top of basic mechanic work. Before starting at the shop, I had never thought of myself as an artist, but for some reason, I could paint the hell out of a bike. The designs just seemed to flow from me, and it was pretty cool.

Even I couldn't deny it. Truth be told, I loved it. We had a really nice Harley Street Glide we were doing a lot of custom work on for a guy out on the west coast. He was some new rock star sensation, but he seemed like a pretty cool fucking dude, not one of those stuck-on-himself-too-cool-to-mingle-with-the-little-guys type.

The finished product was going to be pretty badass, and my paint job was definitely kickass. The tank had a deck of cards flying toward a vanishing point in various positions, as if they were flipping and flying through smoky air. On the front fender, smoky tendrils started, leading to the batwing fairing where a skeleton in a top hat with a red rose and a black bowtie was positioned so he appeared to be the one flipping the cards through the air. You just had to see it to truly appreciate it. Who would have thought a sniper's spotter would end up creating shit like that?

Regardless of how busy I was all day, Becca was never far from my mind, and every time I looked at the clock, it barely seemed to be moving. By the time I noticed it was nearly five, my heart raced erratically as I waited for the last few minutes to tick by while I cleaned up my area. You would think, as much as I looked forward to seeing her again today, I wouldn't be so fucking nervous. It was the anticipation, I guessed.

It was just completely unnerving now that I realized how badly I coveted Becca's heart and soul. Shit, what the fuck was getting into me?

Stop it. I'm not usually so sappy. Don't judge me.

It just felt like I was constantly on edge and waiting for the proverbial other shoe to drop. There was an innate restlessness that was screaming at me to leave now and get to Becca as fast as I could before she could slip away from me. *Fuck.*

Reaper was putting all his tools away, and I told him I'd wait out by the bikes for him. He was talking on his cell and gave me a nod of his head in agreement. The brothers who lived in their own places were starting to trickle out and head home to their families. The music from inside the clubhouse gained intensity as the jukebox was turned up to be heard over the jesting and laughter of the guys. At this time of day, some would be racking up the balls to shoot pool; others were probably sitting at the small bar bullshitting. Still, more would head over to the Oasis, Steph's pub, to hang out and gorge on some of the meals Steph had designed as signature dishes for the Oasis.

"You in a hurry for something, bro?" Reaper was being a cocky asshole with that grin. Fucker knew damn well why I invited myself to dinner—besides Steph's amazing culinary genius, that is. Trying to act relaxed and patient was damn near killing me. My head and heart were about to explode.

By the time Reaper started his bike, smiled, and rolled out of the lot toward his place, I was so anxious to lay my eyes on her, I couldn't stand it. Once we hit the road, I quickly worked through my gears until my bike ate up the few miles to their home. We rolled our bikes up to the garage and set the kickstands. Reaper was still grinning at me with a teasing expression as he got off his bike.

"Shut the fuck up." He hadn't said a word, but I knew what he was thinking, and he needed to just stuff it. Motherfucker. Like he hadn't panted after Steph when he found her again. Despite knowing where I hoped things would end up with Becca, there were no guarantees in this life. What I knew for sure was I wanted her like no one I had ever wanted before. Maybe this wasn't a forever thing. Maybe after a while, I would be able to work her out of my system, but right now, I just knew I wanted her. I wanted to be inside her, wrapped around her and owning her. The thought of that Trevor asshole or any other guy having their hands on her soft skin had me damn near seeing red. Something about her brought out a crazy possessive side of me. Not in like a stalker, creepy way, so don't even go there.

She just felt like… well… like she was mine.

Chapter SEVENTEEN

Becca

STEPH HAD CONCOCTED SOME SORT OF FANCY CHICKEN ON A BED of seasoned rice with Asparagus spears and carrots, seasoned with some kind of deliciousness.

I made… the salad.

Boy, did I feel like I went all out.

Yes, sarcasm intended.

Now, in my defense, I did make my mom's famous coconut cake for dessert. Thanks to my mom, baking was really more my thing. One thing I could say as I sat smelling the amazing aromas that permeated the kitchen was Reaper must never get bored with Steph's food! He better stay active, or he would easily be six hundred pounds one day, I giggled to myself.

My eyes kept darting over to the clock to see how much longer before the guys were home. Every minute crawled by until I heard the rumble of their Harley's as they pulled up out front. One of them said something, and then I heard laughter that sounded like Reaper, but I wasn't sure. The fluttering in my chest and stomach increased.

Looking down, I noticed I had flour on my T-shirt and sticky Remi handprints on my jeans from when I let her lick the bowl of frosting.

Crap!

"I'll be right back!" I shouted to Steph as I raced down the hall to the spare bedroom, stripping out of my clothes as soon as the door closed. As I stood digging through my bag for a clean pair of jeans and a shirt that didn't say I had dressed up for him, but one that didn't make me look like a bum, I heard Reaper coming down the hall. He must be going to their room to get cleaned up too. Okay, good, I had time.

That's when the door burst open and Mason stepped in the room. Whatever he was getting ready to say froze on his tongue, and I was immobilized for a moment in shock before grabbing a pillow off the bed next to me and holding it over myself.

Shit, I was in my underwear! Granted, they were nice ones—my favorite red set—but I wasn't expecting anyone to just come barging in! Damn.

"Excuse me! Do you not know how to *knock?*" It was hell trying to keep my face from giving away the rush I felt just seeing him. I tried to maintain an indignant look. I was sure I failed, but I tried. The man had already seen me in much less, but that was before.

Before what? I don't know... Shut up.

When I saw him close the door softly and lean back against it, I felt my body tingling and a flood of wetness at my core. *Oh man, oh man.* How did he *do* that to me just by *looking* at me?

Oh no, he was not coming toward me with a feral gleam in his eye. No, no, no. Oh shit, yes, he was.

I held a hand out in front of me to ward him off, like I didn't want to crawl up his sexy body like a spider monkey. "Hollywood, what are you doing? No. Don't you come over here! *Hollywood!*" I started to panic at the thought of not being able to control myself if he got too close. But it was already much too late. He gently took the pillow from me and set it on the bed before placing his hands on either side of my neck and sliding them up until his fingers were buried in my curls. I was sure he could hear my heart beating, because it sure as hell felt like it was pounding out of my chest. His lips parted, and he started to lean closer.

When his lips brushed against mine hesitantly at first, I felt a jolt of electricity… or energy… or something… shoot through my entire body. Whatever it was, I didn't want it to stop. When my hands curled up around his body and over his shoulder to pull him closer, the kiss deepened into a crazy, frantic exchange, like we were trying to meld right into each other. My nipples were so hard the friction of them against my lace bra was almost uncomfortable. God knew when his hands slid down to my thighs, but I felt them gliding up from my thighs to cup my ass and pull me tight to his body. Oh wow, he was seriously turned on, unless the large ridge I felt in his jeans was something other than his dick.

My nails dug in to the leather over his shoulders, and I moaned into his mouth as he pulled me even closer, placing pressure on my clit. Sweet baby Jesus, the sensations washing over me made me whimper. He lifted me up until my legs were wrapped around his waist, and I felt his leg rise as he climbed on the bed while holding me. Our kiss broke off as he laid me back across the comforter. A whine slipped out of my mouth at the loss of contact from both his lips and groin.

"Hollywood…" The breathless whine of my voice was foreign to me.

"Mason. For you, it's Mason, not Hollywood." His voice was as breathless as mine.

We were both breathing heavy as he stared into my eyes as the back of his hand skimmed along my skin until his fingertips were running along the inside of my panties. When his fingers dipped down into my folds, I knew he felt how turned on I was. It was evident in the mixed look of triumph and pain in his eyes, which appeared more green than gold. My breath caught at the feeling of his finger slipping in and out of my channel before he added a second digit.

Dear God, don't let him stop…

My head pressed back into the bed, and gasping breaths slipped from my mouth as his fingers moved in and out, curling against just the right place to push me into sensory overload. The heel of his hand placed pressure in circular motions on my clit, and his name whispered from my lips as I grasped desperately at the comforter. "Yes, just like that…" *Was that me hissing out words of encouragement to this gorgeous man with his hand between my legs?* My hands were still wildly grasping the bedding. My subconscious must have thought, if I could get a strong enough grip on something, then I could control the crashing waves of insane desire he was creating in me.

My breasts ached, my entire body quivering and on edge. *Jesus, he is so good at this.* The feeling of absolute fulfillment at his hands was about to overtake me, the ripples starting at the periphery of my being.

"Let go, Becca. Give it up for me. Show me again how fucking gorgeous you are when you come." His words whispered across my neck. He increased the pressure on my clit and his fingers played my G-spot like the most skilled pianist. The pressure kept building, and every muscle in my body tightened in expectation. When the explosion came, I saw white flash behind my closed lids and his name was a groan from deep in my soul. His lips crashed to mine in an effort to contain my moans of ecstasy as his hand continued to work me, squeezing out every bit of pleasure and extending my orgasm until I thought I might completely combust.

When I finally started my descent back to Earth, he broke off from our kiss so we could breathe and rested his forehead against mine. "God, Becca, you're so fucking stunning. I could spend all day in bed with you, making you come, just to see that look on your face. You are so damn amazing to me." His fingers continued to stroke within my core as he kept pressure on my clit, causing me to clench against them in an aftershock of pleasure. When he pulled his hand from my panties and raised it to his lips, I almost died. *Surely he wasn't going to… oh God, he did.* He licked his fingers as if the cream coating them was the sweetest delicacy.

Shit, that was hot.

"Jesus, Mason. What the hell are you doing to me? You're going to drive me crazy if you keep this up." My voice sounded breathless and soft—so foreign to my ears. I watched as he removed his fingers and leaned closer before running his tongue along the shell of my ear, causing goose bumps to erupt along my skin. He then nipped my ear with his teeth.

Mmmm, damn his teeth on my skin were a wild turn-on.

"Becca, baby, I've only just begun to pleasure you. By the time I'm done with you, you'll have forgotten the feel of any other man inside you. The only name that will come to your lips in climax is mine. Your body will crave my touch like an addiction." His breath puffed against my ear and neck as he spoke, causing the chills to ripple through my body with a shudder of desire.

Oh dear God in heaven. What he didn't know was I already did.

Hollywood

"You probably won't believe me, but I really did just come in here to tell you dinner was ready. Then when I saw you standing there in just those tiny scraps of red lace, it was my undoing. You do things to me no other woman ever has." It was important for her to know that while I didn't for a second regret what had just passed between us, I didn't come in here intent of seducing her. Of course, I can't say that wasn't on the agenda for later, but hey, I wasn't admitting that just yet.

She bit that bottom lip between her little white teeth and my cock jerked, reminding me I had neglected it. *Fuck.*

"Becca, please stop that shit or we will *not* be having dinner with everyone." My tongue ran across her bottom lip and teeth, extricating her lip from their punishment and allowing me to gently suck it in before ending in a tender, lingering kiss.

I crawled off the bed, reaching for her hand to help her up. When she stood, I pulled her body gently to mine before placing another soft, chaste kiss on her lips and the tip of her nose. My hands gripped her ass in a possessive hold.

"Baby, we need to talk. Ride with me after dinner." It wasn't really a request, but her green eyes met mine and she nodded before cupping my head and kissing my cheek. She stood there on her tiptoes and held the side of her face to mine for a minute before she spoke.

"I need to get some clothes on, so unless you want me to go out and have dinner dressed like this, you need to let me go." She gave a teasing little grin and stepped back until my hands rested lightly on her hips. The thought of Reaper, or any man, seeing her like this made me feel an irrational burst of jealousy, so I reluctantly let her pull out of my arms to dress.

My eyes devoured her every movement as she stepped into a pair of snug-fitting jeans and slipped on a long-sleeve, black Metallica tee with vintage print across her chest. I had never been more jealous of a band in my life. She sat on the bed to pull on a pair of socks and then walked over to grab a pair of boots. When she bent over to tug them on one at a time, I had to adjust my dick just from the view of her perfect, firm ass and the tiny glimpse of skin where her shirt raised up slightly.

Shit, I'm in trouble with this girl, and I truly don't give a rat's ass.

She straightened up and looked at me. Yeah, totally busted checking her out, and her smirk said she knew exactly what I had been doing. I shrugged my shoulders and gave her a shit-eating grin.

"Hey, what can I say? I'm a red-blooded man and you are one fine-looking woman."

The sound of her laughter made my stomach flip. She raised an eyebrow as she tried to turn the knob and found it locked.

"Well, after I saw you like that, I figured it wouldn't be a good thing for someone to walk in on us while we came to an, uhhhh.... understanding." Winking at her, I reached around and unlocked the door, opened it, and waved her through in a "ladies first" manner.

Best. View. Ever.

Walking behind her was something I could handle doing every day. Well, maybe not. I might end up with a perpetual hard-on. That shit would suck. Hmmm, unless it led to us being in bed. Then, of course, we would never get anything done. No job, no money, no place to live… probably a bad idea.

"Earth to Hollywood, Earth to Hollywood. Are you done checking out Becca's ass? Because I'd like to eat the amazing food my wife made for us sometime tonight." I jumped at the sound of Reaper's voice. He stood in the doorway to the living room with his arms crossed over his chest, trying not to laugh at me. Shit, was I really that engrossed in looking at her ass? Dammit. What the hell was wrong with me? Grinning like an idiot, I decided I really didn't care that he saw me staring. She was like a drug crawling through my blood, and I totally needed to fuck her until I got her out of my system. Then maybe we could go our separate ways.

But if I was just going to fuck her and forget her, why did it piss me off to think of her with someone else after we were done? Because every nerve in my body screamed she was mine every time I saw her.

Chapter EIGHTEEN

Becca

DINNER WAS AMAZING, AS ALWAYS WITH STEPH'S COOKING, BUT also one of the most uncomfortable experiences I'd ever had. First, Remi busted me by asking why "Unco Mason" was in my room. Steph and Reaper tried not to laugh at her innocent question. Then, to top it all off, Mason and his smug little smirk. I was mortified that Steph and Reaper had any idea of what had happened in there. Good Lord. Once upon a time, I would have had no qualms bringing a guy home with Steph being in her room, but now that we were older and it was her house with her *family*, it just seemed, well, awkward. She had *kids* in the house for crying out loud!

I started to help Steph clean up after dinner, but she wouldn't let me, insisting that I go with Hollywood to "relax and enjoy the ride."

She always referred to him as Hollywood; I guessed that was because that was how she was introduced to him. In all honestly, I had been too, but when a guy tells you to call him by his name in the middle of the best orgasm of your life, you call him by his name. At Steph's phrase, I saw Mason waggle his eyebrows, and I knew what kind of "ride" he was thinking of. My eyes rolled at his craziness, but truthfully, I felt a little thrill go through me at the thought of both kinds of "rides."

Yeah, there was still a bit of that wild child in me. Who we were deep in our soul didn't change no matter how hard we tried to subdue it.

Steph loaned me a leather jacket since it had cooled off quite a bit after the sun went down, and Mason and I went out to get on the bike. Several of the guys I was with in college had bikes, so I was no stranger to riding, but it had been awhile, and I was a little nervous. Not to mention, the thought of him being between my legs? Oh damn, that was not a good place for my mind to go while I needed to be paying attention so I didn't fall off the damn bike.

Mason's bike was gorgeous, I had to admit. It was a metallic black with saddle bags that were the same color and a fancy "dashboard" looking thing. I was sure all this stuff had a name, but I wasn't up on my motorcycle lingo. He pulled a half helmet—I knew its name because I remembered one of my ex's talking about the difference between a full-face and a half helmet. See? I wasn't totally bike stupid. As he started the bike up, music began to play, and I laughed because it was Metallica's "Unforgiven II," and I thought of the shirt I had put on. Mason looked at me in question.

"What's so funny?"

Pointing at my shirt, I smiled, watching him read my shirt as I was zipping up the borrowed jacket.

"Yeah, you have nice tits," he said, and I couldn't help but laugh. I gave him a playful punch in the arm, and he motioned for me to climb on as he continued to laugh. *Shithead.*

Some things really were like riding a bike, I guess. No pun intended. Climbing on the bike felt natural, like I had done it all my life. He didn't have a backrest for me, so I had to scoot forward and wrap my arms around his waist. Of course, this pressed my boobs up against his back and my crotch against his ass, not that I could think of a nicer ass to be up against.

Stop it, Becca, you slut! Ugh! I was sooooo bad!

He told me to hang on tight. As we pulled out on to the road and picked up speed, I swore he was intentionally shifting quickly to smash my boobs against him each time. Okay, so I wasn't really complaining. The wind was cool as it rushed by, and it was definitely warmer snuggled up close to him.

He never said where we were going, but I didn't really care. The ride was amazing, and holding his body close to mine was like a little slice of heaven after the magic he had worked on it before dinner.

He started to slow, and I looked over his shoulder to see where we were. We had turned off into a park by the lake and followed the narrow road around the lake until we pulled into a parking area, and he backed us up into a spot and shut off the engine. We sat on the bike for a minute listening to the ticking of the engine and enjoying the warmth of the motor and each other before he pulled off his helmet and hung it over his right-hand mirror. It seemed like a good time to climb off, so I did and worked to get the buckle unlatched on my helmet.

It wasn't cooperating, and I struggled a little before he reached up to help me. My hands fell to my side, and I took in the details of his face as he focused on the buckle and working the strap loose. He was so damn good looking. It should truly be a sin to look as gorgeous as he did. He had tipped his head to the side and bent down a little to see the buckle under my chin, putting him at eye level with me. His lashes were obscenely thick and long, his lips were firm but full, and his jaw was strong, slightly square and had a darker five o'clock shadow coming through. There was a thin scar that cut through his left eyebrow, and I wondered how he had acquired it.

He must have felt my scrutiny of his face because he looked into my eyes as he lifted the helmet from my head, and we just stood there for a moment considering each other while he held the helmet in one hand. He took a deep breath and grabbed my hand as he set my helmet on his bike and led me toward the lake. Just the touch of his hand to mine sent tingles of awareness through my body. It was like electric currents fired from his fingers to mine. He led me over to a little shelter with a couple of picnic tables looking over the lake. It had one wall blocking the wind and the view from the road, leaving us somewhat secluded.

Mason climbed up to sit on the top of the picnic table and reached out a hand to pull me up with him to sit between his legs. After I got settled, he wrapped his arms around me and rested his chin on my shoulder. His scent invaded my senses as we sat quietly. We stayed that way for a while and watched the moonlight as it reflected on the water. Between the breeze and fish out on the lake, it created small waves and ripples so the lake appeared to be glittering. The night was quiet, with only the rustle of the breeze blowing through the trees, the chirp of crickets, and small animals scurrying in the distance.

"Becca, I needed to talk to you away from Steph and Reaper. Look, I know things went to shit in Vegas. It was just a real punch to the gut to find out I was the 'other guy.' There are things about that… well, it's a long story." He took a deep breath. "You said you didn't want to talk about it, but I need to know. I honestly don't know what this is between us, or how long it will last, but I don't want you to go back to him. Stay here with me. See where this goes—no strings, we just see what happens. Right now, I just don't think I can let you go… and the thought of you being with anyone else fills me with an indescribable fury. It makes me feel like I'm completely out of control, and dammit, I have tried so damn hard to get you out of my head for months. You have no idea. I don't understand it, but I think if you left right now, I may just cease to exist. God, that sounds cheesy… Please don't think I'm crazy, because I'm not a pussy, but I guess I feel pretty fucking possessive of you, whether it makes sense or not."

His words caught me completely off guard as I never expected to hear that from him. My heart lurched and my breath felt wedged in my throat. In all the time I had been with Trevor, he had never said such candid things to me. Then it clicked in my head… he thought Trevor and I were still together.

Turning my head and upper body to look at him, I reached up to take his face and look him in the eyes. His scruff was prickly against the soft palms of my hands, and I rubbed my thumbs against it, hearing and feeling the rasp as each hair crossed my skin. "Mason, Trevor and I aren't together anymore. I had told him things were over before I left for Vegas. I wasn't with him when you and I were together there. He didn't want to hear it, and he pressured me into staying in the house to 'work things out' after I got back. But in the end, I couldn't stay with him, because I just knew it wasn't going to work. I moved out months ago. Then I came up here to get away from some stupid crap that happened, not just to visit. I don't know how long I'll be staying, but I can't go back yet. I don't *want* to go back yet, if ever."

His eyes seemed to darken at my admission and his lips parted slightly. His fingers wove through my hair as he grasped it tight to tip my head closer to him. I couldn't help leaning in to him, even with his hand guiding my head. It was like his lips and body were magnets and I was under their pull. My heart lurched when my lips encountered his, and it felt like a thousand butterflies fluttered in my stomach. He tasted like heaven and what started as a gentle meeting evolved quickly into a passionate battle to consume each other.

Hollywood

When her lips touched mine after she told me she wasn't with Trevor, I lost all thought and pulled her up until she was straddling my lap. The chemistry between us was off the charts. Whatever was between us was strong as fuck. No other woman had *ever* affected me like this. Becca was straight-up under my skin. She had crept into my head months ago, and I couldn't get her off my mind no matter how hard I tried. She crept into my very dreams at night. She was becoming as vital as the air I breathed. And that scared the shit out of me.

My hands slipped up under the back of her shirt, and I unhooked her bra before resting them on the silky skin of her back. The heat of that satiny skin against my hands felt like an inferno. She ran her arms around my waist and mimicked my movements by running them up under the back of my shirt. Her lips tasted sweet like the frosting on the cake she had made. Taking her bottom lip with my teeth, I drew it into my mouth and suck gently before moving to kiss along the line of her jaw.

She pressed into me, chest to groin, with a quickly inhaled breath that escaped her lips again in a soft moan. My cock was pressing painfully at the zipper of my jeans, and her grinding against it was bordering on painful but so incredibly arousing I didn't want her to stop. She was pushing me toward insanity, and if I didn't bury my cock in her soon, I might embarrass the shit out of myself. This was happening tonight come hell or high water. She then pulled her body back a little and her hand reached between us. When her nails ran over my jeans from the base of my cock to the tip before she curved her hand around it and squeezed, I groaned in desperation.

Fuck me.

"Becca, I need to be inside you. Now. But I need to be sure you're wanting the same thing. If not, I think we need to leave and I need to take you back before this actually kills me." When she unbuttoned my jeans and lowered the zipper, I grabbed her wrist in my hand. "I need you to say it, Becca. I need you to tell me what you want. There cannot be any doubts or questions, baby. Not this time. I need to know it's just me and you, and we both want this." She looked me dead in the eye and the words that came out of her mouth nearly made my eyes roll in my damn head.

"Hollywood, I want you to fuck me. I want you to bury your cock in me over and over. I want to feel you come in me as I squeeze your cock with my pussy. Is that clear enough?" *Jesus Christ*. Clear enough? Shit, I felt like she drew me a fucking picture, and what a picture it was. Holy hell.

I rolled her over so she was laid out on the tabletop. My jeans rested low on my hips unzipped and unbuttoned thanks to her hands, but I wanted her out of hers. Her boots came off first, and I dropped them haphazardly to the ground. Her jeans were next. There was no patience or carefully sliding them off. They pulled off inside out, and I dropped them to the ground with her boots. Leaning over the table, I ran my hands up the outside of her thighs and buried my face in the lace of her panties, biting her clit through the lace and inhaling the scent of her arousal. When I pushed them to the side and ran my tongue along her slit, she dug her fingers in my hair, pulling me closer.

Her panties slid down her thighs in a rush as I needed to see and taste her unobstructed. My tongue circled her clit before I grabbed it with my teeth and flicked it back and forth with the tip of my tongue. She thrashed and moaned as I slipped two fingers in her slick, wet, heat without letting go of her clit. I knew exactly how to curl my fingers to make her come for me, and I was relentless in my assault on her body and senses. She tensed under me, and her thighs tightened around my head. It didn't matter if it was too much; I pushed her legs open again with my shoulder and my other hand, preventing her from escaping my tongue and fingers. This time, I was intent on driving her over the edge until she essentially fell apart in my hands.

She screamed my road name as I felt her pussy clamp down tight on my fingers. "Mason. Goddammit, call me Mason when we're like this," I heard myself growl into her. I fucking loved that I made her brain scramble, but I wanted the sound of my actual name on her lips as she uttered it in the flood of intense pleasure I had created in her.

She was so damn responsive. Her fluids ran out on my hand as she continued to spasm around my fingers. I continued to stroke her, drawing out her climax as long as I could, pressing kisses to her curls and her belly. Working my way up her body, I pushed her shirt and bra up over her glorious chest. My tongue ran around her belly button and across her ribs until I reached the bottom curve of her breasts. Harder than I intended, I nipped the bottoms, leaving slight pink marks in my wake. God, she had amazing tits.

Suckling one taut nipple, I rolled the other between the thumb and forefinger of my free hand. With the stimulation to both her nipples and her core, she was on sensory overload. Her breaths came in short pants, and she moaned my name once again as I lightly ran my teeth across the nipple I had been suckling.

"Jesus, Mason. I need to feel you. Please." When she whimpered those words, I lost control, hauling her to the end of the table and flipping her over. I pulled out my cock and stroked it a few times with the wetness she had left on my hand before I pushed just the tip into the tight core of her warmth. My other hand stroked her ass before I gripped her hips with both hands. The end of my cock teased her soaking wet pussy by slipping in and out. She cried out in frustration at my teasing actions.

"Tell me how you want it," I rasped.

"I need you, Mason, hard. Now, dammit. Fuck me! Please!" As I drove myself deep into her pussy until my balls hit against her clit, she gasped. My eyes rolled into the back of my head and my knees nearly buckled as her hot sheath tightened around my cock. Fucking A, she was so damn tight I almost lost my shit right then and there. I found myself trying to think of random boring shit just to keep me from blowing my load prematurely.

"Fuck, Becca. Hold still for a second, or this is going to end way too soon." My words were gravely, I knew, and I could barely form a coherent thought. She lay over the table, her forearms and head resting on the table as she panted and moaned. Shit, she was going to kill me. It took everything I had to gather up any vestige of control. When I finally felt like I could move without emptying into her immediately, I slid in and out, building up a steady rhythm. During an outward stroke, I dipped my fingers into her slick wetness, coating them before I circled her puckered ass and slipped the tip of one finger in. "This will be mine soon too," I whispered in her ear. She gasped, and I felt her tighten around me.

"Harder." *Fuck. Hell, yeah, I could accommodate.* Slamming into her until my balls were slapping against her and her tits were bouncing, I listened to her grunts and whimpers of pleasure with each thrust. Her body tensed and her sheath became slightly tighter, telling me she was so very close. I reached around, and my fingers circled her clit at a rapid pace, encouraging her to come with me. The other hand grasped her breast, squeezing her nipple between my fingers. My balls tightened up, and I knew I didn't have much time left.

"Come, Becca. Come now. I'm not going to last much longer, baby." No sooner had I made the request than I felt her hot pussy clamp down viciously tight on my cock, and she screamed my name for the second time that night, but this time it was my actual name… That did me in. Two more thrusts, and I felt my cum explode from my cock and fill her. She continued to squeeze my cock with the spasms of her orgasm, milking every last drop from me until I thought I was going to pass out.

Jesus H. Christ. She was too damn much.

Lying across her back for a moment to get my breath, I pressed my lips to the heated skin of her back. She shivered and moved to stand. My arms held her tight to me as we stood, desperately trying to gain control of our breathing. With my cock still nestled within her wet warmth, I buried my nose in her deep red hair and inhaled the fresh scent of her, feeling like I would never get enough of this woman. She was doing crazy things to my mind, body, and heart—all the things I never thought I would want. She whimpered as I slipped out in a flood of our mixed fluids.

"You. Are. Mine. Stay with me, Becca. Please, don't go…" Though I meant them to be a demand, my words were a murmured plea, as if they slipped uncontrolled from deep in my soul.

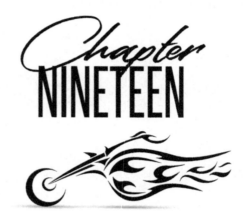

Chapter NINETEEN

Becca

Sex with Mason was mind-blowing and shook me to my core. Never in my life had I been left feeling completely satiated, yet wanting more. He just made me feel things no one else ever had. In his arms, I felt wanton. On the other hand, I also felt protected and cherished, like I was precious and desired. Shit, what was I going to do when he decided he had enough of me? He just wasn't the type to settle down for long.

He'd said he wanted us to see where this… whatever it was… between us, went. However, it seemed as if he thought it was a feeling that we would grow out of or grow tired of. Standing here in the moonlight, wrapped up in his arms, I knew my heart was not coming away from this relationship unscathed. I foolishly cared about him too much already. He wanted me to be addicted to him and his body; well, he got his wish. Just the thought of him walking away was ripping at my heart and making me ache where we had been joined mere moments before. After he was done with me, I knew I would be completely shattered. And walk away, he would. Guys like him just weren't the commitment type. He wanted me to be his, but I doubted he meant forever.

The best thing I could do was cordon off my heart. What I needed to do was tell myself we would just enjoy each other and the sexual chemistry for as long as it lasted. *Yeah right*. Hopefully, after it ended and I went home again, I would wrap up moments like this and relive them when I was alone. What I needed to do and what would actually happen were probably two different things. My hands moved back and forth from his wrists to his elbows, feeling the hills and valleys of his defined muscles in his forearms. He squeezed me tighter, kissing the top of my head. This was the stuff dreams were made of, and I prayed it didn't end in a nightmare for my heart. Speaking of my heart, it lurched at the feel of him burying his nose in my hair and inhaling deeply.

Hefting a sigh, I extricated myself from his arms and rummaged around for my scattered clothing. The lack of his warmth hit me immediately as the cool night air ran over the thin layer of sweat covering me after our exertions. Shit, I was soaked *there* too. I used my underwear to clean up as best I could before he took them from my hands and stuffed them in his pocket with a smirk. *Weirdo*, I laughed to myself. As I redressed, I watched him fasten his pants, taking in the sculpted muscles of his torso. *Gawd*, he was truly divine. Chiseled abs led to that perfect V, which pointed to the part of him that made my mouth water. I took in the colorful tattoos that decorated his arms and torso, again. It should be criminal for him to cover that gorgeous body, I thought as he pulled on his shirt, tugging it down over his body. But damn if I could deny how sexy it was.

"Hollywood, I quit my job down in Council Bluffs," I said

quietly. "I pretty much ran away after some embarrassing pictures of me got leaked out. Granted, they were all from when I was in college, and they weren't really, really bad, but that wasn't how they appeared when they were posted. Someone intended to paint me in the worst light they could, and it worked. The school superintendent asked me to take a leave of absence until this all blew over, but I turned in my resignation. Then, my roommate asked me to leave because she was afraid of the backlash she would face for letting me continue to stay there since she was a teacher too. People were vandalizing her house because of me, so I really don't blame her for asking me to leave. To top it all off, my parents and I had a falling out after I broke it off with Trevor because they felt like he was such a 'catch' and I was foolish to let him go. Just another of my many disappointments to my parents. Well, mostly my mom, but my dad didn't stand up for me, so I couldn't go to my parents either. Steph didn't even know I was coming. She was a sweetheart to let me stay like she has, but I'll have to find a job to pay my way soon. I have some savings I can get by on for a while, but not too long." After that spiel, I took a deep breath and watched his expression for a sign of revulsion or a change of heart after what I had revealed. I just felt the need to tell him everything. He stood half in the shadows, so it was hard to read his face.

"Baby, I don't care. What's in the past is in the past. Trust me when I say I've done some shit that would make yours seem mild I'm sure. People are obviously too busy casting stones to realize they aren't any better than you. And I owe you an apology too." He appeared uncomfortable, and I wondered what he could possibly have to apologize for.

"What are you talking about?" He didn't really owe me any explanations for anything I could think of. He sat on the bench seat of the picnic table, holding his head in his hands and resting his elbows on his knees.

"In Vegas." Yeah, well, Vegas was a big fucked-up mess between us for sure.

"Look, Mason, I know I was a bitch to you too. I really didn't think there was the slightest chance in hell anything lasting could come of that night. We lived hours apart, and I wasn't expecting either of us to commit to any kind of a relationship with those types of terms. Don't worry about it." Granted, I had thought he was being a bit of a self-righteous asshole, but that seemed extra bitchy to bring up.

"I thought you were still with Trevor but messing around with me, Becca. You know the whole 'what happens in Vegas, stays in Vegas' type deal. It pissed me off because I have a rule that I don't mess with people in relationships. It was a promise I made my sister after her ex-husband screwed anything with a pussy, even when they knew he was married. She made me promise to never be a home-wrecker and to never cheat on a woman if I was serious about her." He took a deep breath. "Anyway, when Trevor called that morning and you lied about why I was there, I thought that's what you were doing and that you thought I would be okay with it. I treated you like shit, and I'm sorry. I should have just asked you, but my temper got the better of me that day."

"Wow. So, we both kind of sold ourselves short that weekend. But, Mason, it doesn't matter. Either way, we would have had too much distance between us, and we each had our own reasons to want to stay where we were at the time. I happen to not have anything holding me there right now, but I agree with you that we should just see where this goes." My thigh was against his as I sat down next to him. He reached over and pulled me into his lap, cradling me in his arms.

"Clean slate?" He nuzzled behind my ear. The action sent shivers of desire through me. Damn, he was like a drug, but I was contentedly worn out and basking in the afterglow of what we had just shared.

"Clean slate." We sealed the deal with a chaste kiss. How long we sat out there enjoying the view and the tranquil night sounds, I have no idea, but I had never felt so at peace in my life.

Chapter TWENTY

Hollywood

THAT NIGHT, I HAD WANTED TO BRING BECCA BACK TO MY ROOM with me and keep her locked up there with me forever. Naked. But instead, I had dropped her off at Steph and Reaper's place with a few more fucking amazing kisses and a little roaming of our hands before she braced both hands on my chest and pushed me away with a giggle then quietly entered the house and left me smiling like a fool on the front porch.

Shit had been busy at the club the last week or so, and I hadn't seen her since that night. A few X-rated phone conversations were the extent of my contact with her, and I was about to explode, I was so on edge. Fuck, she was under my skin. If I didn't get my Becca fix soon, I might lose my damn mind.

Our club had been mostly legit for the past year or more, but we still had occasional run-ins with assholes who felt like they wanted to try to take over our shit. We had the shop, a strip club, a tattoo shop we just opened, we had a small interest in Steph's bar, and we were in the process of starting up a construction company to go with the hardware/lumberyard. Yeah, it kept us busy.

Unfortunately, we had been having more issues at the Emerald Shamrock, our strip club, lately. According to the girls, there were some assholes in a cut they didn't recognize who had been harassing them. The shady-ass manager had been kept on when we took over the bar. Several of us thought we should have shitcanned him right away, but the club decided he knew the business, so we would let him keep his job. He was a sleazy little bastard, and he was saying he didn't know who these guys were and they, conveniently, never seemed to show up when we had someone there. The manager was about to get booted because we were pretty sure he was skimming somehow. Cash hadn't been able to track it, but he was thinking it was through the girls' tips. We knew there was no way that bastard could afford the lifestyle he was leading on his salary. Now it was up to us to figure out exactly where he was getting the money.

The latest was something we were not going to let slide. One of the new girls had actually been assaulted and raped during a private dance. The other girls said she entered one of the private rooms with a "skinny creepy looking guy in a cut." Great description, but everyone had been busy that night and, therefore, not paying great attention to who was where. She was still in the hospital in serious condition, so we couldn't get a good description of the asshole assailant. We were not going to put up with any woman being treated like that, but to have it be one of our girls made it a serious fuck up that would absolutely be dealt with.

We had positioned one of the prospects, Soap, there incognito, since the manager didn't know him, and Hacker had tapped into the camera system and added a few extra cameras the manager didn't know about, but so far the other pieces of shit hadn't shown their face. When they did, they were going to learn not to fuck with us.

It became my job to stake out the Shamrock from the little diner across the road, sans cut to stay "undercover." It was a shithole on the surface, but they had great food and even better coffee, so I figured fuck it, there could be worse places to have to watch from. Ordinarily, I wouldn't give a shit how many nights I needed to sit here, but now that I had someone I'd rather be with at night, it was making me antsy as fuck.

So here I was talking to my sexy redhead while I drank coffee and watched the Shamrock. Her voice purred across the line and coiled around my dick, making me fidget in my seat like a kindergarten kid on the last day of school. Damn, I wanted to have her here where she could actually wrap something around my… Shit, I needed to stop thinking about it. These assholes needed to just show up already, so we could report back to Snow who the fuck was on our shit list and then *do* something about it.

"So, what time do you think you'll be done tonight?" *As soon as I slide into you*, is what I want to say, but I half laughed and half moaned instead. I knew that wasn't what she was referring to, but my mind went wicked places when it came to her.

"Shit, baby, not soon enough. But as soon as I'm done, I'm coming by to pick you up. I want you to come back to my room and stay the night with me. We have a ride tomorrow, and I want you to join me. Several of the old ladies will be there. It would give you a change to meet everyone." I couldn't stand another night of not seeing her beautiful face, or smelling her light floral scent, or touching her silky skin.

Fuck. These thoughts are not helping my damn cock.

"Ooooo, a sleepover? Should I bring my sleeping bag, makeup, and hair products to do you up? Are we going to sneak out to chase boys?" Her husky laugh had the bastard in my pants twitching again.

"Hell, baby, you don't need to chase *boys* when you're going to have this *man* under you, over you, and inside you. Oh yeah, I can assure you, you won't need more than this one man." I was smirking, and I knew she was aware I was fucking with her when her laughter rang out.

"Oh ho! Is that so? Well, then I'll start packing my overnight bag, and I'll bring the popcorn and movies!" She sounded more like the feisty Becca I first met, and I loved it. The smile in her voice was unmistakable.

"Yeah, you do that, baby, but don't be disappointed when you never get to watch those movies. Hey, baby, I gotta run. I'll call you before I leave to head your way." I disconnected the call quickly. There was a group of about five or six bikes pulling up out front of the Shamrock, and they weren't ours, that was for damn sure. Knowing I needed to get closer to get a good look at the patch and colors they were throwing, I threw a twenty down on the table and headed across the street just as they all entered the Shamrock.

Entering the strip club after crossing the street, I was assaulted by cigarette smoke, blaring music, and the hooting and hollering of all the guys that were watching the show. Trying to remain inconspicuous, I grabbed a beer at the bar from one of the waitresses. Sparkle, yeah, total stripper name, was doing her number. She always danced with an intricate mask decorated with rhinestones. Her only days she worked were on Friday, Saturday, and Sunday's. It was a mystery what she did during the week, but she brought the crowds in on the weekends, so that's all that mattered to us. Before Becca, I had thought about breaking my redheaded habit for her, but never did because Hacker seemed a little taken with her, and I didn't want to step on his dick. Not only that, she really never gave any of us the time of day.

Catching Soap's eye as I walked in, he gave me a head nod that he saw them come in too. Casually, I made my way through the crowd like I was trying to find someone so I could walk past the bikers who had come in. As I passed by them, I overheard their jeers toward Sparkle and the waitresses. They smelled like shit, and if I was correct, they were high as fuck on something. Their patches didn't look familiar to me, but the name rang bells and the patch itself definitely made the dancers' descriptions of it make sense. It was just a set of red eyes, and their rockers read Demon Runners MC with a Nomad bottom rocker.

Keeping on the move, I wandered back to Soap and clinked beers with him like we were just a couple of buddies meeting up for some beers and a titty show. We didn't want to give away who we were. I took the stool across the table from him and positioned myself so my back could lean against the wall as I surveyed the crowd. Even though years had passed, I still liked to have my back secure and have a clear, unobstructed view of my surroundings whenever I could. Some habits were definitely hard to break.

"You get a good look at the patches?" I asked Soap.

"Yeah, you?" I nodded. "You know them?" he asked me.

"No, but I've heard of them… somewhere. They seem high as shit too. I'm going to send a text to Snow to send a few of the boys over as a little 'show of force' to let them know this is our place and they should maybe get on their fucking bikes and keep 'nomad-ing' on down the road. Stupid fucks." My text complete, I sent it off and waited for the prez's reply.

Snow: Sending the boys your way now

Then we just sat and waited for the guys to show up. Damn, I still fucking hated waiting.

Chapter TWENTY-ONE

Becca

My bag was packed, and I was sitting on the front porch steps waiting for Hollywood to show up. That name still cracked me up, but hell, he sure was hot enough to be a sexy Hollywood actor. He could also be my personal porn star any day of the week. The thought made me snicker to myself.

Steph and the babies had already gone to bed, but the guys were still out doing whatever it was they were doing for the club tonight. Steph told me to get used to hearing the phrase "club business." Ugh, whatever. They could have their little boys club, I just wanted time with my guy.

My guy. Wow, it had been awhile since that term sent a thrill through my belly and a tingle between my legs. Shit, was I rushing things? Doing the right thing? Really, I hadn't been out of my relationship with Trevor for very long. Maybe I was rebounding. No. Trevor and I had been over long before I met Mason and certainly long before I moved out.

Besides, Mason and I had both said we would enjoy this for as long as it lasted. No expectations. No promises of forever. So, no, I wasn't screwing up; I just needed to avoid overanalyzing our relationship because I was really working hard to just let things run their course and not define or rush anything—at least that's what I told myself.

Leave me to my little make-believe world and be quiet.

My elbows leaned back on the step above me, and I looked up at the stars. They were so beautiful out here. It seemed like there were millions more than I used to see in town back home. It had only been just shy of two weeks week since I packed up my meager belongings and showed up on Steph's front door step, but I loved it here already. The more I thought about it, the more I knew I would really like to stay here. Even if things didn't work out between me and Hollywood, which I didn't even want to think about because damn it hurt and it shouldn't, I really loved the feel of this small town. Yeah, I missed my parents, but maybe I needed to spread my wings and fly. Besides, my dad called me yesterday and said he changed his routes so he could swing by to see me every so often. Man, I loved my dad. My mom and I? Yeah, I loved her, but we were still not seeing eye to eye.

The rumble of Harley pipes in the distance broke the silence. Lordy, I didn't know how Reaper didn't wake the kiddos when he came home late at night, because I could hear them from way down the road already. My heart started to pick up speed at the mere thought of Hollywood getting closer to me. Senses on high alert, my entire body tingled in anticipation. When their headlights pulled in the driveway, my belly gave a quick flip.

Shit, I was in trouble if my body was physically reacting to just knowing he was close. It was like I had my own little "Hollywood radar" going off. Hell, it may be entirely too late to guard my heart. Trying to push those thoughts down, I pulled in a deep, fortifying breath.

Both guys pulled up and shut off their bikes. Reaper got off and started toward the house, kissing the top of my head as he passed me on the stairs. "Goodnight, Little Red. Don't do anything I wouldn't do." He smirked, and I laughed, swatting playfully at his leg as he let himself quietly in the house. Shithead. After the door latched, I looked over to Hollywood who was still sitting on his bike looking at me like he was ready to consume me. *Hungry* was the term that described his expression.

"Well, Red, baby, what are you waiting for? Or have you changed your mind?" His voice slid across the night air and ran through my senses like smooth whiskey. My bag was next to me, and I scooped it up as I went down the steps and sauntered over to him. Excitement rippled through me, making me feel like a teenage girl on her first date.

"Does it look like I changed my mind?" My tone was sultry, and I leaned in and nipped his neck before I kissed his night-cooled skin. Then I let my tongue slip out to run up along his jawline, ending in another nip where his jaw ended.

His growl was his only response before he grabbed my waist and lifted me over his bike so I was facing him, straddling his legs with my ass on the tank. His lips on mine were like adding gasoline to a fire as the heat exploded between us. Our kiss was wild and deep, a dueling of tongues and nipping teeth that left us both breathless and wanting as we pulled away from each other slowly. My forehead rested against his and his words feathered over my lips.

"Jesus, baby, I need you. Even more than before. Are you ready to go now? Because if we don't get going soon, like *right now*, I'm going to christen Reaper and Steph's front porch." My smirk earned me a smile and a quick kiss before he smacked my ass and told me to put my bag in the saddle bags and get on the back.

Before I knew it, we were racing down the road. My hair flew like a fiery banner behind me, and I knew it would be tangled as shit by the time we got there, but what a glorious feeling. With my breasts pressed tight against him and my face buried in his back, I inhaled the smell of leather, smoke, and what I could only describe as… Mason. My nipples felt hard enough to cut glass, which had absolutely nothing to do with the temperature, and I was glad for the double barriers of leather, or I would never hear the end of it from him.

By the time we arrived at the clubhouse and rolled through the gate, it was well after one in the morning. The gate closed behind us and we drove behind the building to park and enter the back door. The clubhouse reminded me of an old barn or shop with some serious fencing topped with razor wire. They were *not* playing around with that shit.

Damn.

Hollywood unlocked the door, and after securing it and setting the security code, he took my hand and led me down the back hall of rooms to the second door from the end. Then he unlocked the door and pulled me in behind him to close and lock the door behind us.

No sooner had he locked it than he was grabbing my bag to toss it to the floor and scooping me up in his arms. Our eyes stayed connected, and we were both breathing heavy by the time he stopped at the bed and tossed me to the middle where I bounced then fell back against the pillows. The room was dark except for the moonlight coming in from the high window above the bed. I watched as he stripped off his leather cut and pulled his shirt over his head. That was a view I would never tire of seeing. My tongue ran across my lips unconsciously as his muscles rippled and flexed with each movement.

Sweet baby Jesus.

Everything he stripped off landed on a chair next to the door. The top button of his jeans was next. He sat on the edge of the bed to remove his boots and socks. Did it make me bad that I wanted to lick every rippling muscle on his body?

When he crawled over the bed to me, he straddled me and placed his hands on either side of my shoulders. All I could do was concentrate on breathing and remaining still. He leaned close and buried his face in my hair along my neck. Mmm. His lips tickled the skin on my throat, and I tilted my head to allow him better access.

"God, Becca, you are going to be my undoing." He bit down on my shoulder where my neck joined it and sent shivers racing down my body. *Oh God.*

My clothes seemed to melt away as his hands made quick work of pulling them off me. Every second seemed to tick by in slow motion when he stopped to gently kiss me. Becoming impatient, I reached for his jeans, but he took both my hands and raised them over my head and held my wrists in one of his large, calloused hands while the other ran reverently along my face, down my neck, over my chest to finally cup a breast where his thumb then rubbed back and forth across my nipple. His fingers trailing over my skin pushed my sanity to the brink. My eyes closed, back arched from the bed, and whimpers slipped from my mouth. His touch ignited a fire under my skin. The heat of his mouth closing around the other nipple left me feeling like I was falling apart.

Jesus Martha, what this man did to me.

"Don't move your hands." His voice was a demanding growl by now.

His lips, hands, and tongue trailed down my body until I felt his heated breath against my pussy. The next thing I felt was when he nipped at my clit before going back to my nipples. If one could die from pleasure overload, I might just do that with him. He slid his legs between mine, and the denim from his jeans rubbed against me in a maddening friction as I arched up into his hardness. He groaned against my breast as he pressed into me. In desperation, my legs wrapped around him and pulled him closer, but he rose up, breaking their hold, and shucked off his jeans in record time. The smooth head of his cock slid through my wetness before he slammed into me. Now, I had obviously been with other guys before, but none that made my vision blank to blinding white before a frisson of pure, unadulterated pleasure swept over me.

"Goddamn, baby, you feel so fucking good." His voice was strained and raspy.

His thickness stretched me, and I felt so full, I swore he was rubbing against every sensitive spot I had. Sex with him was on a whole different level. After just a few strokes, I felt my body tensing for the pending explosion.

Holy shit, oh dear God, Fucking A…. I screamed his name as I felt waves of electricity pulse through me and white light flash around me once again. My pussy clenched against him over and over as he continued to bury himself deep into me. Finally coming back down to Earth, I looked at his handsome face and saw his cocky grin.

"Well, that was fast, baby." Before I could catch my breath from my shattering climax, he began moving in me once again. Sweat dotted his brow and shined across his chest. He was grunting with each demanding stroke when he suddenly found my clit with his thumb and circled it until I exploded with intense, earth-shattering pleasure, then buried himself to the hilt and roared with his head tilted to the ceiling. The surging pulse I felt as he filled me was like he was marking me as his, and I freaking loved it.

Hollywood

Jesus fucking H. Christ. Every muscle in my body quivered and tensed as I emptied into her wet warmth. When she came apart under me, I could barely contain myself. My breaths came in rapid succession, and I rained kisses across her tits and up her neck. We were both slick with sweat, and she tasted salty-sweet on my lips. Rolling over, I pulled her to me where she snuggled up against my side and tucked her leg over mine. My hand lazily stroked up and down her back, pausing to grab a handful of her firm, rounded ass. This woman was fucking perfect. Perfect looking, perfect feeling, perfect tasting, and perfect for me. There was no way I was letting her go. Call me crazy, but I needed her like the air I breathed. Inside, I warred with the thoughts of tying myself down versus being ecstatic over claiming her as mine. Yeah, I had told her before that she would crave me and become addicted to me, but I was beginning to realize she was *my* very own drug.

She had a beautiful smile, and I loved her laugh. Those spellbinding green eyes were straight mesmerizing and, whether she was chewing my ass or teasing me, they flashed and sparkled. Shit, listen to me sounding like a fucking poet. No lie, I just loved everything about her. Fuck, I just loved her.

Shit. What the hell?

Jesus.

I loved her.

It was true. I fucking loved this gorgeous woman lying next to me. This was not where I saw this going when I saw her again. In all honesty, I figured I would just be a selfish prick and use her body as long as it was fun for us both, and then we would go our separate ways, like I usually did with the women I was with. Inside, part of me still felt broken and wondered if she would be a balm, or fire, to my somewhat tortured soul. We hadn't really known each other long, but hell if she hadn't crept into every pore of my body. Pulling her close to me, I gave her a tight hug and kissed the top of her crazy wild auburn hair. She gave a soft sigh, and her body curled into me further.

Her breathing was soft and even, and I knew she had fallen asleep.

I love her. I really love her. Fuck, now what?

She seemed cool with us just fucking and having a good time.

When I said no strings, she said okay without hesitation. What if she never felt the same way about me? God, I was a fucking idiot not to have protected my heart better, but I sure as shit didn't think it was capable of actually feeling love in such a way for someone other than my family. Not even with Lorie had I felt so connected. No, I told myself, I just needed to convince her that she couldn't live without me either. My only hesitation was I didn't know if it was a good idea to be pulling her into the shitstorm we had brewing.

When the brothers arrived at the strip joint tonight, we had kicked the Demon Fuckers out and told them they could keep moving on and not to come back. As they all pulled out on their bikes, one of them shouted they would be back and we wouldn't like what happened when they returned. Yeah, well we would be waiting for those dumb fucks. They would learn not to fuck with us. Of course, this meant more time away from her as we stepped up on security at all of the businesses and making sure everything was secure at our storage warehouse.

That just meant I would have to enjoy every damn chance I had with her. It made me want to keep her here, but that would only be okay for a little while. We could talk about looking for a place for the two of us tomorrow. Maybe I was rushing things, but I didn't give a shit. I felt like I had waited my whole life for her, and if there was anything my time in the Army had taught me, it was that life could be short and we needed to grab onto the good shit while we could. She was definitely one of the good things. I closed my eyes and breathed her sweet scent in as I listened to her soft breaths and felt her small puffs of breath against my chest. My last coherent thought was that she was as close to heaven as my tortured soul may ever get.

Kisses feathered across my chest like the flutter of butterfly wings. My cock was pressed into warm softness. When it was suddenly surrounded by wet, tight heat, I woke with a start. My eyes opened to find thick red hair surrounding my face as the greenest eyes stared into mine, and for a moment, I was disoriented and panicky. My knee-jerk reaction was to try to buck her off and push her away from me. Fucking hated it when that shit happened.

"Shhhh, baby, it's just me." Her whispered words were like warm honey, and I groaned as I felt her tighten around me then begin to move against me. With a mind of their own, my hands found the smooth skin covering her hips and guided her pace as she rode my cock. Jesus, I could wake up like this every damn day of my life. *Fuck.*

A rapid pounding on my door, with Hacker's voice hollering at me to cover my dick and answer the door, interrupted what was close to the quickest orgasm I was about to achieve. It obviously didn't stop her as I felt her clench around me and throb over and over as she mewled and dug her nails into my shoulders. Hell, yes, I wanted her to mark me. The sharp pain from the bite of her nails was a welcome one.

"Get lost, fucker! Unless the building is on fire or Snow is calling for me, I'll be out when I'm ready to be out!" I knew the fucktard heard me because I heard him laugh before he beat on the door again. Shit, at this rate, I was never going to finish this morning. Fucking cockblocker.

"Get your dick out of that sweet-as-hell redhead and you two come have breakfast with me."

"Fuck off, asshole! We'll be out when we get out. Wait for us." He was quick on his way to an ass beating.

Becca had the nerve to giggle.

"Oh really? You think this is funny? Mmm, I'll show you what happens to my woman when she laughs at my interrupted orgasm after she already got hers." She laughed as I flipped her over until she was under me and on her belly. She quit real quick when I pulled her hips up, pushed her chest to the mattress, and rammed deep into her soaking wet pussy.

Holy Jesus, she felt like a slice of heaven. When I slapped her ass, she squealed, looking over her shoulder at me in shock. The tightening of her sheath around me belied her expression of disapproval. My hand softly circled the red handprint I left on her creamy-white ass cheek, and my lips and tongue ran up and down her back, my teeth nipping and scraping until she was a quavering, whimpering, incoherent mess.

Only when she was finally *begging* me to fuck her, did I grip her hips tightly and slide almost completely out before slamming into her over and over until I blew my damn load just as her walls tightened and she joined me in my moment of trembling ecstasy.

Yeah, I said trembling—as in my whole body felt like it had earthquake tremors running through it that didn't quit. Hell, my eyes damn near rolled in my head. We both shouted out our satisfaction and collapsed in a tangle of limbs amongst the wrinkled, scattered sheets.

My beautiful girl turned to me smiling and gasping. Damn, she was amazing. My smile mirrored hers, and I slapped her ass, lighter than before. "Come on, woman. Let's get in the shower, unless you want to go have breakfast with Hacker smelling like straight sex." She shot across the room and into the adjoining bathroom faster than I could even roll my ass out of the bed, my laughter hot on her heels.

Sundays were family days. We usually went for a ride, stopped somewhere for dinner, or came back to the clubhouse for a barbecue. If it was winter and too shitty out to ride, we would just barbecue and chill in Reaper and Steph's big-ass barn. Since the weather was nice, we were going for a ride through Fort Defiance, then through the lakes, down through Spencer, and back on Eighteen, to Four, and back to the clubhouse. It was a peaceful, gorgeous ride.

This would be the first time I had ever brought a woman on a ride, and Hacker had given me shit for it all through breakfast—at times making Becca laugh, and at other times, making her face match her fiery hair. She was fricking cute as hell when she blushed because it snaked down her chest and up to her hairline.

Not that I made a big deal about it to anyone, but I bought her a helmet. Iowa didn't have a helmet law, but the club was pretty pro-helmet after Stumpy, one of the founding members, hit a deer and died about ten or eleven years ago. That was way before my time, but just knowing he had been a founding member whose life was cut short, it was sobering. Granted, Reaper and I often went without and would get shit for it, but it was not something I even wanted to contemplate with Becca. So… I got her the helmet.

Really, I wasn't looking for it when I got it. I mean, I had an extra plain black one I was letting her use, but when I had gone to the cycle shop in Spencer to get some parts, I saw it and couldn't resist. It was totally her. With skulls, roses, and wicked-looking butterflies, it was a little badass, a little froufrou, and a little spunky, just like she was. So, it was sitting on the seat of my bike when we went outside, where everyone was gathering before heading out.

Of course, everyone remembered her from Reaper and Steph's wedding, and they all smiled and various greetings rang out to "Red," but they didn't know she and I had history from then, nor that she was now *mine*. The only ones who had any idea we were sort of an item were Reaper and Hacker. So, you can imagine the response when the rest of the brothers saw us walk out of the clubhouse together, after Becca insisted on changing from what she had worn to breakfast into a "better outfit for riding." Personally, I didn't see the difference, but hell if I was telling her that.

As we walked up to my bike and she saw the helmet, all conversation stopped when she squealed. "Oh my God, Mason, you got me my own helmet!" She swooped it up, looked over the entire thing inside and out, hugged it, and then stood on her tippy toes to kiss me. Fuck, now my face was probably the one as red as her hair.

"Um, yeah. I saw it and thought you would like it. And safety. You know...," I mumbled, embarrassed at everyone finding out what I had done. Now, if you don't understand, it's a pretty big deal to get a girl a helmet. Becca didn't know that, but everyone else did, which was why there were some pretty shocked faces, a few jaws scraping the ground, and plenty of raised eyebrows.

Shit. I knew I should have given it to her inside.

"I freaking *love* it, baby!" She ran over to show it to Steph, who made sure to look over Becca's shoulder at me and give me one of her smartass smirks while Reaper looked at her, Becca, and then me before elbowing Hacker, who hadn't been paying attention, and busting a gut laughing. My palm flattened on my forehead and slid down my face.

Hacker was quick to walk over and hand me a ration of shit too.

"Hmm, so your girl, Red, got her very own new helmet, huh? Isn't that *sweeeeet?* So, is the infamous Hollywood getting—" He let out an exaggerated gasp. "—*serious* about a girl? Say it ain't so!"

God, please make it stop. No, of course not. Thanks.

"Fuck off." Grabbing my helmet from my handlebar, I jerked it down over my head and buckled it. By that time, Becca had bounced back over to me, ear-to-ear grin splitting her face, and she hugged me again. She reverently sat the helmet on the seat while she braided her beautiful, deep-red hair and finished it off with a hair tie she had around her tiny wrist. Once she was done, she popped her helmet on and looked at me expectantly.

Most of the brothers were on their bikes because Snow and Vinny were mounted up. Shaking my head at her infectious smile, I laughed before I could say something stupid to Hacker, making my life even suckier. Climbing on first, I motioned for her to get on. Once everyone was on their bikes, they all started them up and, of course, guys on motorcycles being guys on motorcycles, every one of us revved our motors until all you heard were rumbling, roaring, growling thunder. It was fucking awesome every time I heard it. Not gonna lie.

Becca must have loved it too because she was clapping my back, and I could hear her laughter over all the noise. That sound might just rival the sound of our pipes.

Smoke, as our road captain, signaled and we all pulled out, two by two. We were rolling deep with thirteen members and three prospects in our formation today. It was impressive.

Reaper and I rode next to each other, and the girls were both taking pictures of the surrounding scenery, all the bikes, each other, and whatever the hell else they were taking pics of. Looking in my mirrors to check on her, I caught Becca getting some crazy selfies, and I couldn't help but to laugh at her. She made me do that a lot.

Laugh…

With her it was laughter from the heart. It wasn't just me trying to be the life of the party or keeping everyone in a good mood. It wasn't just on the surface. She made me feel light and buoyant inside.

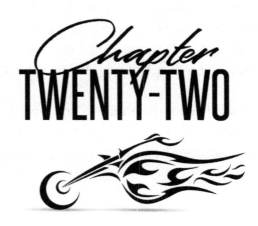

Chapter TWENTY-TWO

Becca

THE BELL RANG AND MY LITTLE STUDENTS FOLLOWED ME OUT THE door single file, followed by my aide, to be picked up by their parents or go to the buses. Surprisingly, I had gotten a job at the local private pre-school and elementary thanks to the amazing reference letter Mr. Strankowski had written for me. It sucked that the teacher I replaced had to quit due to family reasons, but it was a blessing for me.

My children were the brightest little kindergarteners I had ever met, and they had already wormed their way into my heart after only three weeks. It was a trade-off in that I was bummed about not being able to teach just art, but I loved that this school taught year round to ensure continuity of learning and less forgotten skills over the summer break that most schools had. We just had more days off here and there with smaller breaks scheduled in place of an entire summer off.

Usually, it seemed my days ended too quickly with them, but I was excited for it to end today. Hollywood was picking me up because we were going to look for a place for the two of us. We had been staying in his room at the club for the last month, and I had slowly moved more and more of my things into his room.

It was okay, but it was a little weird knowing the other guys who stayed there knew what we were doing after we closed the door at night. It was like sleeping in a guy's dorm room or something. Not to mention, it was a little weird seeing the nasty-ass skanks that rolled out of some of the guys' rooms. It also bothered me because it made me wonder how many times it was Hollywood's room they rolled out of. No, it more than bothered me; it pissed me the hell off. So, when he told me he was thinking of renting a house and asked how I felt about getting a place of our own, I jumped at it, burying any self-doubt that I was rushing into things.

My last little darling was loaded up in their momma's car, so I went back to my room to gather up my things and change into a pair of jeans. When my phone pinged with a message, I grabbed it as I ran into the small bathroom in my room to change, setting it on the counter and opening the message. Braiding my hair as quickly as I could, I read it.

Sexy-Ass Mason: I'm out front baby

I snickered every time I got a call or text from him and saw how I saved him in my phone. My jeans and boots on, I grabbed my purse, stuffing my phone in it as I rushed out the door.

God, he was gorgeous. When I saw him sitting on his bike, looking at his phone, I had to stop and catch my breath. He hadn't seen me yet, and I just stood there drinking in the sight of him. His short-cropped hair was getting longer on the top, and the breeze ruffled it, making it messier than usual. My fingers itched to smooth it, and I swore I could actually feel the strands just looking at him.

His eyes lifted to me and a smile spread across his face. There was no doubt it totally mirrored mine.

He did that to me. That beautiful smile of his was contagious, and he spread it to me all the time. Moving quickly, I tucked my purse in the saddle bag and climbed on behind him. My chin rested on his shoulder.

"Hey, sexy. Wanna take a girl for a ride?"

He chuckled and shook his head. "You may want to rephrase that, or I'll take you for a ride all right." The deep growl of his voice told me that, while he was teasing me, there was truth to his words as well.

"Sheesh! Is that all you think about, you dirty man?" Teasing him, I rubbed my boobs against his back. When he groaned, I knew he was imagining my nipples pebbling from the contact with him.

"Woman! You're trying my damn patience. We need to go look at these houses, and if you keep that up, we won't make it." Laughter bubbled up from deep in my soul. It felt amazing to feel so free emotionally. I kissed his cheek and settled back to wrap my arms around his waist. Unable to refrain from teasing him further, my hands slipped under his shirt and traced over the ripple of his abs before locking low in front of his hips. "Oh fine, let's go, gorgeous!"

"Helmet." His stern command reminded me of my beautiful helmet sitting on the seat of my car. Crap. Hopping off, I grabbed it, locked my car, and shoved the keys in my pocket before jumping back on the bike, helmet in place.

One thing this man could do was ride a motorcycle. We pulled out of the parking lot, and the wind caught my braid, whipping it back as we picked up speed. He drove fast, but with a purpose, and I never feared his ability to safely operate this screaming beast of a bike. Burying the face of my helmet to his back, I could smell his cologne through my open visor, and I breathed it in deep. It was a spicy, woodsy blend that drove me crazy. *Mmm*. Yeah, I could devour him like a chocolate chip cookie fresh out of the oven. He was a delicious specimen of man, and he was *mine*.

The first place we were looking at was about a mile out of town in a newer subdivision. The owners were looking to rent it while they were working out of state for a year. As we pulled up, I took in the faux barn doors on the garage and the rustic-looking pillar by the front door. It was a beautiful home. The property management agent was already waiting in the driveway, and he got out of his car as we pulled up in front of the house. Hollywood shook his hand, and they spoke briefly before he was leading us up to the door. If I remembered correctly, he was a prospect's dad, but hell if I could remember which one.

"I'll show you around first, and then let you take your time looking around." He led us through a sunny foyer and into a spacious living room with cathedral ceilings and a set of French doors that opened onto a large deck. The kitchen was to the left with a breakfast bar separating it from the living room. The cabinets were white barn-like doors, with dark granite countertops. It had stainless steel appliances and a breakfast nook overlooking the backyard. The bedrooms were to the right, off the living room, and were separated by a large shared bathroom. The master bedroom was to the left, next to the kitchen. We wandered around the house after our initial tour, checking out the master bedroom and connected master bath. It was nothing super fancy, but it did have separate sinks, a separate little toilet room, a walk-in shower, and a whirlpool tub. The closet was through the bathroom, and I figured it was big enough to hold my clothes. *Hmmm, what's Hollywood gonna do with his?* I giggled at the thought.

"What's so funny?" His arms wove around my middle, and his chin rested on my shoulder. This was probably my favorite place to be… snuggled in his arms. His nose nuzzled my ear, and his tongue curved around the earlobe, suckling my earring gently into his mouth.

How can his tongue flicking my earring back and forth be a turn-on? I don't have a damn clue, but he sure as hell knows how to make it that way. Damn.

My inner self wanted to strip down naked, rip off his clothes, and jump him right here in someone else's house with the agent outside. *Bad girl! Stop it!*

"Mmm, I have no idea. I can't think when you're doing that."

He chuckled in my ear.

All in all, it was a nice house, but I hated the idea of getting settled in somewhere and having to move out in a year, but with our relationship being so new, maybe that was a good start. A lot could change in a year, especially since we agreed to take things one day at a time and see where this went. Damn, that was depressing. For once in my adult life, I could actually see myself happily settling down and having babies with a guy, and he just wanted a fling with potential expiration date.

Shit, this sucked. Maybe I should tell him how I feel. Fear of scaring him away kept my lips sealed. I wanted to savor what we had for as long as I could.

He stepped around me and grabbed my hand. "Let's go see the next one."

We thanked the agent as we left and promised to let him know what we decided.

The next house was a no-go. It was poorly laid out and needed a lot of updating, regardless of the big size. In my opinion, the rent was way too high anyway.

The last house was a few miles up the road from Steph and Reaper. When I found out where it was, I was hoping this one would be the one, because I would love to be so close to my friend. There was a prominent *For Sale or Rent* sign next to the mailbox at the road.

The driveway was a smooth-packed gravel that wound through the trees before opening in front of an older four-square farmhouse with a perfectly matched addition off the right. Someone had done an amazing job with the addition, keeping true to the style and magic of the home. The driveway curved off to the left side of the house where a small garage had been built with a covered walkway to the back porch.

It was painted a soft taupe color with dark brown trim. There were neatly trimmed rose bushes all along the front porch and the side of the garage. We pulled onto the concrete driveway in front of the garage. The agent wasn't here yet, as we were told to call him as we left the last place. Hell, I couldn't wait for him to arrive.

Hollywood shut off the bike, and we sat looking around for a minute. It was so peacefully quiet. The sounds of chirping birds filtered with the sunlight through the leaves of the giant oaks, which surrounded the house. A light breeze scented with the honeysuckle blossoms that grew near the backyard fence drifted past me. I hopped off the bike and headed around the path to the front porch.

If my dream house had a picture, this was it. My heart pounded as I walked up the front steps. It was like the house called to me as it wrapped its charm around me like a warm cloak in winter. My hands covered my heart as I turned in a rush toward Hollywood, where he stood on the front lawn.

"Oh my God, Hollywood, I'm in love and I haven't even seen the inside!"

Hollywood

The look of rapture on her face as she looked around painted a smile on my face I just couldn't contain. She was so precious, and I knew she had no idea how fucking cute she looked. When she said she was in love, I knew I was right in leaving this one until last. In all truth, I had been looking at this one for a few days, and I was seriously contemplating buying this house, but I needed to know she loved it as much as I did. The other houses were merely decoys, but had she liked them better, I would have conceded to renting one. The visual that planted itself in my mind when I came to look at this house by myself yesterday had her sitting in the living room curled up reading a book. In every room I had walked through, her image and how she would look wandering through our home popped into my head. Yeah, I wanted this to be *our* home. This was a huge step, and the magnitude of it all didn't escape me.

She didn't know I had the key to the place in my pocket. George, DJ's dad, was the listing agent, and he had secretly given me the key when we looked at the first house. My call to him had totally been for show so Becca didn't realize I had already looked at this place. The owners had inherited their parents' home on the family farm, and their children weren't interested in moving in, as they already had homes they were comfortable in. So, they were looking to rent or sell, but I definitely wanted to buy. My hope was that Becca would fall in love with it, just as I did, and I wanted us to start our forever here. I just had to get her on board with me to make it happen.

When I climbed the steps, my gaze was intent on her. She looked like a giddy high school girl. It made me smile just watching her reaction to the home. When I pulled the key out of my pocket and slipped it in the lock, she looked at me in surprise. I opened the door and motioned for her to go ahead and go in. She gazed at me with a confused and questioning look, but she walked in and gasped.

"Oh my fucking God, Hollywood! Have you *seen* this?" She spun slowly in circles as she took in the entryway, the staircase off to the right, and the living room to the left. Squealing like a little girl, she rushed into the living room, which had a wide arch connecting it to the dining room. The owners had taken out the wall between the kitchen and dining room and replaced it with a breakfast bar with a pillar at the end. The kitchen was a shining chef's dream. Stainless steel appliances gleamed from light oak cabinets with a tan-based granite countertop. The owners had put a lot of money into this remodel, but in the end, their family home won out for them. Their loss, I figured.

As I followed her into the kitchen, I knew she was taking in the light sage green walls with an earth-tone tile backsplash over the counters. The windows allowed for an amazing amount of natural light. A door at the back of the kitchen led out to the back porch and the walkway to the garage. There were tall windows in the dining room that spanned the wall facing the backyard, and the wall straight across from the kitchen breakfast bar held the door to the newer addition, where the master bedroom had been built.

When she stepped through the door to the master suite, she gasped and waved her hands around. I followed her in so I could continue to drink in her joy. She rushed through the bedroom where she saw the sitting room, where I secretly hoped to see her nursing our baby in someday. The bathroom was through the sitting room, and I knew she was going to love the sunken oversized tub. Her shriek told me she found it. My smile spread wide at the sight of her jumping up and down clapping her hands. When she spun back to me, her eyes were sparkling and her chest was rising and falling in rapid succession.

"Oh. My *gawd*, Hollywood! I haven't even seen the upstairs, and I am in love. Please, please, please say we can rent this gorgeous house and they won't kick us out because they end up selling it. Holy shit, I love this house!" Her hands were clasped at her chin, and she wound her arms around my neck when I stepped close and rested my hands on her hips.

"What if I told you I wanted to buy it?" My breath held, and I felt as if my heart stuttered waiting for her response.

"Wait. You want to *buy* it? It must be expensive, baby. Are you sure? I mean, I'm not trying to say you can't afford it, but well, I guess I don't know what I'm trying to say. I'll help with the payments. Unless you don't want me to. I don't know if that is forward of me. I'm babbling, aren't I? I just… Wow. I just… *wow*." Her lips pressed firmly to mine, and I grabbed her ass, swinging her around. We broke apart, and we both laughed. Her smile was all I needed. Making her happy would be my number one goal in life, if the reward was that smile.

"Yeah, I'm sure. I looked at it yesterday, after having driven by it several times when George told me it recently went on the market. As soon as I saw it, I knew this was the place. I had been praying you would love it as much as I did. This house… it called to me. Hell if I couldn't see you in every room, but I wasn't going to buy it if you hated it for some reason."

"As if! What the hell is there not to love about this home?" She looked at me in astonishment. My laugh erupted at her expression, and I squeezed her close.

"So, you want me to call George and tell him we want to write up an offer? Speak now or forever hold your peace, baby."

She pulled away and held me at arm's length. Her expression was one of comical deep contemplation. "Hmm…. Well, I suppose we could suffer through and live here." She gave me a smirk before she turned away and raced to look at the upstairs. Her footsteps pounded up the stairs. Her shouts of pleasure reached my ears as I slowly followed her.

The stairs were probably one of my favorite features of this house. They were a dark oak and original to the house. They went up a couple of steps to a small landing where there was a stained glass window with red roses designed in it. Then the stairs rose again to a second landing with a matching stained glass window at the landing, but with pink roses, before it went up the few last stairs to the upper level. There were three bedrooms with a bathroom on the end. All the floors were polished wood, which gleamed in the setting sun. Truth be told, I had imagined filling all of these rooms with our babies, but I didn't know if she was ready to hear that.

I found her sitting cross-legged in the first bedroom, the waning sunlight shining through the window and glinting off her hair, giving it the appearance of flames. Her arms were wrapped around herself, and her eyes were closed. She looked serene and a little wistful.

Settling down next to her, I rested my arm around her, pulling her close so her head rested on my shoulder.

"Hey, baby. What's wrong? Did you change your mind?" Just the thought had my heart feeling like it dropped to the first story. Please, don't let her have changed her mind. Fuck, I needed to tell her how I felt. I needed to tell her my hopes and dreams for the two of us. I needed to tell her how I pictured us together in this home. I needed to try to explain the thoughts and feelings that circled around in my head and heart all day every day. There were a lot of things I *needed* to do. Jesus, it made me feel like a sap.

Reaching around, I rested my hand under her chin and tipped her face toward me. A lone tear slipped from under her closed lashes. Catching it with my fingertips, I feathered a kiss to her lips.

"Baby, talk to me."

"Oh, Hollywood. It's just so perfect. I see us here. And it's breaking my heart. I know we said no strings, but God it will kill me to let you go. I'm so afraid of you having enough of me and cutting me loose. My heart aches and dies a little at the thought. You said we would just enjoy each other and the time we had, and I truly did not enter into this with the intent of falling for you so hard."

Well, hell.

"Becca, look at me. I wanted to wait to tell you because I was afraid of scaring *you* away. You are such a strong and independent woman, I didn't want you to think I was trying to overwhelm you or take away your independence after you just escaped that kind of relationship with Trevor. But, baby, I fucking love you. I know I don't deserve you after all the shit I've done in my life, but you are my *everything*, and I want it all with you. Maybe I'm foolish, and maybe you aren't ready to hear all this. I'm not telling you this shit to guilt you into saying it back so—"

I didn't get any further before she was kissing me madly, wildly, deeply, knocking me flat on my back in the waning sun warming the wood floor. Who knew love could feel so fucking amazing?

Chapter TWENTY-THREE

Becca

When I broke away from our kiss, I was breathless. This man, he just got better and better. Part of me was waiting for the other shoe to drop or for the dream to end and I woke up back in Council Bluffs. He was just straight-up too good to be true.

"Jesus, Hollywood, you are nuts, you know. How could I not be insanely in love with you? You have loved me passionately, without words, since the first night we were together. I was foolish for not ensuring Trevor accepted shit was over before I left and foolish for not taking a crazy chance and following you home from Vegas. I wasted so many months that could have been spent with you, and I beat myself up for it. I've been tearing myself up afraid you would get tired of me and I would be irrevocably damaged because there could never be another love like this for me. And a love like this? I'm telling you, it only comes around once. Now go call the agent and do what you have to do to make this our home." My lips brushed lightly over his open mouth. His eyes were wide before he closed them and kissed me with crazy abandon while his hands slipped under my shirt and across the skin of my back.

"Shit, baby, yeah, I need to call George." He kissed me briefly one last time before he got up and pulled out his phone. I heard him descend the stairs as he spoke on the phone to who I assumed must be the realtor. My arms wrapped around my body again. The room was darkening as the sun continued to slowly set. In my mind's eye, I was imagining a thick rug here on this floor, scattered with blocks and toys as the sound of children's voices echoed through the house. My hand rested on my belly as I imagined it swelling with his baby. A slow smile spread across my face. Someday.

My hair was piled on my head to keep it out of my way as I directed the guys on where furniture and boxes went. We didn't have a lot, but we had bought a bedroom set, and he had a bunch of stuff he had been storing at his parents that they brought over in his dad's enclosed bike trailer. I couldn't believe it was only a month ago I first laid eyes on this home. It felt like it had been ours forever.

Hollywood was firing up the grill as the guys filtered out to the backyard after unloading the last box and grabbing beers from the large ice chest. Watching them all laugh and joke, it was hard to miss how close they all were. They were all dressed in jeans, T-shirts, and a leather vest with the same patch on all their backs, except for a few that had "PROSPECT" in the center instead of the patch with Hades, fresh from battle, surrounded by flame and holding a medieval double-bladed ax in one hand and captured flame in the other. It was a little gruesome but totally badass.

"They are like a bunch of young boys sometimes, aren't they?" I heard from behind me. Turning, I saw Hollywood's mother standing there, watching them as well. She was a beautiful woman for her age. You could tell she was a lot younger than his dad, but they were such a great couple. She had a spark to her, and I sensed a kindred spirit as soon as I met her this morning. Her long hair was pulled back into a braid with escaping tendrils and had very few gray strands mingling with the dark blonde. It was obvious where Hollywood had gotten his dark blond locks.

"I'm so glad he has all the boys. Even though his dad was worried about him joining up with them, it has done him good. Between that and worrying about him when he first came home, every gray hair I have was earned. God, he had terrible nightmares back then. He took so many pills and drank like a fish. We were terrified he was going to kill himself or someone else riding his bike drunk as a skunk." She paused and looked me in the eye. "Maybe I shouldn't be telling you all of this, but I wanted you to understand how much the club has pulled him together, how important it is to him. And now that he has you in his life, he just seems… complete. I knew something was different about him, and when he finally told us about you, after he decided to buy this house, I knew. Mason loves you. Any fool can see it, but a mother knows her son. Take care with his heart, Becca. He acts happy-go-lucky, but he does everything deeply."

I sniffled back my tears and hugged her tightly. "I love him too, Jenny. With all my heart."

When I looked up, I met his eyes. He smiled, raised his beer to me, and lifted it to those sinful lips. My tongue ran across my bottom lip at the thought of tasting his. Yeah, I totally and undeniably loved that gorgeous, tattooed, scarred man. His past demons may haunt him at times, but I would do my best to show him I was here for him.

"Oh my God, Becca. I still cannot believe he bought you this house." Steph came in with little Wyatt in his Baby Bjorn carrier. His chubby little legs wiggled against her belly, and his fist was in his mouth as his dark, downy head rested on her chest. Remi was outside, sitting on her daddy's shoulders, and I could hear her squeal and giggle every time he acted like he was going to drop her.

"He didn't actually buy the house for me, Steph. He loved the house too. It's not like we're married, so it is technically his house." My face was flaming red, and I knew it. Damn, it felt on fire. Both women snorted in a very unladylike manner at my response.

"Yeah, okay, beeotch. You are crazy if you don't think he had you in mind when he went to look at this house and when he made the offer to buy it. He is crazy for you, and I cannot wait to have you two fill this house with babies." Shit, there went my face again.

Oh. My. God. Steph, I am going to kill you.

"Steph!" My eyes flashed to Jenny in embarrassment. After all, this was her son we were talking about. Jenny laughed so hard she had tears leaking from the corners of her eyes. My mortification was complete. God, help me.

"Sweetheart, I would love to have me some grandbabies to spoil. But I'm not rushing you two. I'm going to head out there to bother my old goat of a husband." She kissed my cheek and whispered in my ear, "I'm so glad he found you, young lady. Just be patient with him. He'll have ups and downs, but he deserves to be happy. He deserves you. Thank you." Her hand rested on my cheek for a second before she wandered out back and down into the yard to wrap her arms around her burly husband. I watched as he kissed the top of her head in affection, before I turned back to Steph in frustration.

"Jesus, Steph, you ho! We haven't really talked about having any kids yet. I cannot believe you said that in front of his *mom*. Fucking A, girl. We have only been together for a few months, and we aren't even engaged, for Christ's sake. Ugh!" My eyes rolled at my best friend, who could be a serious pain in my ass at times. It used to be me who was the bossy, crazy one. It seemed my girl had come out of her shell thanks to that sexy-ass biker of hers. She just laughed at me before hooking her arm through mine and leading me out the door and to the backyard to join everyone.

Mason held his arms out as he shouted, “Baby! Get your sexy ass over here and give your old man some much needed loving!” Everyone was laughing as I planted a big smooch on his smiling lips, unconcerned with our audience observing our actions. Yeah, this *was* my man. Come hell or high water, I planned to make this last. There was no way I could see myself without him now. How quickly he had wormed his sexy way into not just my body, but my heart and soul…

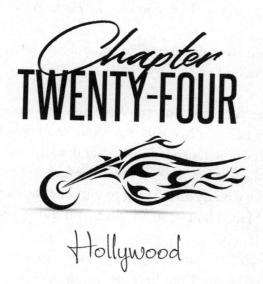

Chapter TWENTY-FOUR

Hollywood

Becca and I had only been moved in for over three weeks and were still getting settled in the house, but I had been on babysitting duty for the past week at the Shamrock. Fuck, I would rather have been home looking at my woman's tits instead of the ones that were flashing from the stage. I mean, don't get me wrong… I was a guy… I liked tits. What red-blooded man, didn't? But there was something about my own woman's that made others pale in comparison. And the cigarette smoke clinging to my hair and clothes every time I left here made my lip curl in disgust. I had to shower as soon as I got home each night, because I wasn't crawling in bed with my beautiful woman, tainted with the smell of a fucking titty bar.

The Demon Runners MC had been harassing the girls as

they left the club at night, so we were taking turns standing guard there. Tonight, it was me and DJ. So far, none of them had shown up, and that dickhead manager, Arnie, kept giving us dirty looks. Motherfucker was forgetting who signed his paychecks.

As the club closed up, DJ and I went outside to our bikes. We planned to sit out here until all the girls left safe and the club was locked up tight. A sickeningly heavy cloud of perfume descended on me, and I saw Cherry closing in on me. *Fuck. What the hell did she want?*

She leaned over my shoulder and rubbed her tits on my arm when she got close.

Really?

"Back the fuck up, Cherry. What the hell do you want?" My patience with her and her shit was slim. She pouted, and her garishly bright red lips looked distorted and nasty, though I was sure she thought she was being sexy. What the fuck did I ever see in that? Clouded by easy pussy and trying to get over Becca was what I had been doing. Man, I had been an idiot. You didn't get over someone like Becca.

Cherry ran her nails along my abs and up my chest before she slipped a hand around the back of my neck. My arm instinctively flung her hand off me.

"Aww, baby, don't be like that. I just need a ride. Sparkle was supposed to give me a ride home, but she got cut early." Fuck, I didn't want to give this bitch a ride anywhere, but I couldn't leave her there unattended, not with those assholes fucking with the girls.

"I'll call you a cab." I pulled out my phone to dial the cab company, but she placed her hand over mine, stopping my call. She leaned close to my ear, letting her lips trail across my neck.

"I don't want you to spend a bunch of money on a cab, baby. You know I live down in Spencer with my sister right now. That would be one hell of a cab fare. I'd rather just pay you for the gas in your bike." She batted her fake eyelashes at me and I rolled my eyes. I actually had no idea where she lived.

"DJ! Give Cherry a ride home." He grinned as he nodded. There, let him sink *his* cock in her nasty ass. He was young and not too particular. Just hoped he used a goddamn condom. He told her to climb on. Cherry was pissed, but she hiked herself on the back of his bike and made sure her short, tight skirt rode up to expose her garters and half of her ass. Whatever. They pulled out as the last girl drove off and Arnie set the security code and locked the door.

Fuck, I was tired, and I couldn't wait to get home to my baby. My bike started up with a deep rumble, and I rolled out of the parking lot toward home. Shit, that sounded good. Home. I smiled all the way home as Linkin Park blared from my speakers and the wind whipped past me.

When I pulled up to the house, the lights were still on in the bedroom. I took the porch steps two at a time and let myself in. Walking with a purpose straight to the bedroom, I was met at the door by gorgeous green eyes, deep auburn curls, and a sexy smirk topped by a silky green barely there nightie.

"Hey, baby…" Her voice was sexy as hell, and it curled right around my heart.

Fuck me.

My hands grabbed her waist and pulled her close. My nose buried in her hair, and I nuzzled her neck. God, this girl always smelled amazing, and my cock jumped at the mere scent and proximity of her, but I felt her stiffen in my arms before she pulled back.

"What the fuck? You smell like cheap perfume, Mason." Her eyes narrowed and she pushed away from me. "And that lipstick on your neck is *certainly* not my shade, asshole! Are you fucking kidding me? I cannot believe this shit!" She stormed off and slammed the bathroom door, while I stop there feeling like I had just been spit out by a tornado.

What the fuck just happened here?

I stormed to the bathroom door and grabbed the knob.

Oh, hell no! She did *not* fucking lock me out! My fists pounded on the door. "Becca! Goddammit, open the fucking door! Now!"

"Screw you!" Her muffled reply through the door only pissed me off more. I hadn't even done anything, and here she was proclaiming me guilty without even letting me explain myself. Closing my eyes and taking a deep breath in an attempt to calm myself, I switched tactics.

"Baby, please open the door. Nothing happened. I promise." Maybe this would work. My mother always said you catch more flies with honey than vinegar. Shit, I always thought that was a dumb expression. My head rested on the door. It cut me deep that she would assume I could ever even consider messing around on her, but I really didn't want to fight with her. Women and their jumping to conclusions—one reason why I had avoided relationships. If I admitted the truth, I was hurt, more than mad, that she could have that little faith and trust in me.

"Becca, baby. Please. Talk to me."

The door flew open, and I was thrown off balance from the sudden motion and felt like I would fall on my face.

Finally.

Well, maybe… She still looked pissed as hell.

"Okay. Then tell me where you were." Her eyebrow raised in question and her arms crossed over her chest, pushing her tits up. My eyes almost popped out of my head, and I had to tear my gaze back to her face. Holy shit, what was it about tits that suck a man's intelligence right the hell out of his head? My head shook to clear my thoughts. *Focus.*

"Baby, you know I can't tell you club business. You just have to trust me when I tell you there is nothing for you to worry about. It's not what you think. I didn't do anything." As pissed as she was, I knew this was not the time to tell her I had been running security at the Shamrock. Shit, I thought steam literally came out of her ears. *Oh hell.* As the door began to slam in my face, my foot shot out to stop it.

"Go away. You have been gone almost every night this week. Every time I ask you where you were, I get 'club business.' Yeah, well, fuck 'club business' because I have had enough of 'club business.' Leave me the hell alone." When I reached for her face to cup her cheek, she jerked away, preventing contact. My hand fell useless to my side.

"Baby, I'm sorry, but have a little faith in me. Shit." My eyes plead with her to understand, but she wouldn't even look at me.

Damn. Without conscious thought, my fist made contact with the wall. Her body jumped slightly at the sound. *Motherfucker!* She damn well knew we had some shit going on at the club. I had *told* her there would be times I may not be able to tell her details of what we were doing. What the hell had crawled up her ass that made tonight any different that she suddenly *now* had to know where I was.

Dammit!

Fine, I wasn't going to keep fucking begging. Damn stubborn woman. My footsteps resounded through the house as I took the stairs two at a time to go to the bathroom upstairs to shower.

Yeah, so I was throwing a bit of a fit as I slammed the door. Fucking sue me. The shower curtain nearly suffered for my mood as I ripped it to the side to start the water. Before the mirror steamed up, I looked at my reflection, seeing the bright red lipstick smeared on my neck. Well, damn. No wonder Becca was a mad motherfucker at me. Cherry sure as shit knew what she was doing, and I was going to have her ass for this. My clothes reeked, and I dropped them to the floor as I peeled them off. When the water was hot, I stepped under it, closed the shower curtain, and dropped my head to let the water pour over me to wash the stress and stink from my skin.

Didn't she know I loved her and I couldn't even *think* of being with another woman? She had me tied in knots and flapping in the wind for her. I said it to her once, and I meant it—she was my *everything*. The thought of her being with someone else… ever… eviscerated me. If she knew the power she had over me….

Maybe I needed to go down to try to talk to her again.

Ah fuck. Never mind. Now was not the time. Not with both of our tempers flaring.

After I dried off, I wrapped the towel around my hips and padded down the hallway runner to the one room we had set up as a guest bedroom. Crawling in between the cold sheets was not how I imagined my night ending. Fuck, I was hoping to crawl between her warm thighs, but that went to shit. My mind wandered as I stared at the moonlit shadows waving across the ceiling. By morning, I didn't remember falling asleep, but I clearly remembered the nightmares that tortured my mind.

Chapter TWENTY-FIVE

Becca

"WHAT DO YOU MEAN YOU NEED TO GO TO THE STORE? I thought we were hanging out here working on decorating your beautiful house? I'm not dressed to be running all over town, you little skank," Steph stood with her hands on her hips. "I look like straight doo-doo."

"Yeah, well, I need to know something for sure. I planned out my whole night, starting with a slow seduction and then on to telling Hollywood my suspicions, but instead, the asshole came home smelling like skanky slut and had cheap-ass-looking red lipstick smeared all across his neck. I wasn't telling him shit after that." My temper was still volatile after last night, especially picturing the garish red lipstick smeared on his neck. The rational side of me said there had to be a good explanation for his condition when he returned home, but right now I didn't want to hear it. Lately, I had been taken over by this crazy, irrational bitch.

"Becca..." Steph grabbed my arm, spinning me back to face her as I was getting ready to slip my feet in my flip-flops. It was a sunny day and promising to be another *hot* early August day. In deference to the weather, I had pulled on a pair of white cutoff shorts and a red tank top. Good Lord, I could tell I hadn't been to the gym in a while because they were a little snugger than the last time I squeezed my ass into them. Of course, that could be... But damn, it was too soon to be getting fat, right?

"Becca! What the ever-living hell? Are you telling me you think you're pregnant?" Steph's eyes were like big, round, blue saucers. When her huge grin broke out, she started to shriek and squeal as she jumped up and down, her thick blonde ponytail swinging around as she jumped.

"Oh my gawd! I don't care if I'm *naked*, we're going to the drugstore right the hell now." She grabbed my hand, and I barely had time to grab my purse from the bench inside the front door and swing the door shut before she was dragging me over to her beautiful new SUV Reaper had bought her. Lucky bitch. He said she needed "something more reliable to haul his babies around in," when he surprised her with it last weekend. It was a week old and still smelled brand new.

"You are a lucky bitch, Steph," I told her as I ran my hands along the supple leather seats after buckling myself in. Her answering grin told me she was digging it too.

"Thanks. Much nicer than my old one, right? But don't go trying to change the subject, bitch monkey. When did you start feeling sick? How far do you think you are? Does Hollywood have any clue at all? Have you talked about kids yet? Whoa, this is almost like déjà vu..." Her questions shot out a hundred miles a minute. My head felt like it was swimming. Damn crazy girl. And bitch monkey? That was a new one. Totally filing it away for later use on her.

"Well, that's just it… I haven't felt sick at all. It just dawned on me yesterday that I couldn't remember when my last period was. I missed a few pills during the move up here and then again when we were staying at the clubhouse, but I had gotten my period and didn't think anything of it. But that was like the third week I was here, and I don't think I've had one since. I've just been so busy that I haven't paid attention. God, I'm such a scatterbrain lately. And talk about bitchy? Hell, I've been irritable and moody. So, I don't know… two maybe three months?" My hair was pissing me off even as I spoke. In resignation, I pulled it up on my head, grabbing the hairband from around my wrist, twisting it around my hair, and pulling the ponytail halfway through.

The fields slipping by as we drove were a blur. If Mason was fucking around on me, how was I going to stay with him? How could I have a baby with him? The mere thought of having an abortion made me feel sick and was completely out of the question. Before, I had been a loudmouth pro-choice advocate, but now that it might be me, it was a totally different story. There was no reason I could think of that justified ending a baby's life.

Looking down, I realized I had unconsciously covered my belly in a protective gesture. Tears welled in my eyes, but I blinked them away before they could fall. Hurt and suspicion were circling in my head, making me dizzy. I hated that it was even there to begin with. It was like my perfect world was falling apart around me, just as I feared.

The trip into the corner drug store in town was a quick one. Steph ran in for me when I told her I couldn't do it. The fear of breaking down in sloppy, snotty tears in the middle of the aisle, or at the register, had me recoiling in terror of stepping foot in there to get the tests. Instead, I shoved some cash in her hand and told her to just go get me some. She hopped back in the SUV and shoved a paper bag at me. When I looked in the bag, I cracked up laughing. "Really, Steph? There must be ten freakin' tests in here!"

She was still laughing as she pulled up in front of my house… oh my God, my house. Tears burst forth like a leaking dam. My words were garbled as Steph pulled me out of the SUV and back into the house. Down the hall and into my beautiful bathroom, we raced, until she stopped and pointed at the toilet.

"Go pee, girl! Now!" My face must have resembled a goldfish out of water, with my mouth flapping open and closed and my eyes bugging out of my head. Words were trapped in my tight, burning throat. I sure as hell wasn't pissing on a stick in front of my friend, no matter how close we were.

"Now?" I squeaked.

"Hell yeah now, girl! Now. Go. Pee!"

Shit. My paper bag and I entered the little toilet room, and I closed the door behind me. It took a few minutes of staring at the bag before I could start moving…

Fifteen minutes later, we sat there looking at the five tests laid out on the counter. Yes, it actually took five little plus signs and double lines to make me believe it wasn't a mistake.

"Damn, this really is déjà vu." We looked at each other and burst out laughing, but it wasn't long before I was crying again and Steph was holding me and stroking my back in an effort to comfort her hormonally crazy friend. *Man, I love this girl.* We'd been through some shit, for sure.

"Becca, baby girl, you need to tell him. This is his baby too. Talk to him. Figure this shit out, but whatever you do, don't wait. That never helps. Trust me." Her soft hands cradled my face as she tucked my stray hairs behind my ears and leaned over to kiss my cheek. I felt like I was going to cry again. *Damn. Come on, God, please help a girl out.*

I prayed my entire pregnancy wouldn't be such an emotional roller coaster. Sighing, I hugged my best friend tight and promised I would talk to Mason as soon as he got home from work.

Chapter TWENTY-SIX

Hollywood

Becca had been sleeping when I left this morning, and I'd been hesitant to wake her. My mood was shit when I awoke due to the nightmares plaguing me through the night. It wasn't often I had them anymore, but every so often they snuck in and wreaked havoc on my mind as I slept. The coffee I poured nonstop down my throat did little to wake me, and I had felt sluggish all day.

Now, as I walked into the beautiful home Becca and I shared, I was hit by the wafting aroma of roast, potatoes, and carrots—one of my favorites and my baby knew it. Hopefully, this meant she had forgiven my ass and we could move on.

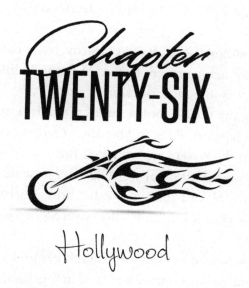

It tore me up that I had to keep her in the dark about stuff with the club, but the less the old ladies knew, the better for them, and in turn, us. It was best to never give our enemies anything they could use against us, especially family. Like I said before, we were mostly legit, but we skated the edge a little.

She was going to be pissed when she found out I had to leave again tonight. It wasn't supposed to be my turn so soon, but Gunner was puking his guts up with the flu and everyone else was tasked out for tonight. So, it was me and Reaper. Hopefully, we could talk a little over dinner and I could get her to understand why I couldn't tell her everything.

She was pulling the roast out of the oven as I entered the kitchen, giving me an amazing view of her ass in her tight little white shorts.

Shit, she does it to me every time.

Adjusting my dick, I took a deep breath, trying to get control of the traitorous bastard. Fuck it. Silently, I crept up behind her as she set the pan on the trivets and shucked the hot pads on the counter. My hands slipped around her waist and my nose nuzzled her neck.

"Hey, baby. Have I told you today how much I love you?" She laughed softly at my question and covered my joined hands with hers.

"No, Mason darling, because you left before I woke up." She had been calling me Mason since we moved in together, and I really loved the sound of my name on her lips. Her head turned to the side and those lips of hers sought mine. Never thought I would love coming home to the same woman, but hell if it didn't feel like everything was right with the world when I did. Our kiss was fleeting, but the love poured from one of us to the other and back in that brief moment. God, I was afraid she might tell me to fuck off for good after last night, and it had me wanting to tie her to the bed so she could never fucking leave me. She had been pissed, and I knew I was asking for it again tonight. No matter how small the disagreement was, I hated arguing with her.

"Dinner is ready if you want to eat." The shower could wait, because I wanted to enjoy this happy moment with her as long as I could before I pissed her off again. Her sensuous body turned until we were chest to chest. Slipping my hands down to her ass, I slapped it as I lifted, encouraging her to jump up in my arms.

Her legs wrapped around me as I buried my face in her neck. God, I needed her right fucking now. As I started walking toward the bedroom, it dawned on her what I was doing.

"Mason, I told you dinner is done. It's going to get cold. What the heck are you doing?" I kept walking until I tossed her on the bed. "Mason!" she squeaked out and tried like hell to crawl off the bed.

Nope. I grabbed her ankles and slid her back toward me as I climbed up on the bed to straddle her, trapping her legs between mine and threading my fingers through the hair on the back of her head. My mouth lowered to her protesting one, and I took unfair advantage of it being open to slip my tongue in. Her protests abruptly ended as her arms circled my sides to dig her fingers into my back.

Using one arm to hold myself up, I unzipped her already unbuttoned shorts. Quicker than she could even start to comprehend, my hand slipped down the front and under her silky panties. Circling her clit briefly, my middle finger slipped down, in and out of her already sopping wet core. When she moaned in encouragement, I entered her wet warmth with first one finger, then two, pushing deep into her pussy and curling. She answered by rubbing up into the heel of my hand.

She was getting more and more erratic with her movements, and I knew she was close. Pulling away from her, I licked my fingers as I stared into her heavy-lidded gaze and heaving chest. God, she was sweet.

"Mason…," she whispered, heavy with need. My pants were shucked in record time as she quickly shoved her shorts down and off, and I knelt above her, dick in hand, stroking slowly before guiding it to her slick folds. In a savage thrust, I buried myself in her until we were one and the same. With each plunge of my cock, she mewled and lifted to meet me to rub her clit against me.

My hand slipped up her shirt and under her bra, carelessly shoving it out of the way. As I tweaked her nipple, my lips and tongue trailed along her shoulder and neck. There was no gentleness in me. There was no room for it. This woman, she made me desperate. Aching. Possessive. Pulling her skin into my mouth, I couldn't help but mark her as mine.

Each stroke into her velvet core was heaven. Her hands grasped at my shirt in desperation, and I knew she was as close as I was. Lifting one leg up and curving it over my arm, I leveraged myself up to change the angle of my entry. With each animalistic thrust, I would grind against her clit. She was going to come before me, or I would die trying. Her breaths were whimpers as her eyes pleaded with me for release. My speed increased, and it was all I could do to hold off my own climax.

"Fuck, baby. Come. Come on my fucking cock. Jesus, I'm almost there. You feel so goddamned good. Come with me, right fucking now!" At my filthy words, I felt her slippery wet channel tighten and spasm around my cock, and I was done. The pleasure knotted in my spine, shooting up my body and through my cock. With a final, deep push, I roared out in absolute rapture.

Her unbelievably tight pussy was damn near strangling my dick, and the sensation became too much. With a lingering kiss, I slid out, feeling our combined fluids slip out with me. Whimpers were her response to her sudden emptiness. My semi-erect cock rested on her as I kissed her again.

"Don't deny it, baby, you love it when I talk dirty to you."

"Shit. I wouldn't even try. Guess you wanted dessert first, huh?" she teased in a breathless voice. I smiled, laughed, and got up to walk to the bathroom.

"Let me just wash up really quick, and I'll be ready to eat, baby. Unless you want to skip dinner and go for round two?"

She laughed and threw her pillow at me, hitting me in the face. "I worked hard on dinner for you!"

Chuckling, I went to the bathroom, wet a washcloth for her, tossing it to where she still lounged, boneless on the bed. A shriek escaped her as the wet rag landed on her belly.

"Oh my God, Mason! You're going to pay for that!"

"I'm sure, and I can't wait." I laughed out. Her answering smirk was met by my own before I returned to the bathroom.

Lathering up my hands and arms, I rinsed the soap off in the sink and dried them with the towel hanging by the sink. Damn, I really was ready to skip dinner and drag her ass back to bed for another round.

When I sat at the table, she had already dished my plate and was setting it in front of me.

The first bite was a heavenly taste explosion, and I couldn't hold in my moan. Damn, this was incredible. She sat watching me with her plump lip held tightly in her teeth. That's when I noticed she hadn't eaten a bite, but held a piece of the meat poised in midair as she watched me for my reaction.

"Holy shit, babe, this is amazing! You absolutely outdid yourself with this meal." Her face flushed in obvious pleasure.

"Well, I have a confession… it's one of Steph's recipes. She brought it over today when I told her I was going to attempt this for you tonight."

"Damn, it's good. And, baby, I'm sorry about not waking you this morning, but I wanted you to be able to sleep in. How was your girl time today? Reaper said the kiddos were at Steph's parents' house for the weekend. What all did you girls do?" My mouth was dying for me to keep feeding it, so I wasn't about to disappoint, and I shoveled the delicious food in like a starving man. The manners my mom taught me flew right out the damn window. When she didn't answer, I looked up and thought she looked a little pale. She was just pushing her food around her plate.

"Umm, not much. We just talked and hung a few pictures. Ran to the store real quick. Nothing much." My girl seemed off somehow.

She was usually gutsy and bold, not this hesitant, quiet thing sitting across from me.

"Everything okay? You seem.... not like my usual feisty girl. You girls have a falling out?" Not that I could see that for a minute, but I was confused at the behavior this gorgeous woman of mine was showing me. It just seemed, well, not her. I was stumped. Shit, I hope she wasn't still pissed at me. She didn't seem like it, but who knew with women?

"No, everything was fine. I guess maybe I just slept like shit without you last night. I don't want to do that again, Mason." Her words were nearly a whisper at the end. She was still pushing her food around and looking down at it absently.

"Okay, baby. That is not a problem, because I slept like shit without you too." I sat my silverware down so I could take her hand. My other hand tipped her chin to bring her face to mine. "Look at me, beautiful. When you are in my bed with me, you hold the nightmares at bay. I hadn't had a single one since we started sleeping together, but last night it was... I don't know... like the dreams knew I was alone, like they preyed on me in my weakest moment." My free hand then ran through my hair and I closed my eyes, grasping my hair in my hand in an attempt to keep the memories of the dream from stealing into my head even now, while I was awake.

It was the God's honest truth too about the dreams preying on me. They slipped in, stalking me when I was vulnerable. Then they ravaged my mind and body as I lay trapped in sleep. At least that was how it seemed, and I fucking hated it. That was something I tried to keep people from knowing. Being vulnerable, having a weakness... no one needed to know that shit.

She pulled my hand up to her mouth to press her lips to my fingers before letting me go, insisting I finish eating before the meal was cold. After I was done, I helped her clear the table and do up the dishes. What I was not ashamed to admit was I could have eaten three more helpings, but I knew I would regret that later when

I was only good for sleeping. She melted in my arms when I held them open, and I kissed her before I smacked her playfully on the ass and told her I was getting in the shower to wash off the smell of sex and grease from the shop. Despite my invite to join me, she laughed, saying, "Babe, I need to start a load of laundry and put the leftovers away. Besides, you have already distracted me enough. You need to behave."

"Never. And you know you love it." Her laughter trickled over my body as I headed back to the bathroom.

My shower was quick because I needed to get my ass in gear if I wanted to have time to talk to her again before I cut out. Damn, I felt like a little chickenshit pussy, dreading telling her I was leaving again—and I *still* wouldn't be able to tell her where I was going. After getting dressed in jeans and a T-shirt, I ran my fingers through my damp hair and called it good. Time to face the dragon. Beautiful though she may be, she was soon to be spitting fire.

She was sitting on the couch reading a book when I came downstairs. Damn if she didn't look exactly as I pictured her when I first looked at this house. For a moment, I just stood there silently drinking her in. My heart gave a lurch at the beautiful sight she made. As if she sensed me in the doorway, her eyes raised to mind and a small smile curved her lips.

With a sigh, I sat down next to her and pulled her into my lap. She wrapped her arms around me, rubbing the tip of her nose against mine.

"Mmm, you smell good. Wanna run up to the Redbox and grab a movie?" she murmured as she kissed the corner of my mouth.

Well hell, here's where shit goes bad.

"Yeah so, about that. I need to run out again. This is the last night this week though, baby, I promise. I wasn't supposed to be tasked tonight, but Gunner is sick as shit. Trust me, if I could stay here, cuddled up with you, I would." Her brow furrowed, and I felt her body tense in my arms.

"Then take me with you." Her chin raised and her gaze bore into me, waiting for my reply.

Fuck.

"Baby, I can't." My head fell back to the couch, and I closed my eyes.

"You can't or you won't? What are you doing while you're gone?" Yeah, this was gonna end as badly as I feared. My lips pressed together in frustration.

"I can't." Sitting up, I looked her in the eyes, silently begging her to let this drop.

"Oh, let me guess, 'club business,'" she said, laced with sarcasm.

"Look, Becca, I told you when we moved in that there were going to be a lot of nights where I was going to be gone." I wished she could just understand I wasn't going out to fucking party. Shit.

"Then at least tell me where you're going." Her expression grew darker. Not a good sign. My head tipped back, and I released a frustrated groan. *Dammit!*

"Baby, I can't," agonized out of me to the ceiling with my eyes closed. She was making this so fucking hard on me, but club business was club business, and there was no way I would betray my brothers or my club, no matter how much I loved her. Besides, if I told her I was at a fucking titty bar all week, I was pretty sure she would totally lose her shit on me. They may find my body in a shallow grave.

"Whatever. Fine. I guess I'll see you when you get home then." She jumped off the couch and stomped into the bedroom, slamming the door, much as I did last night. My hands scrubbed over my face in defeat. When my phone vibrated in my pocket, I pulled it out, swiping to answer.

"Yeah."

"Don't sound so happy to hear from me there, sexy. You ready to be my date tonight?" Reaper chuckled at what he obviously thought was his divine humor. Fucker.

"Man, screw you. Yeah, I'll meet you at your place in fifteen." At least tonight I was with Reaper. Even though I wasn't in the mood for filling in for Gunny, he and I had been a team longer than any of us brothers, so it was a little like old times. We just understood each other and easily anticipated each other's thoughts and moves.

With a heavy feeling of dread, I headed out after hollering through the locked bedroom door that I loved her. Her answer was a mumbled, "Yeah, right. Well, I love you too."

Great. Well, I'm picking that damn lock if it's still locked when I get home tonight.

Chapter TWENTY-SEVEN

Becca

FUCK THAT MOTHERFUCKER IF HE THOUGHT I WAS SITTING HOME like the nice dutiful little woman. What he didn't know was I was changing in the locked bedroom. Because I was going to get to the bottom of this shit. He wasn't going to just go out every night, coming home covered in cheap perfume and cheaper lipstick. Hell no. I was going to find out where the hell he was spending his nights.

When he hollered through the door to tell me he was leaving and he loved me, I was still pissed, but I couldn't let him leave without telling him I loved him. It hurt my heart to fight with him. Like my chest literally ached. This was not how I planned on shit going tonight. Telling him I was pregnant was hard enough as it was. I sure as shit wasn't going to blurt it out in the middle of an argument.

The sound of the front door closing spurred me into action. I grabbed my boots, pulling them on as I worked my way to the door, hopping on one leg at a time. My purse was swooped up, and I grabbed my keys off the hooks by the door. Shutting off the lights to my car so he wouldn't notice me pull out behind him, I watched his bike turn out of the end of the driveway toward town. Slowly easing out onto the road, I kept a close eye on his taillights in the distance. Waiting until he disappeared over a hill in the road, I turned my headlights on. Hopefully, he would just think I was a vehicle that had come off one of the side roads.

It was easy to keep myself at a safe distance with the speed he was traveling. As we neared Reaper and Steph's, I saw another bike pull out as he hit his brakes and they took off together.

Hmmm, so Reaper is going with him tonight. That got me wondering if Steph knew where they were going.

The ringing of her phone echoed over my car speakers as I waited for her to answer.

Come on, girl, answer.

"Wassup, you sexy beeotch?" Despite my mood, I couldn't help but smile at my best friend's peppy-sounding voice.

"Nada, my little ho. Hey, where is your man running off to with mine?" It was a struggle to sound nonchalant. "I'm wondering if I should be jealous of their bromance." She laughed and I knew I had fooled her in regards to my mood. *Good.*

"Hell, chica, I don't know. It's all that-"

"Let me guess, 'club business,' right?" Keeping the snide tone from my voice was impossible this time. She must have picked up on it because her tone sobered.

"Hey. Girl, it's okay. I promise they aren't doing anything they shouldn't. I trust Reaper. Explicitly. Just keep faith in your man, sweetie." Easy for her to say. She wasn't the one whose man was coming home smelling and looking like a hooker had climbed him. "Did you tell him before he left?"

"Ugh! No! I didn't get a chance," I growled in frustration. "Anyway, I gotta run, hoochy. I'll call you tomorrow. Love you."

"Love you too, beeotch." In frustration, I disconnected the call on my car dash. The bikes' headlights were probably a good mile ahead of me, but I could still see them. We were heading toward Spirit Lake and I recognized the glow of the lights of town in the distance. When we pulled into town, they had to slow down, and I started to catch up to them so I had to drop back, barely keeping them in my sight with traffic. The Lakes got busy in the summer with all the tourists who flooded in.

When they turned into a lot with a building trimmed in green lights, I read the sign. The Emerald Shamrock. Flashing in neon was a busty woman with green shamrocks covering her nipples.

What. The. Ever-loving. Fuck?

You have got to be shitting me, I thought as I pulled into the gas station across the road and parked along the side of the building, trying to figure out what to do next. They walked in together, and I saw Reaper laugh at something Mason said.

My temper was boiling. I was ready to punch him right between his gorgeous light hazel eyes. That bastard. And Reaper was with him! Wait until Steph found out where our *loving* men had hightailed it, under the guise of "club fucking business."

Assholes.

How long I sat there stewing and trying to think clearly and form a plan, I had no frickin'clue. Finally, my temper won out and I backed out of my parking spot and waited for an opening in traffic to pull into the packed parking lot across the road. Popular place, I thought snidely. The lot was so flipping full, I ended up having to park toward the back. Of course, they were able to park their bikes right up front. *Dicks.*

After walking around the building, I walked up to the front door and pulled it open, taking a deep, fortifying breath. God, the place was dim and smoky. The bouncer by the door looked at my ID then to my face. Jesus, I wasn't trying to sneak in with a fake ID. His expression became thoughtful before he nodded his head that I could go in. Sheesh. Man of few words, much?

There was a stage situated against the back wall, with a longer section jutting out into the crowd like a runway, lit with green lights around the edge. The bar spanned the entire right side of the club with two burly-looking bartenders manning the bar that was lined up with customers. There were two women dressed in short—and I mean short! Like ass-cheeks-hanging-out short—black shorts and bright green tank tops that were damn near painted on they were so tight. Those, I assumed, were the waitresses. Of course, there were darker green shamrocks printed over their boobs at nipple location. My eyes rolled at the obvious lack of bras on either of them. As perky as those things were, they were fake for sure.

Yeah, I was feeling extra bitchy. Wouldn't you if you just found out your man had been chilling at a titty bar every night since you moved in together?

My eyes were still trying to adjust to the low lighting as I scanned the bar, looking for the guys. The music cranked up as Nine Inch Nails "Closer" began to pump from the speakers. This was one of my favorite songs, so this bitch better not make me hate it by being the one wearing that nasty red lipstick. A busty blonde who looked like she was a naughty acrobat rather than a stripper began to slink her way to the pole.

Rhinestones covered her masquerade-type mask, a short white sparkly skirt and a silver studded halter top completed her outfit. And by the hoots and hollers of the horny bastards lined up around the stage, she was a favorite.

Why the hell I was sitting there watching a stripper's number, I couldn't tell you, but she was mesmerizing. God, she was sexy, yeah, but she was grace and self-confidence and talent. What the hell was she doing working as a stripper in Podunk, Iowa when she could be on Broadway, or something? *Damn, girl.* Shit, was she flexible. By the time she finished her number, she was down to a glittery G-string and some silver nipple cover-thingies. She shook her ass and blew kisses to the crowd as she gathered up the last of the tips thrown up at her and strutted off the stage.

Wow.

Shit. She had distracted me from my mission. My eyes resumed their scan of the room. When they lit on a half-naked, gaudy redhead climbing up to straddle a guy against the wall in the corner, I wanted to gag. Gross. Some guys were sooooo without shame. When I saw Reaper walk up to them and noted his angry body language, my eyes took the disgusting scene in again. No. No way. Blood boiling, I pushed and wove my way through the crowd to the corner and the scene of what was unfolding to be the beginning of the end of my relationship. My heart pounded in anger, denial, and adrenaline.

"What the fucking hell?" Not sure, but I thought I may have shrieked at glass-breaking decibels. The nasty, skanky, redhead turned to me as she slid off what I then knew was *my man's* lap. Bitch had the nerve to give me a dirty look and tell me to fuck off or she would have her boyfriend throw me out.

"Are you fucking kidding me?" My eyes flashed to Mason's shocked hazel ones that were nearly gold tonight. *Yeah, shocked to see me, darling?*

"Babe, I can explain. This is *not* what you think." He turned to skank-face. "Cherry, I told you once, and I'm not telling you again, get the fuck out of here." When he tried to reach for me, I jerked my arm out of his grasp as I back away, breathing labored and so mad I could probably spit damn nails. Fury resonated through my entire body.

"Hollywood, you know we have a good thing going. This scrawny bitch is why you're telling me to leave? Fuck her." She turned to me and spit out, "You aren't wanted bitch, move along and get the hell out of here. You don't fucking belong here." My mind barely registered skank-face telling me he was her man and I needed to get the hell out of there. *I'm the scrawny one*? My focus turned to her, and I was about to punch her boney ass out when Reaper wrapped his arms around me and quietly told me I didn't want to do this here. Hollywood looked furiously at skank-face before he turned back to me. He still looked angry, like I did something wrong. My body jerked and twisted until I pulled out of Reaper's hold, turning on him.

"You! Both of you. Oh my God. I can't even find the words right now. Jesus Christ. I cannot. Just cannot believe this!" Havoc churning through me, I turned and forced my way through the crowd to the door as I felt sobs tear through my body. Through the pounding rush in my ears, I barely heard Mason and Reaper shouting my name. My hand snatched a small stack of napkins from a table as I pass to wipe the tears that were blinding me. Realizing it was a futile endeavor, I shoved them in my pocket and kept moving. All I could focus on was the door and getting the hell out of there. At the last minute, I noticed the back door was closer and diverted my path, bursting out of the door into the humid night air. My hands dropped to my knees and my head hung as I gasped for breath and sobbed.

Not wanting to wait long because I knew the guys were following me, I stood. As I rushed toward my car, fumbling with my keys, the air was knocked out of me as I was tackled from the side, and a hand covered my mouth. We nearly fell to the ground when another set of hands grabbed me, and we were moving toward a dark-colored van. My body started kicking and thrashing, fighting tooth and nail against the slow progression toward the van. Panic like I had never felt engulfed me. How did you process something that only happened in the movies?

Something sickly sweet covered my face, and everything seemed grossly distorted before my vision started to go black.

Heavy.

No breath.

Sinking.

I was sure I heard Mason and Reaper shouting before there was just… nothingness.

Chapter TWENTY-EIGHT

Hollywood

MY MOMMA TAUGHT ME TO NEVER HIT A WOMAN, BUT IF EVER I wanted to plant my fist between a bitch's eyes, it was Cherry. As soon as Reaper and I walked in, she was up my ass. No matter how many times I gave her the brush-off, she kept coming back. After the shitstorm she stirred up with her little stunt last night, I could have easily throttled her with no remorse. This was just icing on the cake of shit she had stirred up.

Reaper had even told her to get lost. That motherfucker can be a scary bastard when he wanted, so she had stayed away just until he left to take a piss. She had slithered up in my lap quicker than I could blink, and I was fighting to shove her off without making a big scene that would call attention to us back in the corner. We were supposed to be observing the comings and goings while being unobtrusive. Every time I pushed to get her off my lap, her arms tightened around my neck. If I peeled her arms from around my neck, she was climbing back in my lap. She was like a fucking octopus.

Reaper came stalking over, looking pissed as hell. *Join the fucking club, buddy.*

"Cherry! Knock it the fuck off!" he growled. "I swear I'm going to lock you in the backroom if you don't get lost. I would have Arnie cut you loose, but your ass wouldn't leave. Now, dammit, Cherry, get the fuck off Hollywood. Now! Don't make me fire your ass and ban you from the place." She looked over at him and batted her fake eyelashes. He rolled his eyes. Little did she know, neither of us had sympathy for her shit.

"*What the fucking hell?*" My eyes closed in dread. That was a voice I was not expecting to hear tonight, especially not at that particular moment. It was one I ordinarily would have loved to hear, but with that slut on my lap, I knew shit looked bad. Real bad. Hell, I wasn't sure how she knew where I was, but it was *not* good.

Cherry slid off my lap, running her hand over my jeans and along my dick as she got off. After having something as golden and good as my girl, this tramp didn't do a damn thing for me. It seemed like she figured that out when I didn't respond to her, so instead, she started running her mouth to Becca after I had already told her ass to beat it.

Becca turned on her, and I thought she was going to jump in her shit with both feet. Reaper must have seen it too, because he wrapped her up and held her, whispering in her ear as she thrashed and fought his hold. I was so pissed at the situation, I could barely think straight.

Becca was a fury as she twisted out of Reaper's arms and lashed out at us both. With every fiber of my being, I wanted to try to explain to her how she misunderstood the whole situation. I wanted to hold her and have everything be okay, but she was pushing her way toward the door by the time I pulled myself out of my agitated inertness. Reaper shoved my shoulder, getting me to move, but by then she had gotten a head start on us. Girl could move. We both rushed to cut her off before she got to the door, when we saw her suddenly cut off and go to the back door.

Shit! Losing precious time, we had to weave back through the place. Of course, it had to be a busy as fuck night.

She was out the door by the time we made it through the crowd. We rushed out the door in time to a sight that was a complete blow to my gut. No, worse. The sight that greeted me eviscerated me.

No. No. No! My heart and lungs near to exposing in my chest, I ran toward the two men who were dragging my girl kicking and fighting toward a plain black panel van. Reaper shouted, hot on my heels. No idea what they had done to her, but I screamed her name just as I saw her go limp and they tossed her in the van like a sack of trash.

The van pealed out as they were still climbing in, doors swinging. My instinct was to jump on my bike and follow them, but Reaper held me back with one arm as he was rapidly talking on his burner phone.

"Stop! Hollywood! Man, I know that's your woman, but we can't follow them blindly. It could be a trap. Snow is pulling everyone from the other tasks and is diverting them here. Hacker is running the plates. I was able to get them before they threw her in." Reaper tried to reason with me, but my mind was shattered. I was seriously losing my shit as I gripped my hair and paced back and forth.

Fuck this shit. I need to go after my girl. Fuck!

Hopping on my bike, I revved it and peeled out, shifting gears like a Grand Prix racer as I tried like hell to keeping the disappearing taillights in my sights as they swerved in and out of traffic down 18th Street. When they turned down a side street, I lost them after a jacked-up truck pulled out in front of me, and I slammed on my brakes to avoid being a bumper sticker.

Reaper skidded to a stop next to me mere seconds later. My

rage knew no bounds as I kicked my kickstand down and jump off my bike. Hands fisted with my arms straight at my sides, I roared in outrage before swinging wildly when Reaper approached me. Vision straight red, it didn't matter who he was, as everything in my body was on disconnect.

"Hollywood! Stop! Fuck!" Reaper's words barely penetrated my haze of wrath. "Let's go back to the main road to meet up with the brothers. We lost them. There is no sense in riding off half-cocked. Man, I told you, this could be a trap to get one of us alone."

Not caring if it was a trap, I was going out of my fucking mind waiting as I headed in the direction of my bike. As I passed by a road sign, I punched the metal. My hand was throbbing, but my adrenaline prevented me from really feeling any damage I may have done.

Let me tell you, I have never been a very religious man, but I prayed to whatever God may listen to me that we found her before anything happened to her.

Deep in my heart, I was terrified I was going to lose her one way or another tonight.

Reaper grabbed my arm, turning me toward him in a blurring half circle. "Hey, Hollywood. Man listen to me. They have an ETA of about five minutes. We're going to find her, bro. You just need to hold your shit together and keep your cool. This is just another mission. Pull yourself together. You can't go racing off and possibly getting yourself killed. We got this, bro, we got this. Now let's head up to the road so they see us. Okay?"

The breath I was holding came out in a rush. He was right, and I knew it, but fuck if I wasn't coming unraveled inside. The woman I loved had been taken, and I knew those fucking piece-of-shit Demon Runners had her. But why? Why her? Did they figure out she was the old lady of a patched member? Regardless, they had signed their death warrant. Legit be damned. Even if it meant turning in my cut, I would hunt down every one of those worthless bastards and kill them slowly if they harm her in any way.

My leg swung over my bike as I settled in, anxious to take off. Reaper and I rode up to a gas station and sat waiting for the guys to get here. Less than five minutes later, we heard the roar of their bikes, but hell if it didn't feel like five hours. Snow, Vinny, DJ, Soap, Hacker, Two-Speed, and Dice all pulled into the lot and stopped in front of us.

"Hacker says the van is stolen. Go figure. Good news is, your woman had her phone on her. We were able to trace the tracker you had him put on it, but that's only as good as the signal. He's tracking her now. Brother, we're going to get her back. No one takes one of ours without retaliation. Now keep your damn head screwed on straight and we'll get her. Let's ride out, boys." Snow was calm, but I could see in his eyes he was pissed that these motherfuckers had taken it to this level. Like I said before, we'd been trying our best to stay legit and on the right side of the law for a while, but fuck with our families and all bets were off.

"We need to get moving. They're moving at a fast rate, and they have a good head start on us." Hacker was messing with his phone. He was one wicked-smart motherfucker. Like, I mean the man was seriously tested as a genius. He could crack almost any program out there, and the ones he actually designed blew my mind. Thankfully, he had his tracking program tied to his phone so he could follow through his GPS and shit. My agitation level was exploding, because I'd been ready to go before they arrived. I needed to get this show on the damn road.

We all pulled out in a tight formation and roared off into the night. Even though Snow, as prez, would usually be in lead, Hacker was this time due to the tracking program he had running. By this time, we were heading down toward Spencer when Hacker motioned we were turning off the highway soon. The gravel roads meant we had to slow down. When Hacker motioned for us to stop, I was pissed.

What the fuck now?

"Damn, I think they ditched her phone," he exclaimed. I watched helplessly as Hacker worked furiously with his phone. My heart felt like it had been ripped out while it was still beating, the pain was so great.

"What happened? What do you mean you think they ditched it?" My frustration was building, and I was starting to come unraveled again.

"I mean, it's showing her phone is right here." He motioned toward the ditch. "They had to have thrown it out," he said as he scanned the ditch with a high-powered flashlight. "Either they found the tracking program, which I doubt, because it was embedded pretty deep and saved to look like it was just a random background program running, or they were just being cautious. There is nothing out this way except for a few old farms and fields. Bro, I'm sorry." Hacker looked like I felt. It wasn't often he was bested. This was damn near Steph's situation on repeat, and I knew how that had played out. My nausea circled and churned in my gut.

"Fuck!"

We all got off our bikes and walked the ditch in search of Becca's phone. Not that it would do us much good, but maybe Hacker could get something off it. He had done some kind of CSI shit in the Marines with the Force Recon. Searching the overgrown grass for a cell phone felt like the proverbial needle in a haystack search.

"Hey! I think I got it!" Soap yelled out. He used his bandana to scoop it up before he came running over to Hacker with it. Hacker stowed it in one of his saddlebags to go through it when we got back to the clubhouse.

"Since we're out here, let's check out the farms along here to see if they're using one as a home base or a place to keep her. We can't all go, because all these bikes would sound like the sky is raining down. Soap, your bike is the quietest since you're running stock, so I want you to ride past the few farmsteads along this road. If you notice anything, keep moving and call us when you get to the end of the road." In a different time, I would have laughed at the slam to Soap's bike; at that time, I just wanted to get going. Snow returned to his bike. "All right, we wait here until we hear from Soap."

More fucking waiting. Dammit.

When my phone started ringing, I was pissed. *Who the fuck is calling me?* I did *not* have time for stupid bullshit right now.

Digging my phone out of the inside pocket of my cut, I saw it was a restricted call. My eyes met every brother standing around before I answered the call.

"Yeah?"

"Is this 'Sexy-Ass Mason'?" a snide, gravelly voice asked me.

"This is Mason. Who the fuck is this?" Right away, I knew this had something to do with those fuckers who had Becca. I knew I needed to keep my cool because I didn't want to give anything away in my temper.

"We have something that belongs to you. Listen carefully, because I won't repeat myself. Get in contact with the Demented Sons MC and tell them we have your hot little number… you know… a certain pretty little redheaded dancer… and if they don't want to keep losing their little dancers, they'll meet us unarmed at a time and an address I will text to you in the morning. If you value your woman, you will convince them to be there. If they don't show up, it won't be just dancers they start losing." He laughed before the line went dead.

"Stupid motherfucker doesn't know who he has. They think they have one of the dancers. They want me to 'get in contact with the Demented Sons MC' and tell them to meet them *unarmed* at a location and time they will text me in the morning. If we don't show, they said it won't just be dancers we start losing." My expression wavered between angry and bleak, my fists clenched in rage. For a moment, everyone was silent before Snow spoke up.

"All right, Soap, get moving. As soon as he scopes out this road, brothers, let's head back toward home. Get your families and get to the clubhouse ASAP. We're on lockdown until we find the sonofabitches. You got me?" Grimly, everyone nodded.

Soap took off down the road, his taillights blinking out when he shut down his lights to decrease his visibility. It wasn't long before Snow's phone rang, and he looked at me shaking his head. We mounted up and headed back toward home, frustrated and on edge. It killed me to turn my back and not search every road in the county in an attempt to find them tonight, but I knew I wasn't thinking rationally. So, I followed Reaper to his house since there was nothing for me at mine. Just the thought made me want to explode. Made me want to scream into the dark night sky. Made me want to rip my own heart from my chest to alleviate the retching pain crushing it.

Reaper woke Steph and told her to get Remi, Wyatt, and enough stuff for a few days. Steph looked at him in concern as she quickly carried Wyatt and his car seat out from the back bedroom. He carried a sleeping Remi, and I took the packed bag from him to carry it out to their SUV. Steph looked at me after securing the babies, and her question took me out at the knees.

"Where's Becca, Hollywood?" her soft voice whispered with blue eyes full of worry.

Grabbing my hair in both fists, I turned away before I completely lost it. Panted breaths rasped from my lungs as I struggled to breathe.

Breathe.

Breathe.

Just fucking breathe.

Gasping, heart shredded, I faintly registered Reaper speaking to Steph in a low tone. My eyes sought the bright stars as I fought to keep my sob at bay—a desperate, aching sob that I was afraid would mirror the one I heard slip from Steph.

Jesus, I don't fucking cry.

Please, God, if you're listening, please bring my baby back to me safe. I fucking need her.

Chapter TWENTY-NINE

Becca

God, my head is pounding. I feel like I sucked on cotton balls all night, too. My eyes don't want to focus, and my bed feels like it's hard as concrete this morning. When I try to roll over, my limbs are so heavy I can barely move. There's a bright-ass light shining right in my eyes, making it hard to find where my pillow went. My arm is like a lead weight when I move to throw it over my blinded eyes. Why don't I remember drinking last night? Man, I must have been trashed to be this hungover. Sleep. Sleep sounds so damn good...

Waking with a start, I realized I must have dozed off again. *Shit.* Oh God, my stomach roiled, and I felt like I was going to puke. My quivering arms finally supported me enough to rise to a sitting position, and I pushed my tangled hair out of my face.

What the fuck?

As my eyes slowly began to focus and take in my surroundings, my heart jumped into my throat and tried to choke me.

Where the hell am I and how did I get here?

Looking around, I realized I was obviously in a small basement room because there was a little window high in the wall, and other than that, the room consisted of four cinder-block walls, a single metal door, and a concrete floor with a drain in the center.

Panic welled inside me and alarm bells were resonating in my head. My memories were vague, and I grabbed my head as if I could hold onto those elusive memories and get my head to quit spinning.

Slowly, flashes started to sift through my mind.

A strip club, Mason, Reaper, the redheaded skank, rushing outside, and a van…

Holy Mary, mother of God…

Shit, I had been tackled and thrown into a van. My head was still pounding and the most revolting taste was stuck to my tongue. Sickly sweet. Rancid. My eyes flashed to the small window.

Was it last night? How long had I been lying here? Where the hell am I?

My bladder felt like it was going to explode, and in a panic, my hand hovered over my belly.

Oh shit, what did they drug me with? Please God, don't let it have hurt my little peanut…

My bladder near to bursting, I couldn't hold it anymore, and I sure as shit wasn't going to sit here and piss myself, so I crawled on quivering arms and legs to the drain. Geez, I felt like a newborn colt! *Please don't let anyone walk in while I'm in this ridiculous position.* Squatting over a nasty drain cover on a floor to piss was not where I ever in a million years saw myself, but necessity ruled in that moment.

Great, no fricking toilet paper in my palatial accommodations.

In a desperate attempt to prevent my anxiety and terror from taking over, I tried to latch onto anger and sarcasm. Staying calm was essential, I knew, but I was struggling. Bad.

Shit, the napkins… Pulling the wad of napkins out, I counted them. There were five. They were the small ones like you put drinks on, but if I opened it up, it would work, and I could ration them out for a little bit. My brain blocked out the thoughts of how long I may or may not be here and *why* I was here. The used one got tossed in the corner furthest from me. Jesus, it didn't escape me that I was rationing napkins for pissing. What the fuck?

Crawling back to the corner furthest from the door, I sat with my arms wrapped around my legs, my knees pulled up tight to my chest. *Dear God, help me. Mason, anyone, please be looking for me and find me soon.*

My throat tightened, and my heart pounded like it may burst. I'd watched too many fucking scary movies and knew the girl never made it out of crap like this unscathed. Sometimes she didn't make it at all… *Please, God, I don't want to die,* ran on repeat through my brain as I sat there thinking about all of the things I had to live for, and my baby, tiny and nestled in my abdomen, was at the top of the list. Mason didn't even know he was going to be a daddy.

Maybe he wouldn't even look for me. I really thought he loved me, but now I wasn't sure. Was I deluding myself? How could he love me but be at a strip joint with sleazy skanks climbing all over him? My rational side told me there had to be more to what I saw, but my hormonal, irrational, hurt side was angry and spiteful.

Guess I dozed off again, leaning against the wall with my forehead on my knees, because I woke with my neck was killing me from the awkward angle. The direction of the light had changed, so a few hours must have passed by. My mouth was still so dry, and I was hungry. Really freaking hungry.

When the doorknob rattled, I was instantly alert. The door opened slowly, and a lanky man with greasy hair and filthy looking jeans walked in. The dirty leather vest he wore had a patch that read

"Rat," and I thought how fitting that name was with his beady eyes, pointed nose, and weak-looking, set-back chin. Though I didn't want to, my eyes met his, and I tried not to show fear, even though I was sure he could smell it coming off me in waves.

"Well, lookee here, you're awake. I was hoping to have a little fun with you, but I was told to just check on you and bring you some food and water." He walked closer and crouched in front of me. Gross... his teeth were nasty and his breath was worse. Violently, my stomach rebelled at the smell emanating from him, and I prayed I didn't hurl in his face. Without warning, his hand shot out, grabbing my breast and twisting painfully. Despite my attempt to maintain a cool façade, I cried out in pain.

"Those are some nice titties. Mmm, yeah, I can't wait to have a round with you. We need those Demented Assholes to show up so we can kill them all. Man, I sure hope you don't get caught in the crossfire, 'cause I want to bury myself in you something fierce after they're dead. Maybe, if you're lucky, they'll let me claim you as mine."

Lucky? Yeah, not so much, you delusional asshole.

When he reached out to touch my hair, my cringe was involuntary, and he laughed as he stood up. My gag reflex was working overtime as he stroked his dick through his pants then readjusted it before walking to the door. He reached outside the door and threw a bottle of water and a gas-station-style sandwich at me.

The dirty patch on the back of his leather vest as he walked away read "Nomads" under a patch with some kind of ugly creature with red eyes and fangs and "Demon Runners" above it. I filed that away, trying to remember every detail I could in case I lived through this and was able to tell the police.

Right now, the odds of that seem really, really shitty...

"Rat, cut your shit out. Get upstairs before I gut your nasty, greasy ass. Go take a damn shower, for fuck's sake." If I thought fear rolled off me with Rat, I felt sheer terror rise in me at the man who walked into the waning light coming from the small window.

Not because he was scarred or ugly, but because this man had dark, cold, dead eyes. His hair was slicked back and held in a ponytail. If it weren't for his eyes, he would have actually been a good-looking guy, but those black eyes were just plain flat and emotionless. His threat to Rat seemed extremely plausible, and I believed he would do it with relish, not remorse.

Fine tremors skated down my spine as he ambled to me, and I glanced to the open door, weighing the chances of making it past him and out the door before he could catch me. When I looked back to him, he had a feral grin as he narrowed his eyes at me.

"I wouldn't if I were you." My eyes widened slightly at the thought that he could read my mind.

"What's your name, Red?" God, I hated that he called me that after Mason and his club called me that with affection.

Fucking asshole.

My gaze continued to meet his, but I remained mute.

Quick as lightning, his hand reached out to grab my jaw in a punishing grip, bringing immediate tears to my eyes. Blinking to hold them at bay, I tried desperately not to let them fall.

"Answer me, *before* I break this delicate little jaw." Jesus, he was crazy, but I believed him. Of course, just because I believed him, didn't mean I was giving in easy. I'd always been too damn stubborn for my own good, but I wasn't stupid enough to think they were going to actually let me go after this.

"Fuck you," I spat through the pain. His other hand shot out and backhanded me, knocking my head back against the wall. Fuck, the pounding in my head reached epic proportions, and a warm sensation trickled down my face, so I was pretty sure his ring had done some damage to my cheek. *Dickhead.* Without warning, he grabbed my hair in his fist, jerking my head so my face was mere inches from his.

"You think I care that you have tits and a pussy? I really don't. I tried to ask you nicely, didn't I? Now, what… is… your… name? So I can make sure those Demented Pussies know which one of their little dancers we have." He took his finger and caught the blood trickling down my cheek. When he put his finger in his mouth and sucked my blood off, my stomach cramped and heaved. My lips pressed together in defiance, despite my rising fear of what he may do to me.

"Stupid bitch." His soft-spoken tone were in blatant contrast to the words themselves.

My fear was well placed as he punched me in the face, and my eye instantly began to swell shut. He was so fast, I didn't even see it coming.

Holy shit.

My head was now throbbing at a vicious pace, and I truly believed he was actually ripping my hair from my head, his grip was so tight. Though I desperately tried to block it, his next punch still caught my lip, and I tasted the metallic evidence of the damage before he punched me again and again. Black dots danced in my vision, and if he hadn't been holding me up by my hair, I was pretty sure I would have collapsed in a boneless heap.

When he grabbed the front of my shirt in his meaty, bloody fist and ripped it straight down, I felt cool air hit my stomach. Pure instinct had my hands attempting to cover myself and protect my defenseless baby.

With a jerk, my legs were pulled out straight by the ankle until I slid down the wall and my head hit the floor. As he braced his foot on my chest to hold me down, he began to pull my boots off. Sheer desperation had me trying to kick out and fight him, but I could barely breathe with the pressure he was exerting on my chest. Hands clawing at his boot in an attempt to allow expansion for my lungs, I felt hysteria creeping in.

God, I'm going to suffocate.

Panic built like a tsunami in me, and I felt sure he had cracked some of my ribs by this time. He knelt down, replacing the boot on my chest with his knee, and then easily unbuttoned my jeans and ripped them off.

Jesus God, help me. Tears coursed down my cheeks, my sobs stuck in my chest.

Cruelly, his hand seized me by the pubic bone, pushing my underwear down before his fingers shoved into me. Fuck, it hurt so fricking bad. If I could have screamed, I would have, but I couldn't even breathe! Tears continued to leak from the corners of my eyes as he jerked my panties down further to midthigh.

Please no…

"This would be all you're good for, but I don't like dry, cold bitches." His fingers pulled out and shoved painfully into me once more before he finally decided he was done with me.

There I lay on the floor, gasping to regain my breath after he removed his knee from my chest. My ribs hurt with each expansion. A big fist gripped my hair again, and a whimper slipped from my cracked and bleeding lips. Effortlessly, he lifted me off the floor by my hair until I was close to his emotionless face.

"Don't worry, that's not a problem we can't fix. They can try to identify your body when we're done with you. It makes no difference to me. I'll be back, and you better hope I've heard from them, or you get to suffer for their stupidity. As it is, your boyfriend will see what his little stripper girlfriend looks like now." When he released my hair, I fell over and he kicked me in the thigh. Vaguely, I heard a clicking sound and looked up with my one barely open eye to see he had a phone out and he was taking pictures of me.

Stripper? What the hell? Does he really think I am one of the strippers from that place? Jesus. And my boyfriend? Shit, they're sending these to Mason. Oh, God. If they have his number, then I guess that answers what happened to my cell phone.

Little does this asshole know, Mason probably wouldn't even give a shit about what happened to me since it seemed everything we had was a sham. I prayed he at least looked for me for Steph's sake, since she was his brother's wife and my best friend, but I wasn't holding my breath. Trembling, I watched as he walked out of the room with my pants and boots, leaving me lying on the cold concrete in my panties, bra, and torn shirt.

Time ceased to exist as minute ran into minute while I lay in a crumpled heap, tears running to the concrete floor. But I was starving, and through blurred vision, I saw the sandwich Rat threw at me. Even though it pissed me off to accept anything from these assholes, I knew I need to eat something if I wanted to maintain my strength in case the opportunity arose to escape. Also, my baby needed whatever I could get.

The thought of the innocent life in me not getting a chance to grow and see the world broke my heart. Why had I been so stupid? Despite knowing better, I completely disregarded my surroundings when I left the strip joint. That was one thing my dad had always drilled into me.

Oh God, my parents.

If I died, they were going to be devastated. Self-pity overwhelmed me as I continued to cry over my situation, until I finally felt like I was just completely out of tears.

The water felt good on my dry, parched throat, but the process of drinking and eating the nasty gas station sandwich broke my lip open again and I tasted blood. Every part of my body ached and burned. When my nausea built, I leaned against the wall and closed my eyes, taking deep breaths. Slowly, it began to ebb. The urge to cry pressed at my eyes and throat like hot pokers, but I told myself it wouldn't help me. It was time to get my shit in one basket and do what I could to get out of here.

When I tried to stand, my leg almost gave out on me. Rubbing on the area, I felt the hard, swollen knot in my thigh. Shit, there was swelling and a large purple bruise forming already. My head was *still* pounding, I hurt like hell all over, and I could barely see out of one eye. Reaching toward the window, I found it nailed shut. *Of course.* Briefly, I considered using my shirt around my hand and trying to break the glass, but I knew I wouldn't fit through the window, and even if I could, I wouldn't be able to pull myself up to it to save my soul.

Slumping to the floor in defeat, I curled in a tight ball and silently prayed for someone to find me before it was too late. The silence was deafening, and defeat crept over me like a wraith.

Chapter THIRTY

Hollywood

THE TEXT WITH THE ADDRESS OF THE MEETING PLACE AND TIME came through at about eleven the next morning. Bodily and mentally exhausted, I had barely slept all night worrying about Becca and if she was still okay. My girl was feisty and strong, but I honestly didn't know how much she could take in a situation like that.

My fist raised to knock on Snow's door, and he answered after a grumbled, "yeah, hold on." When he threw the door open, I saw Cammie sprawled in the bed behind him. Despite averting my eyes as quickly as they registered his glare, I still backed up and looked down the hall. Clearing my throat, I gave him the info from the text message.

"Call everyone in for church. I'll be there in five." He closed the door.

I did what he asked, my body moving on autopilot. We were all hastily taking our seats when Snow entered the room and sat at the head of the table. He ran his hand through his dark brown hair, causing it to stand up. Not sure I'd ever seen him look so weary, and lines of stress creased his forehead. During times like this, we all knew he carried a heavy burden and none of us envied the responsibility he shouldered.

"These assholes have been a thorn in our sides for too long now. We have a meeting place and time for early tomorrow morning, but I don't trust them. They say they want to make a deal to split the small gun transport we operate, and they're demanding a share in the area for drugs, which will happen over my dead body. You all know I don't give a shit about the weed, but I'll be damned if I let them bring meth into our area. Fuck that shit. And we're not stupid enough to believe this isn't a setup. Reaper, I want you and Hollywood to work with Hacker to see if there's any video surveillance we can tap into in the area. We also need a good location to set you two up in a position to cover us and take out as many as you can. They fucked up when they started to mess with us, but they signed their death warrants when they took Hollywood's old lady and threatened our families."

We continued to work out all the details, and then Snow adjourned the meeting. Reaper and I headed toward bed to try to catch a little sleep before we had to leave to set up. We were all passing through the doors, grabbing our phones from the basket we placed them in prior to going into church. Looking at the screen, I saw five missed messages. Opening them, it first read:

Unknown: in case you needed incentive to get them to listen to you

The pictures began loading and I doubled over from the torment that hit me like a punch to the gut. Grasping desperately at the wall, a roaring sound filled my ears. Reaper yelled my name as my knees hit the floor and my phone dropped from my lifeless fingers. The visions of those photos were forever etched in my brain, and I felt physically ill at the thought of what all she must have endured.

"Jesus." Reaper looked at my phone and handed it off to Snow as he covered his mouth with his free hand. Steph ran up to Reaper, and I could barely make out her frantic whispering to him. Being Becca's best friend, I knew this was killing her too. Not to mention, it probably brought back bad memories for her. Snow was talking to me, but I barely heard a word he said. My jaw and fists were clenching, and my chest heaved with ferocious breaths.

I am going to kill them all. Every fucking one of them.

Of course, there were no camera systems in the shitty area they wanted us to meet, so we were going in blind. It was a vacant, condemned, old slaughterhouse on the edge of town. Much like our sniper missions, we had arrived hours ago to ensure we were set up and ready before they got there. We stealthily moved in under the cover of darkness, dressed all in black with nothing but our eyes exposed, and even those were blacked as best we could. Since she had been taken, I had only slept in short spurts, but my adrenaline was pumping, keeping me alert. It felt like Reaper and I were back in time on another mission.

We had brought the portable video equipment and had explicit instructions from Hacker on what he wanted to be able to see to help determine placement of the cameras. We waited patiently on the roof of a grain elevator located on the property next to the packing plant, after setting up the surveillance. We had already run a recon of the building and surrounding area upon our arrival. Everything was clear.

Fuck, they were idiots. From our rooftop location, we had an unobstructed view of the inside of the old factory, thanks to the majority of the windows being shattered.

It was nearly three in the morning and the meeting was set for five. It would still be fairly dark by then, and I knew they were planning on having the advantage.

Stupid fucks.

Unlike our missions in the Army, I was not just operating as a spotter. This time, I was prepared with my own sniper rifle. Yeah, I may not be as good a shot as Reaper, but I was still better than most. Growing up hunting with my dad came in handy at times like this.

We still didn't know where they were keeping Becca, so our instructions were to allow one or two to escape so we could tail them back to wherever they were hiding out. Silently, I prayed they would lead us to her and we would be able to rescue her in time. Fuck, I prayed she was still alive… Unbidden, thoughts of what Steph had endured at the hands of that psycho raced through my mind, and I prayed some more.

Personally, I would've rather just spare one of them and slowly torture the location out of him, but that was my anger feeding itself and another reason I was glad I wasn't the prez. Times like this, I was grateful for Snow's level head, but it didn't stop me from wanting to make them all suffer.

Before we headed over, Reaper talked to me and did his best to get me focused on the mission. He seemed nearly as angry as I was, and I knew Steph had begged for us to bring her friend home safe. She was distraught, and every time she looked at me, she hugged me and cried. If my brain had been functioning better at that time, I might have questioned the crazy, frantic despair in her eyes.

The air was cool, but I felt like I was sweating bullets. My eyes closed and my breaths slowed as I worked to focus my mind and body.

Breathe.

In.

Out.

Focus.

Everything dissipated except for our immediate situation. It had been a while, but I channeled the soldier I once was. The rooftop we rested on was pebbled, and it seemed as if we'd been laid out on the uneven surface forever, though the discomfort barely registered as we maintained focus, diligently watching for our targets.

These pieces of shit were stupid for not keeping someone at this location all night. Showed they were straight fucking amateurs. Vicious ones, but amateurs just the same.

When we saw movement, we looked through our night vision lenses to see a single person checking out the area. The bright green glow in his hand told us he was using a phone, probably to let his dipshit brothers know the coast was clear. Little did he know…

Two others joined him. We continued to watch them as they set up in what they obviously believed were hidden locations. These dumbasses had clearly never trained or lived like Reaper and I had. They were absolute incompetents, and I almost felt sorry for them. Almost.

We held steady and waited. The waiting was always the worst, but we had learned patience for this exact type of situation over the years together. It did, however, take everything I had to keep the personal nature of the situation to the back of my mind. I knew I needed to stay impartial to maintain my focus.

ETA of our brothers was still about forty-five minutes out, so it didn't surprise us when we saw more of their guys rolling in and parking their bikes back behind the vacant building.

We counted seven guys in total. Three that had set up in advance, and the four that had just showed up. They entered the factory through a side door to wait for our guys. We radioed in to Hacker to give him verbal updates to coincide with the video feed. We were also connected to Snow and the guys through the high-tech earpieces that were nearly invisible in the dim light. It was amazing what you could acquire with the right contacts and money.

What we weren't expecting was the panel van that pulled up. Pretty sure it was the same one Becca had been thrown into, and my eyes flashed over to meet Reaper's. He nodded and returned his focus to the scene unfolding below us. We silently watched as the overhead door opened, the van drove in and they quickly closed the door. The driver got out and spoke to the four in the factory. It appeared the driver was alone. My senses were on high-alert. Something just didn't feel right.

Right on time, we watched our guys as they rolled up the deserted road toward us. Everyone was present except for the two prospects that had stayed behind to watch over the families back at the clubhouse. They arrived "slick back"—no cuts—in two of our blacked out SUV's, coasting up to park up the road, and then walked in as silently as possible. Hacker was in our van with a prospect as a driver so he could operate a command center of sorts. He had the video and audio feed working as our third set of eyes. We were well aware we would need the advantage as long as possible.

The stupid fucks should have posted someone up the road to call in and notify their guys we were arriving. Like I said… amateurs.

Our brothers all quietly sounded off, giving us the sign they were hearing us clearly. We reported our observations to them as they worked their way through the darkest shadows toward the factory. Having most of our brothers as prior military sure helped in situations like this.

As they neared the entrance to the building, Reaper and I zeroed in on the assholes who *thought* they were hiding. We knew we had mere seconds to hit the first of our targets before moving to the next—two each. The safety of our brothers depended heavily on us.

Because we were focused on our targets, we missed the activity by the van until I heard Snow whisper, "Shit," but I didn't dare waver from my focus. Reaper spoke to the brothers, asking if there was a problem or change of plans. Hacker advised us to stay on course and wait for the predetermined signal from Snow to take out our targets before we moved on to the assholes left standing. Had I wavered my focus from my target, I would have picked up on the hesitation in Hacker's voice and I would have seen one of my worst nightmares unfold.

Chapter THIRTY-ONE

Becca

YOU NEVER REALLY KNEW HOW STRONG YOU WERE UNTIL YOU had a tiny human relying on you to protect it. Despite this, however, I couldn't lie and say I hadn't momentarily prayed for death because of the pain. I was pretty damn sure my ribs were cracked, if not broken. There was no way it could hurt that much to breathe and my ribs still be intact. Also, I was pretty sure my body looked like it'd been used as a punching bag.

Oh wait, it was. For the last twenty-four or more hours, because honestly, I had lost track, the raspy voiced asshole had systematically beat the ever-loving shit out of me. The scariest part of it all was he didn't even seem angry as he punched or slapped me.

The cold-hearted bastard remained flat faced, yet I swore he enjoyed every minute. He would ask me what I knew about the club. How many members there were. Which of the members I "belonged to." What Mason's connection to the club was. Since he and I were probably over, I wasn't lying when I told him none of them. He told me repeatedly how "they" would learn this was no longer "their" territory. I could only assume he meant Mason's MC.

No matter how many times I tried to tell him I wasn't one of the MC's strippers, he wouldn't listen to me, and he would punish me for "speaking without permission."

There had never been a moment in my life where I hated someone as much as I hated that bastard. The terror of the beatings harming my baby nearly broke me, but I forced myself to hold it together. Time drifted and blended, merging in a kaleidoscope of horrific moments twisting around in my head.

My consciousness had obviously drifted in and out, because I didn't remember being loaded back in the shitty van, but I sure as hell felt someone dragging me out of the van by my hair. When my battered body bounced off the side door and hit the concrete, I whimpered at the jarring to my numerous injuries. After that, he continued to drag me a few steps away from the van before dropping me to the ground.

It was so cold. Was I completely naked? It was hard to tell if you had clothing on when your very skin hurt and the pain traveled straight to the bone. Not to mention, I was nearly covered in dried blood. My breaths came in rapid gasps to prevent deep breaths, which caused excruciating pain. There was a ringing in my ears, so I could only hear a hum of voices. I was sure they brought me here to finish me off, but I remembered what the greasy one named Rat said about it being an ambush.

Through blurred vision, I swore I saw some of the guys from Mason's club. My voice escaped me and my mind wouldn't connect with my mouth to form words. There was no way for me to warn them that this was a trap. Even though he and I had gone to shit, my heart still ached at the thought of his beautiful, smiling face, or any of the others, going still in death. In the last few months, I had become close with all of them through Mason, Steph, and Reaper. They'd become like family to me, and I felt sick inside at my helplessness.

Blackness snuck in from my peripheral vision when I heard shouts and gunshots. Silent sobs tortured my body as I imagined their blood flooding the cold concrete. Vaguely, I was aware of squealing tires and the sound of motorcycles roaring away from here. My consciousness wavered as my eyes grew heavy.

When a blanket covered me, I wondered if I was dead and being covered by paramedics, or maybe that asshole because he assumed I was dead. No, he wouldn't have cared one way or the other and would have been just as happy to leave me lying on the side of the road like unwanted refuse.

A hand brushed my hair, stiff with blood, out of my face. Muted voices sounded around me, but I had no idea who had me. My eyelids were weighted and refused to open. Carefully, my body was gathered up and gently laid down again. As my consciousness continued to fade in and out, I heard faint, sporadic words with "got you" and "safe" being the only words I caught. The rest, like the voice, were muffled and recognition alluded me. My heart wanted it to be Mason, but my mind knew it couldn't be. Wouldn't be.

The last thing I remembered before the darkness completely enveloped me was cringing away from painfully bright lights as someone pried my eyelids open and being jostled so bad the pain took my breath away.

My head was foggy as hell and I was so freaking thirsty. Damn, my eyelids were heavy, like fifty-pound weights were attached to them, but they finally flickered open briefly. I must have been hallucinating the sandy, tousled head of hair resting on the edge of my bed, but before I could blink to see if it was real, my eyes just couldn't stay open any longer. A warm, calloused hand held mine, and I knew with every fiber of my being it was Mason. So tired though. Just needed to rest my eyes for a teeny tiny bit…

The steady beep of the machines surrounding my bed woke me and my eyes actually cooperated and stayed open. When I looked around, I took in the obvious. I was in a hospital room. In the chair angled next to me, Mason slouched with his head tipped over the back and his mouth slightly open in sleep. His hand held mine on the bed and his booted feet were propped on my bed next to my own. He looked rumpled and his face was no longer clean shaven, but covered in a darker scruff. Why it struck me as funny that his beard was so much darker than his hair, I had no idea, but when my giggle slipped out, I groaned at the sharp pain it caused.

His eyes popped open, and he jolted upright, feet dropping to the ground but never losing his grip on my hand.

"Becca! Oh my God, baby. You're awake! Shit, I dozed off. I'm so sorry." His words rushed out of those beautiful lips that my traitorous side was longing to kiss. His eyes were a stormy-looking green, and his hair stuck up every which way. Despite it all, he had never looked sexier… and I had never wanted to escape him more. My heart still hurt from what I saw at that stupid strip club, especially after he had been so self-righteous about cheating back in Vegas.

My faith in him had been demolished, and I felt like I could never trust him again. He made me feel like he had been playing me. Because I loved him with every fiber of my being, it had crushed my heart. Even though I was pretty sure I wasn't thinking clearly or rationally, I wanted to get up and run as far away as I could.

My attempt to speak came out as more of a croak, and he rushed to press a red button on my bed and then came back to me with a cup of ice chips that he spooned into my mouth. Accepting it with unimaginable gratitude, I almost moaned in ecstasy. The cold ice melting across my tongue was like manna from heaven.

"The doctor said if you woke up to call the nurse and that I could give you ice chips, but that you should only have a few at a time until we know if your stomach will tolerate it." The look of concern on his face left me feeling confused, and I hated it. I wanted to hate *him.* I wanted to tell him to leave, but I couldn't make my mouth say the words. It left me torn between wanting him to hold me and wanting to scream at him to get out. Fatigue had me opting to just have my questions answered.

"How long?" I croaked, hoping he understood I was asking how long I'd been there. He spooned more ice chips toward my mouth, which I readily accepted.

"You've been out for nearly five days. There was a small area of bleeding on your brain that resolved itself, but with the swelling added to it, the doctors wanted your brain to rest so it could heal. They just stopped the shit that was keeping you under this morning."

"What… what did the doctor tell you?" The ice chips were helping moisten my mouth, but I still felt like my voice was rusty. With every word from my lips, my ribs felt on fire.

I prayed the doctor didn't tell him about the baby. I really prayed I didn't *lose* the baby.

I wasn't ready to tell him yet. I would, but I just wasn't ready yet.

God, I needed to talk to Steph. I really needed my friend.

"Baby, you were pretty beat up. Luckily, you didn't have anything broken, but nearly every rib on your right side is cracked. And you had significant head injuries, a bruised kidney…" His voice cracked. "Jesus, baby, it was just so much. I really don't know where to even begin. I'm so fucking sorry. If I had left you alone, you wouldn't be here like this. I'm so fucking selfish, I know, but I can't give you up. Not for anything." He let out a deep breath and held my hand in both of his, resting it against his cheek.

An older lady in scrubs entered my room and announced she was my nurse and she was pleased to see me awake. She asked me a few questions, took my vitals, asked if I needed anything else, and said the doctor would be in to see me shortly. Nodding my head hurt, so I closed my eyes again.

"Steph. I need to see Steph." With great effort, I open my eyes and my gaze pleaded with him.

"She's actually on her way. She's dropping the babies off at her mom's, and she'll be here soon. She texted me earlier as she was leaving their house to see if you'd woken up yet. God, I have been so worried about you, babe. I was so afraid of losing you… especially with the way we left things. We need to talk, baby."

"Mason, I don't know." I felt so discombobulated. My heart was begging me to pull him up into the bed with me, to have him just hold me, but my mind was screaming to tell him to get the hell out of my room. My body felt like I had been run over by a steamroller, but I wanted the comfort of his arms despite being hurt and angry at his betrayal at the strip club, which led to my abduction. The battle between the two sides of my heart was making me dizzy.

"It's okay. We don't need to do it now. I don't want to put unnecessary stress on you while you're trying to recover. When you get home and are feeling better, we *will* talk. Okay?" His voice poured over my soul like a healing balm, and I hated my capricious heart.

"Yeah." It was the most noncommittal answer I could bring to mind.

That was when I heard the one person I'd been waiting for, but I hated the tremor I heard in her voice. My friend had been through so much in the last several years. I hated that I was adding more to burden her.

"Hey, my little hooch." She was attempting to maintain a sense of normalcy, but I still heard the shaky quality of her voice.

The sterile almost chemical smell of the hospital room was making me slightly ill. My eyes pled with her as I looked briefly at Mason, and I hoped she understood I was asking her to convince him to leave so we could talk.

"Awww, Hollywood, baby, why don't you go on home and get cleaned up. Now that our girl is awake, I can stay here with her for you. She isn't going anywhere." *Thank you, thank you, thank, my friend.* My eyes closed as I tried to gain control of my thoughts and words.

"No. I'm not leaving her." He sounded angry, and in surprise, I looked at him. His eyes were turbulent and golden in his anger.

"I'll be fine, honest. Steph will be here, and she's right, I'm not going anywhere. Go home, shower, and get a little rest." *Please, please,* my mind pled. I needed answers that I could only get from Steph after he was gone.

He appeared to waver in indecision before he got up and kissed me, running his hand along my face before framing it with his hands. He kissed my forehead, whispering, "I love you, beautiful," and walked to the doorway. "I'll be back, baby. We can talk a little when I get back," were his parting words.

"Sure." I attempted to reassure him so he would leave.

Steph sat next to me in the seat Hollywood had vacated. He looked at us both once more before reluctantly leaving the room. Then we heard his footsteps fade down the hall. Her hand grabbed mine, and I watched as tears filled her eyes and spilled over. Considering it wasn't that long ago the roles had been reversed, I hated that she had to be here and have this reminder. More guilt on my plate. Heap it on.

"Steph, do you know? Did the doctor say? Oh, God, Steph, I need to know about my baby. The doctor hasn't come in yet." Her tears worried me, and my heart began to ache. Praying to God, I just needed to know.

"Becca, honey, I don't know. The doctors wouldn't tell me much because I wasn't family. Hollywood told them he was your husband, so we found out most things through him, but I don't know what all they told him. Do you want me to go find a doctor or your nurse?" When I nodded, she stood and walked out of the room. The nurse was supposed to be getting the doctor, but she must have gotten side-tracked.

Steph came back with both the nurse and the doctor in tow. Loved my girl. She made things happen. The nurse proceeded to get another temp and recorded another set of vitals off the machines attached to me. Geez, how many times did they do that in a day?

The doctor was a woman with graying blonde hair pulled up in a bun, which wasn't doing a great job of keeping said hair contained. She was wearing light blue scrubs with a white lab coat and carried a clipboard stuffed with papers. Her kind eyes were complete with laugh lines, and she made me feel more at ease than I had been.

"I'm Dr. Cavanaugh, and I'm pleased to see you awake and talking, Mrs. Kannan. Your friend tells me you have some questions. I'd like to do a quick exam, and then we can talk, if that's okay." I nodded to her, anxious to get the answers I needed. She called me *Mrs. Kannan;* they must have assumed Mason's last name was Kannan since he said he was my husband when they admitted me. Hell, I wasn't going to correct her assumption.

Steph left the room to give us privacy as the nurse closed the door and pulled the curtain in the room. She proceeded to check me out head to toe. When she was finished, she asked, "Do you want your friend to come back in or would you rather talk in private?"

"No, I want her here," I answered, so the nurse went to bring her back in. Steph followed the nurse in and sat down next to me, gathering my cold hand in her warm one as she rubbed soothing circles on the tops of my fingers. My other hand clenched and unclenched in the white, woven cotton blanket.

The doctor pulled up the other chair next to my bed and proceeded to tell me about the damages to my body and how I was fairing as a result. She still hadn't touched on what I was impatiently awaiting to hear.

"Dr. Cavanaugh? What about my baby? Is it… I need to know…" My throat clogged with tears and a sob hiccupped, unbidden from my lips. When she grew quiet and reached out to hold my rapidly fidgeting hand, I feared the worst.

"Mrs. Kannan… Becca… your baby is fine." The breath I didn't know I was holding was expelled in a mix between a laugh and a sob. "I'm not going to lie, we were concerned for the first couple of days, so we didn't say anything to your husband. When he didn't ask, we assumed he didn't know yet." Her eyes looked at me in question for confirmation of her assumption. My bottom lip held between my teeth, I nodded.

"Your baby's fetal heart tones were checked this morning when your husband went to get a cup of coffee. They were steady and within acceptable limits. We want to conduct another ultrasound. One was done in the emergency room after your blood tests came back positive on the HCG qualitative, but the dopler wasn't picking up a heartbeat. Going by the measurements of the baby, it appears you are about thirteen weeks. Does that sound about right to you?" My heart leapt at the thought. *Holy crap*. I was right, I had gotten pregnant almost right away. What if he thought I did it on purpose? My mind was worrying itself in circles with a million what-ifs flying through it and bouncing off each other.

"Ummm, yeah, that could be possible. In all the stress before I left Council Bluffs and after I got here, I missed a pill… a few times." *Stupid, Becca. Seriously stupid.*

"Well, it only takes one, you know. Not to mention, the pill isn't 100 percent effective… nothing but abstinence really is." Her laughter was soft and soothing, but did little to calm my nerves as they jumped and fluttered in my stomach. Except it wouldn't stop. My hand went to my barely raised belly. It was hard, but it hardly seemed big enough for me to be thirteen weeks already. The fluttering came again, startling me, and I let out a surprised, "Oh!"

"Sorry! My nerves are so bad, my stomach is all fluttering." The outburst was a little embarrassing to top off my distress. My cheeks puffed out, and I blew out my breath.

"Well, actually that could be quickening," the doctor said, "and with this being your first baby, this could be about the right time for you."

"Quickening?" What the hell was that? Now I felt really stupid. There wasn't a chance for me to get any pregnancy books, and I had wanted to make an appointment with a doctor before I jumped the gun. My circumstances had changed all that it seemed, and there was no doubt that I was pregnant now.

"The first time you feel the baby move." Steph squeezed my hand as she smiled through her tears. "Oh, Becca, isn't it an amazing feeling?"

My hand continued to rest on my slightly curved belly. I didn't feel anything with my hand. It had just felt like a goldfish was fluttering in my belly. Or like I had gas. The movement had stopped, and I began to panic a little.

"It stopped! Is he okay? And why aren't I feeling it with my hand? Does that mean he's weak? Geez, it seems like it's been forever since I took any classes on a baby's development. I admit I didn't pay great attention to any of the stuff on pregnancy because, at that time, I wasn't really thinking of having children. I don't remember *any* of this." Alarm was setting in. For someone who never thought they would have children, this tiny little life growing inside me already meant the world to me.

Dr. Cavanaugh smiled as she reassured me that was normal. She pulled a little black box that looked like it had a mini microphone attached to it out of her pocket.

"Just to make you feel better, let's listen to your little one, okay?" Nodding my head was all I could do as words escaped me. She squirted some gel on me, then placed the microphone-looking thing to the blob of gel, spreading it around until we all heard a steady *whoosh-whoosh-whoosh-whoosh*. Tears sprung to my eyes.

"Listen to that! Sounds beautiful." She listened for a few more seconds before she removed the gel with a paper towel and cleaned up her little device.

She told me they would get another ultrasound to ascertain possible issues with the placenta or amniotic sac this afternoon and keep me another night for observation to ensure I wouldn't have any lingering issues from the sedative I was given. If all was well by morning, I should be able to go home sometime tomorrow afternoon. After I told her I didn't have any other questions, she excused herself to order the ultrasound. Even though she said it was normal, I wanted to stop on my way home tomorrow to get a pregnancy book.

"Becca, you have to tell Hollywood… *today*." Steph's soft voice broke into my thoughts, causing my heart rate to increase and sweat to break out on my forehead and down my back. My eyes closed and my head fell back to the pillow in resignation. Considering I wasn't really sure where we stood, I was so afraid this would send him running if he wasn't happy with my news. Our relationship was so fragile at this point. Getting pregnant had been the last thing I planned, but what if he didn't believe that? Maybe I could wait just a few more days to see where we were… also, I certainly didn't want him to want to be with me just because of the baby.

"Becca, did you hear me? And no, you cannot wait any longer. I see those thoughts going through your head as if they are written across your face. He deserves to know. He either wants the baby with you or he can hit the hills, sweetie, but either way, you need to tell him. Trust me on this one. I would know." Steph's tone took on a stubborn note, and I knew she was right. It didn't mean I was happy about it, but I knew I *did* need to tell him.

Chapter THIRTY-TWO

Hollywood

When I left the hospital, I was pissed. Hell no, I didn't want to leave Becca's side, but I knew I smelled like ass and I needed to get a few hours of decent sleep. There was a crick in my neck that hurt like a motherfucker from sleeping in that chair by her bed, but I would do it all over again to be close to her.

Maybe I fucked up by not telling her what was going on, but I didn't want to land my ass in a sling by disclosing club business. Shit. There were now a few things I would have to tell her that she pretty much already knew because of those assholes kidnapping her.

I decided to go to the clubhouse to shower and nap since it was closer to the hospital, and I needed to check in anyway. After checking in with Snow and giving him an update on Becca, I went to clean up.

Trudging into the room I had shared with my woman before we bought our home, I had fleeting memories assail me of wild nights and lazy mornings. Would we ever have that again? Would she forgive me for not telling her what I was working on? Forgive me for not telling her I was at the Shamrock so she wouldn't follow me or come to the absolute worst conclusion every time?

Sometimes I hated that club business had to be so tight, but I knew that for the safety of every member, and in turn their families, it was important. No matter how much we may believe we loved someone, at any point they could shitcan you or vice versa. Brothers were forever. Bitches, even old ladies, could come and go. Becca was never just a "bitch" to me, but I had to keep everything in perspective.

Who the hell was I kidding? I was fucking insane for her. There was no "perspective," because I couldn't tell up from down when I was near her.

My brain knew I needed that shower, but hell if I could summon the energy to make my way to the bathroom. My body crashed on the bed, face down. No matter how hard I tried, I couldn't keep the bruised and battered vision of my baby's face and body out of my mind. By association with me and my club, I had done this to her. *Fuck.*

There was no one who had ever held my heart in the palm of their hand like she did, and I knew there never would be again, but I couldn't keep myself from thinking maybe she was better off without me.

Drifting off to sleep, I thought I smelled her fresh scent, and it tortured my body, mind, and soul to be away from her. Despite realizing I should, I had no idea how I would ever let her go.

Thrashing in the bed, screaming, was how I awoke from my fitful sleep. *Fucking A.* My heart was beating so hard and so fast I thought it would burst through my chest wall. Vivid images of the accident had been running through my dreams, but instead of our interpreter next to me, it had been Becca. Nausea roiled through me at the thought of those images. Shit. Maybe I needed to start taking those damn pills for my nightmares again. Fucking pills. Hated 'em.

The clock on the beat-up stand by the bed read 1400. Shit, I needed to get back to the hospital.

Rolling to my back, I threw my arm over my eyes. Battling with the thoughts in my head wasn't helping me, so I rolled my ass out of the bed and shuffled to the bathroom. Flipping the shower knob all the way on, I waited for the hot water to make its way to my room. As I undressed, I caught my reflection in the mirror. Despite my recent sleep, I had dark circles under my eyes. Damn, I looked like fucking shit. I took in the scars covered by tats and the ones that weren't. I was only twenty-eight, but I looked much older at that particular moment, and I felt at least eighty.

The hot water scalded me when I stepped into the shower, and I quickly turned it down before closing my eyes and letting the water run over my head and face. My thoughts assaulted me from all directions, and it was nearly impossible to sort through them all at once. With a roar, I hit the shower wall with both fists, leaving them resting where they landed, and pressed my forehead to the cool tile. Tears, which I tried to deny, ran from my eyes, mixing with the rivulets of water.

Chapter THIRTY-THREE

Becca

After several attempts to reach Mason, I gave up and told the doctor to let the ultrasound technician know I was ready. I was disappointed because I had hoped he would be back in time for me to tell him about the baby and for him to be here to see it.

Due to my still "fragile state"—the doc's words, not mine—the doctor didn't want me going down to the imaging department and instead was having the tech bring the ultrasound machine to my room. Steph was still sitting with me holding my hand as we watched, but paid little attention to, something on the Food Network. If nothing else, at least I had her with me.

When the ridiculously bubbly tech rolled the machine in and was setting up, the voice I had hoped to hear over the phone boomed from the doorway.

"What the fuck? What're you doing to my old lady? What's going on in here?" *Shit*. Mason had stopped in his tracks a couple steps in the doorway at the sight of the unfamiliar machine in my room. His expression was one of mixed anger and fear. His eyes flitted franticly from the tech to me then Steph. I could tell he was going to lose his shit if I didn't intervene soon.

"Umm, can you give us a few minutes, please?" My eyes pleaded with the tech and Steph to understand. The poor tech stuttered a "uh, yeah, sure, I'll just go, uh, to the bathroom, uh, and be back," before she rushed out of the room, avoiding Mason in all his menacing glory, like the plague.

Steph leaned over and kissed my head and squeezed my hand. Her expression and small, reassuring smile told me to be strong. As she walked past Mason, she placed her hand gently on the leather vest covering his chest. She looked at him, though his eyes were still boring into mine, and gave him a supportive pat before telling us she would be back in a little while.

"Becca? What the fuck? What's going on? Are you okay?" His voice wavered slightly, giving away the deep emotion he was holding at bay. He still hadn't moved, and I held my hand out to him, wordlessly calling him to my side. He seemed to shake himself loose and walked closer to me, sitting by my bed before gently gathering me close. Even that slight movement created pain in my ribs, but I ignored it as best I could. My head rested on his shoulder, tucked under his chin, with his arm supporting my back, and I inhaled the familiar smell of leather, cologne, and motorcycle exhaust for fortification.

"Mason…." The rest of the words were lodged in my throat. His one hand smoothed my hair while the other gently squeezed my arm where he held me. Shit, I didn't know what to say.

"Baby, what is it? What's going on? Are you okay or not? Did they find something else? Whatever it is, we'll get through it. You hear me? Together, baby, we got this." His soothing words calmed me slightly, and I prayed he remembered them after I told him the news. I pushed him back from me slightly so I could look him in the eyes. Where my hand rested on his chest, I felt his heart beating in time with mine.

Who was I fooling? I was still crazy about him. He was my sun and moon. The question was whether he was going to freak when I told him and bolt.

Taking a deep, painfully fortifying breath, I spoke. "The night I was… taken…" *Shit, this was hard.* "That day when Steph came over…"

"Baby, you're worrying me. Just spit it out. There isn't anything we can't deal with together." His beautiful light hazel eyes met mine, and before I became totally lost in them, I blurted out what should have been said the same day I found out.

"I'm pregnant."

Total silence.

Like, I'm talking… crickets. I thought time may have briefly stopped as neither of us breathed, nor did the usual hospital noises intrude from the background. His breath finally escaped in a rush and his eyes closed tight.

"Say something. Please." His heart raced under my hand, and I felt him inhale a shaky breath. My hand slipped up to cup his cheek, running my thumb along his bottom lip. "Baby?"

"Are you sure? Fuck, Becca, you were hurt so bad. Oh God, what if it… Shit. Holy Crap. Becca. I'm going to be a dad?" His eyes looked to mine in hope, concern, and confusion.

"Yes, I'm sure. And they did an ultrasound when I was first admitted after my labs showed I was pregnant. The doc said everything seemed fine, the heartbeat was strong and steady, but they wanted to get another one to be sure." I nodded toward the ultrasound machine. "Which is what you walked in on. I tried to call you to see if you were coming back soon. I was really hoping to talk to you before the tech got here so I could see if you wanted to be here for it, or if you wanted to be with me at all. We haven't really talked, and I wasn't sure where we stood, let alone how you would feel about a baby. So much has happened, and I was afraid you would be angry, or that you were waiting for me to get better to tell me you decided we were a mistake…" My rushed words trailed off as I ran out of breath.

"Fuck, Becca. How could you think I had changed my mind about you? I love you. You're my baby girl, and there is no way I would let you go or risk what we have for some skank like Cherry. What you saw was not what you thought, but we can talk about that later. When I first looked at our house, all I could picture was you with our babies in every room I walked through. I wanted to fill that big house with the patter of little feet, and I wanted to plant my babies in your belly as often as I could to show everyone you were *mine.* Maybe that sounds crazy, but I fucking love you, woman. I'm not letting you go. Ever. You have made me the happiest man in the world with this gift. I'm just sorry about everything that happened to you because of the club, and I pray that you don't think we, or our baby, are mistakes." His lips brushed across mine gently, before his tongue pushed its way between my lips to tangle with mine. He leaned back, breaking the kiss, and tucked my hair behind my ear.

"Now where is that tech? Holy Fuck… I wanna see my baby." His grin was infectious as I felt myself smile.

Hollywood

There were few moments in a man's life where he truly felt humbled and awestruck. Seeing the little fuzzy image on the screen and hearing someone call it "your baby" would definitely qualify as one of them. Becca was squeezing my hand and covering her mouth with the other as we sat mesmerized, listening to the tech point out the little head, arms, legs, fingers, and toes. It was hard to wrap my head around the fact that I was going to be a daddy, let alone that we had pretty much missed the first three months or so of her pregnancy.

When the tech asked if we wanted to try to see the sex, our eyes collided. *Shit.* We never even thought about that, but there wasn't much time to really talk about it.

"Ummm, isn't it too early to tell?" Becca questioned the tech.

"Well, ordinarily, yes, but this is a 3D Ultrasound machine, and it's much easier to tell. Well, that's if you want to know." The tech looked at me nervously, making me feel bad for scaring the shit out of her when I first came in the room.

"Mason, do you want to know?" Becca bit her bottom lip, and her brow furrowed. Fuck, she was cute. And hell yeah I wanted to know, but not if she wanted to keep it a surprise.

"Well, what do you want?"

"I want to know, but not if you don't..." Her cheeks took on a rosy blush over the fading bruises. Grinning, I looked at the tech.

"Yes, ma'am... please let me know if I have to worry about one dick in town or all of them. I need to know if I have enough fire-power at home." The pretty tech blushed when I winked at her after my answer. Funny that before Becca, I would have probably tried to get this girl's number, and now it just felt good that I could still make a female blush, because the only pants I wanted in now were Becca's. Obviously, I had done a pretty good job of it too, and my swimmers were more potent than her birth control. I laughed to myself.

"Well, Mr. and Mrs. Kannan, it looks like you better pick out some boy names because he definitely has boy parts!" Mentally, I did a fist pump. Nothing got a man feeling incredibly caveman-like than finding out he made a boy. Not that I would have loved a little tiny Becca any less, 'cause I wanted a few of those too, but hell, I needed to make sure I had the big brother first to watch out for assholes messing with his little sisters when I wasn't around. And I didn't give a shit that the tech called me by Becca's last name. We were gonna rectify that, though…

"Fuck yeah!" *Okay, oops, that totally slipped out.* But hell if I regretted it. I was proud as fuck right about then. Becca was laughing at my antics, and I kissed her loudly on the lips before I kissed her on the top of her beautiful head.

"But are you sure?" I questioned. "It looks awful tiny." My skepticism crept in upon closer inspection of the still frame she had on the screen with a little arrow with the words "IT'S A BOY!" pointing at the tiniest little stem I had ever seen.

Becca laughed… "Considering he is only about the size of a peapod or a lemon, that's probably about right, babe." I looked at her in disbelief.

"Are you serious? How do you even know that? And there is no way. My boy is at least as big as an avocado." I was trying to be serious in the face of Becca's uproarious laughter. She seriously had tears leaking from the corners of her eyes, she was laughing at me so hard, and I failed to see the humor in this. This was my son we were talking about.

"Here you go. I printed out several of the pics of little junior for you guys." The tech was grinning wide as she handed the strip of sepia-colored pictures to us. She appeared to be over being afraid of me and my pissy mood I was in when I arrived back at the room. "I'll leave you to battle out the particulars of your little man. Congratulations, you two!" As she wheeled her machine out of the room, I snatched the printouts from Becca's still laughing ass. I shot her a glower intended to make her quit, before studying the pictures closer.

Of course, her ass still laughed.

"Stop it. The nurse said they took your catheter out. You'll pee yourself, and I'm not cleaning your bed." In her defense, she did try to hold her laughter in, but when she burst out laughing before she held her ribs and groaned again, I frowned at her in mock annoyance.

"Baby, I love you. And I'm sure he is just fine in his man parts.

Now, let me see the pictures of our son." Whoa. If that wasn't ice water to the face. Our son. Never thought two little words would hit me with such a gamut of emotion. Happiness. Pride. Love. Fear. Excitement. All just hit the tip of the iceberg. And who knew a little lemon would have my heart so tight in its tiny-fingered grasp?

"Our son. Holy crap. Becca, this is our son. You're giving me a son. I saw his heart beating. He moved and wiggled. After everything you went through, he's okay. You kept him safe, baby. Thank you. God, I can't thank you enough. Shit. I need to call my parents." At my last words, my beautiful girl's smile dropped from her face. "Baby? You okay?"

"My parents… shit. I haven't even really talked to my mom since I've been here. I've talked to my dad, but not a lot. I don't want them to know about what happened to me. Please, Mason. Promise me you won't ever tell them. I'll tell them about the baby after I get home and I'm all healed up. Okay?" She was grasping my hand in a near death grip. *Damn.*

We had talked a little about what had happened between her parents and her when she told them she was leaving dickface, and I thought it was fucked up that they wouldn't be in their own daughter's corner, but I didn't say anything at the time.

"Baby, it's fine. You tell them when you're ready. And I'll be here for you when you do. I've got your back, baby… always." After giving her a quick kiss, I pulled out my phone to call my mom. She was going to absolutely shit. My heart raced a little in excitement.

A dad. I was going to be a dad. *Fuck me.*

It felt like forever since we had entered our own house. Well, shit, I guess it had been quite a while. Honestly, I hadn't come home once since she'd been taken, because I couldn't bear to see the memory of her in every room. Yeah, this house was mine, but who was I kidding?

It was hers. Totally hers. Just like my fucking heart.

Walking into the bedroom, we set her plastic "patient belonging bags" down on the floor. We could deal with them later. Pretty sure she would want to burn everything in there anyway. She stood looking out the window with her arms wrapped tight around her middle and clutching her sides. Curling my body around hers from behind, I gathered her in my arms and pulled her close. Silence enveloped us as we stood melded together.

My brain was running in crazy circles wanting to know what all had happened to her, yet terrified to have my worst fears confirmed. Instead of pushing her to talk, I allowed her to just absorb my strength as I held her close. Experience had taught me you couldn't force someone to dump their emotional burdens on you, but it'd also shown me how destructive it could be to compartmentalize one's feelings and stuff them away in the darkest corners of your mind.

My lips placed gentle kisses at the crown of her silky burgundy tresses and trailed along the side of her neck. This wasn't an attempt to be sexual, just to connect to her and absorb everything sweet that was just… Becca. When I bent to kiss her shoulder, I felt and saw her break out in a wave of goose bumps as a soft moan slipped from her perfect lips.

"How are you feeling, baby?"

"God, I just want a shower. Join me? Please?" Hell, she didn't have to ask me twice. She turned in my arms and slipped her hands around my waist. Briefly, her head rested on my chest before she untangled herself from my arms, and I followed her to the bathroom. Allowing her space, I quietly watched as she set the water temperature in the shower and then wasted no time in peeling off my clothes. When I reached for the button of her jeans without thought, she jumped and a startled squeak escaped her. Tremors consumed her body.

"Sorry, baby, I didn't mean to scare you." Her pulse raced under my lips as I kissed beneath her jaw. Kneading her tense shoulders, I rested my chin over her head, attempting to ground her. She reached up and covered my hands with her shaking ones.

"No, I'm sorry. It… it startled me, is all. When he…" Her voice trailed off to a whisper, and rage ripped through my soul at the thought of anyone violating her in such a way. The need to kill him with my bare hands nearly devoured me from the inside out.

Guilt consumed me because I knew, deep down, this happening to her was my fault. Her connection to me and the club was the catalyst to her abduction. If she had never come here and gotten involved with me, she would have never been in that position.

Not to mention she was carrying our baby at the time. Had I known, not only the woman I loved but my son as well, were both nearly ripped from me, I may have went out of my mind while we waited. Even now, the thought sent waves of despair over me at what could have happened. My heart felt shredded. As I had done while she was still in the hospital, I told myself she would be better off if I let her go and sent her home to her parents.

Just thinking about losing her nearly brought me to my knees.

No, fuck that. She wasn't leaving me. She was mine.

She suddenly reached up, cradling my face and pulling my lips to hers. What started as a soft, tentative kiss, quickly evolved into a passionate twining of tongues as we tasted and consumed each other. We broke apart, our breathing coming uneven and gasping. She quickly divested herself of her clothing and backed into the shower, her passion-glazed eyes never breaking contact with mine.

Telling myself I needed to give her time and let her just heal, I closed the door behind me after stepping into the shower with her. Despite my resolutions to keep this detached and to only assist her with strictly showering, our bodies drew together like the strongest of magnets, and our lips connecting was like lightning striking. My hands hesitantly slid down her smooth skin to grab her lush ass in both hands, squeezing her as I lifted her body to mine, and she wrapped her legs around my waist.

Her sudden intake of breath reminded me her ribs were still sore, and I tried to break free and set her down, but she only kissed me deeper with a slight shake of her head as her legs gripped me firmer. My cock was hard and aching to feel her slick heat wrapped tightly around me. It made me feel like the worst kind of asshole.

"Please, Mason," she whispered. Every tightly clutched shred of resolve I had unraveled, and with a tilt of my hips, I rubbed the tip of my cock in her slick folds before I broke free from our kiss, resting my forehead to hers. My chest heaved with the effort to breathe in enough oxygen to keep me conscious.

"I don't want to hurt you, baby," growled out of me. Her answer was to grip my waist even tighter with her legs, raising herself slightly before sliding down and sheathing me deep inside her luscious warmth in one single stroke. No matter how fucked up the world may seem… no matter how fucked up in the head I felt… connected to this woman, I felt centered and invincible.

By the time we were done in the shower, the water had grown cold and we were sated and sleepy. In worshipful silence, I gently dried every gorgeous inch of her body, cataloging every fading bruise and placing loving kisses over each one, before quickly drying myself. Wrapping a towel around her wet hair, I cautiously scooped her up in my arms, climbed in the bed, and held her against me.

My eyes grew heavy after I heard her breaths slow, even out, and deepen. Pulling her closer to my body, careful not to crush her healing ribs, I wrapped her in my arms with her head resting on my chest and one leg curled over my own. Contented, I slipped off to sleep knowing this was exactly where she belonged.

Chapter THIRTY-FOUR

Becca

IT HAD BEEN JUST SHY OF TWO WEEKS SINCE I HAD COME HOME from the hospital. Heavens, it was so good to be in my own bed, but I was sleeping like shit. In my dreams, I relived the torment of being beaten over and over. It was becoming the norm to wake up screaming with Mason holding me and trying to soothe me each night.

Sitting at the table drinking orange juice, I knew I needed to go back to work soon, but I was terrified to leave the house. What the hell was I going to do? There was no way I wanted to give up my job. I loved it. I loved my little kiddos.

A knock at the door had me jumping and spilling my juice in my lap. Shit!

The doorknob rattled and my hands shook as my heart raced, wondering if they were coming for me again. After another several knocks, I slowly crept to the front door. At the sound of Steph's shout from outside to open the door, my relief was palpable. Fingers trembling, I quickly unlocked the door and opened it with a shaky smile. Steph's confused look met me as I opened the door fully to admit her, Remi, and Wyatt.

"Hey, you! Let me run and change really quick, I spilled OJ on myself." Remi ran into the living room to pull out one of the books I kept in a basket for her, and Steph went to sit on the couch with Wyatt. Scanning around outside briefly before I closed and locked the front door didn't make me feel any better.

I changed quickly into some yoga pants and a tank top and headed back out to join my friend. Since coming home, none of my pants wanted to fit comfortably. Go figure. Time to go shopping, it would appear. Yeah, not looking forward to that.

As I settled in to the couch and held my arms out to a drooling, grinning Wyatt, Steph sat frowning at me. Wyatt was slapping my face and pulling my hair as I looked at her and questioned, "What?" His little chubby knee caught my ribs, and I winced at the brief sharp pain. *Damn, were they ever going to heal?*

"Your door was locked. Becca, your door is never locked. Hollywood said you also haven't been sleeping well." Steph's expression wavered between concern and confusion as she sat with her arms crossed, impatiently waiting for my response. I had been able to put off anyone visiting since I came home by saying I was still so tired, but it was really because I just wasn't ready to talk to anyone. It was bad enough I had to tell some of the club members everything I remembered about my abduction.

"Yeah, well, he talks too much. Besides, I now have reason to ensure my home is secure. Complacency is what got me abducted in the first place. I'm just being careful." I tried desperately to maintain a tone of practicality. I didn't want to admit to Steph that I was scared shitless to leave my home or to be home alone.

"Becca, do you forget who my husband is? Do you forget who *your* man is? Do you think Hollywood can't spot how you're feeling? Maybe you need to talk to him. You can't stay holed up in here forever."

There wasn't anything wrong with me other than I was a little more nervous than usual. It was pissing me off that it seemed everyone was making more out of this than there really was. I was understandably upset, that was all there was to it. Time was all I needed to just get over it all.

"It's only been a few days since I came home, but okay, Steph. No problem. I'll talk to him tonight, if it makes you feel better, okay?" A subject change was in order. "So… we're having a boy." I couldn't hold back my smile. I had wanted to wait to share the news with everyone until I was able to talk with my parents, but I really needed to tell someone, besides Steph was my best friend. Not to mention, I hadn't had the courage to call my parents and tell them. The way my mom acted about Steph marrying Reaper, I knew she was going to flip a lid when she found out I was pregnant with a "biker's" baby.

Top it off with us not being married, and that was a recipe for a disastrous conversation with my mother. I also hadn't wanted to call after what had happened to me because it made me feel like they would just *know,* and I didn't want to talk about it. With anyone. Not even Mason, even though I had just promised Steph I would. And especially with a counselor like Mason, Reaper, and Steph thought I needed to.

"What? Oh my gosh! I wanted to be in there, but I knew it was a time for the two of you. I'm so happy for you! Oh! I can save Wyatt's things for you! Unless, of course, you want to get all new. I mean, it is your first child, so I would totally understand if you don't want to use hand-me-downs." At the mention of his name, little Wyatt leaning toward his mom, so I handed him back into her waiting arms. He proceeded to snuggle into her shoulder and chew on his hand, drool running across his fist and down his arm.

"Jesus, Steph… I wasn't raised to be a snob. I'm not above accepting hand-me-downs for this little guy." I grabbed a tissue from the side table and wiped up Wyatt's drool. My hand palmed my belly where my little peanut was safely nestled. Right at that moment, the wiggly goldfish feeling fluttered through me. My laughter bubbled out as my eyes met Steph's.

"He's moving?" Steph looked at me with her puppy-dog, yearning eyes and I knew she was remembering this feeling.

"Yeah, he is. I can't wait until I can feel him kicking from the outside. I want to be able to share it with Mason. We've talked a little about what happened that night before… well, you know… and I believe he wasn't doing anything, but I'm still upset that he didn't just tell me what was going on so I didn't feel the need to follow him. Our relationship's a little precarious, at best, right now. It feels like we have pretty much called a truce for the baby's sake. I want so bad to believe he loves me and wants a life with me, but he seems content to just let things roll along like they are. It's so frustrating." Dang, it was good to have my best friend here to discuss all the crap that had been rolling around in my head since coming home from the hospital. Despite feeling I just needed time, and maybe I did, it was nice to unload a little.

"Good God almighty, that man is insanely crazy for you. I honestly never thought I would see him settle down with one woman, but I'm happy to see he has, and I'm ecstatic that it's with my best friend, especially considering how close he and Reaper are. It makes it feel like we are truly family now. For a while, I was really getting worried that he would die of some rare venereal disease before he ever settled down!"

Wow. She got my best "did you really just fucking say that?" expression.

"Ummm, well, you know what I mean." Steph's face went beet red at the realization of her comments. "But for real, Bec, he loves you. A man doesn't buy a house like this and move his girl in without having some deep feelings. Not to mention, he never left your side the whole time you were in the hospital."

"I know, and I keep trying to tell myself all that. He has told me over and over how much he loves me, and I know he was there in the hospital, but what if it's all just guilt?" Self-doubt was eating me up. The hundreds of what-ifs that bombarded me were tearing at my confidence in our relationship.

"There's no way that it's just guilt. No. Way. You need to stop worrying about all this so much. It's not good for the baby, honey. What do you say we take these two monsters and grab a nice relaxing lunch? Well, as relaxing as it can be with a toddler and a baby. We can go to the Oasis and have something from my new lunch menu..." Steph had bought the Oasis from one of the old ladies in the MC when her husband entered into "retired" status with the MC and they decided to do some traveling. After Wyatt, Steph had hired a manager to take on the brunt of the work, leaving her to have more time with the children. She still created the menus and even cooked some days when the itch to be a chef again struck her.

"Actually, I'm really tired and thought I would take a nap. Maybe next time. Raincheck?" The thought of going out in public had my heart racing, and I grabbed my hair, pulling it into a ponytail to hide the shaking of my hands. "Little Mason must be pushing on my bladder because I really need to pee too. I'm sorry, hon."

Steph looked crestfallen that I didn't want to go with her, and I felt bad, but the thought of leaving the safety of my home was worse.

"Then I'll just stay here and make us all lunch! You can nap afterward. After all, you need to feed that little guy." Steph popped up from the couch after pointing at my tiny baby bump and placed Wyatt on a blanket on the floor. She set up a little mobile play thing to keep him occupied and stimulated and went to rummage through my pantry and cupboards in search of her latest culinary masterpiece. Of course, the woman could make an award-winning dish with cardboard and bread, so I wasn't too worried about if I had everything she needed.

"I'll be right back." Hastily, I made my exit to the bathroom as I felt my anxiety level increasing, and I was afraid it would develop into a full-blown panic attack in front of Steph and the babies. My back slammed into the back of my bathroom door as I closed it, and I covered my mouth and nose with my cupped hands in an attempt to calm my breathing before I hyperventilated. Tears formed in my eyes, and it felt like I was going to literally fall apart. My body shook from head to toe, and I wondered how I was going to maintain in front of everyone for much longer.

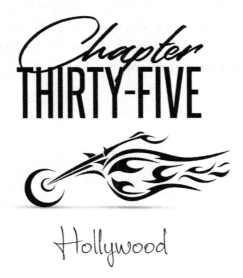

Chapter THIRTY-FIVE

Hollywood

"Hey, Reaper, bro, do you have a minute?" Things with Becca had been tense since she came home from the hospital. I was doing my best to remain calm and act like life was normal, but deep inside I knew things were unraveling with her, and if she didn't get some help, it was going to cripple our relationship. I couldn't help but think of how Reaper and I handled shit at first, and I didn't want to see Becca fall into that same rut, especially with our baby growing in her. She was already barely holding everything together, and I knew it was a matter of time before she couldn't keep everything buried. Of course, every time I mentioned her talking to someone, she got pissed at me.

"Yeah, bro, what's up?" Reaper wiped his hands on a shop rag and walked toward the cooler for a bottle of water. I grabbed a bottle of water as well and cracked open the lid, taking a long chug of the ice-cold liquid. Leaning against the tool bench along the wall, he drank his water and waited for me to talk.

"Shit, Reaper, I'm really worried about Becca. She's not dealing well, but she keeps trying to act like there's nothing wrong, like I can't spot that shit. We both know she's not okay, but she refuses to talk to anyone. She's carrying my baby, bro, and I know this can't be good for him. Besides how much *she* means to me, if anything happened to that baby, I don't know what the fuck I would do. How does a baby I haven't even seen yet have me so protective and overwhelmed with love for it? It's got me feeling like an emotional wreck, like I'm growing a fucking vagina, for fuck's sake!" Setting the bottle down on the bench, I ran my hands through my short hair in frustration.

"Hollywood, bro, trust me, those little munchkins weave a spell around you as soon as you know they're coming. I don't know how or why, but they sure as hell do. Has she talked to her family yet? Maybe talking to them will help her work through some of this. If nothing else, planning for the baby with them may help preoccupy her mind. And whoa, hold up! Did you say 'him'? Did y'all find out it was a boy and you didn't tell me? Hell, Wyatt and your little guy running around this town together? It may not survive them! Shit, *we* may not survive the two of them together!"

I couldn't help but laugh at the visual of our two boys as teenagers.

"Yeah, they'll be hell on wheels, and no, she refuses to call her mom or dad yet, because she doesn't want them to know about the kidnapping and assault. You know I get that, but I don't think it's healthy either, bro. Not only that, but I feel like she doesn't want them to know about us, like she's ashamed of us." That last was what cut the deepest, and saying it out loud hurt even more. My feelings had never been so deep for another woman in my entire life. Honestly, I didn't want that before Becca, which was part of the reason I was a love 'em and leave 'em kind of guy. The doubt wasn't in whether she loved me back, but whether she was proud to love me. Yeah, serious vagina growth going on here. Fuck.

"Hey, fucker, don't say shit like that. I highly doubt she's ashamed of you, but you have to admit, she has faced a lot of crazy shit since she got here. I can see why she wouldn't want to tell her parents everything and risk having them think she made a bad choice in coming up here, but I don't think that involves the choice she made with you. That woman is crazy about you, bro. Trust me. All I fuckin' hear from Steph is how Becca 'gushes' over you." I couldn't help but laugh at seeing Reaper roll his eyes and make the quote signs with his fingers as he said the word "gushes."

My humor was short-lived, however, because reality crashed down on me, and I still couldn't help but feel like she was ashamed of me. Part of me, with the heart of stone, said fuck her if she was ashamed of me. The other part of me ached at the thought that maybe I really wasn't good enough for her. No matter how I tried to be the happy-go-lucky guy everyone thought I was, I knew I was still broken inside. Sometimes, I was still seriously fucked up in my head—I was just good at keeping it buried deep.

"She was supposed to go back to work this Monday, but she called her boss and told him that she was taking an unpaid leave of absence due to 'issues with her pregnancy.' She couldn't understand why that pissed me off. That's like inviting bad juju and shit, for one. For the other, I know how much she loves her students, and I think it would have been good for her to be around them again." I finished off the last of my bottle of water, which had started to grow warm. As I pushed off from leaning on the tool bench, I crushed the water bottle, screwed the lid back on, and tossed it into the nearby recycle bin.

"Steph said she was heading over to y'all's house today to drag Becca out for lunch. Hopefully, she was able to talk to her. When Steph went through her shit, her counselor was great. Maybe she can get Becca to make an appointment with her."

Steph had been stalked, kidnapped, and tortured by her ex-boyfriend before Reaper had been able to rescue her. It was a tough time for them, but she had made it through with the love, help, and support of Reaper and her family.

"Maybe you could ask her to bring it up if she wasn't able to today. Anyway, thanks for listening to me bitch, Reaper. I think I'm going to clean up my area and call it a day. I'm going to go home and talk to Becca. Maybe I can get somewhere with her. If nothing else, I can make sure she knows I'm here for her." I wasn't going to lose her. No fucking way. The problem was, I could feel her slipping away from me little by little.

Hacker entered the garage, making a beeline for us. My chin tipped up in acknowledgement.

"What's up, bro?" Reaper greeted him.

"You got a minute, Hollywood?" The grim expression on his face had me curious, and my senses were pinging.

"Yeah, sure. Talk to me while I clean up?" At his affirmative nod, I began to put my tools and supplies away.

"Remember when you asked me to look into those pictures and shit that were posted on Becca's school back in Council Bluffs?" I nodded. "Well, I figured out where it all originated."

That had me stopped in my tracks. "Yeah?"

"Yeah. It was her piece-of-shit ex. He e-mailed the pics on her laptop to himself, and even though he deleted the e-mails from her computer, he didn't count on me. He's pretty good at hacking into simple stuff like social media sites, but he's got nothing on me. The dumb shit left a trail a mile long leading right to his digital door." That had him grinning. "Found e-mails he had with another computer geek about how he was sure it would make her go running back to him."

"Oh really? So maybe we need to return the favor to him? Just don't ruin him too bad—after all, his actions brought her to me. And *you're* a computer geek your damn self!" I laughed.

"No. I prefer computer genius. Do I look like a geek to you?" He held his tatted arms out to his sides, and I had to admit he was a buff motherfucker and about the furthest thing from a geek as there was. Laughing again, I shook my head at him and pitched a cleaning rag his way.

"You definitely don't fit the stereotype, bro," I agreed. My grin lasted until he gave me a mock salute and headed back toward his room.

That piece-of-shit asshole, Trevor, pissed me off because he hurt Becca, and for that I wanted to dot his eye, but I couldn't hate him because he unwittingly chased her into my arms instead of his. Between the number he pulled on her and the shit she had gone through thanks to the fucking Demon Runners, my baby was broken. Maybe I couldn't completely fix myself, but I would do everything in my power to fix her.

"Daddy!" My heart gave the same familiar lurch when Reaper's little girl, Remi, came running in with pigtails flying. Her little red converse shoes patted on the floor as she barreled into him. He scooped her up and spun her giggling bunch of preciousness in circles before plating a big kiss on her cheek. Her little arms wrapped tight around his neck as he stood next to me watching Steph approach him holding their stout little chunker, Wyatt. He had her blonde hair clenched tight in both chubby fists trying to shove it in his mouth despite Steph working diligently to get it loose of his grip.

God, I wanted that someday. Now it would seem it was becoming a reality. That was if I could get Bec through all this shit. Fuck, I was worried about her.

"Hey, beautiful. You see Becca today?" I kissed her on the cheek, earning a growl from Reaper. Laughing, I took Wyatt from her arms. I loved fucking with Reaper's possessive ass, especially since we both knew it was in fun and there were no worries.

"Yeah, hon. The kiddos and I had lunch with her. She seems to be doing okay, but she still seems a little… off. I tried to convince her to talk with my therapist, but I don't know how successful I was. Maybe mention it to her when you get home." Nodding, I kissed little Wyatt on his cheek and handed him back to his momma. Lastly, I patted Reaper on the shoulder, and he gave me a hug.

"Thanks, babe. I gotta finish cleaning up so I can get out of here. Talk to you guys later."

After everything was in its place, I walked out to my bike. Tossing a wave to Reaper, Steph, and some of the other guys who were heading out or into the back toward the clubhouse, I shrugged on my cut, straddled my ride, and started her up. Her rumble briefly soothed my soul, and I closed my eyes for a second to just simply *feel* before I revved the throttle, nodded my chin to the guys, and peeled out of the lot.

The ride home was short, but hell if I didn't still enjoy it. I shut off my stereo and let the wind, the hum of the tires on the asphalt, and the throaty rumble of my pipes all converge into my perfect form of meditation. The phrase "wind therapy" was not an incorrect rationalization for the feeling riding gave me.

As I pulled into the driveway, I stopped at the entrance for a moment to absorb the view of the house I had bought for Becca, our home. The love I felt for her rushed over me, and I knew I needed to get her to agree to seeking help so we could move forward for our baby boy.

After taking a fortifying breath, I glided up in front of the garage and came to a stop, pushed the kickstand down, turned the front wheel, and shut my bike off. The ticking of the motor followed me as I walked up the porch steps.

The house was quiet as I entered, and I tried to keep my noise level down so I didn't wake her. Lately, she had been so tired. Maybe I should plan a little getaway for us this weekend and take her out to the lake and rent one of the little cabins out there. We could have some alone time together. I dropped my keys on the table and wandered over to the couch.

After pulling my boots off and setting them at the end of the couch, I stood and walked to the bedroom. The door was open and the light was off, but there was no Becca lying in the bed. The bathroom was empty as well. So, she wasn't relaxing in the bedroom or the bath, maybe she was working on the rooms upstairs. I called out her name, and it seemed to resonate portentously in the empty house. She didn't answer, so I began to systematically search the house room by room, though deep down I knew I wasn't going to find her here.

Thumping down the steps, I told myself she must have decided to go out somewhere after all. My assumption that her car was in the garage must have been erroneous. I was surprised, but hopeful that she was coming around. When I pulled my phone out of my back pocket and dialed Becca, it went straight to voice mail. She must have left her charger behind again. She was always doing that despite me riding her ass about keeping one in her purse. It scared the shit out of me to think of her out there and not having a way to call for help or for us to find her if, God forbid, she found herself in another situation like before.

My next call was to Steph to see if Becca had called her or stopped by. As the phone rang, I walked back through the living room toward the kitchen. Passing the table, my gaze caught on a piece of paper I had missed when I came in and tossed my keys down. I began to read the note Becca left as I walked toward the kitchen for a beer.

The words seemed to crowd in my vision as I disconnected the call. My hand fisted around my phone, and the hand holding the paper clenched until the paper was no longer readable. My heart pounded and my breath caught before I launched my phone across the room, shattering it against the wall and leaving a dent in the sheetrock. It took me a few seconds for it to register that agonized cry I heard came from deep in my soul.

I drove like a raving lunatic down to Reaper and Steph's. My bike tore up the driveway, skidding to a stop and throwing small bits of loose asphalt as I reached the end of the driveway. Mind racing, my chest heaved with the inability to catch enough air in my lungs. I felt disconnected and my hands shook as I climb the stairs of their porch and banged on the door.

"Hollywood—" Steph started to greet me with a smile that quickly disintegrated as she took in my disheveled and frantic appearance.

"Where is she? Is she here?" In my anger and unraveled state, I barged into the house yelling Becca's name. Reaper came from the living room with a beer in his hand as I was pushing past Steph.

"Bro, what the fuck? I love you, but if you touch my wife like that again, you'll be picking your ass up off the floor. That's if you get up at all." Reaper looked at me with a mix of anger and astonishment in his ice blue eyes. My brain registered what he said, and I looked to Steph as understanding of my behavior sank in.

"Steph, babe, I'm… I'm sorry. My mind is not thinking right. Is she here?" Steph glanced to Reaper and held a hand up to him before looking me in the eye.

"What are you talking about? Becca? She was home and said she was going to take a nap when I left after lunch. Did you call her?" Steph looked at me with concern in her eyes. I had no idea if that concern was for Becca or me and my insane, unfamiliar behavior.

"Yes, of course I tried to call her. I just got voice mail." I shoved the crumpled letter at her because I didn't trust myself to speak more than I had. My brain felt on the verge of shutting down. Goddammit this was why I had never wanted to share my heart. Moisture battled behind my rapidly blinking eyes, and my hands gripped tightly in my hair as I slid down the wall to sit on the floor. She didn't have to read the letter out loud. It was burned in my memory already.

Mason,

I'm so sorry for handling things this way. You deserve better than this, but I need to get away. It's just all too much right now, and I need to get my head straight. Please don't try to find me, because I know you will, but I need some space to think. No matter what I decide, I won't keep your son from you, but I can't be there right now. Maybe ever. I just don't know. When I can, I'll be in touch.

Please know that I love you with all my heart, but I just don't know if that is enough. My mind is all over the place. I feel like I'm unraveling, and I can't put this on you while I try to get myself right. Take care of yourself.

Becca

"Oh my God, Hollywood. I'm so sorry. I didn't know. She didn't say anything about this to me today. I swear." She handed the crumpled-up note to Reaper before crouching down next to me. Her hand rested on my shoulder, and my agonized eyes met hers as I tried to figure out how I was going to just let her go. Despite telling myself it would be for the best, I couldn't do it. She was mine, and I loved her. Now I just needed to find her and show her she was stronger than she thought and we were even stronger together.

Chapter THIRTY-SIX

Becca

My mind continued to aimlessly wander as I stared out the window at the fields rushing by. The sky was so blue and the clouds were obscenely soft looking. They tempted me to reach up and try to grab ahold of them. The whine of the diesel engine lulled me into a peaceful stupor. My father was casting surreptitious glances my direction, but respected my fragile state for now and remained quiet.

He had called me shortly after Steph left with Remi and Wyatt and told me he was driving through. Imagine his surprise when I asked him to come by the house to pick me up and then when I walked out of my house with a bag in hand and climbed in his truck. Something told me he wasn't expecting me to go with him, even though I had asked him to get me.

Surprise, Dad!

He had met Mason once when he stopped on his way through town with a load on his way to Minneapolis. We had all had lunch, but I had introduced him as Mason and never mentioned that he was a member of the local MC. After my mother's reaction to Reaper and Steph, I just didn't want to give her a reason to call me and remind me how much I had disappointed her. Again.

My dad and Mason seemed to get along really well and had talked Army and classic cars through the entire lunch. As I hugged him goodbye that day, I had asked him not to mention Mason to Mom because I didn't want to endure her million questions about him and our relationship.

So, I knew he was dying to ask me what had happened and why I was heading down the highway with him. When I could pull the words together, I would talk to him, but at that moment, it was all I could do to hold myself together. As the miles continued to fly by, I felt myself drift off to sleep. My dreams were filled with the scent and feel of Mason wrapped all around me.

The truck coming to a stop woke me from my blissfully diverting dreams. For a moment, I was disoriented, until I remembered making the impulsive decision to leave with my truck driving father after he called. After hanging up with my dad, I had scratched out a hasty note to Mason and thrown a little bit of the clothing that still fit me and a few toiletries in a small duffle bag then raced out the door when my dad pulled up. At the time, it seemed like the perfect solution to my problems. Now I wasn't so sure, but I told myself the time away was going to do me good.

"Hey, Becca-girl, you sleep good? You can go lay in the back if you want to stretch out. I just need to fill up and stretch these old legs and we'll be back on the road. No pressure, sweetheart, but I'm heading into South Dakota with a load I'm dropping off tonight and then taking a load back down to Nebraska. After that, I was heading home for a few days. So, when you feel like talking, you need to let me know if you're coming home with me or what your plans are. Okay?" My gaze flickered over to my father, taking in his full, red beard with the gray weaving through it. A small, fleeting smile crossed my face at the memories of being a little girl and braiding his beard. My bear of a father was such a gentle giant my whole life, and he never let me forget I was the best thing that ever happened to him.

"I know, Daddy. Thank you." The truth was, I didn't really know what the hell I was doing. Guilt was beginning to eat away at me for my cowardly escape. Mason didn't deserve what I had done. God, I fucked up. Making a mental note to call him after my dad and I talked, I rested my head back on the seat and stared listlessly out the window. My dad slipped out a frustrated sigh, climbed down from the driver's seat, and began to pump fuel in his truck. He climbed back in and pulled forward to park his truck in preparation to go inside the truck stop. Once he backed in to an empty spot, he started to get out of the truck.

"I'm pregnant, Dad." It was a soft whisper, and I wasn't sure if he would even hear me. I just needed to get it out. Silence greeted me, but I knew he was still facing me as he had begun to step down and froze.

"Becca?" My dad's strong, gruff voice quivered as he said my name. Tears streaked down my cheeks in wavering rivulets, and my breath came in shaky bursts. My hand covered my mouth as if it could hold in my silent sob. What I had always imagined as a happy, excited time in my life, which would be shared with my parents in a moment of joy, was blurted out in emotional strife. After all, my parents were going to be grandparents; I was going to be a mother. This should be a time of celebration and happiness, right?

My father had yet to move, and I knew he was waiting for confirmation of what he thought he heard. It felt like an impossibility to turn my head and meet my father's eyes. Shame flooded me. Not because I was pregnant and not married. Not because the father of my child was a biker. Shame because I had waited so long to tell them and because I was being a coward by running. Once again.

"Yeah, Dad. You're going to be a grandpa…" Slowly turning my gaze to him, I worried my bottom lip with my teeth. "The baby is Mason's." Well, that was dumb and obvious, I supposed.

"Well… Becca… honey. I, uh, I don't know what to say. The thought of becoming a grandfather warms my old soul, Becca-girl, but you don't seem happy, and… well… you're here with me and that baby's father is back in Grantsville. Do you want to come in and have a cup of coffee with me and we can talk? Damn, you really know how to catch an old man off guard, sweetheart. Give an old man a little warning before dropping bombs like that."

A blubbering laugh escaped my lips briefly at my dad's ability to bring humor to my moment of recklessness. Today I had acted without thought. My impulsive decision to leave was affecting not just me, but Mason, my friends, my family, and my unborn baby, whom my hand rested softly over. Steph didn't even know where I had gone, or the I had gone *at all.*

Incapable of words at that moment, I just nodded and climbed out of the truck. My feet shuffled in trepidation, like a prisoner off to the gallows, as I made my way around the truck to face my father. Damn, I hated the thought of disappointing my dad. As I came face to face with the man I loved more than life itself and who loved me unconditionally, I expected disappointment to emanate from him, but I saw only worry and love as he held his arms wide open for me to fall into.

"Daddy…" My sobs broke through, and I stood in a busy truck stop soaking my dad's red plaid shirt with tears that wouldn't stop as he held me, smoothing my hair and whispering soothing words of comfort into my ear.

Chapter THIRTY-SEVEN

Hollywood

I was exhausted as I pulled my bike up in front of the rust-colored house with scattered spots where the paint was peeling away from the siding. White trim surrounded the windows and the porch. The yard was well kept and the flower beds were meticulous. The breeze coming off the lake felt good as it blew gently through my hair, which stood on end after I pulled off my helmet.

By the time I got Becca's parents' address out of Steph it was after seven. Another three hours to get here, and it was now after ten at night. Was it too late to knock on the door? I hated to be a dick and wake up Becca's parents, but I didn't think I could wait until tomorrow to see her. Deep inside, I knew she had run home. There was nowhere else I could imagine her going, and believe me, I searched.

Hacker had checked her credit card and bank card for activity, but nothing.

It ripped me in two to think she ran from me, that she didn't have the faith or trust in me to wait and talk to me, but I wasn't going to give up on her. For about two seconds, my anger turned me defensive and I was pissed at her and told myself, if she didn't want to be with me, then fuck her, but deep down I knew that was bullshit and I would die fighting to keep her. Some things in life were worth fighting for. My family was one of those things.

After I set my helmet up on top of my right mirror, I swung my leg off my bike and stood looking at the front door of the house. Stretching out my tired muscles, my eyes glanced briefly at a weather old "Semi Parking Only" sign. Becca's dad's sign. The one her dad boasted she bought him when she was a young teen. Her father was a big, gruff dude, and he and I hit it off right away the day we had lunch with him. I hadn't met her mom, but with a nervous breath, I knew that was about to change.

Placing one heavy foot in front of another, I moved closer to the door. My fist raised and knocked three short raps on the door. Silence met my knocks. My fist was raising to knock again, when the porch light flicked on and I heard movement on the other side of the door. The door opened with the chain still in place, and Becca's green eyes in the face of an older woman with blonde hair looked at me with reservation.

"Mrs. Kannan?"

"Yes?" She continued to look at me with question and suspicion in her eyes.

"Ummm, my name is Mason. I'm…" I didn't even get the rest of the words out before the door slammed shut. *Well fuck*. Then I heard the scrape of the chain and the door flew open.

"Oh my God. You're Becca's man! Come in, come in!" *Becca's man…* why did I love the sound of that so damn much? She ushered me in and motioned for me to follow her into the kitchen. My eyes took in my surroundings, out of habit, and I noticed a comfortable and extremely neat home. In my mind, I pictured Becca running through the house at various stages of her life. Unbidden, I felt a smile take over my face.

"I made a chocolate cream pie today. Would you like a slice? Sit down, sit down! Make yourself at home." She bustled around the kitchen, pulling out small plates, cups, and silverware. Evidently, no answer was a "yes" for Becca's mom. She sliced a healthy piece of pie and set it in front of me. "What can I get you to drink?"

"Water, please, ma'am." Becca must have gone to bed, so I settled in to visit with her mother while she rested. Now that I had made it here, there was time for me to talk to her in the morning. Since she hadn't been sleeping well, maybe being safe in her childhood home would give her the peace she would need to sleep well.

"'Ma'am'? Oh hell, don't make me feel old! Please, call me Gina. I must say, you made quite an impression on Rob, my husband. He spoke very highly of you, and that doesn't happen very often. Becca is the apple of his eye, and I don't think anyone has ever been good enough for our girl in his eyes." She smiled at me, causing small creases to form around her bright green eyes. "Now tell me, what do I owe the pleasure? Did you have business in town? Is Becca coming too?"

"Wait. What? She's not here?" My heart began to pound as adrenaline pulsed through my veins. I thought for sure she had headed here. My fork dropped next to my plate and my appetite disappeared like a wisp of smoke.

"Here? Why would she be here, Mason? She has a new job and well… you now. I can't lie to you and tell you that it hasn't torn me up inside that she rarely calls me anymore, but I know she needed time to get past her anger with me. I really only wanted what I thought was best for her. She's my only baby, you know. I just want her to be settled and happy." Her face showed grief, and it aged her immediately, though it didn't diminish her beauty. It was easy to see where

Becca had gotten her stunning looks from. Her mother was an attractive older woman.

"Mrs. Kannan—Gina, Becca left earlier today. She, well, I guess we had a falling out, and I thought she came here. Steph gave me your address, and I got here as quickly as I could. You haven't talked to her? She's not answering her phone to me. She's having, ummm, a hard time, and I thought she came here to ground herself again." My hand mussed my hair as it ran absently through it. Her expression told me she hadn't spoken with Becca and had no idea what I was talking about.

"Mason, she hasn't called me in ages now. She's definitely not here. Wait, let me call Rob, maybe he's talked to her. Unfortunately, he tends to talk to her more than I do lately." She appeared sad. Then she jumped up and grabbed a cell phone from the counter by the back door. My patience was wearing thin, and my anxiety was rising by the minute.

Where the fuck are you, Becca? I tried to utilize the breathing exercises my shrink had me try way back when, but it wasn't really helping.

"Rob? Have you heard from Becca? Mason is here because he thought she was here. Now I'm starting to get worried.... What? What the hell, Rob? Why didn't you call me?.... Okay. Sure, hon, I understand. She's okay, though?.... Okay, yes, baby, I'll keep him right here." Her eyes met mine, and her eyebrows raised at me as if she was daring me to argue. My hands raised in mock surrender. "Yes, I love you too. Okay, I'll see you late tomorrow morning. Drive safe." She pressed the end button and set her phone down on the table.

"What did he say? Is Becca okay? He talked to her?" I wanted to shake her, but I was trying desperately to hold my shit together. Patience was waning fast with me, but it wasn't her fault.

"She's with him now." Relief flooded through me. "He couldn't call earlier because she has been awake and upset. She just dozed off, and he hadn't had a chance to call me. He told me to keep you here if it meant I had to tie you to a chair. Do you want to tell me what that is all about?" Her expression was one I had seen my own mother use when she was waiting for me to explain my actions after I got in trouble for some wild stunt or another as a kid.

"Gina, I think we need to let Becca fill you in. She wouldn't appreciate me running my mouth, and I am so tired I can barely think straight anyway. Now, if you trust me enough that I won't leave town after driving all this way to find her, I'm going to try to get a hotel room." Wearily, I rose from the table. Her hand shot out and grasped mine.

"Nonsense. I have two spare rooms, well, one is technically still Becca's, but either way, they are both available. You can stay here, and I'm not taking no for an answer. It's not that I don't trust you, but you may as well be here when she gets here. Okay?" Her expression brooked no argument.

"If you're sure. I don't want to burden you or anything." Her eyebrow raised, and I tiredly smiled at her tenacity. "Okay, I'll go grab my bag from my bike, and I'll be right back in." When I stood, she followed suit and then embraced me. It was a little awkward at first, but she grasped my upper arms in her hands as she pulled back, and I saw her eyes glisten with unshed tears.

"No burden at all. Rob told me how happy you've made our girl. She may not believe me, but I've only ever wanted the best for her. While I'm not a big fan of those crazy bikes you and your friends ride, I really just want my baby girl to be happy. Please don't let me down."

"No, ma'am—um, Gina. I sure don't intend to." Becca and I had a lot to discuss when she got here. First thing being that she was not ever running off on me again. The next being where we went from here. One thing I knew for sure was that Becca and our son were everything to me and she was coming home with me. There was no way I was taking no for an answer, and if I had to stay here to convince her, I would stay as long as it took.

Sleeping in Becca's childhood bed without her left me with one of the worst night's sleep in a long time. Should have slept in the spare bed, but I thought being in her old bed would make me feel closer to her as I slept. Unfortunately, my nightmares haunted me each time she wasn't physically there to ground my soul. The only problem with her winding herself so deep into my heart and soul was she also became leverage for my demons. My dreams were filled with images of her being part of all the worst memories of my military missions. That was something that really fucked with my head.

So, it was no wonder I woke feeling like I had been in a cage fight all night. Between hauling ass down here on my bike, staying up talking with her mom all night, then add my restless sleep to the mix, and I was sucking when I rolled over and literally fell out of the full-sized bed. Fuck, I missed my king-sized bed I shared with her.

The smell of bacon cooking led me straight to the kitchen, and I had to look at the time to see if I had inadvertently slept in too late. I was usually an early riser, but after the night I'd had, it wouldn't have surprised me. It would seem Gina was an even earlier riser than me.

Gina was piling bacon onto a plate lined with paper towels, and she looked up as I walked in the doorway. Another plate was full of scrambled eggs, and the toaster popped up just as she moved the pan from the burner and turned off the stovetop.

"Good morning, Mason. Sleep well?" she asked.

"Yes, ma'am. Thank you." No way was I telling her about my night. Some things you just didn't go sharing with everyone.

"Now what did I tell you about that 'ma'am' business, young man?" She gave me a stern look as she held a clean plate out to me. "Help yourself. I'm pretty sure you didn't feed yourself before heading down here, so you must be hungry."

"Hungry? Yes, ma—uh, I mean, Gina. I could eat, that's for sure.

Thank you." Accepting the plate she gave me, I motioned for her to dish up her plate first. "Ladies first."

Her cheeks flushed and she shook her head at me but added food to her plate. "Coffee is in the pot over there on the counter."

Filling the cup she'd left sitting by the pot, I inhaled the rich smell of the dark coffee before carrying the cup and my plate to the table and having a seat. We ate in companionable silence for a bit before I asked, "Did Rob say what time he expected to arrive?"

"He has to drop his current load in Lincoln at about seven, so by the time he unloads, drives here, drops the trailer off at the shop, then bobtails back here, I'm guessing about ten at the latest." She sipped her coffee. "So, it may be my husband's place to ask this, but may I ask what your intentions are with my little girl? You two have been living together, and she hasn't talked to me much, so I wasn't sure… well… Look, it has really bothered me that things between her and I have deteriorated. I'm not sure what all she told you about it." Her eyes stayed trained on the cup she held cradled in her hands.

"So, first answer, I don't plan on letting her get away from me, and I'm hoping she'll make an honest man of me." I grinned, and she looked up at me and laughed. That was better. "Second, she didn't really get into details, just that you disagreed with her decision to leave that ass—uh, the guy she was dating." Shit, my mouth was gonna ruin me with Becca's mom if I wasn't careful. She probably wouldn't understand what years of working combat arms in the Army, being in the Ranger Bat., and then the last few years surrounded by bikers did to your language. Either way, they were both men's worlds, but come to think of it, I needed to watch my mouth anyway, or my boy's first word was going to be shit, fuck, or asshole.

"Trevor was a nice guy, and I can't lie and tell you I wasn't disappointed when they split, but I've had time to think about it, and never in a million years would I want her to stay in a relationship that didn't make her happy. And I would say that about the two of you as well. I'm not just saying that because they ended. Mason, she's my little girl. The only one I had and the only one I'll ever have. When I said I want her happy, I meant it." She had just stood to take her plate to the sink when there was a knock on the door.

We both looked at the clock and she said, "It's definitely too early for it to be Rob and Becca. I'll be right back." Finishing my coffee, I nodded then took my plate to the sink. Her voice murmured at the door with whoever was there, then I heard the other voice raise, before she yelled, "Trevor!" in shock.

Spinning to face the kitchen doorway, I prepared for the footsteps I heard heading my way.

"Who the hell are you?" A man about my height with dark brown hair and squinted eyes shouted as he entered the kitchen. "I saw a bike out front, and I knew there was no one they knew who had a bike. So, who are you and what the hell are you doing here? Gina! Is Becca messing around with this piece of shit? Is that why you wouldn't tell me where she was?" he yelled at Gina.

This motherfucker was about to get up close and personal with my fist if he didn't stop where he was, but nope, he had to keep closing in on me. If there was one thing I could say about myself, it was I didn't like being cornered, and I sure as shit didn't like people I didn't know getting up in my personal space.

"Dude, you might want to stop right there. I don't fucking know you, and you sure as shit don't need to raise your voice to Gina or me unless you want your fucking ass kicked." There goes my mouth again. He may have been my height, but he was a skinny asshole. Some might call him "lean," but I liked to tell it like it was—he was a scrawny bastard. There wasn't a doubt in my mind I could take him blindfolded, but I would prefer it not be in Becca's parents' home.

He bristled at my words and stuck out his chest, trying to look tough. Damn, what the fuck had she seen in this dumbass? Shaking my head and laughing at him, because I knew that would piss him off more than words, I reached over to the door going to the backyard from the kitchen.

"Why don't we go outside to talk like men. This doesn't really concern Gina." Talking wasn't exactly what I had in mind, but I figured if I asked him to come outside so I could kick his ass, he probably wouldn't be too keen on that. Gina stood out in the front hall looking in the kitchen with her phone clutched tight to her chest. Man, I hoped she didn't call the cops, because I wanted to deal with this asshole myself. Catching eye contact with her, I gave a slight shake of my head for her not to do or say anything.

As he advanced on me, I reached behind me and opened the door, backing out onto the back patio. Let him think I was backing away from him because I was afraid. Stupid prick. I was afraid of no man.

Making sure I was plenty far from the house and any patio furniture that would get in the way, I braced myself for the attack I knew this dumb fucker was going to try.

"I don't know who you are, but what I do know is you're nothing but trash, and it's only a matter of time before Becca comes back to me where she belongs. Just because she and I had a falling out, don't think things are over with us. She loves me. We've been together too long for her to just throw us away. By the looks of you and that crappy bike, you will never be able to provide for her like I can," he sneered. Goddamn, this guy was completely delusional.

"Look, buddy, you're fooling yourself if you think you have a snowball's chance in hell at Becca going back to you. She fucking lives with me. Sleeps in my bed every fucking night. Not to mention, the stupid shit you pulled with posting those pics sealed the deal. Were you really dumb enough to think that was going to make her go running back to you?" Laughing and shaking my head at him in an attempt to egg him on, I watched him closely for the moment he snapped. Aaaaaand there it was.

He charged me.

What I wasn't expecting was the dumbass to have a gun that he pulled out and pointed at me before he ran toward me with it pointing right at my head. Well, this fucker just made things interesting. My piece was tucked neatly in the back waist of my pants, but he was unstable and I didn't want my movements to cause him to shoot my ass. *Why me, Lord, why me?*

"Whoa, man, what the hell? There's no need for that shit. We're at Becca's family's *home*. You don't want to do this here." Both of my hands were held up where he could see them. You know, kind of like I was surrendering, which I sure as shit wasn't. Trevor lurched and pointed the gun at me with a shaking hand until it was within inches of my nose. Jesus, it was dumbasses like this tool that gave guns and people with concealed carry licenses a bad name.

"Shut up! We're going to leave here. You're going to come with me, and you're not going to try anything funny," he spat out at me.

Okay. Right. Time out. So, let me explain something to you. I was a little crazy, right? Hell, ask the VA. "Reckless behavior, PTSD, non-compliant, poor decision making," blah, blah, blah… Not all true, but a semblance of truth in it all. Anyway, not all of my decisions were the best, but I'd be damned if someone was going to threaten me, and not only that, but do it in my girl's family's fucking backyard. So, I kind of made a dumb decision here. Sorry.

"Fuck off," I sneered at him. Right before I punched him square in the face.

Thankfully, it worked out in my benefit, and when blood sprayed from his nose, he reached up—gun still in his hand, by the way—to cover it with both hands. So, I flat-hand shoved the side of the gun into his already broken nose, twisted it out of his hand, and punched him in the gut. That was enough to drop him down to his knees before I kicked him backward.

He was rolling around on the ground crying and holding his nose like the little pussy he was. When Gina pushed out through the screen door, I was bent over slightly with the gun still clutched in my hand, my other hand resting on my knee.

"Oh my God, Mason! Trevor! What the heck are you two doing?"

she exclaimed in shock.

"Ma—I mean, Gina, now would be a good time to call the police, unless our friend Trevor wants to just call his behavior stupid and leave. For good." *Please say you'll leave, fucker.* I really didn't want the fucking cops there, but the asshole took things a little far, and I didn't want someone getting hurt by this lunatic. If we had been anywhere but there, I would have beat the ever-loving shit out of him.

"I'll go. I'll go! Leave the cops out of it. I'll lose my job if you call the cops. It's bad enough that I'm on administrative leave because I got hacked and all my shit is fucked up. They'll fire me for sure if you call the cops." The pussy whined like a baby. Fucker should lose his job, but I just wanted him gone and out of Becca's and my life for good.

"Then take your stupid ass and get out of here. If you so much as drive by this house, they will be calling the cops on your ass. You get me?" I did my very best not to kick him square in his head with my boot. If Gina hadn't have been out there, I probably would have. My teeth ground in frustration.

True to his word, he rolled over to his knees with his head on the ground before he got up and rushed out the gate of the backyard. I tucked his gun into my inner pocket of my cut after wrapping it in my bandana. He sure wasn't getting it back. Dumb fuck.

"Gina, I'm sorry that happened here." Goddammit, I hoped I didn't just fuck myself with her.

"Mason, no, I'm just so glad you were here. He's been coming by asking about Becca since she left. Never in a million years… Lord, I never thought he would do anything like that. Are you okay? You have blood on your hand." She reached for my right hand, but I deftly pulled it back.

"I'm okay. Are you all right?" She looked shaken, but she was holding it together pretty good.

"Of course I am. I'm just in shock that he would behave like that. My God, what if Becca had stayed with him and he had done something to her? How on Earth could I have been so wrong about him? I can't thank you enough for being here. Jesus Lord. Let's go inside and get you cleaned up." She turned and headed inside, and I followed. Her words about Becca with him had my temper boiling. Yeah, I was a possessive fucker, and I hated to think of her with that douche. It also pissed me off that I couldn't leave more of an impression on him.

Damn, I hated to have to tell Becca about this, but I knew I would. What I *was* looking forward to telling her was how Hacker had transferred all his money out of his bank account and into multiple other bank accounts with bogus names, trashed his credit, and cancelled all of his insurances. This was after taking out multiple credit cards in his name and then maxing them out on porn sites. It was going to take him forever to get shit straightened out. Inwardly, I chuckled, imagining the mess he had to deal with. Served him right.

Chapter THIRTY-EIGHT

Becca

My dad had dropped his trailer off after unloading outside of Omaha and we were bobtailing back home. Despite my ire with my mother and the events of the last several months, I was looking forward to being home and seeing her. Regardless of all the bullshit, I loved her and I hated that I left with things so crappy between us. More guilt assuaged me as I thought about my piss-poor choices lately.

Dad and I had been talking a lot since yesterday. I had cried and bitched and cried some more. He took every tirade and bout of blubbering in stride, though I knew it pushed him well out of his comfort zone—just another reason I loved him. He would move the moon and stars for me and not grumble a bit. My hormones at that point in time were really pushing the limits of his abilities though.

The familiar curves of the roads on Lake Manawa shook me out of my introspection. The memories of my youth assailed me as they did every time I drove out to my parents' home. When the familiar red house came into view, my heart jumped into my throat. Sitting in the driveway of my childhood home was a familiar motorcycle. When I realized I was holding my breath, I looked over to my father with wild eyes before looking back to the bike and nervously rolling the hem of my hoodie.

"Daddy, no. Turn around, keep going, whatever, just no. No. Not yet. No." I wasn't ready to face Hollywood yet. I just couldn't. He was going to be so pissed and disappointed in me. Even though I knew I'd been a coward to leave like I did, at the time, I just needed to get away. I needed time to regroup and ground myself here.

"Becca-girl, look at me." My father's deep voice was soft, but his tone tolerated no argument. It was one I was very familiar with. My eyes reluctantly met his again, and I swallowed the lump lodged deep in my throat.

"That man is the father of your baby, and if I'm not mistaken, he loves you and that baby. A man doesn't drive over three hours in the middle of the night chasing after a woman that he doesn't care about. From everything we talked about last night and this morning, I'm also assuming you love him too. So, it seems to me, you owe it to that grandbaby of mine to talk things out and get this situation figured out. Now whatever you decide, we'll be here for you, and you always have a home with us, but you already know that. I didn't say a word to your mother about the baby. I figured you could share that joy with her yourself. I love you, Becca-girl."

My father, the gruff, burly truck driver was the last one you would expect to be compassionate and observant. And well, I knew he was right. I needed to talk to Mason. It was time to put my big girl panties on and figure this shit out.

The truck rumbled then went silent as my dad turned off the

ignition. Lost in thought, I sat staring at the house, unmoving for a moment before I pulled up those figurative big girl panties and looked at my dad. He clasped my hand in his large one, eclipsing mine. With his gentle squeeze and a nod toward the house, I slowly and reluctantly opened the truck door and climbed down. My eyes met my dad's one last time before I shuffled up to the door and reached for the doorknob.

Here goes nothing.

My mom's head peeked around the doorway to the kitchen, and when it registered with her who was coming in, she ran toward me and hugged me tightly to her. Once again, I found myself fighting to hold back tears. "Mom…"

"Oh, baby, I've missed you. I wish you hadn't just run off after all that business with those computer pictures. No one who matters believes any of that crap, but I'm not going to go on about that. There is someone here who has been waiting for you."

Like I hadn't figured that out when I saw the bike in the driveway, Mom. Thanks for stating the obvious. I knew she didn't mean anything by it, so I kept my mocking thoughts to myself.

I didn't even have to see him to sense him. It was like my very molecules were attuned to him. My hand sought the comfort of my mother's hand, and I walked with her to the kitchen. Golden eyes raised to mine, and Mason stood, for once looking uncertain in my presence. My mom squeezed my hand as she released me. Of their own volition, my feet took two steps toward him, and he stepped toward me. God, he was so gorgeous. My chest fluttered just being near him. There was no question, I loved this man with all my heart.

His hands reverently framed my face, and he brushed a loose curl behind my ear. His hand gently raised my chin until I was looking him full in the eye.

"God, baby, don't ever do that to me again. You are my world, my *everything.* You have no idea how bad you scared me. And the heartache… shit, baby. How are you feeling? How's the—" My finger came up to rest on his lips as I stole a furtive glance toward my mom, only to realize she had silently left the room to leave us alone to talk.

"Let's go for a walk, okay?" This just wasn't the place for us to talk, so I led him out into the yard and, looking both ways like I was taught as a child, tugged him across the road to the edge of the lake. We were away from the beach area, so the grass went nearly to the edge, only a one to two-foot section of rocky, pebbly sand separating it from the water. This was my quiet place, and I had come here often as a child and teen to absorb the peaceful lap of the water at the shore. My dad and I had fished here, rarely catching anything worth a damn, but enjoying each other's company nonetheless. It was here that I dropped to the ground and waited for Mason to sit next to me.

Our fingers twined as he settled next to me, his jeans barely brushing against my thigh, our joined hands resting in my lap.

"I'm so sorry for running off like I did. My mind has been so messed up. I'm stupid paranoid. The dreams… they're just… God, I don't know. Horrible. I don't want my parents to know about the kidnapping. For one, I don't want them to blame you and your club, but also, I don't want them to worry and stress over something they cannot change." I took a deep, fortifying breath. "And I'll go to therapy, if you think it will help."

My eyes met his. The breeze ruffled the hair on the top of his head and blew a tendril of my dark red locks across my face, which he once again tucked behind my ear.

"Baby, I'm not trying to be an ass about the therapy, really I'm not, but I'm terrified to think of you letting this all build until I find my beautiful woman in the same boat as Reaper was when I found him again. Believe me when I say I know how hard it can be to feel 'normal' after something traumatic like that happens, and that is *not* a place I ever want you to be. I try so hard to stay the upbeat, happy-go-lucky guy that let's everything roll off my back, but, baby, I'm fucked up inside too. The club? They help me because I trust them, and I know they have my back in any situation. But you? Baby, you keep me sane. I just want you to have the best chance to work through all of this and come out with the ability to cope with what happened. I want us to be able to be there for each other and to be the best parents possible for our little man." He leaned in, cradling the back of my neck with his hand. As he leaned closer to press his lips to mine, I started to lay back, bringing him with me. We were right along the road, but the steep slope of the bank concealed us from passersby.

He pulled back slightly and my lips quivered in disappointment.

"Bec, baby." He closed his eyes briefly before looking me in the eyes and shocking the ever-loving shit out of me. "Trevor stopped by this morning. It turned into a shitshow, but he's gone, and he won't be bothering you again." Then he proceeded to tell me what happened and about how Hacker had found out it was Trevor who posted those pictures, hoping I would run back to him for comfort and a place to live when I lost my job. Damn, I thought Trevor was a dull bookworm, geek type. Who would have thought he would be capable of all that?

Though I hated that he and Mason had the altercation in my parents' backyard, I was glad Mason had been there to handle the situation. What if he had used the gun on my mom? Or me if I had been there? God, my life had become a TV drama series.

My hand reached up to brush along the firmness of Mason's cheek, bristling against the short growth of beard he had going on.

"Thank you for coming for me. Thank you for being there for my mom. Even though I ran off like a fool, thank you for not giving up on me." My hands urged him toward me to finish the kiss we were so close to before.

When his lips met mine, I felt that same tingle and rush that I felt every single time. He twisted his upper body to rest on one elbow, allowing his other hand to slide up my thigh and tuck into the hem of my shorts, where he just let it rest, but lightly rubbed small circles with his fingertips. We broke the soft kiss, looking into each other's eyes for God only knows how long.

"God, Becca, I love you. That's something I never thought I would say to any woman other than my mother, but I do. I fucking love the hell out of you. We can do this together. I swear to you."

"I love you too, Mason. So very much."

Hollywood

Becca and I lay in the grass alongside the lake for at least an hour. We just held each other, touching each other to reassure ourselves that the other was really still there. Fluffy clouds skittered across the expanse of soft blue as we enjoyed the sound of the water lapping at the shore. The sun rose higher in the sky, and I heard her stomach rumble before her slender hand went to it as if she could silence it.

She was so fucking cute. My hand covered hers and slid lower to cradle the little bump that existed below her belly button. How I had missed the slight changes in her body was a fucking mystery. In my defense, she still didn't look like she was as far along as she was. It was hard to believe my son was growing in that diminutive mound. It just didn't seem possible. Also still amazing to me was how happy the news of pending fatherhood had made me. Yeah, I had been a little envious of what Reaper and Steph had—a family—but I always saw myself as someone who would be happy spoiling everyone else's kids. It just goes to show, despite our firmest resolutions, sometimes life takes us by the balls and runs with us. All we can hope for is to hold on.

And make new resolutions.

In reverence, I leaned forward to place a kiss over his current cozy home and to whisper words that were just between me and my boy. Becca's fingers ran through my hair, and I rested my ear to her belly as if my little man would speak back to me.

When I raised my head to look at her, her hand slid to rest on my neck.

"Becca, baby, my son and I have been talking." She giggled at my serious tone as I told her about my father-son conversation. "What? You doubt me?" I asked in mock indignation.

"Oh, no," she laughingly replied. "Please do tell."

"Hmph! Well… as I was saying before I was so rudely interrupted, my son and I have been talking, and he told me—" I paused to glare at her while really trying hard not to smile, daring her to interrupt me again. "—he doesn't want his daddy to be a single father, and he would really like his mommy and him to have the same last name as his daddy. He really wants us to be a real family, and I can't seem to find a reason to disagree with him. So… what do you think? Will you do me the honor of becoming my wife and making an honest man of me? We need to set a good example for our little man and teach him that living in sin is totally unacceptable. I don't have a ring yet, because this wasn't exactly how I planned to do this, but sometimes the right time hits us when we don't see it coming."

At the catch in her breath, my grin broke through all my attempts at holding a straight face. Her face registered shock and happiness, and her eyes welled with tears before she grabbed my face, pulling me up until our noses touched.

"God, yes. Yes, I will make an honest man of you and set a good example for our son. I will be your wife and our son's mommy, making us our own special little family. I love you, Mason. Yes. Yes, I will marry you! And I don't care about the ring at all." Her lips parted, and I kissed her like it was my last kiss on earth. She was going to be mine. Irrefutably, undeniably mine. When we broke apart for air, I rested my forehead against hers and spoke through my shortness of breath.

"Then I would say we have quite a bit to talk to your parents about. And we need to feed my growing boy." I stood, reaching down to grab her hands and pull her up against me as she stood. My hands slipped around her, and I grabbed her ass, hiking her up against me, and she wrapped her legs around me. I walked up the hill, careful not to drop my precious treasure, looked both ways, and ran across the road with her bouncing and giggling against me.

"Put me down, you nut!" I loved the sound of her laughter, but I wasn't stopping until we had her parents as witness to her agreeing to be my wife, so I bounded up the stairs and released her with one hand briefly to open the door.

"Rob! Gina! Where are you? Your daughter has something to tell you!" I shouted out as she laughed and attempted to cover my mouth, but I shook her hands away. They came from the hall and stopped with Rob resting his hands on Gina's shoulders. He gave me an approving grin, and Gina looked at us expectantly.

"Oh hell, I didn't expect to tell you all like this, but... Mom? You're going to be a grandma and Mason has asked me to marry him. I said yes." She bit her full bottom lip and worried it between her beautiful white teeth. Hearing her say yes out loud again tripped my heart into overdrive. She may or may not know it, but she had just made me the happiest fucker that ever existed.

Gina covered her mouth with both hands, her eyes grew wide and glossy before turning quickly to face her husband. "Rob! Did you know about this?"

"She just told me about the baby, sweetheart. I promise I haven't kept anything from you, honey." He stroked the back of her hair and placed a kiss to her forehead. That was what I hoped to have between Becca and me after as many years. "Now, son, what if I told you that you don't have my permission to marry my daughter?" He raised an eyebrow at me as he continued to look sternly at me. The twinkle in his eye gave away the true nature of his mood.

"Well, sir, I would have to tell you that while I respect you, the decision is up to your beautiful daughter... and I promise to protect and cherish her and our baby for the rest of my days on this earth. I love your daughter and our baby more than life itself, and I need her in my life because of that love…" Besides, there was no way in hell anyone was telling me I couldn't be with them, but I wasn't going to push my luck. I set Becca down and kissed her cheek. She smelled like sunshine, fresh air, and heaven.

"Stop it, Daddy! *Gawd!*" Becca rolled her eyes as she turned and pressed her back to my front. My arms wrapped around her, pulling her close to me, and her hands rested on my arms. My heart felt near to bursting with the love and happiness she brought into my life.

"Mom, Dad… Trust me, it was a surprise to Mason and me too. I'm over a third way through my pregnancy, and I haven't even known for that long. Sooo… you're going to have a grandson. It's a boy!" Becca squealed. Gina squealed. And I grinned like a fool.

Becca's mom rushed to her, framing Becca's face with her hands. I gently released Becca from the cradle of my arms as she embraced her mom. They both began with the waterworks, and Rob rolled his eyes as he walked over, placed a kiss on his daughter's and wife's heads, and said to me, "Come on, son, let's leave these two blubbering women to plan baby and wedding stuff and go out back to have a cold beer to celebrate."

Grinning ear to ear, I followed Becca's burly giant of a father out to the back-yard after he grabbed two beers from the fridge. Hell, I was glad he hadn't decided to punch me for this situation, because he would have crippled my ass. Damn, he was a big ol' dude. We settled into a couple of Adirondack chairs and enjoyed the wind rustling through the leaves of the shade trees in the back-yard.

As I sipped my beer, he looked me in the eye. "Gina told me about the visit from Trevor. Thank you for being here for her. Never really liked that guy, but I thought Becca and her mother did, so I supported what I thought was Becca's choice. Then when they broke up, Gina was so sure it was a mistake and, well, she's my wife. You'll learn that sometimes it pays to not make waves. But it seems in this case, I really messed up."

His hand scrubbed down his face, pulling on his beard at the end. “I want your word that you will protect my baby girl and my grandson with your life. Treat her like the treasure she is, and we’ll be good. She’s my only child, and I couldn’t handle it if anything happened to her or I lost her.” His words were softly spoken and gruff.

“Not an issue whatsoever.” That was a promise I would easily keep, as they were my life too. The thought of what she had already endured made me doubly vested in ensuring her safety. Never again would she be in danger if I could help it. We clinked bottles and got lost in our thoughts during the comfortable silence that stretched between us.

If I had stuck to my stupid resolution to stay away from relationships, she wouldn’t be in my life and my baby wouldn’t have been conceived. Funny how fate changed everything we thought we knew.

Becca Lange… Man, I loved the sound of that…

Epilogue

Gabriel Mason Lange made his debut into the big bad world in the wee hours of the morning… the very day after his parents were married. No wedding night bliss or happy honeymoon for them. His mom and dad were both exhausted after seven hours of hard labor on no sleep, but as the nurse laid him on his mother's chest, she gently stroked his silky golden hair and ran a finger along his rosy, round cheek. His daddy nearly cried when she asked him if he wanted to hold his son, but he would never in a million years admit it. His hands shook slightly as he reached for his little man. He tucked him in close to his body and bowed his head to whisper in his baby boy's ear.

"Now we both can keep your mommy safe, little guy. And when your sister comes along, I'm going to need you to watch out for her too. But we won't tell Mommy we're planning a little sister for you yet. On second thought, maybe you need a little brother so the three of us can watch over your momma. She's feisty and stubborn, so we may need back-up."

Mason would have sworn his son smiled at him in agreement; his mommy would have said it was gas. Either way, the love emanating from the room was nearly palpable as little Gabriel's grandparents and multiple "uncles" poured into the room later that morning. Reaper clapped Hollywood on the back, congratulating him while Steph kissed Becca and told her what a great job she had done. Everyone was so excited to see the newest addition to the family that Hacker went unnoticed as he leaned in the corner with a desolate expression.

Becca held tight to Mason's hand as everyone fawned over little Gabriel. She couldn't believe how much her life had changed from a year ago. She now had a husband, who she was over the moon for, and a son that she loved so much it made her ache. The mask was gone and her heart was wild.

The End

Enjoy a preview of Kassi and Erik's story…

Chapter ONE

Kassi

"This is bullshit, Kassi, and you know it! I hate you going there to dance, knowing all those fucking perverts are staring at you and touching you. It's not right. Let me get a job to help with the bills so you can get a *normal* job somewhere." Matt followed me across our tiny living room to the front door as I prepared to leave for work.

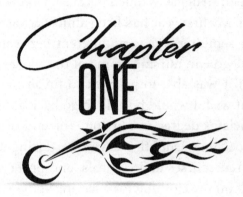

"Watch your mouth, Matthew. And *no!* For the last time, you are not getting a job. I want you to be able to concentrate on school and football this year. It's your senior year, and it's important for you to excel so you can have a chance at some good scholarships. They're watching you for football scholarships, and that's important. I've got things covered. Also, no one's allowed to touch us on stage unless we give permission. Okay? So, don't worry about me, I've got this." We had this same argument nearly every night I went to work at the Emerald Shamrock. No, it had never been my ambition to be an exotic dancer—oh hell, I was a stripper, let's be honest—but it paid the bills better than the waitressing position I started with, and certainly better than working at the hardware store.

Once Matt graduated high school and went on to college, I wouldn't have to struggle as much because, God willing, I would be a nurse by then. My first year had been almost a waste because the curriculum each semester was very different between a bachelor's and an associate degree in nursing. Some of the classes applied, but most wouldn't until I was able to go back to finish my bachelor's. If everything went well, I would be able to go back soon after graduating with an Associate's degree in nursing. The end of my final semester was fast approaching. Until that day came, during the week I was taking my required courses and clinicals, and on Friday, Saturday, and Sunday I took off my clothing for a leering audience.

Yeah, that was my life for the time being, but I *would* make it through this.

"Oh come on, Kassi, my grades are good *every* year. You know they have been. I'm sure taking a part-time job isn't going to kill my grades. Besides, I don't even know if I want to go to college right away. I've been thinking a lot about joining the Marine Corps after graduation. And I hate that you gave up your dreams and opportunities for me." He tucked his hands in the front pockets of his jeans and looked away from me. My heart dropped to my feet when he said that.

"Don't be hasty, okay? Wait to see what offers you get before you decide to run off to the military. Those recruiters will make everything sound right as rain, and then once you sign on the dotted line, they tell you 'oh, sorry, but you belong to Uncle Sam now, so you'll do what we want.' I don't want to see you shipped off to Afghanistan and then get a knock on the door that my little brother is gone. Please, promise me you'll wait."

My eyes plead with him as he looked at me out of the corner of his eyes before he tipped his head back and looked at the ceiling in frustration. Tossing my bag that held my costumes on the old microfiber couch we had grown up with, I stepped closer to him and held his shoulders to make him look at me.

"I didn't throw away my dreams, Matt... I'll still finish nursing school. It's just going to be taking me a little longer to get my BSN, and by different route, but I would do it over again as many times as I needed to in order to keep us together."

Since our parents died, I'd struggled to keep what was left of our family together. Both Mom and Dad were only children, and our grandparents had passed away at various intervals as we grew up. The only family we had left were some very distant cousins near Chicago. Tooth and nail, I had fought to gain custody of Matt so he didn't go into the foster care system. The state didn't want to grant custody to me at first because I was only nineteen myself, almost twenty. They didn't think I was prepared to take on the responsibility of becoming a mother figure to a fifteen-year-old.

At the time, I was working at a hardware store in Ames and had finished the first year of nursing school at Iowa State. Now I was almost done with nursing school. Literally, I had less than a single semester left. Well, for my associates anyway. My plans had originally been to go to Iowa State University to get my Bachelor's in Nursing. Matt was right that I gave up my scholarship, but I didn't regret it. A scholarship didn't keep me and my brother together.

So, I had moved home, enrolled in the community college, and was lucky enough to get into the program relatively soon thanks to my grades, the classes I had already taken, and my scores on the nursing entrance exam. Initially, I was working at the hardware store here that was affiliated with the one back in Ames, but the pay sucked.

Unfortunately, after our parents died, we had to sell our

childhood home because I just couldn't afford the house payment and taxes. Mom and Dad had a little more debt than we realized, so almost all of the life insurance they had went to bury them and to pay off their bills. We had enough left over to get a reliable car and pay the deposits on this one-bedroom apartment. Because he was a growing young man, I felt he needed his own space to get away to do homework and just be alone, so I gave up the single bedroom for Matt. I slept on the couch in the living room, and we just made it work. We shared the closet, since it was the only big thing in the whole apartment, spanning the entire length of the bedroom.

After custody was finally granted, I quit my job at the hardware store and took the job at the Shamrock so I could support the two of us and afford to go to the community college. It also gave me weeknights to be around to help Matt with school work, study my own stuff, and have dinner at a decent time. It worked, but I'd be lying if I said it wasn't exhausting. Sometimes I slipped back into my anger stage of grief and found myself being angry at our parents for leaving us and taking away my dreams. Blame was easy to throw around when I was angry.

Those were the times I really had to work hard to remember they would've never purposefully left us alone. We'd been a close family, and it never occurred to any of us that we wouldn't be there for each other forever. Sometimes shit just happened and life sucked.

Not to mention, it had been scary as hell being the main parental figure for my brother, knowing I hadn't made all the best decisions growing up. Yeah, here I was, far from perfect and yet responsible for guiding my brother toward success. Between the grief of losing both of our parents in one fell swoop and the sudden changes we were forced to deal with, it was rough at first. It took some time, but we worked through it and learned as we went along. Never did I try to be his "mom" though, and we both relied on each other to pull things together.

Now, a little over three years later, my little brother was nearly a grown man, I just turned twenty-three, and I was praying to finish nursing school without anyone finding out I worked as a stripper.

Ugh!

That was the biggest reason we had moved over to Spirt Lake after we sold the house, fear of running into the people we knew from our small town every day and having them ask what I was up to now. Thankfully, I had been able to land this job through a girl I used to work with at the hardware store. Her cousin was one of the other dancers, and they helped me get hired on a mostly cash basis with my position being listed as "waitress" so I wouldn't have the awesome extraordinary job title of "stripper" show up on a background investigation or to hit the CPS radar since they still liked to nose in our business every so often. It all made me feel like I continuously walked a tightrope.

My eyes flicked to my watch, which had belonged to our mother, before returning to Matt. Hell if he wasn't starting to look more and more like our dad every day. It was both heartbreaking and heartwarming to look at him. He had dark brown, nearly black hair and sky-blue eyes, which were identical to mine. Of course, that was where the similarities ended, because where I was lean and willowy like our mom, he was getting broad and muscular like our dad. Man, he was going to break hearts in college. Already, he looked more like a man than a boy as he dropped onto the couch with a scowl.

Preparing to leave for work, I leaned over to kiss him on the cheek and ruffle his hair. Geez, it felt weird to feel stubble on my little brother's cheeks at the end of the day. My hand then rested on his cheek for a minute before I pulled him in for a quick hug.

"Love you, little brother. No wild parties while I'm gone." My words were a standing joke, because that was something I had no worries of whatsoever. We had both been so afraid of CPS getting involved again, and then being separated after we worked so hard to stay together, that we never threw parties or did anything to have attention drawn to us. Thankfully, Matt was a responsible young man who had always been mature for his age. His face lit up as he wiggled his eyebrows at me and grinned; then the mutinous expression returned before he answered me.

"Just please be careful, sis. Even though I'm almost old enough to be on my own, I don't want to lose you. Physically or mentally... you're all I have." The last was spoken so quietly I wasn't sure that I was meant to hear it. He got back up and followed me to the door. My arms wrapped around him in a brief, but tight, hug. Gathering up my bag again, I scooped my keys off the hook by the door. Before I could catch further lecturing by my *younger* brother, I quickly descended the stairs outside our apartment and climbed in our dark blue Honda Accord and backed out. I cast one last wave to my brother before he went inside, and I put the car in drive and headed to work.

Chapter TWO

Kassi

"You're up in five, Sparkle!" I double checked the bobby pins holding my wig to the wig cap, ensuring they were secure and took a last look in the cracked mirror at my station. Crazy what a blonde wig and an elaborate rhinestone-encrusted eye mask did to totally disguise my appearance. Looking back from the mirror sat a stranger's image. No matter how many nights I saw this blonde woman staring back at me through the glass, I couldn't reconcile her image with my own. Maybe that was a good thing. Shaking my head to dispel the image from my head as I stood, the sound of the crowd cheering signaled the end of Candy's routine and told me it was time to shake my money-maker, so to speak.

My eyes closed, and I took a deep breath, inhaling the persona of "Sparkle" and strutting out on to the darkened stage to take my opening place. The lights on stage were out until the opening strains of my favorite routine song began. As Jason Derulo's "Talk Dirty to Me" began to play, the spotlight lit me up. The heat from the spotlight warded off the chill I was experiencing, being so ridiculously, scantily clad, and the familiar smells of smoke, spilled alcohol, body odor, sweat, and cheap perfume assailed my nostrils.

My costume for this routine started out with a short, silver, fringed skirt, which barely covered my ass, a cropped, sparkling silver top that tied between my very full breasts, a silver and black lace bra, and a lacy black thong with rhinestones decorating the front.

The club followed a combination of dress codes that were required by law and imposed by the owners, the Demented Sons MC. Our nipples remained covered by various pasties of our choice, and we wore the skimpiest thongs we could get by with because it generated better tips. After nearly three years of this, I had grown comfortable with being nearly nude on stage. Whether that was good or bad, I wasn't sure, but I had perfected stepping into Sparkle's persona, which was brimming with attitude and confidence. In a way, it was like becoming a completely different person; one with endless spunk, sexual confidence, and total control of her world.

As usual, the crowd hooted and hollered from around the stage that jutted out into the bar. They weren't allowed to touch us inappropriately, as I told Matt, but if you wanted better tips, they always wanted to tuck them in the band of your thong during and at the end of our routines. Some nights I had to really grit my teeth at the "accidental" wandering, grazing fingers.

Tonight was one of those nights.

It wasn't that they scared me; it just pissed me off that these assholes all assumed because I took off my clothes for them, I wanted their grimy hands all over me. But at least it was a lot safer since the guys from the MC had bumped up security after a few incidents with one of the girls getting beat up pretty bad and then one of the old ladies being kidnapped by a rival club because they thought she was one of the dancers. It was some scary shit and something I would *never* tell my brother, but they were doing their best to keep us safe, which was more than I could say for some of the other strip clubs.

Toward the end of my routine, I was hanging upside down from the pole in just my thong and the glittery pasties when my eyes met with the narrowed gaze of one of the MC members. He was sitting back against the wall, and I just happened to see him through the crowd as people jostled each other near the stage. For that split second, I felt my chest and face flush more than it already was from the exertion of my performance. My heart raced, and it seemed wetness flooded between my legs. Embarrassed, I flipped backward off the pole with my heels dropping in a single staccato beat before strutting, dipping, and shaking my ass off stage as I gathered the last of my tips.

Fuck. It wasn't like I had never seen a hot guy before—hell, damn near every guy in the MC was hot as hell. Nor was this guy new to me. He had been here a lot lately, pulling extra security, and I knew his name was Hacker. It seemed like the poor bastard was stuck with the weekend shift a lot lately.

Damn, he was a sexy specimen of a man, and he made all my girly bits stand up and take notice, but I had steered clear of men in general, just like I steered clear of doing private dances because I needed to maintain *some* of my dignity, and because I never wanted to get too close to anyone and risk blowing my disguise. There was just too much at stake in my life right now.

Cinnamon was heading out after me, and as I passed her she spoke quickly to me. "Hey, girl, you have a customer in the Red Room requesting a dance." Shocked, I looked up from tying the top back over my boobs.

"What? No. I don't do private dances. Everyone knows this." My nerves were on edge, and I was getting pissy with Cinnamon when it wasn't her fault. The hurt look on her face told me I shouldn't have tried to kill the messenger. She was the one who got me my job here and the only dancer who knew my true story. I really liked her, and she had sat listening to me many a night when I started to feel overwhelmed by the responsibilities in my life.

"From what I hear, when Shirley told him that, he told her he was paying extra in order to get you to go in there and it would be in your best interest to go. Do what you want, but if it's who I think it is, you may want to take this one." Before I could argue further with her, she bussed my cheek and rushed toward the curtain and out on stage.

My blood was boiling. Dammit, I made good enough money dancing without having to be groped by some drunk-ass, rich businessman. That type of degradation was too much for me to deal with, so I set off toward the Red Room to tell the guy thanks, but no thanks. Even though I was working this job, I had my limits.

The rooms were actually clean and nice with a small stage around a pole, a leather love seat, facing the door, and a music system in the corner where you could choose the song you wanted to perform to. The particular room I was heading to was lit up with hundreds of twinkling red party lights suspended from the ceiling. Each room had a different color—hence the Red Room, Blue Room, Green Room, and Purple Room.

Pushing the door open, I barged in still dressed in just my thong and top, with the rest of my costume clutched in my hand, and stopped dead in my tracks. Reclined on the seat sat Hacker, and my planned tirade froze on my tongue.

Shit, he was hot.

My brain may have actually frozen too, because the diatribe I had planned was just swirling aimlessly in my head.

"Close and lock the door." His deep voice poured over me like warm honey. It curled around me, thick and warm until I felt like I was momentarily floating.

Doing something I never did, and unsure why I did it then, I followed his instructions, shooting him a curious look over my shoulder. With the door closed, the sounds out in the club were reduced to a barely audible hum. After the door was shut and locked, I turned around and pressed my back to the cold door. My heart pounded, and my hands shook slightly. Thoughts jumbled around in my head, refusing to form complete sentences, and I was still at a complete and total loss for words.

"Ummm, so I don't usually do private dances, and I'm pretty sure, uhhh, all of you know this." My eyebrow arched up in question, and I tugged my bottom lip with my teeth.

"And I don't normally pay for one." His smirk should have pissed me off, but it just made my thong wetter. *Holy shit.* And those damn sexy eyes shifted from blue to greenish blue as he sat studying me in the red glow of the room. His tattooed arms were crossed over his chest, and I couldn't help but appreciate the definition in them. Damn, I loved a guy with great arms… and… wait for it… he had a neatly trimmed *beard*.

Be still my heart.

"So, I guess, uhhhmm, I guess I could dance if you really wanted me to, and since you guys pretty much, umm, sign my checks. Just don't expect this every night I work," stuttering, I felt the need to set some boundaries after all. "Okay? Do you, umm, have any requests?" Jesus, I sounded like a freaking idiot.

Why couldn't I form intelligent sentences in front of him? Where had "Sparkle" gone? This was ridiculous! Dammit! And *why* was I entertaining this?

"Yeah, I do. Put on "Emotionless" by Red Sun Rising." I did what he said, and as the music started to fill the small room, I grabbed the pole, cool in my hands, and stepped up on the small stage. Closing my eyes in an attempt to channel Sparkle once again, I swayed and slid along the pole. As I wrapped a leg around the pole, I imagined wrapping my legs around his hips as I sank down…. *Holy shit! Stop it, Kassi!*

Taking a deep breath, I inhaled the spirit behind the music, the faint smell of his leather cut, and a hint of whatever cologne he was wearing. His scent caused shivers of awareness through my body, head to toe.

"Open your eyes. Look at me." My eyes opened, and I realized he had leaned forward, resting his forearms on his knees as he watched me move on the pole. Silently, he held out a hand to me, and without thought, I reached out, taking his hand in mine. As soon as his fingers wrapped around mine, I felt a jolt of electrical awareness.

He gently tugged me down off the stage until I stood between his spread legs. My breath caught and my lips parted as my tongue nervously traced over my bottom lip. I never saw his other hand coming until it was too late. My voice was a breathless whisper as I realized he was removing the rhinestone-encrusted filigree mask.

"No!"

Chapter THREE

Hacker

NEVER HAD I WANTED *ANYTHING* TO DO WITH ANY OF THE dancers at the Shamrock. Sticking my dick in somewhere I knew half the male population had already been just didn't hold a lot of interest for me. Never had. Besides, that hadn't worked out too well for Hollywood and that nasty bitch Cherry. Still didn't know what he was thinking there, but at least he and Becca were happy and things had worked out between the two of them. Just because I didn't want a relationship didn't mean I begrudged my brothers who did.

The guys gave me shit all the time because I never had women hanging on me or crawling out of my bed in the morning. Just because I could count on my two hands the number of women I'd been with since I left college over eight years ago, it wasn't a crime.

It was my fucking life. Now, I'm not saying I was a choirboy, because of course I'd experienced a few one-night stands and quick fucks in the back of the clubhouse, but none of them held my interest long, and none of them stayed in my bed. I didn't *sleep* with any of them. I fucked them. That was it.

No breakfast the next morning. No misleading soft words. Just sex. Nothing more, nothing less.

Thanks to the trouble we were having with the Nomad Demon Runners, we had all been pulling extra duty at the Emerald Shamrock, which further cut back on any free time I might have had. Of course, I knew Sparkle only danced on Friday, Saturday, and Sundays. After the first time I saw her dance, I had volunteered for the weekend shifts, using the excuse that the other brothers had families to spend their weekends with and I never really had plans.

Truth? I couldn't get enough of the sexy blonde that wasn't a blonde at all. Her wig was good, but I could tell it wasn't her hair. Her skin was too warm and olive tinted to be a blonde. Despite the false image and the fact she hid behind a mask, there was no way to fight the draw I felt toward her every time she brought that sexy ass out on the stage. She was my own personal siren, and I had a bad feeling she would lure me to my destruction.

She had a body to die for—long, muscular legs; curvy hips; big, perfectly shaped breasts; full red lips that caused to a man to think crazy, dirty things; and those bright blue eyes that a man could drown himself in.

Her pink tongue running along her bottom lip was nearly my undoing. When I reached for her mask, it was instinctual and without thought or plan. I just knew I needed to see her. Really see her.

When she grabbed for my hand a second too late, her eyes wide and her grip firm, my eyes narrowed. What did she have to hide that she always wore the mask? Not that it mattered, because I wasn't planning on asking her to marry me. Like I said… fuck relationships.

What I was having a hard time fighting was the uncontrollable need to see her unfettered and coming unraveled in my arms. It was so strong, it was nearly a tangible thing.

"Shhhh." My hand set the mask next to me on the couch and reached out to cup her neck, drawing her and her full red lips closer to my own. Her hands dropped to my shoulders to maintain her balance as she leaned toward me. When our lips brushed against each other with the barest whisper of contact, it was like a frisson of electricity ten times as strong as the one I felt when our hands first touched.

The kiss was deep and frantic before either of us comprehended, and our tongues lashed and teeth nipped at each other's lips in a rush. Her hands clutched at my shoulders, and mine reached for her hips and pulled her on to my lap until she straddled my throbbing cock.

Fuck, she was going to kill me. Who the hell was this girl?

Her fingers tangled in my hair and grasped at the front of my cut as mine reached around her to cradle her close to me at her back and hips. Her barely covered pussy ground against my cock as we sat there dry humping like a couple of high school kids. One hand slipped around to knead her perfect, firm, full tit through her barely there shirt. *Goddamn, they were totally real.* She moaned as my hand continued to stroke and knead first one then the other of her beautiful tits. *Shit. What the hell was I doing?*

Sanity broke through the muddled haze that was my brain, and I gently broke away from the magnetic pull of her lips. We both were breathing heavily; her with her forehead resting on my shoulder and me with my face in her hair. The hairs of the wig were soft, but I craved the sight and feel of her own hair.

"Let me see your hair, beautiful."

"You can see it," she mumbled into my shoulder. A chuckle slipped from me, and I leaned back to tip her chin up to look at me. Her eyes were downcast, and I tipped my head at an angle to place myself in her field of vision.

"Sparkle—no, what's your real name, sweetheart?"

Her teeth grabbed her bottom lip and worried it in indecision. She took a deep breath before she met my eyes with her beautiful blue eyes, rimmed in thick dark lashes. This soft, sweet girl was nothing like the alluring seductress, Sparkle, that took the stage, but I liked this side of her even more than I would have thought.

"Look, I don't do this. I came in here to *tell* you I don't do this. I don't know what came over me, and I have to say, I really feel a little like a slut right now. I need to go. I still have two more sets tonight because Monique called in sick." Her eyes begged me to believe her words as she tried to back off my lap. While I understood she needed to go back to work, I wasn't ready to let her warm body go. My arms held her hips in place, which caused her to press into my cock again. We both groaned at the jolt of pleasure from just that little bit of contact. Something told me that fucking her would be unlike anything I had ever experienced, like it may be so explosive I may be tempted to consider… no. Never mind that thought.

"Relax, babe. Despite how tempted I am, I'd rather not have the first time with you here in a strip joint, and that wasn't my intent, okay? I just wanted to talk to you. Just needed to have you to myself for ten minutes. But mark my words, my cock will be buried in that warm, wet pussy of yours sooner rather than later. You feel me?" My words were whispered in her ear as I tried to calm my raging hormones and work up the ability to let her go.

Shit, I felt like a teenage boy with his first real hard-on. What the hell kind of magic was she weaving? What the hell was happening to me?

Her quick intake of air was the only response I got before I loosened my hold on her and she rapidly scrambled off my lap then grabbed her costume pieces and held them as if they could cover her near nakedness. She could wrap herself in a gunny sack, and I would still think she was beautiful, so I didn't know why she was worried about covering herself.

"I'll be here until you get off. Let me take you home after your shift is over." She had reached the door and stopped with her hand on the knob as she looked over her shoulder at me with an expression of surprise and an emotion I couldn't quite place.

"No. You can't come to my home." Her eyes were wide and startled, much like a deer in the headlights look, before she put her mask back on and slipped out the door. My eyebrows raised in surprise, and then anger bubbled up in me. Wondering if she was looking down on me and thinking I wasn't good enough for her because I was a member of the MC had me instantly pissed. Then my mind quickly wandered to another conclusion. *Don't fucking tell me she has a damn old man waiting on her at home! Motherfucker.*

My fist dented the door slightly when it met the metal surface. What the hell was getting into me? I really didn't even know this girl. Why the fuck did it matter if she was with someone? It shouldn't matter to me. She was just some girl I drooled over on a stripper pole. Right? Yeah, of course.

And hell, it wasn't like I couldn't find out every second of her life if I really wanted to, but I would rather she give in and let me in on her own. The normal, sane Hacker would have just said "fuck it" and went about his way alone. Instead, I pushed those semi-lucid thoughts away and allowed the anger to suck me in again.

Simmering in my irritation, I slammed out of the private room and stormed down the hall toward the front door and outside to get some air. I paced the parking lot several times before I came to a decision and re-entered the club looking for Bo, the bartender. He knew all the girls, and I was going to get some answers from him about little Miss Sparkle instead of hacking into her life like I was tempted to. If she actually did have a man at home, I didn't know what the fuck I was going to do, because I didn't poach, but this minx had my insides in fucking knots.

I wanted her, and that said something considering my history.

I was so fucked, and I just didn't realize it yet.

Acknowledgements

I cannot believe this is my second book. There are so many people I have to thank for everything they did to inspire and motivate me to bring life to Mason and Becca. I'm not even sure where to begin.

First, I'm thanking my readers. I can't lie and say I was sure you would exist when I first released Colton. You surprised me from the beginning, and every day since. Never in a million years would I have thought so many of you would buy and then actually *love* my writing. My heart overflows with gratitude to you all, because honestly, without each and every one of you, there would be no Mason.

Next, I will thank Penny. You were my go-to gal (paragraph by paragraph some nights). You believed in me from the beginning and continued to encourage me when I felt like Colton may be my "one hit wonder." Oh and yes, I still promise if they ever make a movie out of my books you can be there when they select the cast (She's sure that will happen someday).

Charrissa, my fellow book-junkie. Thank you for reading Mason while Bobby was sick on my couch from "Texas Cedar Fever." Also, thank you for helping moderate the newly coined Facebook Group "Kristine's Krazy Fangirls." I miss you, and you need to move back to Texas soon.

Once again, thank you to the fabulous author, Sybil Bartel. Sybil, you are my hero. Your ever positive nature, steamy-hot books, and general awesomeness, inspired me to get moving on Mason and get him out to the best readers in the world, all as quick as I could. Keep the fans happy! (By the way, if you haven't read Sybil's books yet… what are you waiting for?!)

Clarise of CT Cover Creations, you did it again! Thank you for making Mason as gorgeous and perfect as Colton. You made them both look so amazing, especially sitting side by side! You're a true genius.

The ladies at Hot Tree Editing gave my words polish and professionalism and there is never thanks enough for that! (I know if any of you read this part, you're probably cringing at all of my grammatical oopsies since I'm writing how I speak. Heehee.) Thank you Virginia and Kristina, for loving my characters and catching all my faux pas.

Stacy at Champagne Formats, you are absolutely a formatting Goddess and you can tell your children I said so! When my major fiasco happened with Colton, you calmly fixed everything and turned my world right-side up again. Mason will be just as beautiful "between the covers" thanks to you. I still thank my lucky stars I chose you to handle my formatting needs! (Thank you to Sybil for that too!)

And as always, my last-but-never-least, a massive thank you to America's servicemen and women who protect our freedom on a daily basis. They do their duty, leaving their families for weeks, months, and years at a time, without asking for praise or thanks. I would also like to remind the readers that not all combat injuries are visible nor do they heal easily. These silent, wicked injuries wreak havoc on their minds and hearts while we go about our days completely oblivious.

About the Author

Kristine Allen lives in beautiful Central Texas with her adoring husband. They have four brilliant, wacky and wonderful children. She is surrounded by twenty six acres, where her seven horses, six dogs and three cats run the place. Kristine realized her dream of becoming a contemporary romance author after years of reading books like they were going out of style and having her own stories running rampant through her head. She works as a nurse, but in stolen moments, taps out ideas and storylines until they culminate in characters and plots that pull her readers in and keep them entranced for hours.

If you enjoyed this story, please consider leaving a review on Amazon or Goodreads, to share your experience with other interested readers. Thank you!

Twitter @KAllenAuthor
Facebook @kristineallenauthor

Made in the USA
Coppell, TX
18 May 2020

25342137R00174